Sleep, Baby, Sleep

Sleep, Baby, Sleep

M. J. Hardy

ISBN-13: 9781505853292
ISBN-10: 150585329X

DEDICATION

*In memory of Donna, Cynthia, Sheila, Mark, Jane, Jill,
Kristine, Timothy, Kimberly, and their families.*

*To my mother, who was a victim in more ways than one:
betrayed by her own flesh and blood, allowed
to be sexually assaulted by a relative.*

ACKNOWLEDGMENTS

To those who supported the effort along the way. First, Eleanor Evangelides, who revived the story of Mark, Jill, Kristine, and Timothy; Camille McClure, Paige Hardy, and Melissa Wetherbee, whose initial reviews and editorial comments were instrumental in the development process. Second, Dr. Brad Gericke, Dr. Greg Tomlin, Mary Fitzgerald Feola, and Priya Sethi for their reviews and editorial comments that were key in the final stages, and Heather Morado, attorney, who guided me through the legal process. Finally, the staff at both CreateSpace and Writer's Digest: Krista Rea, Ashleigh Powell, Jeff Suess, and most notably Cherri Randall and Joe Stollenwerk, whose support was invaluable.

To my own family, who have brought me more riches than one could imagine.

INTRODUCTION

Oakland County in Southeastern Michigan was a magical place to grow up in the 1960s and '70s. The county is part of the greater Detroit metropolitan area, consisting of hardworking, working-class cities like Oak Park, Royal Oak, and Berkley; middle-class cities like Southfield, Birmingham, Auburn Hills, and Farmington Hills; and wealthier cities such as Troy, Bloomfield Hills, and West Bloomfield, with their artistic or eclectic downtowns exemplified by Franklin Village. Notwithstanding the economic disparity between the cities, the automotive industry is woven within the fabric of this area.

The county was dominated by the automotive industry. According to Fortune 500, in 1977 General Motors was the second largest corporation in the world, while Ford was the third largest, and Chrysler the tenth.[i] They dominated the economy of greater Detroit, not to mention all the large, medium, and small businesses that supported the industry. Names like Lee Iacocca, the president of both Ford and Chrysler, who was responsible for the creation of the Ford

Mustang and Chrysler Minivan, and John DeLorean, the flamboyant auto designer who created the DeLorean DMC-12 made famous in the movie *Back to the Future*, were synonymous with Detroit.

Adding to the uniqueness of the area was the creative talent in the arts. Celebrities such as Kristen Bell, Eminem, Kid Rock, Madonna, Glenn Frye of the Eagles, Barry Gordy and Motown Records, Diana Ross and the Supremes, Jerry Bruckheimer, S. Epatha Merkerson, Mitch Ryder and the Detroit Wheels, Bob Seger, Ted Nugent, Tim Allen, Michael Moore, and Sam Raimi are all products of the greater metro Detroit area.

The greater metro Detroit area also inspired art and architecture movements in America. Stretching along Woodward Avenue is the impressive 319-acre campus of the Cranbrook Educational Community, which consists of the Cranbrook Institute of Science, the Cranbrook Art Museum, the Cranbrook Academy of Art, and the Cranbrook House and Gardens in Bloomfield Hills. Cranbrook is known internationally for its place in the modernism movement as well as some of its community of artists such as famous architects such Albert Kahn, Eliel Saarinen, and Charles and Ray Eames.[ii]

Additionally, crime in this area was low, and crime directed against children was unfathomable, yet the abductions and eventual murders of four children had an impact on everyone who lived there. What once was a safe place was thrust into the throes of fear for thirteen months, from February 1976 to March 1977. Parents no longer allowed their kids to roam or play outside unsupervised. Residents now locked their once-open doors and placed placards in the windows identifying safe homes for children to run to in emergencies. The people of the greater Detroit area lived a collective nightmare that year. This fabulous place to live and raise a family became the setting of a horror story.

The unknown serial killer came to be referred to as the Oakland County Child Killer (OCCK) or by the more chilling and sinister nickname, "The Babysitter." The killer earned this moniker for the length of time the abducted children were held and the attention paid to them during their captivity. The killer held the children anywhere from four to nineteen days: feeding them well, bathing them, pressing their clothes and dressing them while in captivity, and then leaving their bodies in a cradle position in very open and public areas for discovery.

According to the Michigan State Police task force report,[iii] Mark Stebbins, age twelve, was abducted on February 15, 1976, while walking a few short blocks from the American Legion Hall to his home. Four days later his body was found in the parking lot of a shopping center. Jill Robinson, twelve, was seized on December 22, 1976, while riding her bike along Woodward Avenue to her father's apartment in Birmingham less than a mile away. Her body was left along the side of the highway the morning after Christmas.

The next victim, Kristine Mihelich, ten, was abducted on January 2, 1977, in front of the 7-Eleven across the street from her apartment building and along a major road. Kristine was held for nineteen days before her body was left at the end of a cul-de-sac in Franklin. Timothy King, eleven, was taken on March 16, 1977, from a local pharmacy while his parents were eating dinner at a restaurant just across the street. Six days later his body was dumped along the side of the road. The map that follows, courtesy of Martha Thierry of the *Detroit Free Press*,[iv] depicts the specific locations in Oakland and Wayne Counties where the children were abducted and where their bodies were found.

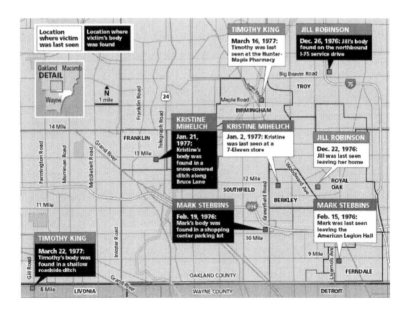

This was an unusually dark and scary time for the residents of Oakland County. Everyone felt terrible for the victimized children and their families, while selfishly in their hearts they were thankful it hadn't happened to them. Every child, teenager, or adult living during that time has his or her own vivid memories of the events of that year.

Our family remembers the time when my parents and younger sister arrived home only to find a police cruiser sitting in the driveway. At the time, we lived a few blocks away from Valley Woods Elementary School and could see the law enforcement activities on a daily basis.

As my parents walked up the drive, the officer got out of his car and met them. He asked if he could speak to my father in private, and as my mother and sister entered the house, the police officer informed my father that they had received a call that someone was acting suspiciously around our house.

He pointed to the window with the yellow curtains that overlooked the front yard and asked whose bedroom it was. My father told the officer that my sister lived in that room. The officer told my father that he had found footprints at the window, indicating that someone had been peering into the room. My sister was thirteen at the time.

What follows is a <u>fictional account</u> of the events that changed not only the families of the victims, but all citizens of Oakland County, forever. In my desire to achieve a certain amount of authenticity and mood, I've used information made public through various sources that the reader can find at the end of the story. Thus, some of the locations, times and dates, and events surrounding the crimes are as close to the actual events as possible; however, names of victims and family members, persons of interest, characters, and incidents are the product of my imagination or used fictitiously.

I realize the story being presented may be uncomfortable for some, but we cannot forget these children, and by keeping their story and their memory in our minds, we can hope to avoid similar tragedies or even bring eventual justice in these cases.

To this day the crimes remain unsolved. If you have any information or tip (no matter how small or insignificant it may seem) that may be helpful in the ongoing investigation, please contact the Michigan State Police or the Oakland or Wayne County Prosecutor's Offices.

—MJH

Sleep, baby, sleep
Our cottage vale is deep
The little lamb is on the green
With snowy fleece so soft and clean
Sleep, baby, sleep
Sleep, baby, sleep

Sleep, baby, sleep
I would not, would not weep
The little lamb he never cries
And bright and happy are his eyes
Sleep, baby, sleep

Sleep, baby, sleep
Near where the woodbines creep
Be always like the lamb so mild,
A kind and sweet and gentle child,
Sleep, baby, sleep

Sleep, baby sleep
Thy rest shall angels keep
While on the grass the lamb shall feed
And never suffer want nor need
Sleep, baby, sleep
Sleep, baby, sleep

—A children's lullaby[v]

ALEX SIMPSON'S STORY

I gasp for air. The next time I'd not be so fortunate. I know the pain she can inflict upon me.

Sister Charity smiles menacingly at me with her little crooked yellow teeth. The tiny wrinkled woman with translucent skin looks at me with ice-cold blue eyes. Her arm rises slowly, and her bony finger points at me from the end of her pitch-black habit. I edge closer to my classmates circled around the tour guide and try to appear interested in the words coming from the tour guide's mouth.

I love the Cranbrook Art Museum, with its incredibly cool artwork, but even it couldn't save me from Sister Charity's oppressive presence. We move to the next display when I see this stunning woman standing next to a statue.

My eyes travel up from her black patent leather high heels with small bows, along her shapely legs, to her charcoal gray wool dress accented by a two-inch-wide black wool belt.

My eyes pause for a moment and focus on her narrow waist. Then I look up at her elegant neck and flawless face with dark-brown hair piled high, not a single strand out of place.

I'm embarrassed. My eyes move from her to my own pathetic Catholic school uniform: the black-and-white saddle shoes, the navy-blue stockings, and the unflattering kelly-green and navy-blue tartan skirt that hangs just below my knees, to the navy-blue blazer and light-blue cotton button-down (oxford) shirt with navy-blue bow tie and matching plaid headband, which keeps my unremarkable mousy brown hair pulled back. Naked of any accessories, I'm not allowed to wear any makeup or earrings; I wouldn't dream of facing the wrath of the nuns.

I remember watching in horror as Sister Charity once ripped a pierced earring from the earlobe of a classmate who had worn a pair in defiance of the repressive dress code. In front of us, Sister Charity called the girl to the front of the classroom. The sinister woman commented on how beautiful the earrings looked. Like a cobra, her hand struck the teenager's ear. The girl's mouth opened wide, the tears welling in her eyes, as she crumpled to the floor in pain and shame. Sister Charity smiled and pointed her wooden yardstick at the rest of us. "Don't ever think this couldn't happen to you."

My mind returns. The tour guide is continuing, "Ladies, I would like you to meet one of the museum's most supportive benefactors. Following in her father's footsteps, she's a great contributor to the museum. We are very fortunate to have her support." As our tour guide finishes her introduction, I clap too eagerly, too loudly. My classmates turn and look at me disapprovingly.

I don't care what they think. I'm completely mesmerized. I know it's foolish and childish to think a woman like her could ever be attracted to me. My own inadequacies kick into high gear.

"Mrs. Bronson, you're much too kind. Ladies, I hope that you enjoy the rest of the exhibits," she says, before she turns purposefully and walks toward the next exhibit.

After the tour, we're allowed to explore the museum on our own. I break free from my classmates and Sister Charity's clutches. I try to decide what to do for the next two hours. I impulsively begin to look for the woman.

I finally spot her studying, appreciating an abstract painting. As she slowly moves from piece to piece, I hear her high heels click against the granite floor. I choose to follow her. I try to act nonchalant, keep my distance, and hide my obvious curiosity. I study her as she moves gracefully from room to room, taking in each piece. The artwork pales in her presence.

Her head unexpectedly turns toward me. I reactively jump back and hope she hasn't noticed me. I curse myself for my immaturity. I quickly walk over and stand in front of a contemporary painting of an artist whose name I don't recognize. I try to gain my composure.

I hear the high heels click on the floor toward me and eventually stop behind me. My face is flushed, and the tips of my ears burn with embarrassment. I feel her presence. Her scent is enticing. I hear the smooth and husky voice.

"Excuse me, young lady."

"Yes?" I say as I turn and look at the object of my longing.

"Are you following me?"

"No…no, I was just admiring your outfit. Chanel?"

"No, a Dior…" She takes a long, hard look at me. "I see you have an eye for fashion. I don't meet too many girls your age who possess a sense of style," she continues, eyeing me carefully.

"I'm sorry, I didn't mean to intrude or seem like I was spying on you."

"What's your name?"

"Alex," I say nervously.

"Alex, I was going to look around for a little while longer. Would you care to join me? We both seem to appreciate art, fashion, and beauty. It might be fun."

Before I can utter a word, she smiles, wraps her arm around mine, and takes us on a private tour of the museum. We spend the rest of the afternoon looking at the artwork and expand our conversation to include music and food. My mother used to make me feel this way—warm, special, appreciated.

She glances calmly at her watch, making me realize I've lost track of time. She looks at me with intensity and bends toward me. I breathe in her perfume and feel flighty. I hope she's going to kiss me. Instead, she whispers in my ear.

"I'm sorry, but I've got another engagement. Would you like to meet again?"

"Yes," I whisper back.

She pulls on her black leather gloves and reaches into her purse. She slips a card into my hand and then turns and walks away. When she is about fifty feet away, she turns back, smiles contemplatively, and finally walks away. I stare at her in utter disbelief and try to contain my excitement. Eventually, I look down at the creamy white business card; embossed in slightly raised gold lettering is the name Marilyn Smith and a phone number. I pray sincerely for the first time in a long time that my needs may be answered.

I shiver as a chill runs through me. I look around anxiously. Sister Charity is staring at me. Her brow is furrowed, and then she leers menacingly.

BIRMINGHAM
SUNDAY, DECEMBER 24, 1961

The frigid air captures my breath in midair. I bounce from foot to foot, waiting, trying to keep warm, while thoughts of Marilyn wrap around me like a rich and luxurious cashmere shawl. Between the cold and my excitement, I fight the urge to pee.

The stars above shimmer like diamonds strewn across black velvet, sparkling in the clear, dark sky. The sound of the Salvation Army volunteer's bell ringing from a distant corner carries through the night. Soon the stores will close, their lights darkening as the last-minute shoppers depart. Any other night, I'd feel abandoned, lonely, depressed. Not tonight; I'm so excited by the cheerful mood from all the

Christmas decorations. The warm glow of Christmas lights in blue, green, red, and orange adds to my strange and wondrous feeling. It's my favorite time of year.

I look down at my brown-and-pink Crowley's department store bag with each gift wrapped in pretty paper and bows. I hope she likes the beautiful silk scarf and gold pendant. *What do you get a woman who seems to have everything? We've just barely met and already I've bought her gifts—I hope she doesn't think poorly of me.*

I'm uptight; a thousand thoughts run through my head. *Marilyn is timeless—everything I ever imagined. She's confident and mature and knows what she wants out of life. She's perfect. I love everything about her. What if she thinks I'm too immature and inexperienced?*

Finally, I see her across the street. Marilyn smiles and waves to me. Trying to contain my excitement, I move slowly to the crosswalk to greet her. She's dressed more casually: a black turtleneck and black wool stretch pants with a leopard-print coat.

I'm so self-conscious that I hope she approves of my outfit. I'm wearing a charcoal-gray topcoat over my favorite cranberry sleeveless angora sweater with matching cardigan; a knee-length, dark-gray, pleated wool skirt; and ruby-colored clip-on earrings.

As we hug, she holds my arms and pulls me closer, lightly kissing each of my cheeks. She holds me at arm's length, sizing me up. "Well done. A vast improvement from our first meeting," she says. "Those uniforms are a detriment to good taste and style. So, how are you doing?"

My heart flutters. "I'm…just so happy to see you. It's been only a week, but the days seemed to drag on forever. I thought this moment would never arrive."

Marilyn grins. "If you don't mind, I've got a change of plans."

"Sure."

"Great. We'll take my car," she says.

The drive is a short one, and it isn't long before we pull into her driveway and walk together along the front sidewalk. The evening looks and feels like a page from one of those romance novels I always read.

As we enter through the front door, she flicks on a few light switches. The concealed lights at the ground and ceiling level reveal her living room. Her home is so cool. I've entered her world.

She walks over to the Christmas tree decorated in gold bead strings, red ornaments of various sizes, and small glittering white lights and sets my bag down.

"I'm a bit of a traditionalist. Gifts shouldn't be opened until Christmas morning," she says.

"We usually open them after midnight mass," I say. "That way everyone can sleep in."

"Nonsense. We'll open our gifts together on Christmas morning."

"Christmas morning? I don't know—my dad and step-mother, they might freak," I say as I bite my lip.

We make our way through the house to the lower-level family room. I look out the window at the dark, secluded ravine that gives me an eerie cold feeling. I wrap my arms around myself for warmth and protection.

"Have a seat; make yourself comfortable. You know I don't bite." Marilyn gestures for me to sit down on the orange-and-red-striped sofa.

"You have a beautiful home. I really like it. My parents' house is so boring and predictable." I unbutton and take off my overcoat and place it on the sofa next to me. I kick off my shoes, settle onto the couch, and draw my legs up underneath me.

Like a powerful, sleek cat, she moves effortlessly and purposefully around the room. I watch her. I like watching her.

Marilyn slides out of her leopard-print coat and tosses it on the back of a chair. She kicks off her leopard-print high heels. Her clothing accentuates her long, firm body. Her lipstick and nail polish are a dark blood red. Tonight, she's wearing her hair down, and it curls at her shoulders.

She walks over to the record albums stacked against the walnut record player lying on the coffee-colored shag rug. She picks out an album, and the black disk slides out of its cover and into her long thin fingers. "I think you'll like this." Marilyn sets the needle to a selected track and a soft bossa nova begins to play.

Winking at me, she does an improvised cha-cha-cha over to the wet bar. She takes two tumblers down from the shelf behind the bar. Opening the small refrigerator and grabbing the ice tray, she places a few cubes in each glass and opens a bottle of whiskey, pouring a healthy portion of the amber liquid into each glass.

Her legs cross over one another as she walks toward me. She sits down beside me and hands me a glass. "Cheers." Our ice-filled tumblers clink together.

I sip the chilled liquid. The whiskey burns my throat, and I feel my face warm up. I try not to scrunch my face from the bitter taste. "I'm sorry. I'm not very good at this."

"That's alright," she says.

She gently caresses my fingers as she takes the glass out of my hand and sets both of them on the coffee table. She gets off the couch and stands in front of me, looking at me seductively. She reaches down, takes my hands, and pulls me up off the couch and into her arms. We slow dance around the room to the smooth, rhythmic music.

Her hand slides down to the small of my back. Eventually, her right hand glides further down and rests on my butt. She gently squeezes. Then she pulls me tight against her body. It feels heavenly.

I look up and stare into her clear, deep-blue eyes. I sense that she can see through me down to my soul. Marilyn thoughtfully asks, "Are you afraid?"

I shake my head slowly, hesitant to tell her the truth—how a neighborhood teenage girl had taken advantage of me when I was younger. "No. I just don't want you to be disappointed."

Marilyn looks at me intensely. "You won't. Nothing pleases me more than hearing the soft cry of pleasure and feeling the quiver of a young woman from my touch."

Marilyn smiles and brings her face in close, her cheek touching mine. She softly whispers in my ear, "Do you like to be touched this way?"

"Yes." I breathe heavily. Her touch is devastating. My heart pounds against my chest, my ears ring, and my body is hot. Her perfume is intoxicating, and I allow my body to be embraced by hers. I'm gone. She stares into my eyes with such intensity and fierceness that she penetrates my soul.

Suddenly, she throws me down on the couch, pinning my arms back, with a force that I never felt before. I'm confused—is this a game? This can't be happening...again. I struggle, but to no avail.

My heart sinks. My emotions crisscross from exhilaration to despair, anticipation to surprise, and submission to contempt. From behind the couch, she grabs and forces a restraint around my right wrist, and then my left.

"You're hurting me." I'm scared, shocked, and I want her to let me go. "I won't tell anyone. I promise. Please, just let me go. You're hurting me. I thought—"

Tears run out of the corners of my eyes, blurring my vision.

"You thought what, Alex, that we would be lovers?" She laughs in astonishment. "I know what you want. I've known all along what you need. You were practically shouting at me to seduce you. Well, Alex, I'm going to give you what you've wanted for a long time."

I strain against the ties, but the more I fight, the more aroused she becomes. Her hands close over my mouth and pinch my nose. Despite all my efforts, I can't shake her. Tighter...I'm suffocating. Tighter...I plead with my eyes. Tighter...the lights start to fade. Tighter...I lose strength. Tighter...the room goes black.

My body shivers, registering the cold. I'm cold, so cold. My body shakes harder. I try to roll over and curl up into a ball. I can't. My hand tries to reach down to pull up my bed sheet and blanket. I can't.

I'm groggy. I struggle to get up, but I can't move my arms or legs. I try to comprehend what is happening. My mind focuses a little more. I'm cold, yet parts of my body are on fire.

I try harder. "Help!" I scream at the top of my lungs though it comes as an inaudible croak. I focus harder, but my mind only welcomes the pain and coldness.

My mind slowly starts to recognize little things, unimportant things—cold, damp, and darkness. I see someone standing in the distance. "Help. Please help me. Why won't you help me?" I don't understand. I'm only met with complete silence and utter darkness; I'm embraced by despair. I feel what little strength I have evaporate. My eyes close.

I'm jarred awake from my body convulsing. My swollen eyes flutter open and register the sliver of light coming through a small rectangular basement window. I try to move; furiously I pull and kick my arms and legs, but the thin white nylon clothesline cuts farther into my skin. My eyes follow the rope wrapped and knotted to my ankles and wrists to the four corners of a cast-iron bed.

My mouth is sore and swollen from the gag. I long to lick my dry lips. My shoulders ache from the restraints. I turn my head to hide my shame. Sobbing, I blame myself.

Time seems to drag on as I lie naked and restrained. I look around the gray cinderblock walls of my prison room. There is a white wooden chair with my white cotton bra and panties neatly folded on it. My clothes are cleaned and pressed on a wire hanger.

I hear a door creak open. I smell her perfume before I see her long, shapely legs striding toward me. She stands in front of me.

"How's my sleepyhead doing?" She smiles, spinning in front of me. "How do you like my outfit? That's right, it's a Dior. I prefer him so much more than Cassini. I find all of the publicity over him and Jackie tiresome. I think a woman should make her own fashion statement, don't you?"

I'm confused by her conversation.

"Oh, see how the scarf and brooch that you bought for me go so well with my outfit," she says. "I can't wait for you to open your gift. I think you'll really like it."

She sits next to me on the bed. She gently strokes my face and neck. "I know that you must be uncomfortable, but it'll soon be over. You can take a luxurious bubble bath, and I'll fix you something delicious to eat. Your favorite meal."

She removes the gag from my mouth. "Please let me go…I want to go home." My voice is barely audible.

"Shhh," she whispers.

"Why, Marilyn?…Why?"

She leans over me, smiles down thoughtfully, and gently strokes my hair. "I don't know what got over me. Normally, I prefer them a little younger. You looked so young, inno-cent...vulnerable. I must have got caught up in the whole Catholic schoolgirl thing. Now, shhh," she quietly commands with her mouth next to my ear. My stomach turns at the smell of her perfume. She pulls the sheet and blanket over me and tucks me in. I feel her hot breath on my neck. "Shhh." As she places her hands over my mouth and nose, I hear her whisper for the last time.

"Sleep, baby..."

LAUREN RING'S STORY

It is a gorgeous sunny September day, and Lake St. Clair has never looked more breathtakingly beautiful as sunlight sparkles on the deep-blue water. There are still a few boats gliding across the water, with boaters taking advantage of the season before winter settles in. We hop into her car, a black Corvette Stingray convertible with its top down. We make our way west on Nine Mile and jump onto Interstate 94. She looks over at me, smiles, and steps on the accelerator. The force pushes me into the seat as an astronaut rocketing skyward. We blast past the other cars along the highway to the 696 to Interstate 75.

I look at her. She's wearing something fantastic—slim, navy-blue, knee-length skirt and a deep-purple silk blouse with a denim jacket. Her blouse is unbuttoned just enough to reveal part of her cleavage, enhanced by her lacy purple bra. Her perfectly painted nails wrap around the steering wheel. I can't keep my eyes off her.

I'm not sure where we're going, but I don't really care. She looks at me and yells over the wind and car noise, "I've got an idea. Trust me?"

I enthusiastically shake my head and think, *Take me anywhere.*

Eventually, we leave the highway and make our way through the peaceful tree-lined streets and expansive yards of the suburbs. Having been here previously with my mother, I instantly recognize Birmingham, with its smart downtown. As we continue our drive through the upscale area, I observe the outstanding blend of trendy boutiques, specialty stores, beauty salons, churches, and local government buildings.

We park the car and spend the late afternoon shopping, looking at the stunning women's clothing and picking out outfits for each other. A feeling comes over me, a feeling that I've never had with anyone before—a feeling of intimacy. I look at her and wonder if she feels it, too. She looks up from the clothes rack and smiles back at me.

As we finish shopping, she suggests that we go back to her place for a little more privacy. I'm eager to spend more time with her and readily agree. The thought of her showing me her home and spending the evening with me seems unbelievable.

She pulls into the driveway. The front yard is pristinely landscaped with maples, evergreens, and hedges, providing her ranch-style brick house with privacy from passersby. She pulls into the garage, throws the car into park, and shuts off the powerful engine.

"It's really not much," she says, "but it is home sweet home."

"I'm sure it's fantastic," I say.

We walk up the front sidewalk past the well-manicured lawn and enter through the front door. She already has everything that I could want, now and in the future: her hairstyle, makeup, perfume, clothes, and car. Her house is no different. I'm immediately taken in by the décor: sensible, simple, but highlighted by sophistication.

"I love your house." The walls are painted a subtle off-white shade, the polished hardwood floor covered with a thick, oriental red-and-black rug with gold trim. The highly polished teak Scandinavian furniture displays Krenit bowls, with their matte-black exteriors and inside clear lacquers of yellow, orange, and red. Throughout the room are several architectural pieces of pottery in white, powerful in their simplicity.

"Thank you," she says. "I've worked really hard, and I'm very selective in everything I choose."

We walk through her house, taking time to look at each room. She puts her hand on the small of my back; my body tingles with excitement. I feel a little light-headed. I'm overwhelmed with my feelings going crazy.

"This is so cool," I say. I cringe, regretting the immature words the moment they leave my lips. I notice how every room is tastefully decorated, from the paint on the walls to the displayed art to the furniture selection and location all chosen so carefully.

"I've never seen anything like this," I say.

"You mean because I don't have the usual gold shag rugs, avocado-colored kitchen appliances, lava lamps, and bean bag chairs?"

"Yeah, exactly," I say.

"Those colors remind me of some type of terrible baby food," she says. "I'm sorry that the house is a mess, but I didn't get a chance to clean it. I had to rush home from work, get ready, and drive over to meet you."

"Oh my God. Your house is spotless," I say. "There isn't a speck of dust to be seen or anything out of place." I can hear my mom's voice harping to pick up after myself and take care of my things.

"Lauren, it's amazing what you can find in garage sales around here. People will stick the furniture in their garages, attics, or, worse, their basements. I'm so thankful that they don't realize the treasures they're throwing away." She points to the two chairs in front of the window. "Those two open-arm chairs are made by a company in Denmark, and I practically got them for free. A little polish and tender loving care is all they needed."

I hope she doesn't think of me as a piece of furniture. "They're so cool. You must be really smart." I'm embarrassed again. *Great, Lauren. Another really stupid thing to say.*

"Follow me," she says.

She seems not to notice or else forgives my inept comments as we continue with my personal tour. As we step inside each room, she takes time to highlight a particular piece of artwork or furniture and gives a brief synopsis of how she has come into possession of each and the painstaking time and effort she has committed in their selection and purchase. *I love her house.*

I want her so bad. She leads me to her last room. Her bedroom. This is it.

A fusion of contemporary and Asian design, it looks like an upscale hotel with the perfect blends of tans, purples, browns, and reds. The milk-chocolate hardwood floors are polished to a gloss and covered with Persian rugs of rich golds and reds. The bed is hardwood, low to the ground with curved legs and a wicker headrest and covered with inviting, soft cream-colored sheets. To either side of the bed are small lamp tables with Asian-inspired ceramic lamps.

"Just don't ask to see my bedroom," I say. "I'm so embarrassed." I think of the differences between her room—the room of an adult—and mine.

Above the bed, my eyes are drawn to an erotic charcoal drawing of a young woman and teenage girl. The attractive woman sits looking to the left with her arm around the small of the girl's back. The girl's head is bent and resting on top of the woman's with her bare back to the viewer, and her arm is gently pressed against the woman's breasts, covering her areolas. They are discreetly covered, yet obviously nude.

"Beautiful, aren't they?" she asks.

I nod my head in agreement. "Yes."

The picture speaks to me on so many different levels. *I want to be the little girl in her arms—naked, safe, loved, and content.*

I want to be the young woman. She's so captivating. I like how, when she looks at you, there is nobody else more important than you. I can only wish that I could be as captivating as her. I think how different we are—my lackluster, dishwater-blond hair; my nonexistent breasts and hips.

I suddenly feel embarrassed by a tremendous sense of insecurity crawling around inside of me. *There is no way I will be able to keep her interest. There is no way I can compete.*

She stands alongside me, looks at me, and then observes the painting. "I apologize. I've been a rude host and haven't offered you anything. Would you care to join me for a glass of wine?"

Before I can respond, she tells me to follow her.

Like the rest of the house, the kitchen is immaculate. We could eat off the floor. However, this room is a little more 1960s and modernist. The refrigerator, stove, and oven door are an upbeat turquoise, and the bright-white kitchen table has matching chairs with bright-red padding.

As she removes a bottle of wine from the rack, I remember how my friends and I, thinking we were so cool and mature getting totally drunk on a bottle of Mad Dog 20/20 wine, piled into a car racing across the Ambassador Bridge to Windsor, Canada, this summer. I have a feeling this is going to be a more mature experience. Opening one of the kitchen drawers, she quickly finds the bottle opener and deftly removes the cork.

She selects two wine glasses from the shelves and pours each of us half a glass. She gently clinks her glass with mine.

"Cheers, Lauren."

"Cheers."

"Follow me."

She opens a door in the kitchen, and we begin to descend the stairs to her basement. Long, sleek, and narrow, the basement is a party room straight from a modernist magazine. I sip my wine, feeling tipsy, as I look at the careful use of bright-colored area rugs accented with comfortable, neutral-colored chairs and a sofa centered on the brick fireplace at the far end of the room.

Standing in the middle of the basement, she takes the wine glass from my hand and puts the glasses on the table. Seductively, she walks toward me, takes my hand, and spins me slowly around. She pulls me close, and her right hand gently cups my left breast. My body is on fire; I lean into her and gently rub against her. Standing behind and very close to me, she seductively says, "Lauren, now for the pièce de résistance."

Suddenly, she slaps me hard across the face. The pain and shock cause me to double over. I desperately try to comprehend what is taking place. Before I know it, she has dragged me through a false wall and throws me on the bed. She straddles me, her knees pinning down my arms, and ties me to the iron railings of the headboard.

"I won't tell anyone. I promise. Please, just let me go. You're hurting me," I beg, but my pleas and prayers go unanswered.

Time passes. She has held me captive for what seems an eternity. She often lies next to me on the bed, gently stroking me. I'm sick to my stomach...feeling helpless to stop her.

On the third day, I can hear her singing. The singing gets louder as she nears the bedroom.

"Happy birthday, to you..."

She enters the cramped room carrying a birthday cake with candles.

"Happy Birthday, Lauren. I looked at your driver's license and saw today is your day."

"You freak! Let me go!"

My anger turning to desperation, I sob, "Just please let me go...just please let me go."

I spend my seventeenth birthday in fear and despair. Sometimes, she'll release me and allow me to eat and bathe. She has me wear other clothes. My own clothes, washed and ironed, hang on the wall. I plead with her, beg her for my release, but instead she smiles.

"Now, Lauren, don't be silly. You know that's not possible. Besides, don't you like it here? Remember how you looked at me in the restaurant when we first met? You were the one who kept staring at me. You agreed to meet with me. You got all dressed up to try and impress me. Lauren, I did you a favor. You wanted me so much that it clouded your judgment. We both know that you longed to have another woman make you feel like a 'real' woman. To help you come to grips with your sexuality."

She gets up off the bed and makes her way to the door. Turning off the lights as she departs, she turns in the doorway and looks at me. "This isn't how I planned my life. It's not my fault what happened to me."

A few days after my birthday, she sits on the edge of the bed, gently stroking my hair out of my face. She asks what kind of food I like.

Tonight, she smiles at me as she unties the cloth wrapped around my wrists and ankles.

"I've got something special for you, but you need to prepare for dinner."

I rub my wrist, trying to get the circulation going. "I'm fine…really. I don't need anything special. I just want to go home…please." Tears well in my eyes and begin to cascade down.

"Don't be silly." She takes me by my hand and leads me upstairs. I want to run. I'm exhausted, embarrassed, and scared. But she's read my mind.

"Don't even think it. You can't get out, and no one can hear you. Let's just try and enjoy our time together."

She leads me into the bathroom. The tub is full of water. I'm trying to figure out what she has planned for me.

"Well, get in," she says. "I'd think by this time that you would love to take a bath."

I dip my toe into the water—it feels warm and soothing. I place my right foot in and then my left. I slowly lower my whole body into the water. The water brings instant relief to my tired and sore muscles.

She sits on the edge of the tub, puts on a large cloth glove, and squirts white liquid from a recognizable green plastic bottle with a white top. She rubs the glove all over my body.

"I've heard they want to ban this. I'm not sure why. I used it all the time when I was growing up." She lifts up the hand-sized bottle and inspects it. "I should probably buy a case of it. What do you think?"

I shrug my shoulders. She continues washing my body. Her gloved hand glides over my shoulders, back, and breasts. She continues her conversation as she washes.

"It does such a great job cleaning your skin, especially acne. Yours has cleared nicely since you've been with me. I love the feel of warm water and soap on my body. Doesn't this make you feel special?"

I mumble, "I guess so."

"Stand up. Every nook and cranny has to be cleaned." She watches intently as the glove moves in circular motions on across my stomach, up and down my legs, and between my thighs.

She opens the drain and turns on the faucet. She pours the fresh water over my head and body, removing any soap residue.

"Almost done." She pats my body dry with a large, soft, white plush towel. She then wraps my body and head with towels. She has me sit on the toilet seat cover. She takes out nail clippers and a file. She clips and files my nails just right.

She smiles at me now. "Time to get dressed. By the time you come downstairs, I'll have dinner ready for us." She hands me back my clothes, bra, panties, and silk stockings.

"Thank you."

"Hurry up. We don't want your dinner getting cold."

She leaves the bathroom, and I can hear her in the kitchen. For the first time, I allow myself just a glimmer of hope. My heart starts to beat a little faster knowing that I might finally be getting back home. Just the thought makes me cry.

I walk downstairs to see her leaning against the kitchen counter.

"Don't you look special. Ta-da." She waves her hand toward the kitchen table.

My favorite meal is all laid out. I'm elated, feeling rejuvenated by the bath and wearing my own clothes. And now the delicious meal waits for me. As quickly, my heart sinks. I feel the bile coming up into my throat. I have a dire premonition. *I am being fed my last meal.*

ST. CLAIR SHORES
TUESDAY, OCTOBER 10, 1972

Charlie watched the woman's hand visibly shake as she took the business card. Margaret Ring sat back in her chair, and the knuckles of her left hand were white as they gripped the arm of the chair. Margaret Ring looked down at the business card with the name Doctor Charlie Taylor embossed on it, and then she looked back at Charlie noting the disparity of the doctor's masculine name and chosen profession and the slender Asian woman siting before her. She reached up with her index finger wrapped with a white handkerchief and placed it under her runny nose, trying to compose herself. She looked off into space contemplatively before she finally responded. "Dr. Taylor..."

"Charlie, please."

"Charlie, what would a medical doctor have to do with my daughter's disappearance?"

"I've received my medical degree, and now I have a four-year residency to get my doctorate in psychiatry. My specialty is in criminal behavior."

"What does that have to do with my daughter's disappearance? Shouldn't the police be here or out on the streets trying to find her?"

"I want you to know that everyone is looking very hard to find Lauren. That is why I'm here; I bring a different perspective to the investigation. I study both the victim and the clues surrounding the crime. I'm able to develop a picture of the suspect. I can't tell the police who the suspect is, but what traits or characteristics the suspect might possess."

"It's hard for me to focus. I'm still confused."

"I'm sorry. I can't tell the police that a specific perpetrator abducted your daughter, but I can tell them they are looking for a white male, twenty-five to thirty-five years of age, a loner, who has mid to high IQ, is not well educated, has trouble communicating, and is socially inept. This way the police can narrow the scope of their investigation and focus their efforts."

"Is this common practice?" Margaret asked as she bent the business card in her hand.

"No, it's a new concept being tried here in the state; however, it has proven successful in other cities such as New York."

"And you think this will help us find Lauren?"

"I do. If you don't mind, what can you tell me about Lauren?"

Margaret Ring sat forward, looking down, and began to fiddle with her charm bracelet. Her thumb and index finger held a heart-shaped charm. "All parents want their child to be happy and successful, to realize and reach their potential. Lauren was a difficult child. No matter what we did, she was never happy. As a child, she was withdrawn and had a hard time getting along with the other kids. The boys would joke about her size and looks…the girls weren't much better. Most times, she was just overlooked."

"What about now?"

"It's only gotten worse. I'd take her shopping, you know, trying to cheer her up, but it only made matters worse. All the sales clerks would mistake her for a thirteen-year-old and show her training bras. I'd tell her that some women's bodies take longer to develop, but she just thinks it's another cruel joke. Reality can be pretty devastating."

"What did Lauren like to do?"

"She'd spend hours in her room. What she did up there I'm not really sure. I tried to give her some space. Who knows? Maybe I should have been more involved with her life."

"Please don't blame yourself. You had nothing to do with her disappearance. You're obviously a very loving and caring parent. Do you mind if I look at Lauren's room?"

"No, I'll show you upstairs."

As the women walked up the stairs, Charlie asked, "Did Lauren have any close girlfriends or even a boyfriend?"

"Not really. There was a boy, actually a young man, who started to call the house. You'd think that I'd be overjoyed with the idea of a boy being interested in Lauren, but actually I wasn't too excited. He was older, twenty-five or so, and on his way to Vietnam. It just seemed like trouble to me."

"Do you think you could provide me with a list of her friends or classmates who might be able to provide some more information?"

"Sure, but it's not much of a list," Margaret said as she opened the bedroom door.

"Do you mind if I look in her room by myself?"

"No, I'm sorry. I'll be downstairs. I'll put together that list. Can I fix you a cup of coffee?"

"Yes, that would be great."

Charlie closed the bedroom door to shut out possible distractions and looked around. The wallpaper was dark green with large, bright daisies, the bedspread a bright yellow with hooked rug pillows in shades of greens and yellows. Posters of Susan Dey from *The Partridge Family* were taped to the walls, gum-wrapper chains hung from the corner of the mirror, and fashion magazines were thrown about. Shoes were scattered across the floor, and clothes were piled high on the desk chair. Charlie smiled. Everything was pretty age appropriate.

Charlie began her search methodically going through the room in a clockwise fashion, making sure that her hands and eyes moved simultaneously. Charlie too often saw how the police would inadvertently miss something because they'd get ahead of themselves.

Her hands slid between the mattress and box springs, and she got on her hands and knees looking up under the bed. Charlie picked up the pillows, squeezed them, and thoughtfully replaced them on the bed. She was looking for a potential clue; each little knickknack gave insight into the victim's heart and passions.

Charlie had almost finished her search. She grasped the brass rings and pulled opened the last drawer. It was Lauren's underwear drawer. *Typical of police to feel uncomfortable going through a teenage girl's lingerie.* Charlie's hand sorted through the cotton bras and panties in all different colors, but the drawer yield nothing.

Charlie sat back on her haunches. *Damn*, she thought and closed the drawer. The drawer wasn't flush with the others. Charlie tried again. Charlie pulled the drawer out further and reached back behind the drawer. Her fingers ran across the rough pine wood until they touched something else.

Charlie's heart skipped a beat as she pulled out a leather-bound book with a little gold clasp. Charlie undid the clasp and opened the book—Lauren's diary.

Charlie turned the pages slowly. From them poured a teenage girl's tortured emotions of pain and anguish. Charlie looked at Lauren's self-portraits in black-and-blue inks of herself looking sad or with tears falling down her cheeks. The pages were covered with doodles—not of hearts or suns or flowers, but of barren and withered trees. Charlie tried to remain clinically detached, but a small part of her heart went out to the despondent girl.

However, for the entry on Wednesday, September 27, the page came alive like Dorothy leaving bleak and gloomy Kansas and arriving in the bright and colorful Oz. The page was filled with flowers and hearts, the inks changed to reds and pinks. Lauren had expressed feelings of hope and rejuvenation—of being alive.

The last entry, on Thursday, September 28, told of a pending date. Charlie looked at the flowers and hearts drawn all over the page. She heard a noise and looked up.

Margaret Ring stood at the door holding two cups of coffee. "Did you find anything of interest?"

"I found Lauren's diary."

"I didn't realize she even kept one." Tears started to well in her eyes and slowly rolled down her checks. "What else have I been missing?"

Charlie got up from the bed and took the cups from the mother's hands. She slowly guided the woman to the bed to sit down and then sat beside her. Margaret laid her head on Charlie's shoulder and wept.

Eventually, when Margaret's sobs had subsided, Charlie asked, "There is something significant about Wednesday the twenty-seventh. Do you have any ideas what it might have been?"

Margaret Ring shook her head no.

RAY TOWNSHIP
FRIDAY, OCTOBER 20, 1972

A predawn call had woken Charlie from a deep sleep and had brought her onto the roads of neighboring Oakland and Macomb Counties in the early morning hours. Charlie exited off the Christopher Columbus Highway and turned onto rural Twenty-Seven Mile Road. She flipped her visor down and adjusted her sunglasses. Charlie pressed down on the gas, and the powerful engine of her dark-green 1968 Mustang responded without a moment's hesitation.

Traveling east, she shot past the small farms, framed houses, and street-side mailboxes standing like lonely sentries. In the distance, Charlie could make out an ambulance alongside several marked and unmarked cars parked along the side of the road. Her car swiftly covered the distance.

Although there wasn't another car on the road, she instinctively turned on her blinker, slowed the car down, and pulled onto the shoulder. A small group had congregated around the all-too-familiar white tarp covering a body. As she opened the door and climbed out of her car, she was taken aback by the remoteness of the area. She walked toward the group, observing the surroundings and familiarizing herself familiar with the sights and sounds. She held out her hand.

"Sheriff, Dr. Charlie Taylor."

The large man took the cigarette from the corner of his mouth and exhaled the steel-blue smoke into the air before responding. Looking downward, he took a hard drag on the cigarette before he threw it down and buried the butt into the ground with his spit-polished black cowboy boot.

"Do you have some identification?" the sheriff asked.

Charlie reached into her leather bag, pulled out her identification wallet, and held it out. The sheriff snatched the wallet with his bulky, nicotine-stained fingers and studied it for what seemed like an eternity.

The sheriff handed back the wallet. "Let's just say, I was expecting someone else."

Charlie's skin began to crawl.

"Dr. Taylor. I'm Sheriff Roy Green, Ray Township. This here is one of my deputies, Bobby Patterson."

The young deputy, trying to ingratiate himself with his boss, chimed in, "Fooled the shit outta of me."

Charlie looked over at the third man leaning against a metallic-blue 1970 AMC Javelin. She thought it an odd choice, but who was she to criticize someone's choice in cars. She drove a Mustang. The good-looking man pulled off his Persol 714 Ratti, folded them, and slipped them into the inside pocket of his suit coat.

"Pete West, special investigator for the Michigan State Police."

Charlie shook Pete's extended hand and replied, "Dr. Charlie Taylor."

"Headquarters called and said you were coming," Pete said. He then turned to the sheriff and his deputy. "Dr. Taylor works with the Michigan State Police on a new law enforcement concept. She comes highly recommended. Not only does she have a medical degree and she studies criminal behavior, but she's made it through our training, too."

"Women's lib...I wouldn't be surprised if she has burned her bra. You wouldn't catch my old lady doing this," Deputy Patterson said.

"Deputy, she's here to help us...more you than me..." Pete said.

Interrupting the conversation, Charlie asked the three men, "What can you tell me?"

Before either man could answer, Charlie crouched next to the body, turned back the tarp, and began to convey the facts. "Female, not more than five foot one, ninety to one hundred pounds, and approximately fifteen to eighteen years of age…"

"Shit, she can't be more than thirteen. She's flat as a board," Deputy Patterson quipped, grinning at his own joke.

Charlie looked at the deputy with contempt before she continued with her observations of the victim. "She hasn't been dead long, probably within last four to five hours. Looks like asphyxiation. Despite the slight ligature marks on her wrists and ankles, she seems like she's in rather good shape," Charlie said as she scrutinized the young woman more closely.

"Why did you say that?" Pete asked as he walked over and squatted next to Charlie.

"I'm sure this is Lauren Ring. She's been missing for over a month, and if I'm right about when she died, then some-one has been taking care of her. No signs of dehydration or malnutrition."

Charlie turned and watched Pete as he stared down at the lifeless body of the good-looking teenage girl. "What are you thinking?" she asked.

"I think it's a shame this girl's life has ended before she even got a chance to really live. I don't know why I'm still shocked or surprised by the cruel ways that evil can be expressed. I've seen it all before—'Nam, Detroit," Pete said, concerned.

"Her clothes look expensive?" Pete asked as he turned to Charlie.

"Yes. Diane von Furstenberg." Charlie looked at the simple black-and-white-print dress; sheer, black thigh-high silk stockings; black platform shoes, and a simple watch with a black leather wristband.

"Sexually assaulted?" Pete asked.

Charlie respectively lifted up the skirt and pulled down lacy black silk panties. "There doesn't seem to be any redness or swelling to the vagina, but it's hard to tell. We'll know once the autopsy's completed," Charlie said, her brow furrowed and mouth pursed.

"What else?" Pete asked.

"Whomever she met or was going to meet must have been someone special."

"Why do you say that?"

"Most girls her age are wearing Love's Baby Soft perfume, bubblegum lip gloss, jeans, blouse, and Earth Shoes."

"What aren't you telling me, Dr. Taylor?"

Charlie lifted up the young woman's hand. "Look at her nails. They're clean, manicured, and polished. Her clothes are well maintained. She certainly hasn't been wearing this outfit for the past thirty days. So it's out of the ordinary the way the killer has taken care of her."

Charlie and Pete stood up and faced the sheriff, deputy, and two medical technicians. "Sheriff, thanks very much for calling us. We won't know for sure until the autopsy is completed, but Dr. Taylor and I believe that the body is that of a missing teenage girl by the name of Lauren Ring. Lauren is from St. Clair Shores and disappeared on Friday the twenty-ninth. The circumstances surrounding her disappearance are shaky at best," Pete said.

Charlie added, "Her mother thought she was going out to meet someone, a kind of secret rendezvous with some boy she had a crush on. Her mother had talked about a young man who was on his way to Vietnam. She said Lauren had gotten dressed up and was very secretive of the whole affair. Her friends thought she had skipped school a couple of days prior and had hitchhiked to the beach. They thought she might have met someone there. So far none of it has panned out."

Charlie and Pete nodded at the sheriff and deputy, turned, and walked to their cars before the men could respond.

"Back there, thanks. But I can hold my own," Charlie said, nodding, her back toward the sheriff and the deputy.

"I wasn't worried about what they might do to you, but what you might do to them. Your rep has gotten around..." Pete said.

"The guy was a jerk and deserved it," Charlie said.

"I wasn't referring to that incident...just let's say that you're overachieving a bit."

"Man's world," Charlie said and then stopped, turned, and faced Pete. "I can't shake a couple of things. Besides holding her captive for almost a month, he seems to have taken pretty good care of her. But what a remote area to leave her body in, yet out in the open for someone to eventually find."

Pete nodded in agreement and pulled out his sunglasses. "I'll give you a call as soon as I hear something from the coroner."

JACKSON
WEDNESDAY, OCTOBER 25, 1972

"Hey, baby, why don't you suck on this for a while? Come on, honey." Charlie could hear the numerous obscenities being hurled at her over the slamming of the steel doors being shut from the distant cells.

"Dr. Taylor," Charlie answered into the heavy black phone that smelled of nicotine and coffee from the previous users.

"It's Pete West. You know, you're a hard woman to track down, and I'm pretty good at it. What takes you to our fine state facility?"

"My residency has me bouncing all over the place. If I'm going to understand criminal behavior, I've got to go where they are. I can only learn so much from a book. What's up?"

"Hey, your assessment was pretty accurate. She died of asphyxiation. She hadn't been sexually assaulted, which would explain why there was no presence of semen. With the exception of the minor abrasions to her wrists and ankles, she had been well cared for—her whole body had been bathed. Absolutely no traces of any type of evidence left behind by the killer. They also found the remnants of her last meal—a hamburger and French fries still in her stomach."

"Her favorite meal."

"How'd you know that?"

"Her mother told me when I interviewed her." *Her poor mother. She must be going crazy. I need to call her.*

"Are you still there?" Pete asked.

"Yes, I'm sorry. Zoned out for a moment."

What are you thinking?" Pete asked

"Can you give me a couple more days? There are a few things I need to research, and you'll have my profile by Monday."

"Works for me. The leads are drying up pretty fast. The local LE doesn't have much to go on at this point."

"Thanks, Detective West. I'll call you Monday."

ANN ARBOR
MONDAY, OCTOBER 30, 1972

"The killer is twenty-five to thirty-five years old, attractive and confident, anal retentive, incredibly neat, car and home well maintained, well organized, thoughtful, deliberate, fashion conscious. The killer somehow knew Lauren's weaknesses," Charlie said.

"Interesting. It's not what I expected. Any theories?" Pete asked.

"Lauren was very a vulnerable person. She definitely had a lot of issues in her life. She felt unattractive, unloved, and unnoticed. The killer must be charismatic. He was quickly able to gain Lauren's confidence, maybe to the point of seduction. Lauren met the killer on Wednesday, and they made plans for a 'date' on Friday under the auspice of a potential relationship. For the first time in her life, Lauren was filled with happiness.

"She dressed up for this secret rendezvous, not in jeans and a blouse, but a designer dress and black silk lingerie. It screamed intimacy. At some point, the killer lured her to his apartment or house and then holds her captive over a long period of time. Maybe she has become his sexual obsession. Eventually, he tired of her and killed her." Charlie caught her breath.

"Interesting," Pete said. "I'm intrigued. Unfortunately, none of our leads has led us to a person of this nature. I'm afraid everything will start to go cold, very cold, and very quickly."

BIRMINGHAM
WEDNESDAY, NOVEMBER 22, 1972

Pete looked over at the dirty office phone that at one time had been beige, annoyed at the constant ringing coming from it. S*hit, the day before Thanksgiving…People, give me a break!* He was hoping to get out of the office at a decent time. Pete picked up the telephone. "Pete West…"

"Detective West, it's Charlie Taylor…"

"Charlie, if this is in response to Lauren Ring, we've got nothing. Absolutely nothing," Pete said.

"You need to have the locals canvas the stores and restaurants about that Wednesday to see if anyone remembers seeing Lauren. Her family and friends aren't going to be able to provide us anything," Charlie said.

"Charlie, they've already been down that road. No one seems to remember seeing her."

"Poor kid," Charlie said. "She seems to be the forgettable girl in life and in death."

"Can I ask why the interest? You've been very persistent. I'd think your residency requirements would keep you pretty busy. It's not like you're responsible for finding her killer."

"It's hard to explain. I just feel a connection, that's all."

"Well, I wish that I had better news to give you. Happy Thanksgiving."

"Happy Thanksgiving to you and your family, too." Charlie hung up the phone.

Charlie looked around her father's home office, trying to fight off the pangs of anxiety. Home was always such a mixed bag of conflicted feelings. She'd never been able to successfully reconcile the love/hate she felt toward her parents, especially her mother. As she left her father's office and walked upstairs, she hoped that, at worst, the weekend would be merely uncomfortable.

Charlie opened the door to her old bedroom and threw her weekend bag on the floor. She sat on the edge of her bed and looked around. The twenty-seven-year-old ran both hands backward through her hair and exhaled. *Why does life always seem so hard and unfair?* She had always been able to easily manage the stressors in her life: never meeting her parents' expectations, always having to prove herself to her parents, her classmates—especially in medical school—and now law enforcement professionals. It was the constant suffocating feeling of hostility and abandonment she had felt since her undergraduate days.

Charlie buried her face in her hands, trying to ease the pain and aggravation. She lifted her face up and looked around her room for solace. Despite her mother's threats of throwing away her "junk" if she didn't come home soon and claim it, the memorabilia remained just has Charlie had left it.

Pinned to the wall was a '68 Detroit Tigers World Series pennant, the year they came from behind to beat the Cardinals in seven games. Hanging from the corners of her mirror were University of Michigan pom-poms.

The bookcases were jammed with old textbooks, binders stuffed with tests and papers that she had written over the years, and spiral notebooks filled with class notes. She picked up her old teddy bear, with one eye missing and cross-stitches marking several areas of home surgery to mend his holes and keep in his stuffing. She held him to her breast—he had always brought her comfort in the past.

I could have used you these past couple of months. She laid him gently down on the bed and then stood up and stretched. "I could use a run," she said to the bear.

Charlie pulled off her purple turtleneck sweater and tossed it onto the bed, unbuttoning her low-riding hip-hugger jeans and pulling them off. Charlie reached into her bag and pulled out a maize-colored University of Michigan

T-shirt, navy-blue shorts, a faded gray hooded sweatshirt, and matching sweatpants.

Charlie knew her mother's reaction had she known Charlie would be running around town in a sweatshirt that had holes from so many machine washings. To Charlie, her running gear was like her favorite pair of blue jeans—they only got better with age.

Charlie pulled her hair into a ponytail as she walked down the hallway. She stopped at the closed door of her grand-mother's room. Her hand reached out to the doorknob, but she hesitated before deciding to open it. On the other side of the door, the lingering smell of Oriental herbs triggered hundreds of memories of her old Korean grandmother, her *hal-mun-ee.*

Charlie hadn't had the courage to enter her grandmother's room since she had passed away the year before. She opened the door, entered the room, and looked around. Folded at the end of the bed was the familiar heavy bright-pink synthetic "mink" blanket that had kept the old woman warm even on the coldest days. Charlie could still see her grandmother, with her smooth, dark-olive complexion, her silver hair pulled back, and her lively dark-brown eyes.

After school, Charlie would come into the room and see Hal-mun-ee sitting in the rocking chair smiling back at her. Charlie would kneel at her feet to be hugged and have her head patted and her hair smoothed. Her grandmother had always provided so much comfort and had been a source of strength for her. When Charlie was nineteen, she had returned home from college unexpectedly. Hal-mun-ee looked into Charlie's eyes and knew the bewildered, hurt, and shattered look. Charlie sat at her grandmother's feet and rested her head against her knee. The woman gently stroked Charlie's head and began to speak.

"It must have been around 1905…I couldn't have been more than five when the Japanese soldiers came marching into Seoul. I held my mother's hand while the others waved their flags. It all seemed very exciting to me—the military uniforms, the marching band, everyone waving flags and cheering. I watched in awe as the soldiers marched precisely in their tan uniforms, rifles slung over their shoulders, and the sun reflecting off the long, thin, razor-sharp bayonets past us. I looked up at my mother and smiled. I was so young and naive that I didn't recognize the concern in her eyes when she smiled back at me and squeezed my hand.

"It was all very confusing to a little girl. New roads and buildings were being built. New stores and businesses began to pop up like wild flowers in springtime, but at night I could hear my parents whispering. I could hear the concern in their voices. Then one day, I came home and saw soldiers standing in front of our house. Two soldiers held my mother by her arms, and she was crying.

"Two other soldiers escorted my father from our house. He was carrying a small suitcase in his hand. I could see tears in the corner of his eyes as he looked at my mother and shook his head no, trying to calm her fears. I ran toward him, yelling, 'Abeoji.' A soldier stepped forward and grabbed me. My mother and I cried and called out to him as we watched my father escorted away.

"Over the years, I learned that my father was a very high and powerful bureaucrat in the Seoul city government. They had taken him away like so many other wealthy and influential Korean men to work on the railroads. Most didn't survive the harsh and tyrannical treatment. It was the last time we ever saw him.

"In grade school, we were given their names. We spoke their language, studied their culture, ate their food, and any mention of our own heritage brought strict punishment. My mother did everything she could for us to survive. An aristocratic and proud woman, she worked in restaurants waiting on tables and washing dishes. At night sometimes they would come to our home.

"She did everything she could to protect and shield me, especially as I got older and started to become a woman. They eventually took notice and started to come around. Through her and my father's former connections, my mother eventually was able to secure a spot for me in Seoul University by giving up her home, and I went to live with a distant cousin.

"It was an exciting time to be with young men and women your own age and background. For a short time, we selfishly put aside our fears and hatred and went about our studying and social activities. However, reality set in, and we wanted our country back. We started to hold secretive meetings, planning and plotting.

"He arrived in the summer of 1918. General Heitaro Utsunomiya, a martinet, clamped down on student activities, but his actions only motivated us more. At first, we started small by sabotaging their vehicles and attacking isolated drunken soldiers staggering home from the bars at night. Our actions brought more severe and retaliatory punishments, but we were not to be deterred.

"It came to a head in the spring of 1919. We declared our own independence day. The students and soldiers clashed in the streets of Seoul. We were no match for their guns and long bayonets. I saw my classmates lying dead on the ground or crying out in pain.

"Those of us who weren't killed were arrested. Some were taken to the red brick buildings of Seodaemun Gamok, where they were tortured, found guilty, and hung. For us more fortunate, we were taken to Ryu San, the Imperial headquarters just south of Namsan next to the Han River. During the day, we cooked their food, washed and darned their uniforms, and polished their boots. At night, we were required to sleep with them. I was lucky; I was responsible for the officers.

"Eventually, I was able to escape. I hid on a boat that went to Hawaii. I worked in the pineapple fields and eventually met a nice man. We married and had a family. Your mother was my firstborn, born in the year of the tiger, at night. She should've been a boy."

My grandmother took my hand. "You're strong. Whatever has happened, you can overcome it. Don't give up."

Charlie could still feel her hal-mun-ee's presence in the room. She said a prayer in honor and thanks and then closed the door. She smiled and wiped a tear from the corner of her eye before making her way downstairs.

Charlie laced up her shoes, closed the front door, and began her run. As the daylight began to fade, she started with a loop around Quarton Lake. She looked at the impressive homes with their expansive lawns.

By the time Charlie had completed her loop, she had established a regular rhythm. Her body was running smoothly and efficiently and was beginning to derive pleasure from a runner's high. She picked up her pace and made her way toward downtown.

Running harder, her arms were slightly bent at the elbows, hands slightly closed, her legs turning over faster. Despite the cold, crisp air, she could feel the sweat starting to trickle down the side of her face.

The experience was liberating. Running here any time of the year was a pleasure that she never tired of—a perfect experience. She entered downtown proper, running past the familiar landmarks.

SS Kresge's dime store with its big red block letters with its bank of large glass fishbowls full of penny candies—Squirrels, Mary Janes, and jawbreakers. Next door was Sanders, celebrating its centennial with its to-die-for hot fudge ice cream sundaes and hot fudge cream puffs, and no birthday was complete if it didn't consist of their "bumpy cake."

How ironic that something so heavenly would be a piece of devil's food cake with stripes of buttercream covered with pourable fudge frosting.

She ran past the storefronts, checking her form in the reflection of the windows. She loved running through downtown to take in all the window displays and relive so many wonderful memories. It wasn't just Charlie who loved downtown—people all over the greater metro Detroit area would come to shop in Birmingham for the experience.

Heading west on Maple Road, Charlie ran along the sidewalks, dodging the shoppers as she went. She could feel their stares. She was an oddity—not only a runner, but a female runner. She ran past the landmark brown brick buildings of Jacobson's department store, or Jake's to the locals.

Charlie loved shopping at Jake's—it was a family tradition and a real treat. She remembered walking into Jake's as a child and being overwhelmed by the store's elegant displays. She had tried on several occasions to explain the experience for those who had never been to their stores. Usually not lost for words, Charlie's description could not do the store justice.

Jake's had a sophisticated ambiance that blended home furnishings, designer jewelry, superb personalized customer service, and fashion shows that showcased men's, women's, and children's clothing. Charlie thought she'd go shopping with her mom and her sister Susan and spoil herself with a skirt and blouse. She knew she was in dire need of a professional wardrobe.

She continued along Maple, past Wilson Drug store, and right onto Woodward Avenue, one of Detroit's most famous icons, known for drawing car enthusiast of all ages and walks of life. Charlie turned on Forest, across Old Woodward Avenue, and onto East Brown. The sun had set. It was dark, the air cold and crisp. She kept pumping.

Charlie liked running in the early evening hours. Coming into the home stretch, she picked up the pace. She was pushing her body to its limit. Her thoughts, on overdrive, shifted from the local setting to imagining she was Bobbi Gibb, the first woman to complete the Boston Marathon. Sprinting to an imaginary finish line, she made her way up Pierce and finished in the middle of Shane Park.

Charlie laughed to herself as the sweat stung her eyes and plastered her hair to her forehead. *If horses sweat, men perspire, and women merely glow, then I am certainly glowing.* Cooling off, she strolled through the park where kids played on the swings, slides, and merry-go-round to let off some of their restless energy as the moms took a needed break from shopping. Charlie walked over to her favorite store.

Unlike the malls that were dominated by chain stores, Birmingham's downtown hosted unique, one-of-a-kind stores like the Varsity Shop. Feeling nostalgic, Charlie opened the front door of her favorite store. She walked down the steps of the cramped store, looking at the numerous photos of Detroit Tigers, Lions, Pistons, and Red Wings players scattered among the University of Michigan sports teams and local Little League team memorabilia. She moved among the local high school and college student athletes there to buy their letterman jackets and sporting equipment.

From the Varsity Shop, she walked across the park to the Sportsman Store, whose architecture was something she would expect from an A. Quincy Jones design. The store's walls were adorned with wild animal trophies. Shelves were filled with Pendleton shirts, corduroys, luxurious wool sweaters, and fishing waders: everything a customer would need to be properly outfitted to appear on a segment of ABC's *The American Sportsman* hosted by Curt Gowdy.

Charlie finally started to jog back to her parents' home. By the time she arrived, her running euphoria had evaporated. As Charlie stood on the front porch, her sweat was causing her to shiver. She entered the house fighting the feeling of depression that was creeping up on her.

KATIE HILL'S STORY

Her lips are soft and moist. I never imagine that kisses could feel so good. I hold her breast and gently squeeze while I nibble on her neck. Janie lets out a noise, not quite a sigh, not quite a giggle. Her head presses against mine. I focus on pleasing her, but she's already managed to unbutton my jeans, and her fingers glide up and down my cotton panties.

Added to the excitement is the knowledge that Janie's folks are upstairs and can, at any moment, come downstairs and find us locked in a passionate embrace–my sweater pushed up and her shirt unbuttoned, bras undone, breasts heaving, and cheeks flushed with passion.

"Shit," we declare simultaneously. Our heads rest on each other's shoulders, and we catch our breath and eventually untangle ourselves.

I think back to before we met. For as long as I could remember, I've hidden my true feelings from family, friends, and, most frustratingly, myself. I never thought even in my wildest dreams that I'd ever get to feel such excitement and passion.

I remember it was a Friday night when I slept over at Janie's house. After a long night of eating Little Caesar's pizza, drinking Faygo Red Pop, watching a late night scary movie, and the National Anthem playing at the end of the broadcast, we went to sleep. Sometime during the early morning hours, we could feel each other's restlessness—tossing and turning, trying to find a comfortable position.

I wanted to touch her so bad, kiss her. My body ached, but I was so scared. I don't know who was first to start it. We still tease each other about who was the first to touch the other. All I know is when the sun came shining through the tiny rectangular basement window, I found peace and happiness for the first time.

My mind returns to the present, and I look at her, smile, and help button her blouse while she gently removes a wisp of hair from my face. We can hear heels clicking on the kitchen floor, and the basement door opens. Janie's mom shouts down, "Katie, it's your mom on the phone."

"Thanks, Mrs. Almonte. I'll be right up."

We giggle as I hook my bra, pull my sweater down, and take a quick check in the mirror to make sure nothing is out of place.

Like an alarm, the hinges of the basement door squeak.

"Katie, honey, hurry up. Your mom's waiting."

"Mrs. Almonte, I'm coming."

As I race up the stairs, I think about my last declaration. That it was not too far from the truth—just a few more minutes of heavy petting. *Whew, that was close!*

"Hi, Mom."

"Honey, how much longer are you going to be at Janie's house?"

"Not much longer. What time is it anyway?"

"It's seven thirty. Have you had dinner?"

"Yeah, Janie's mom fixed us dinner."

"Make sure you say thank you, but not much longer. Remember, we have to be on the road early tomorrow, and you haven't even packed yet. I love you."

"I'll be home shortly. I love you, too."

I come back to Janie's bedroom. She is sitting on her bed and looks up at me with an incredible smile. I will never tire of that smile.

"What did she want?"

I roll my eyes. "Yep, just checking."

"Do you think she suspects anything?"

"No way! No diary, no notes, no cards, not a thing. Oh, babes, I know that you would love for us to be more open and be able to express our feelings. So would I, but if our parents ever found out they would flip, and that wouldn't be the end of it. We would be tormented in school, and this town is too damn backward to ever handle our feelings for one another. We'd be paraded around like some circus freaks."

"You know…before, I met you…" Janie looks a little uncomfortable.

"Don't ever talk about her again…do you understand? It's just me and you."

"OK…I'm sorry…it's just…"

I walk over to her and place my hand over her mouth and look into her eyes. I can feel both the rage of jealousy and my desires for her. "Shhh…" I say.

Janie pulls my hand down. "Then can you sleep over this weekend?" Janie's smile changes, sliding into an enticing stare.

"I would love to, but we're taking off for our cabin tomorrow after my stepdad gets off work." My mood changes immediately.

"It would be fun! Just remember the first time we dis-covered that we had the hots for each other? Lying in bed together, pretending we're asleep, and allowing our legs and arms to accidently touch each other," Janie says.

"I know, but maybe next time."

"Besides, it's New Year's Eve, and we've got a lot to cel-ebrate. You'll be sorry."

"I'm never sorry when I'm with you," I say. "It's been a great year. My best year ever, and this one's going to be even better. Hey, I know it's a sorry substitute for spending the night together, but I still have time for a quickie. Game?"

"You read my mind," Janie says.

I dive at her on the bed. We lock and wrap ourselves in a passionate embrace.

An hour later, we are standing by the front door. Janie wraps the plaid scarf she bought me for Christmas around my neck as I button up my wool coat.

"God, this weather sucks. I'm going to freeze," I say.

"Run home quickly and call me when you get back next Sunday." Janie looks around and then reaches up, grabs my coat collar, pulls me down, and kisses me good-bye. "Happy New Year. Now go, or I'll drag you back in here against your will."

ROSEVILLE
WEDNESDAY, DECEMBER 31, 1975

The car idled in the distance, the heater softly humming along with the radio. The snow began to come down harder. Across the street, the two teenagers hugged, kissed passionately, laughed, and waved good-bye. The driver watched as the teenager pulled up her coat collar, keeping her head down to avoid the wet snowflakes as they stuck to her hair and clothing. The driver watched and smiled.

The teen was deep in thought, her shoulders hunched and head tucked in as far as it would go inside her collar. She made her way along the lonely, deserted street. The light of the street lamps reflecting off the snow gave the scene a surreal feeling.

The driver put the car in gear and inched down the street. The car pulled even with her and the passenger's side window slid open.

"Do you need a ride?" The sound was lost among the snowflakes.

The driver honked the horn to get the teenager's attention. She must have heard or seen something because she finally looked up and around.

"Excuse me?" the girl shouted.

"Do you need a ride?"

"What?"

The driver beckoned the girl to the car. "Do you need a ride?"

"No, my folks' place is just down the road a bit."

"This weather is nasty. All the more reason to jump in."

"You're right about that. It really sucks. Ah, why not. Hey, thanks. I hope that I'm not going to ruin your nice leather interior."

"No problem." The driver's voice was smooth and inviting.

"This is a hot car."

The green light from the dashboard eerily highlighted the driver's features. The young woman stared, her mind racing, trying to put where and when she had heard the driver's voice.

"I get the feeling we've met before. You look familiar. Have we met?"

"No, I don't think so."

"I'm sorry. I just get this feeling we have met before or I have seen you some place. Just make a left turn at the light. My folks' place is down two blocks on the left."

As the car rolled through the intersection, the teenager turned to face the driver. "Hey, you missed the light. Why did you do that? Hey, listen, you need to turn around."

She tried to open the door, but it was locked. "Let me out of here right now. You need to let me out right now!"

The driver calmly looked over at her.

A moment passed, and the young woman's head exploded with pain. Tears sprang to her eyes, and she could taste blood in her mouth where the blow had caught her on the side of the jaw. Before she could recover, the car jerked to the right, stopping. The driver violently yanked her by her hair, whipping her head back and forth, driving her face into the dashboard. The woman's lip and nose split open. Nauseous, her ears ringing, she was hanging onto consciousness when the next blow drove her into a black chasm.

ANN ARBOR
WEDNESDAY, DECEMBER 31, 1975

"I'm sorry. I know I haven't visited in a long time…It's just that I've been really busy. I know its New Year's…No, I don't have any plans, maybe a run. Dad, I'm sorry…I've got to go. Someone's at the front door. Give my best to mom, Susan, and the kids. Happy New Year…I love you, too." Charlie hung up the phone, raced to the front door of her ranch home, and opened it. Standing on the porch was a petite, attractive woman with long, red, curly-on-the-verge-of-frizzy hair and a big smile. Charlie looked into the big deep hazel eyes and freckled face.

"I'm glad I found you here."

"Annie, what a surprise." She let her friend in.

"The cavalry has arrived to save you from yourself." Annie walked into Charlie's foyer.

"What does the cavalry have in mind?"

Annie thrust a bottle into Charlie's hand and proceeded to unbutton her navy-blue peacoat.

"What's this?"

"It's champagne. What else do you drink to celebrate? Wait—dumb question. You probably have a blender full of wheat germ and carrot juice. Besides, we've got a lot to celebrate," Annie said, handing her coat to Charlie.

"We do?" Charlie said.

"You're impossible. Completing your residency and starting a new job, I'd say that's a lot," Annie said, walking toward the family room with Charlie in tow.

"I'd say it was awful presumptuous for you to think I'd be here. Who knows? I could've been out with a hot guy."

"It's freezing outside, but hell hasn't frozen over yet," Annie said.

"I'm not that bad, am I?" Charlie asked

"Let's put it this way: Mother Superior has nothing on you," Annie said, tearing off the aluminum foil cover of the champagne bottle as she began to struggle with the plastic cork.

"God, you sound like my parents and sister. Besides, you never know; at any moment my mystery date may be on the other side of that door," Charlie said, taking the bottle from Annie and gripping both the bottle and cork tightly.

The loud pop of the cork was followed by the sparkling wine flowing from the bottle. Annie grabbed the bottle, placed her mouth over the top of the bottle, and drank the wine before any spilled on the rug.

"Unfortunately, I'm pretty experienced at anticipating premature emissions. At least this tastes good and I'll get a buzz from it. Usually what follows is the loud sound of snoring coming from the other side of the bed," Annie said.

Charlie shook her head, taking the bottle from Annie. "I think I've got some glasses." The front doorbell rang. Charlie and Annie looked quizzically at each other.

"You see, my intuition never fails me...I told you, it's my mystery date behind the door ready to carry me away." Charlie winked at Annie as she got up to answer her front door.

"I hope there are two of them. Knowing my luck...I'll get the dud," Annie said.

Moments later, Charlie came back into the living room carrying a pizza box with plates, silverware, napkins, and glasses balanced on top. "Not exactly what I envisioned for Prince Charming," Charlie said, placing the pizza box on the coffee table and opening the top, allowing the fragrant full garlic smell to fill the room.

"At least yours brings you something delicious. The only type of yeast I get is in an infection from mine," Annie said, taking a piece of the pizza with the mozzarella strings hanging down. She deftly folded the slice in half. "Speaking of your parents, how are they doing? Shouldn't you be spending time with them?"

"I just got done speaking with them right before you arrived. I thought about it, thought the better of it, and decided to spend a quiet evening here."

"What did you tell them?"

"The usual," Charlie said, placing a slice of pizza on a plate as she began to cut it with a knife and fork.

"Pathetic," Annie said, watching Charlie as she cut her pizza and placed a forkful in her mouth.

"Which, my plans or how I'm eating my pizza?" Charlie said, holding up her fork and knife.

"Both. Were they upset?"

"No, their usual disappointment."

Annie took a napkin off the table and wiped her mouth. "Look at us—two hot women. We should have guys banging on the door trying to get at us. You more than me. I know I tease you about your obsession with running and diet, but your body is incredible. Don't get me started on the rest of you; your lips, your coloring...you barely wear makeup. Anyway...Instead, we're drinking champagne, eating pizza, watching *Dick Clark's Rockin' New Year's Eve*, and sitting by the fire like two old spinsters. We're sad."

"Speaking of family and not being with them, where are your munchkins?" Charlie asked, shaking her head in disbelief.

"They're with my mom and dad. They were bummed they couldn't spend the night with their favorite aunt," Annie said, nodding at the TV. "Do you think he's real?"

"Who? Dick Clark," Charlie asked.

"Yeah, the guy doesn't age. I think he died years ago and is filled with embalming fluid and they just wheel him out every year for the New Year's celebration."

"You nut, that's blasphemous to speak of Dick Clark like that," Charlie said.

The women spent the rest of the evening chatting about everything and nothing, watching TV, and eventually falling asleep where they lay. Hours later, Charlie stirred and happened to glance up at the clock. "It's almost midnight. Where did the time go?" Charlie stood up, feeling a little unbalanced from the buzz from the champagne. She looked around her at the damage on the large square orange shag rug—a grease-stained pizza, bottles, and chocolate wrappers.

Annie sat up and surveyed the disaster. "Looks like my house every day of the week."

Both women turned toward the TV and watched as Dick Clark counted off the last ten seconds of 1975. Loud cheers of the crowd gathered in New York's Times Square came from the TV. Charlie and Annie hugged each other.

"Time to forget our past, time for a new chapter," Annie said, rubbing Charlie's back.

"To a New Year filled with great joy and happiness," Charlie said,

ANN ARBOR
THURSDAY, JANUARY 1, 1976

Charlie could hear the phone ringing somewhere in her subconscious. She struggled to determine where the sound was coming from. Eventually, her mind shook off the blankets of sleep and realized the ringing was her phone on the bedside stand. Her eyes refused to cooperate, half closed, dry, and burning. She used all her energy to focus on reaching for the phone. "Yes?" Charlie answered with a raspy voice. She swung her legs to the floor and pulled the blankets up around her.

"Dr. Taylor?" a deep male voice asked.

"Yes."

"My name is Sergeant Jon Bailey, Bloomfield Township Police. Dr. Taylor, sorry to disturb you at this hour, but we were directed by the prosecutor's office to contact you."

"Yes, I'm sorry. What's this in reference to?" Charlie said, staring at the green lights glowing 4:00 a.m. from the clock radio.

"We've found a body of a young woman, and the DA would like you to come to the murder scene."

"Yes, yes. I'll be there as soon as possible. Where is the body located?"

"Ma'am, we're at the intersection of Franklin Road and Fourteen Mile Road. Are you familiar with the area?"

"Thank you, Sergeant. Yes, I'll be there as soon as I can." Charlie hung up the phone and gathered her thoughts. *I guess I start my job sooner than I thought.*

Charlie ran for the bathroom for a quick pee, ran a brush through her hair, and took a swig of Listerine to eradicate any morning breath. She looked around the floor for her cotton panties and bra. She pulled them on while continuing to look for her blue jeans and black turtleneck. She hesitated for a moment, looking at the rumpled blankets and sheets. She quickly ran from the room.

FRANKLIN VILLAGE
THURSDAY, JANUARY 1, 1976

Charlie raced the powerful Mustang along the deserted highways from Ann Arbor toward eclectic Franklin Village. She pushed the car as hard as she could as she entered the interstate, the light poles whipping by in a blur. Adrenaline pumping through her veins, Charlie tried to contain herself, knowing that she was going to a tragedy and not some sporting event.

Eventually, she left well-lit highways behind her and drove along the dark and empty suburban roads. Snowflakes started to fall and float and swirl across the blackened sky as they drifted to the ground. The car meandered north along Franklin Road.

Staring out the windshield, Charlie was lost in thought about her past: the events that had shaped her life to this point. *Why couldn't I be like everyone else? Why couldn't I desire a safe and predictable existence that mainly consisted of a handsome, thoughtful, loving husband, two gorgeous children, a pleasant home, and making baked goods for PTO fundraisers? What's wrong with being like June Cleaver?*

Charlie continued her drive, making out the familiar landmarks and sights. She allowed herself a moment of happiness and became lost in her own thoughts. Franklin was a great place to grow up as a kid. It had outstanding schools and safe neighborhoods where kids could ride their bikes or explore the woods for hours on end.

She thought about her own childhood, how she, Susan, and their friends would play hide-and-seek and tag among the expansive lawns. They rode their bikes past the picture-perfect homes situated along the ravine, along the paths that would take them to the river to explore.

Her thoughts were a like an old silent movie, slowly illuminating Franklin Village. As she passed Fourteen Mile Road, she could just make out the shadow of the Cider Mill when the whole area became a blaze of headlights, spotlights, and the flashing red-and-blue lights of emergency vehicles.

Charlie parked in the Cider Mill's parking area, got out of the car, and pulled up her collar to protect herself against the bitter cold and the wet snowflakes. *How pleasant life can be one moment and then reality comes crashing in all around you.* She walked over to the nearest policeman and showed her identification.

He directed her to a man standing in the middle of all the lights wearing an olive-green belted trench coat, brown faded corduroy pants, and black galoshes with the buckles all undone. He kept trying to comb his sparse hair in place but was losing the battle badly.

"Hi, Detective Stone, I'm Dr. Charlie Taylor." The detective eyed Charlie apprehensively for a moment. "Is there a problem, Detective?"

"No, no, I was just expecting to see someone else," he said and then blew into his hands.

"You mean like a man?"

"Well, sort of, and someone with more experience."

"Detective Stone, I understand. I get that a lot."

"Well, she's over here." Detective Stone pointed in the direction of all the commotion and started walking toward it. "Hey, Doc, I was warned by a guy from MSP that you might be coming, but I didn't believe him. But thanks anyway for coming out here on such short notice."

As they approached the body, Charlie observed the technicians and other detectives examining the body and crime scene. "Let me warn you, this isn't pleasant," Detective Stone said. "I've been at this job for over twenty-five years, and I've never seen anything like this. Honestly, we could use your help."

"I'll try. Why don't we start with what we know?"

"The body was discovered by a couple on their way home from a party." The police officer pointed at a young couple sitting in the back of a police cruiser.

"Can I see the victim?"

"Brace yourself."

Charlie walked over and looked down at the body. Her mind whirled as it registered all the facts. She had observed hundreds and hundreds of crime scene photos. Charlie thought she'd heard it all from her prison interviews with the sickest, cruelest, and most brutal of them all. They'd muse with a sadistic glee in their eyes and describe in great detail the things they had done to a "tasty treat."

But she wasn't prepared for what lay in front of her. She looked down at the beautiful girl. The sheer anger and rage exhibited was obvious.

The young woman lay prostrate in the snow, brutally exposed and discarded like a piece of trash. Her skin was slightly bluish; her large breasts hung down at her side. Charlie tried to imagine that her face was once beautiful, but now it was puffy and black and blue from the blows she had received. Her nose was slightly askew, possibly broken, with drops of blood trickled out. Her forehead had a gaping wound: one and a quarter inches long by three-eighths of an inch wide. The injuries to her vagina and anus looked painful even in death.

Charlie studied the brutality for a while longer and then stepped back to observe the crime scene. She wrapped her arms around herself to keep from shivering as the cold early morning sun came up. Charlie's eyes were tired, but she shook off any exhaustion. She went back to her car and leaned her backside against it, deep in thought. She heard the approaching footsteps crunching on the snow and gravel but didn't respond to them. A gloved hand holding a Styrofoam cup of coffee with steam pouring out the top extended out to her. She reached up and took the cup.

Charlie tasted the burned bitter coffee that had been cooking far too long. "Thanks," she murmured, looking up at the face.

"I thought you could use it." Pete leaned against the car beside Charlie. "What's it been, about five years?"

"That sounds about right," Charlie said.

"What was her name?"

"Lauren Ring."

"That's right. You know we never found the guy…the secret lover. Case went completely cold. I've heard they lost some of the files associated with the case."

Charlie shook her head. "Why am I not surprised? What brings you out here?"

"The same as you: early morning call. This is a local homicide, but anything that has to do with children or teenagers, the locals know to call me."

Charlie nodded in acknowledgment.

"This wasn't what I was looking for," Pete said.

Charlie turned her head and looked at Pete, trying to register his last comment.

Pete stared straight ahead. "I'm looking for any information that will lead me to the Brotherhood."

"The Brotherhood?"

"It's a name I've given to the fraternity of pedophiles— they're a group of very influential men who get their rocks off at the expense of little boys and girls. My boss thinks that I'm wasting my time, that I'm chasing some ghosts, but I know they're out there. I just can't find that one clue that will prove I'm right. Yourself?"

"My new job," Charlie said.

"That's right, I heard something to the effect that you were going to work for the Ice Princess."

"Who?"

"Don't tell me you haven't heard that before? You're good at what you do. You'll find out soon enough. What's your initial impression?"

Charlie smiled at Pete. She liked his cynicism. "It's hard for me to make a very accurate assessment, but looking at the victim, I'd say the assailant or assailants are white males, twenty-five to thirty years of age. The offender is asserting his or their power. The massive blows to the head, disposing of the victim's body like trash, no signs from the crime scene for us to look at. This type of offender probably drives a meticulously cleaned pickup truck and gets off on looking at hard-core porn magazines. I'll be able to validate those impressions once I get to know the victim…and if I ever get to see where the actual murder took place."

Pete looked at Charlie thoughtfully. "I see you haven't lost your touch." Charlie nodded her head in acknowledgment.

"Watch yourself. You know there are those in LE who'll think you're nothing more than a modern-day witch doctor."

Charlie smiled sardonically. "I'm not much different than they are. I study the crime scene, gather information on the victim, note the behaviors involved, and arrive at an informed judgment about the characteristics and traits of an unidentified offender. Scotland Yard developed a profile of Jack the Ripper. Think about Sherlock Holmes. 'You see, but you do not observe. The distinction is clear.'"

"Oh, now that you put it that way, it makes perfect sense—'elementary.' I'll reference all missing children reports in the last twenty-four to forty-eight hours. I'll let you know if I hear anything." Pete pushed himself up off the car. "Good luck with your boss." He waved good-bye without looking back.

LANSING
MONDAY, JANUARY 5, 1976

Pete sat across the dark walnut desk of his mentor, who just happened to have the name Abraham Lincoln. The imposing black man closed the file on his desk and then sat back and looked apprehensively at Pete.

"How are you holding up?" Abraham asked, taking the football off his desk and spinning it in the air.

"I'm fine," Pete said.

"Gabrielle, the kids—how are they? I'm still trying to figure out what that beautiful black woman is doing with the likes of you," Abraham said, tossing the football at Pete.

Pete's hands instinctively reached up and snapped the ball in the air. "You Moo U guys never understood the power of Maize and Blue and the effect that it had on women."

Both men had played for the cross-state rival football teams, and they never missed an opportunity to needle each other.

"She's good, I guess. If my Jacobson's bill is any indication, she should be ecstatic. The kids' behavior is all age appropriate. Doing well in school, seem to be relatively happy."

"That boy of yours…"

"He's got a great arm. At first I was thinking wideout, maybe a safety like his old man, but now I'm thinking maybe QB," Pete said, throwing the football back at Abraham.

"Seriously, Pete, anytime you want out of this, just say the word. There isn't a department that wouldn't take you in a heartbeat."

Pete looked away. "I'm fine, really. I appreciate the concern. You'll be the first to know when I'm ready. But not until I'm good and ready. Besides, I'm getting close. I can feel it."

"That's right, getting close to this mythical organization? What do you call them…the fraternity?"

"You bastard…you know that I call 'em the Brotherhood. You also know that based upon previous arrests there is some very compelling evidence that the pedophiles operating in and out of Cass Corridor may be linked to these suburb parties. Bottom line, we've known that it wouldn't take long before someone realized they could make a lot of money selling children and child pornography," Pete said, raising his right arm, placing it on the arm of the chair, and resting his chin on his fist.

"They've taken the pages from the playbook of some of the state's very own successful multilevel marketing businesses. These guys are sitting at the top of the pyramid. The concept is simple and almost foolproof. They're able to siphon money right off the top based upon the actions of others. But there is no direct linkage. If I didn't hate them so much, I'd marvel at the simplicity and effectiveness."

"Come on, Pete, really? Multilevel marketing?"

"Let's start with the bottom-feeders—men who go out and pick up the children. They transport and deliver the goods, such as eight-millimeter rolls of film and pictures and even in some cases the kids themselves. Most of these guys come from the ranks of previously abused and exploited children and are scraping the bottom of the barrel financially, socially, and emotionally. Having been manipulated most of their lives, it's not a stretch for pedofilism to continue in their adult lives. You know the streets better than I do. What do your intel sources say?" Pete asked as he sat forward in his seat.

"We know they're targeting children of prostitutes and unwed mothers living and hanging out on the street," Abraham said.

"After my last arrests, these guys are getting about ten percent of every dollar collected and never know where the money goes. They just leave it at designated drop-off points, and if they're ever arrested, they're simply out of luck," Pete said, running his hand through his close-clipped, graying blond hair.

"If that isn't bad enough, it's our own kind that really has me pissed off: white-collar professionals who are attending parties held at various houses throughout the suburbs. They're not interested in what they describe as 'skanky inner-city kids—who are smelly, dirty, or disease carrying.' This level requires a better class of victims: kids from their own neighborhoods. So they recruit a more sophisticated bottom-feeder.

"They recruit guys right out of the college ranks. During the summers, they volunteer to coach local Little League teams or work as camp counselors. Their clients, like ordering from a restaurant menu, make their desires for little boys known, and then boys from seven to thirteen come rolling in. Blue eyed and blond is the most prized. They scour team rosters for a boy who might fit the bill. Big money is involved, so these guys go after their marks with a passion and zeal that'd make most used car salesmen envious," Pete said, sitting back in his chair.

"My friend, I'm on your side. I want these guys as bad as you do, but up to this point all you've got is a compelling theory. Right now, all you're doing is kicking field goals. Score me a touchdown."

"I think it's through their connections that I haven't been able to nail them to the cross," Pete said.

"Now we're talking conspiracy theories? Dammit, I've got access to some of the very best intelligence sources, and they're not able to give me anything. Don't you think I'd have found a leak? You know how hard it is to keep a secret among these guys. Honor among thieves, and all that."

"Abraham, these 'prominent' citizens are taking advantage of our most vulnerable, and they can go screw themselves if they think I'm going to stop because I've become a nuisance. We're not talking about interrupting their bridge game. They're selling these kids like they're pieces of property."

"Why in the hell would rich and powerful men be abusing and selling kids?"

"Because it's the ultimate aphrodisiac: power over their victims, sexual gratification, and money," Pete said.

"You know that I've got your back," Abraham said, raising both arms in the air like he was being held up. "But, my friend, I won't be able to protect you if you insist on making accusations at some of society's most prominent citizens. Enough of the Brotherhood for now. Tell me about the latest."

"We don't have a positive ID, but we think she's the missing teenager from Roseville. We'll know later today. The parents are coming in to identify the body. I'll pass onto local LE what I've learned. It's their case. Don't see it associated with anything that I'm working on."

ROSEVILLE
WEDNESDAY, JANUARY 7, 1976

"My understanding is that you and Katie were close. Her parents said you were inseparable." Charlie looked at the devastated teenager crumpled in the plastic chair.

Jane Almonte looked up at Charlie, her nostrils painfully raw and red, her eyes swollen. "Is it true? You know...what they say happened to her?"

71

Charlie looked at the girl. "It's best that you remember her the way she was." Charlie watched as the young woman had another round of painful sobbing. "Tell me about her. She sounds very unique."

"She was the best. My life sucked before I met her. This is so corny, but I felt like Dorothy after she left Kansas and arrived in Oz. Everything here is shades of blue and grays. Nothing bright or colorful ever seems to survive here. Everyone is so damn depressing around here. All they ever do is bitch about their jobs, politicians, anyone not like them.

"Everyone does the same thing; my dad, my brothers, and their friends go to ballgames, play poker, smoke Lucky Strikes, slug down Stroh's beer, and run Brylcreem through their hair. My mother and her friends spend their time going to Tupperware parties, collecting coupons, wearing faux furs and Hawaiian choker necklaces, and trying to keep it all in place with Playtex Living bras and girdles.

"For real excitement, Friday nights are for all-male or all-female bowling leagues, while Saturday nights are devoted to mixed bowling leagues. If they aren't bowling, they're heading north to Grayling or Gaylord.

"Just like Dorothy, the light went on in my world, and it was finally filled with color. She was so different from anyone I had ever met. Katie and I first met at school one day in the hallway. We ran into each other, our books and notes scattering all over the crowded hallway. We were crawling on our hands and knees, trying to avoid being kicked and stepped on. We just grabbed anything we could get our hands on. We got up and looked at each other and decided to go to the library to sort out the mess of papers and books.

"'I think this one is yours…' I asked. I looked across the table at this big girl, and she's dressed like everyone else in jeans and flannel shirt. I really hadn't paid much attention to her, but out of the blue she asks, 'Do you like Vonnegut?' I hand her back a paperback copy of *Breakfast of Champions*.

"I shrug. 'He's OK…I'm reading Joyce Carol Oates's *Do with Me What You Will*. It takes place in Detroit. I can kind of relate to the character…You know she used to live here?'

"'Who?'

"'Joyce Carol Oates. What are you reading now?'

"She looks around to see if anyone could hear us. 'Please don't tell anyone…if my folks ever found out they'd ground me forever.'

"I'm getting excited about the conversation, so I'm looking to my left and right to make sure no one can hear us.

"'Promise?' she asks me.

"I shake my head emphatically. 'Promise.'

"'I got my hands on a copy of *The Catcher in the Rye*. I love it. I can really relate to Holden.'

"'Really? Can I read it after you're done?'

"She smiles. 'Sure.…You're the first person I've met who likes to read…I mean really read. I'm Katie.'

"'I'm Janie.' I smile at her. The school bell rings, and we both realize we're late for class and tear out of there.

"We soon started to meet in the library after school and walk home together while talking about books. Sometimes, we'd go get something to eat. I never had a close friend until I met Katie."

"It sounds like the two of you had a very special bond. You're fortunate. Most people go through their lives never having a friendship like yours. Jane, I'm sorry, but since you were so close, I'd like to ask you some personal questions about Katie."

"Why?"

Charlie noticed the sudden defensive posture. "Good question. Teenage girls are more likely to share sensitive information with their close friends than they would with their parents, clergy, or teachers. More importantly, if I have a better understanding of Katie, then I can help the police. We all want to catch the guy who did this. Help us help Katie. Please."

Jane finally nodded.

"Was there someone special in her life, like a boyfriend, a secret admirer, or a crush?"

Jane shook her head. "She wasn't the type."

Charlie got up from her chair and looked around Jane's basement bedroom. She saw numerous pictures of Jane and Katie pinned to the corkboard on the wall. Charlie went and examined the pictures. "These are great. Where was this one taken?"

Jane smiled. "Boblo Island. We had such a great time."

"God, I haven't been there in years. My sister and I use to dare each other to ride the Wild Mouse." Charlie turned and smiled at Jane. "OK, she didn't have any love interest. What about enemies? I know how mean teenage girls can be."

"No. Katie would've beaten them up. They were afraid of her."

"Really? Why?"

"One time this girl started to pick on me in the girls' locker room. One moment she's teasing me about my breasts and the next moment she's on the floor. She didn't know what hit her. Nobody ever messed with Katie or me again. She could be pretty protective of me."

"Tell me about the last time you were together."

Jane chewed on her fingernail. "We were just hanging out in my bedroom, down in the basement, just goofing."

"Did she seem anxious or upset about anything?"

Jane shook her head no vigorously. "I mean, she wasn't exactly thrilled about going to the cabin with her folks. We wanted to spend New Year's Eve together, but she wasn't upset or anxious about anything."

"When you said good-bye to each other, did you notice anything suspicious? Like a car or someone around your house?" Charlie asked as she sat back down and crossed her leg over her knee.

"No, it had started to snow heavily. I watched her walk away from the house for as long as I could. It was like the night and snow just swallowed her up."

Charlie stood up, closed her notebook, and then gently touched Jane on the shoulder. "Jane, thanks. I think I've got a pretty good idea of who Katie was and how special your relationship was. If you remember anything else, please call me. Will you?" Charlie left the girl to her grieving. As she walked out of the basement, she thought to herself that she had seen relationships like Katie and Jane's before.

Charlie hopped into her car and made her way onto Interstate 696 heading west. As she drove, Charlie was trying to comprehend why Katie's killer would risk so much by driving so far from Roseville to Franklin. The killer had too much to lose unless he had something else in mind.

ANN ARBOR
WEDNESDAY, JANUARY 7, 1976

Charlie entered her 1950's ranch-style home and picked up the mail that had been dropped through the slot. She leafed through the letters, alphabetizing them as she went. She entered the study off the foyer and placed the envelopes with the other unanswered mail next to the answering machine with the flashing red light announcing all the messages that had gone unanswered. She hadn't touched any of the holiday's well-wishes mixed among the sales promotions and bills.

She sighed; she didn't even have the motivation to go for a run. She thought about pouring herself a stiff drink, but that seemed so unsatisfactory. Maybe if she ate something she might feel better.

Charlie made her way to the kitchen. She opened the cupboards—nothing appealed to her. Charlie opened the refrigerator and looked at its contents. She was left uninspired. Charlie's arm wrapped around the door as she continued to stare at the contents. Her conversation with Jane Almonte had struck a chord with her.

Charlie was happy that Jane had found happiness and hoped she could again in the future. Charlie thought about her own personal life, wondering if she'd ever find someone as special as Jane had found with Katie.

Charlie was never alone—she was just lonely. Her parents' and sister's constant intrusions about her own life left her exhausted. Their invariable prodding to get out and date—*to find that special someone*—made her defensive. She slammed the kitchen door and heard the bottles rattling.

She made her way into the family room and turned on the TV. She threw herself down on the couch and rubbed her temples. She looked over at the wall clock and thought about how she'd occupy the night. The prattle coming from the TV left her numb. Charlie closed her eyes and curled into a fetal position.

She could feel it coming on: the nagging darkness that would slither into her world. The feeling that mostly stayed hidden, repressed in the recesses of her mind. It would come out uninvited and unannounced. It would just wind itself around her self-confidence, slowly squeezing, tightening. She'd fight back with all her might to try and overcome it. She'd try sleeping, drinking, and rationalizing it away. But it always seemed to overpower her.

She could feel the cold scales wrapped tightly around her, suffocating her. She'd start to think about the ways she'd do it: drugs and alcohol, warm water and a sharp razor, or going out to the garage and starting the car—simply going to sleep. Leave a letter explaining her actions. How she was tired and wanted it to end—how the serpent had won.

She found it easy to help others. See them through their dilemmas, carefully guiding them, providing candlelight through their own darkness—a way out, hope. She was a respected doctor. She had family and friends who loved her. And so she questioned why she always felt so empty.

She had the occasional lover, but that didn't seem to work either. The only thing that seemed to fight the darkness was her work, to keep herself so consumed with it that it was the only thing that held the serpent at bay.

Her phone rang. She was going to let it go to the answering machine where it could enter the queue like all the other messages. But she looked at the phone as she heard a familiar voice.

"Hey, girl, it's me, Annie. We'd love to have you over for dinner on Saturday night around six thirty. Nothing fancy— just lasagna, salad, and wine. See you then. Love ya."

The slithering serpent quickly recessed back into the darkness. Charlie breathed a sigh of relief with the thought that her plans would have to wait a little while longer.

SHELLY COLEMAN'S STORY

"**H**oney, time to go night, night. Sleep tight." I love her toothy little grin. I pull her blanket up and hand her bottle to her. I turn on her nightlight and close the door. I can hear her sucking on her bottle. It won't be long before she's asleep.

I go to the TV room and turn the TV on. I turn the dial to channel 7, *On the Rocks*, no thanks. I turn the dial to channel 4, *Invisible Man*, too scary, and then I turn the dial to channel 2, *Rhoda*...great. I grab my soda and bowl of chips and just sit down when I think I hear a noise downstairs.

At first, I think nothing of it. It's probably just Steve and Melissa coming home from their dinner. Then I hear the noise again...Was that the kitchen door opening and closing? I can hear the footsteps of someone walking across the kitchen floor. Why haven't they yelled up to me like they always do? Maybe they don't want to wake the baby.

"Steve, is that you? Melissa? I'm upstairs."

Nothing. Silence. I get off the couch and creep over to the TV and turn it off. I can hear the clock ticking and feel my heart starting to beat a little faster, pounding against my chest.

I hear the first step creaking…"Hello?" I call out with less confidence. Still nothing. I'm really beginning to get scared. I'm paralyzed.

Now I hear footsteps pounding up the stairs and down the hallway toward me.

"Help…please…no…don't."

BIRMINGHAM
MONDAY, JANUARY 19, 1976

"Now, George, do you really need to be shoveling snow off the roof at this hour?"

"No, Helen, I really do not want to be climbing the roof and shoveling snow off at this hour, but I do not want to wake up in the middle of the night with our roof caved in, dear, because of the weight of the snow either!"

"Just be careful."

"Yes, my darling." *Damn roof—so much for architectural appeal.*

"Hey, Helen, where did you pack my hat and gloves? I can never find anything around this place. Where in the hell did you move them?"

"I didn't touch 'em. They're probably in the same place that you left them."

"Thanks, I found them." *She's always moving my stuff.*

George made his way to the garage, flipped on the light switch, and pushed the garage door opener. As the door opened, he could feel the cold wind rushing into the garage, hitting him like a ton of bricks.

"Shit."

He took down a ladder, walked outside, and placed it against the gutter.

Thank God this is a ranch. It would really suck if I had to climb two stories.

He went back into the garage, got the snow shovel, and shortly began his ascent, muttering to himself about the crappy winter. It was bitterly cold, and with no Christmas lights or holidays to look forward to, the snow's appeal had already evaporated.

He had been shoveling for only a short time when he shivered not from the cold, but an eerie sensation that gripped his body. He stood straight up and looked down the street, but all was quiet. Only the occasional bark of a neighbor's dog off in the distance disturbed the night. He wondered why noise traveled so freely at night. He would never be able to articulate why he happened to glance across the street at his neighbor's house before resuming his shoveling, but something had caught his attention in the far recesses of his brain.

At first the scene before him seemed so surreal, the savagery and viciousness was hard to fathom. He hadn't seen anything like it since World War II. Time crawled to a standstill like some bad dream where George couldn't will himself to run. His legs would not move.

His body would not respond to his mind. George did the only thing his body would allow.

He screamed at the top of his lungs.

BIRMINGHAM
MONDAY, JANUARY 19, 1976

This was Pete's favorite time of day, his salvation. They had finished dinner. He marched the kids upstairs and ensured they were bathed, read to, and tucked into bed. As he came downstairs, Gabrielle met him at the foot of the stairs with a smile and a glass with two fingers of scotch over ice. They moved into the cozy family room, turning off the lights, lighting the candles, and turning on the stereo as they settled into their favorite piece of furniture: a large, comfortable leather sofa.

Gabrielle sat at one end and stretched her legs across so her feet settled into Pete's lap. Pete stared into the fire and listened to the soft jazz sounds that had a hypnotic effect on him as he unconsciously and methodically massaged her feet. His mind began to relax and wander. He wasn't sure if it was the music, the candles, the alcohol, or the sofa itself that had led to all the nights of passion. A smile came to his face.

"What are you thinking?" Gabrielle asked.

His smile grew, both because of his thoughts and the fact that she had caught him.

"I was just thinking about all the great nights that we have shared on this sofa together and that at least one of the nights had led to a conception of a child."

"Peter J., you're a dog."

"Busted."

He thought of all the others that had preceded Gabrielle. The women he termed Barbies, the eye-catching blondes who were either cheerleader this or homecoming that, but he found them tiresome, predictable, and boring. Gabrielle was none of those things. He always found her looks compelling: the color of her skin, her exotic hazel eyes, and her shapely body that was to die for.

He never tired of her company; he loved the way she made him feel. She was his soul mate, and together they had scratched out a life that neither of them thought was imaginable.

The phone rang, jolting them both back to reality.

"I'll get it," Gabrielle declared, swinging her feet around and quickly scooting to pick up the phone.

"I hope to God it's Becky wanting a cup of sugar or sandwich bags," Pete yelled out.

"West residence. Hi, John! No problem...Yes, he's right here...Yes, I absolutely understand. Honey, for you. It's John."

Pete got up and walked over to the phone, took the receiver from Gabrielle, and slapped her lightly on the butt as she walked away.

"Hey, John, what's up?"

"Pete, sorry to disturb you at home, but we have a homicide, and it's not a pretty one. We need you over here right away."

"Where are you?"

"Lodge Street."

"Shit, that's just a few blocks from here. How bad?"

John took a deep breath. "Looks like a break-in and robbery gone wrong, a teenage girl raped and shot multiple times. Normally, this would be a local issue, but it looks somewhat similar to the other girl we found in Franklin a couple of nights ago."

"Thanks, John. I'm on my way."

As he hung up the phone, he looked at Gabrielle and forced a smile. "Sorry, I gotta go."

Gabrielle looked at him with concern. "Doesn't sound good."

"Unfortunately, it's not. I'll probably be very late, so please don't wait up." Pete knew that she wouldn't listen: he'd most likely find her fast asleep in her chair with a book on her lap. He went to his office, where he kept his personal items. In one smooth motion, he reached for his service revolver, clipped it to his belt, grabbed his wallet and keys, and made his way to the door.

Gabrielle waited for him with his coat and helped him put it on. They hugged and kissed each other good-bye.

"Wake me when you get in, and we'll work on making number three."

Pete smiled, knowing thoughts of her would carry him into the night and many more to come.

BIRMINGHAM
MONDAY, JANUARY 19, 1976

Pete parked his car and made his way toward the commotion. He flashed his badge, and the patrolman who was controlling the gawkers and press directed him to the house. Pete walked through the front door into the comfortable home. He took in the surroundings, noting everything—a lesson he had learned in Vietnam—when he heard his name called.

"Hey, Pete, up here."

Pete climbed the stairs, meeting John at the top. "Hey, John."

"She's over here. It's tragic." John pointed in the direction of the crime scene.

"Aren't they all?"

"This is especially sad. Both parents are dead—died in a car crash a couple of years ago. This is her older brother's house. She was babysitting her niece. Nine months old."

"Baby?" Pete asked.

"The baby is fine," John said.

Pete walked over to Shelly Coleman's body and looked at the butchery. Her clothes had been ripped off her body and discarded around the room. The face of the young girl on the verge of womanhood was bruised, her body showing signs of rape and sodomy.

"It wasn't enough for the killer to do this to her. He emptied his .22 caliber pistol into her face and body," John said.

Pete's mind flashed back to Vietnam, to another young woman. His face turned hard—what his teammates used to call his "game face."

"Any witnesses?"

"Yes, we're in luck for once. The neighbor across the street saw the whole thing. By the time the guy left the house, several neighbors had congregated at the end of the driveway across the street. Listen to this. The guy comes out of the house, strolls down the drive, and nonchalantly walks up to the crowd and asks what's happening. He then turns and goes to his car, a white Cadillac, and drives away."

"And no one stops him?"

"I think they were in shock."

"Description?"

"He's a white male, about eighteen to twenty-two years of age, five foot ten inches to six foot tall, lean, scraggly beard."

Pete was about to ask his next question when he heard a commotion behind him. He and John turned in the direction of the loud conversation. Pete saw Charlie handing her ID to the patrolman, trying to explain who she was. Pete yelled over to the patrolman, "She's with the prosecutor's office. She's one of us."

The skeptical officer handed Charlie back her ID and stepped aside. Charlie walked up, joining Pete and John.

"Thanks."

"John, Dr. Charlie Taylor. Charlie, Detective John Gonzalez. Dr. Taylor works for Sydney White."

"Aw, the…" John started to speak.

"I already warned her." Pete smiled. "APB called in?"

"Yes."

"Make sure the state troopers have it, too. This guy might make a run for Ohio. Hopefully he hasn't outrun our radios."

"Will do."

"Thanks, John. Charlie, she's over here." Pete and Charlie walked over to look at the teenager. Pete stepped back and allowed Charlie to absorb the scene. Charlie looked at the battered and bloody face, the bruises to the body, and the girl's discarded clothes around the room.

"OK, Holmes, what do you think?" Pete asked, looking at Charlie. "Do you think it could be the same perp who killed Katie Hill?"

"Similar, but slightly different. This killer achieved power through his rape fantasy and left a mess; the rape and murder are the goals. I'd say he's much younger than the other assailant. He's probably eighteen to twenty-two years of age. He's probably around six feet tall; he had bad acne as a teenager, so he's trying to grow facial hair. He makes up for his physical and economic limitations through another means like driving an expensive car, either a Cadillac or Lincoln."

"Tell me you overheard us talking."

Charlie looked down and smiled to herself for a moment. "No, I really didn't hear anything before I came here and observed the murder scene. It's probably not healthy, but I'm obsessed by all of this. When I'm not actually looking at a crime scene, I'm reading everything I can get my hands on. And when I tire of reading, I'm spending time with some of our most illustrious patrons of Jackson State Prison. Pete, I'm a woman in a man's world. I can't afford not to be good."

Pete listened thoughtfully. "We've got eyewitnesses, and if it's any consolation, you were dead on in your description. I'm sure the locals will have this wrapped up pretty quickly."

Charlie looked back over at Shelly. "I don't think the Brotherhood had anything to do with this crime."

"No, I'm afraid you're right about that, too."

"One more thing…tell them to look down river or inner city. He's not from around here. It seems like our year is off to an auspicious start," Charlie said as she started to walk away.

PONTIAC
FRIDAY, JANUARY 23, 1976

Charlie surveyed the Oakland County Prosecutor's Office with its massive and beautiful mahogany desk, the large plush weave rug, and complementing chairs and sofa for the staff and visiting politicians to grovel before one of the most powerful political officers in the state. She respected the "trophy" or "I love me" wall adorned with diplomas from the best university acknowledging the highest academic achievement. Next to the diplomas displayed prominently were photos of the prosecutor standing alongside a president, the governor, and several local politicians. Several framed letters of appreciation with gold emblazoned emblems from the highest offices articulating the signers' heartfelt thanks hung on the walls.

What wasn't on display, but equally impressive, were the carnage and destruction undertaken to achieve this position. *Ice Princess—wasn't that the term of endearment used to describe Sydney White?*

Was it the lack of compassion that Sydney demonstrated toward her opposing counsel and their clients, taking every opportunity to step on their necks? Was it used to describe her physical appearance, most notably her striking platinum-blond hair? Was it the fact that she steadfastly remained celibate, leaving many men who had tried to win her affection in the deep freeze?

Charlie watched the staff closely. The tension was evident in the occasional cracking of knuckles, nail biting, and the apprehensive glances at the clock and looks toward the heavy wood door that led to her inner office.

Charlie had been observing their behavior the past month. They were sitting in the conference room of Sydney White, Oakland County prosecutor, for the weekly Friday morning meeting. Regardless of what others thought, Sydney White was a maverick, a pioneer. She was the first woman to win a seat in the Oakland County prosecutor's office. She had taken on the political bosses and beaten them at their own game. Now there was even talk that she was fighting to get the party's support to run for governor.

When the door opened, Sydney White strode confidently into the conference room and took the seat at the head of the table. Charlie looked at the attractive woman with her platinum-blond hair pulled tight into a ponytail—not a hair out of place. She was wearing a mocha neck-tie blouse with a chocolate skirt. She immediately took charge of the meeting. Sydney looked around the room.

"Let's get started. Bill?"

Bill Choate, her trusted deputy, ran down the cases that were currently on trial and then the pending cases. He navigated deftly around the land mines that would trigger his boss's explosions. Everyone seemed to be holding their own until she asked about the two teenagers' deaths.

"What do we have on the two girls' deaths?" The question was met with uneasy silence. "What, you think your silence is going to stop me from asking? What do we know about these girls' deaths?" There was a knock at the door. "Yes?" Sydney answered.

"Ma'am, it's nine thirty. You've got thirty minutes before the press conference," her assistant informed her. "The list of attendees' names and the organizations they represent are on your desk, too."

"Helen, thank you, and yes, I believe that I'm ready." As Helen shut the door to her boss's office, Charlie couldn't imagine a time that Sydney White wasn't prepared.

Charlie watched and listened as Sydney White's voice rose in volume and deliberateness. "All right, gentlemen, you've heard the woman. I've got a press conference in thirty minutes, and I'm going to have to give them something. So what do we know?"

Charlie could feel the heat and smell the fear as Sydney slammed both hands on the table. "For Christ's sake, we've had two teenage girls killed within a couple of weeks of each other. You haven't produced anything: no eyewitnesses, no leads. Come on, people, let's get it together. We're acting like a bunch of JV players."

Finally, Bill cleared his throat and spoke up as he slid several pictures across the large mahogany conference table. Sydney looked at the photos briefly and then passed them onto Charlie. Charlie looked at Katie's school photo, which showed a beautiful young lady, a good student with a nice family, a good friend, and compared it with the crime scene photos revealing the sadistic nature of the wounds inflicted on this young woman during the heinous crime.

For a brief moment, Charlie let her feelings stir for Katie's parents, who would have a difficult time recognizing their own daughter from the crime scene photos. She had already seen how this case had garnered a lot of attention from the public and media. This was going to be a career maker or breaker for all involved.

Bill Choate cleared his throat and spoke. "I've heard through some of my informants that a few members from a local gang might be involved. Rumor has it that maybe one of the gang member's girlfriends may have the young woman's clothing. For the killer or killers to abduct her in Roseville and drive all the way out to a rather remote area of Franklin Village is of interest. No history of drugs or misbehavior. Despite her modest background, Katie was clearly college bound."

He went on, "From Dr. Taylor's conversations with family and friends, we know she wasn't the type to go off on a whim or hang with the wrong crowd to inflict pain and anguish on her parents. She was careful and cautious, so she wasn't likely to engage in any risky behavior like going hitchhiking. Although she was a very attractive girl, she hadn't been dating anyone. No one steady, so most likely there was no jealousy angle there."

"What about our most recent victim?" Sydney asked.

Bill waited a moment to give others the opportunity to speak, but hearing none he continued. "The second victim was Shelly Coleman, a fourteen-year-old orphan who lived with her brother. On Monday the nineteenth, Shelly was babysitting in an upstairs room when the perp broke into the house. Apparently, he had broken into other houses in the neighborhood. She was just at the wrong place and time."

"Witnesses?" Sydney asked.

"Several. A horrified neighbor across the street on his roof had been shoveling snow when he witnessed the murder through an uncurtained window. He was the one who reported the crime.

"The perp took with him what valuables he could find. He then strolled out of the house, saw several of the neighbors gathered across the street, asked what happened, and then calmly got into a '67 Cadillac parked along the street and drove away. Despite all this information of the man and car, we haven't been able to locate him."

There was another knock on the door. Sydney White's assistant poked her head in. "Time to go."

"Thanks, Helen. All right, gentlemen, we're done for now."

Charlie eyed Sydney.

Sydney saw Charlie staring at her and continued on barking orders. "I want to meet again on Monday, and I better have something to go on." Sydney stood and gathered her notes. "Dr. Taylor, follow me."

Charlie and Sydney strode down the hallway toward the elevator. When they reached the doors, Sydney stopped and asked, "What do you think?"

"I don't know if I should be flattered to be considered one of the boys, but I don't think that's what you had in mind. Do I think they're related? No, although there are some similar patterns."

"Except for Bill, I don't trust those idiots. I need you to be my eyes and ears on these investigations. I need somebody out there that I can trust." The two women stepped on the elevator, and Sydney pushed the button for the first floor, which would take them down to the redesigned briefing room. As the doors opened, Charlie could feel the charged excitement in the air. Charlie watched Sydney purposefully walk toward the oak door where an aged cop stood guard.

Sydney smiled and asked, "Frank, how's the leg?"

The guard laughed. "Like a weather barometer, and with all this cold air and snow this past month—a living hell. Only one year left till retirement."

He opened the door, and as Sydney strode past, she said to him, "If I do not solve this case, I may be forced to join you."

Then she whispered for Charlie's benefit, "Useless. Should've retired years ago." She climbed the two stairs, put her notes on the podium, and looked down briefly. She gathered her thoughts one last time.

Charlie stood at the back of the filled briefing room packed with reporters, cameramen, and photographers.

"Ladies and gentlemen, as you well know, we've got an eyewitness, a description of the assailant, and his car. He doesn't just disappear into thin air. We're going to catch this perpetrator. It's just a matter of time."

FRANKLIN
SATURDAY, JANUARY 31, 1976

"Are you ready? Hold on tight." Charlie held the little girl between her legs, placed her feet on the Flexible Flyer's handles, and pushed off with her hands. The red grooved steel runners flew over the hard-packed, almost icy snow. Charlie pushed hard on the right handle and then the left.

The sled's runners responded, digging into the packed snow as they serpentined down the hill. The wind whipped at their faces as they raced down the large hill. They soared past the deserted Little League baseball fields, past the converted tennis courts where the figure skaters and hockey players shared the ice. They had covered the whole community church's commons.

Charlie and Missy fell on their sides laughing as the sled finally came to a halt.

"Let's do it again!" Annie's daughter, Missy, shouted as Annie and her son, Josh, ran up to them.

"Mom, she always gets to ride with Aunt Charlie," Josh complained.

"What am I, chopped liver? Don't you like riding with me?" Annie asked.

"Mom, you don't like going to the top of the hill." Annie's son pleaded his case.

"Good point." Annie looked to the top of the large, formidable hill, which dissuaded the faint of heart from pulling their sleds, toboggans, and saucers to the top. Before Annie could respond, Charlie chimed in.

"How about this…Josh and I'll go down the hill a couple of times, and Missy, you go with your mom."

Annie mouthed the words "thank you."

"Afterward, I'll treat everyone to a big cup of hot chocolate with marshmallows, the works." Charlie smiled at the rosy-cheeked children. "All right, Josh, I'll race you to the top of the hill." Charlie grabbed the rope and started running hard toward the hill with the sled and Josh trailing after her.

"Cheater!" Josh yelled. "You got a head start."

An hour later, shadows formed on the top of the hill as the winter sun began to set early in the cold afternoon sky. The kids pulled their sleds toward the car. Following behind, Annie and Charlie walked side by side.

"Thanks for a great afternoon. We've all been cooped up in the house way too long." Annie looked around. "It's gorgeous around here. It looks like a picturesque postcard."

"It does, doesn't it?" Charlie said. "Franklin truly is 'The Town That Time Forgot.'"

They passed the church with its majestic white steeple with a clock and bell, a circular drive, and large double doors—it was a great place for a wedding.

"My sister, Susan, was married here. It included a horse-drawn carriage that carried them away after the ceremony."

"It must have been incredible," Annie said, "It's like every little girl's fantasy."

"It was. It's too bad our fantasies don't live up to our reality." Charlie felt the darkness start to creep out of the recesses of her mind.

"Aren't we the cynic?" Annie bumped Charlie with her hip.

"Sorry, don't mean to put a damper on a great day." As Charlie pointed out the sights, Annie took her arm. "Susan and I would ride our horses around here. God, I haven't been riding in years. I hope it's like riding a bicycle. I'll have to take Missy riding someday."

"She'd love it, but I want to go, too," Annie said.

"Mom, hurry up. We're cold," Josh yelled.

Hearing the children's pleas, Annie yelled back, "We'll be there in just a minute."

CODY EDWARDS'S STORY

"**M**om, can I go to the hobby shop?" I ask.

"Honey, can't you see that I'm busy at work. I can't leave work and drive you up there," Mom says.

"I'll walk," I say.

"I know marines are tough, but no way, mister, not today, not ever. Now go and join your brother. Kyle is playing pool with Jack."

"But, Mom, I'm bored and there is nothing to do around here."

"Honey, please don't beg. Now, you have already been there once this week and you used up your allowance."

"Come on, Mom, this guy said he was bringing his neat car, and I really wanted to see it."

"Which guy?"

"You know, the guy I told you about. The one who has the neat cars."

"Cody, you know I don't like you hanging around those older boys. The answer is no, young man."

"Mom?"

"Cody."

"OK, OK, but can I go home and watch a movie?" I grab my red jacket off the chair in hope of her saying yes.

"All right, head straight home and watch your movie." She messes with my blondish hair and kisses me good-bye.

"Love ya, Mom," I say.

"Honey, I love you, too."

I zip up my jacket and say good-bye to everyone. As I walk out of the restaurant, the wind takes my breath away. I am freezing, so I pull up my sweatshirt hood. I don't have any gloves, so I put my hands into my pants pockets and start walking home.

As I walk along Nine Mile, I think. *I just wanted to race my car. My other friends will be there. Their parents let them go…why can't I? I hope Chris isn't too mad that I didn't show today. He said he was going to be bringing his car that's really fast and he was going to even let me have a turn. Mom treats me like a baby sometimes. It just isn't fair.*

It's so cold. I'm freezing. The wind keeps blowing my hood off. *I can't wait for summer.* It almost seems like nighttime. The sky is dark gray, and the snow is no longer white, but covered with black dirt.

I try to cheer myself up. At least I can watch John Wayne in *The Sands of Iwo Jima.* I've got the house to myself.

I stop at Woodward Avenue and wait for the light to turn green. My hands and ears start to hurt. I try to cover my ears with my hands to warm them up, but my hands only hurt more. They are beet red. I try blowing on them, but nothing works.

The light changes, and I cross the big street. Not much farther. I am almost home when the car pulls alongside me. It is so cool looking it reminds me of some of the slot cars I'd seen. The driver waves at me and rolls down the window. "Come here…you look so cold. Jump in."

FERNDALE
SUNDAY, FEBRUARY 15, 1976

Carolyn Edwards looked at her watch. *Damn, two hours to go.* She was feeling a little guilty for being short with him. She thought, *my little marine has been so courageous through the divorce, even with his father abandoning both him and Kyle.*

"Just a minute, Frank. I'll be right with you."

From the payphone in the lobby, Carolyn dialed the number to her house. As she waited for Cody to answer, she was inclined to doodle as she looked at the notes scribbled around the phone and on the Yellow Pages. The phone had rung numerous times, and he still hadn't picked up.

Hmmm, that's just not like him. Where could he be?

Carolyn finished wiping down tables, resetting the place settings and refilling the salt and pepper shakers before she punched out and she and Kyle began the short walk to their house. Carolyn shivered from the cold and moisture in the air—the potential for a pleasant walk home didn't exist. She rolled up her collar and walked a little faster.

Carolyn's mind kept returning to Cody. He had always been a cheerful, happy kid, but he had been thrown for a loop when she and Fred had divorced. He was more cautious, quiet, and reserved. Carolyn was trying to gauge her response when she saw him. Hug him, run her fingers through his hair, and say, "Hey, Jarhead...hungry?" *Or,* she mused, *should I let him know how upset I was when he didn't pick up the phone?*

When Carolyn could see her house, she was surprised that there were no outside lights on. She was even more surprised when she noticed the house was dark. Carolyn turned her key in the lock, opened the door, and stepped inside.

"Cody, we're home. Honey?"

Carolyn expected to hear, "Hey, Mom, I'm in here watching TV." However, the house was eerily silent. There was no response. Carolyn made her way through the house, flipping on the lights. She went into Cody's room, turning on the light. She looked around for some clue or hint of where he might be. Her eyes caught the pencil marks on the doorjamb marking Cody's age and height. Her heart began to sink.

"Mom, I've checked everywhere downstairs, even his favorite hiding places," Kyle said. "Where could he be?"

"Honey, I don't know, but when I get my hands on him..." Carolyn tried to hide her concern. "Kyle, honey, run over to the Whites' and see if he's there."

"I sure he's at one of his friends'. Cody is a great kid, and he wouldn't do anything stupid. He'll be all right."

"Thanks, honey, I'm sure you're right. Just check with the Whites." Her body shivered as fear gripped her, making her feel the same cold she had felt walking home. Carolyn waited an hour before she decided to call the police, hoping that Cody would come bounding through the front door, apologizing profusely for scaring his mother half to death. She did not want to give into her fear.

"Ferndale police?"

"Hi, my name is Carolyn Edwards, and my son is missing," Carolyn said as she rubbed her temple with her free hand.

"How old is he, ma'am?"

"He's...he's twelve years old."

"Ma'am, I'm sure that he's all right. He's probably just hanging at some friend's house."

"You don't understand. We've checked with his friends. No one has seen him. He's a good boy."

"Ma'am, I'm sure we'll find him quickly. We haven't had a kidnapping in over ten years. I'm sure that he'll return home at any moment. I'd like to send out a report ASAP, but I'll need a description of him."

"Sure...of course...sure. His name is Cody Edwards. He's twelve years old. He's about one hundred pounds and four feet eight inches tall. He has sandy-blond hair."

"That's very helpful, ma'am. What clothes was he wearing?"

"He's wearing a bright-red nylon jacket, yellow hooded sweatshirt underneath, blue jeans, and black rubber boots."

"Can I have your address and phone number? Thanks, Mrs. Edwards. I'll send a report out ASAP. But please call us back if he returns home."

Carolyn hung up the phone and sat quietly. The minutes passed with eerie determination. Minutes turned into hours and hours into days.

FERNDALE
WEDNESDAY, FEBRUARY 18, 1976

The door opened and a small, frail woman looked out at Charlie with tired, painfully exhausted eyes.

"Hi, Mrs. Edwards, my name is Dr. Charlie Taylor. We spoke on the phone yesterday."

"Oh, yes...hi...Please come in."

Charlie entered the small living room. The furniture was not expensive or new, but everything was very well maintained, clean, and orderly. Charlie could tell that Carolyn Edwards was an attentive mother and took her responsibilities seriously.

"Do you mind if we stay in the kitchen? I want to be near a phone in case someone calls with news."

"Of course. Wherever you're the most comfortable."

Charlie followed Carolyn through the living room into the kitchen. "Care for coffee?"

"Yes, coffee would be nice." Charlie watched Carolyn's hands shake as she poured the coffee into the two large mugs.

"Cream…sugar?"

"Please."

The two women sat at the small kitchen table. Charlie observed the three place settings. She did not say anything, allowing the distraught mother time to compose herself. Carolyn traced an imaginary line in the table with her right index figure.

"Everyone has been so thoughtful. The police and community are searching anywhere and everywhere for him, putting up posters. And the guys, the guys from the American Legion, are conducting their own searches like a military operation."

"My understanding is that Cody was walking home from the American Legion."

Carolyn nodded her head. "He was complaining that he was bored and wanted to go to the hobby shop. I said no… Maybe if I had just…"

"Stop. This isn't your fault. You had no way of knowing that anything like this was going to happen."

"I know, but I can't help myself. The pain is so great. I don't know what I'll do if something happens to him."

"You said the hobby shop?"

"Yes, it's the place up on Woodward Avenue near Thirteen Mile Road. The kids go there to race their slot cars."

"So what happened next?"

"When I wouldn't cave in to his demands…he asked if he could go home to watch a John Wayne movie on Bill Kennedy's show. It was some marine movie…Cody wants to be a marine so badly."

"Tell me about Cody's dad. What is he like?"

A spark flashed in Carolyn's eye—she looked up with a vengeance. "That bastard left us, all of us, for his goddamned secretary."

"I'm sorry. How did Cody take the divorce and his departure?"

"Hard, but he tried so hard to be brave…a real marine." Carolyn smiled for a brief moment.

"Do you think he could have anything to do with this? Could Cody be with him? The start of a rebellious teen… 'Mom won't let me go to the hobby shop. I'll show her, I'll go see Dad.'"

"No, no. My ex-husband's a first-class jerk, but he'd never do anything to harm Cody. I've already checked…Cody's not with him."

"Tell me about the American Legion."

"I waitress there, and I'd bring the boys because I couldn't leave them at home by themselves. The guys adopted them like they were their own."

"Could someone have followed Cody home?"

"No, no way. Those men adore the boys. No one there would ever do them any harm. The Legion's been a significant part of his life. Cody's father walked out on him when he was only three years old. It may sound cliché, but he learned about duty, honor, and country from these men. They were more like fathers to him than his real dad had ever been. They adopted us and looked after us like we were their own. No one ever complained, and the boys soaked up the stories—it never got old. They would take the boys to Tigers games and make sure they'd get their homework done."

"Maybe not a regular, but how about someone else who just happened to be there?"

"No, I don't remember anyone new or unfamiliar."

"Did Cody mention anything or anyone?"

"No, no, I don't remember anything different."

"Carolyn, thanks for meeting with me. We are all trying very hard to find Cody, and I'm sure it won't be long before we do." Charlie took Carolyn into her arms and hugged her tightly and could feel the mother's pain and anguish as her body shook and the tears streamed down her face.

"Why, why did I let him go?" Carolyn sobbed.

FERNDALE

WEDNESDAY, FEBRUARY 18, 1976

It was barely one in the afternoon, and the day was already dark and depressing when Charlie walked out of the small brick home and jumped into her car. The winter had long ago stopped being enjoyable. The sky was covered with desperately gray clouds. Charlie pulled her collar up and adjusted her scarf, but there was no escaping the cold. She turned on the ignition and felt the power of the 390 V8. She put the gearshift into reverse and backed out of the driveway.

Charlie drove the four short blocks from Cody's home to the American Legion. Cody would have walked along Nine Mile, a busy thoroughfare, and then had to cross over Woodward Avenue, hardly a secluded area. Charlie observed the pictures of Cody stapled to every telephone pole. She could see groups of people going door to door. The community had pulled together. Charlie turned off Nine Mile onto the tree-lined Livernois Avenue and pulled into the parking area of the American Legion. Charlie got out of her car and looked at the red brick building.

She took in her surroundings, looking at the large sign announcing Cody's disappearance and the phone number to the Ferndale police. Charlie remembered how her father used to take her to an American Legion. Her mother always refused to go. She couldn't stand how some vets would stare at her as if she was Tokyo Rose herself. Charlie and her father did all the Thursday all-you-can-eat buffet dinners, Friday night fish fries, Saturday dances, and Sunday brunches. Charlie thought they were the staples of Americana.

She smiled to herself, thinking in some ways she was no different than Cody. She had loved to hear the good-hearted bantering that went on between the services: army versus the marines, marines versus the navy, and everyone piling on the air force. Her father, a "flyboy" during the war, was often the brunt of much good-hearted ribbing.

However, she knew that they knew in their hearts that they had all served, had all seen their fair share of horror, and all knew that few could comprehend or appreciate giving their lives in service to their country. It was a deep and common bond, though rarely spoken. So she was not surprised by the response of members of the Legion to Cody's disappearance. Someone had taken one of their own.

Charlie walked into the foyer. There was a restaurant on the left, a bar on the right, and a sign that directed the customers to the basement for weekly bingo. Charlie went into the restaurant and sat at the light-green Formica table, with its heavy aluminum legs and matching dark-green chairs. Charlie needed some comfort food and tossed her regular fastidious diet aside and placed her order of a hamburger, grilled onions, mustard and mayonnaise, French fries, and a chocolate shake.

While Charlie waited for her food, she reviewed her notes. Although Cody came from a broken family, he was not a high-risk child. His mother was responsible and caring, and there was a terrific support system in place. Charlie knew she was probably looking for a white male, twenty-five to thirty-five years of age. Her challenge was to figure out his logic and methodology when it seemed to defy both. After lunch, her next stop would be the hobby shop on Woodward Avenue.

Charlie left the American Legion and then drove along Nine Mile Road and maneuvered along Woodward Avenue South until she was able to U-turn onto Woodward Avenue North. She stopped at a red light, and a car pulled alongside of her. Charlie looked over at the car, a metallic-blue 1974 Nova. The driver was a young man dressed in a plaid sport coat and large knotted tie. He casually looked at Charlie and then back out his windshield and began to rev his engine. The light changed, and the young man jumped on the accelerator. His rear tires squealed, and his car rocketed up Woodward. Charlie gripped her steering wheel tightly and thought to herself, *Another day, hot shot.* She drove the remaining three miles uneventfully and turned off Woodward and parked the car in front of the hobby shop.

Charlie walked through the front door and looked around. She walked through the aisles, looking at all the model cars, the airplanes, the small bottles of Testors paint on display with their kaleidoscope of colors: Hot Magenta, Napoleonic Purple, and Black Pearl. The next aisle was devoted to Estes rockets in all sizes and contained all the other utensils and tools any hobby enthusiast would need.

Charlie looked at the center of the store—the main attraction. There were two large HO-scale slot car racing tracks, with little scaled cars speeding around the track with a distinctive whine. Two twentysomething men playing hooky from work were racing their cars. Charlie walked up to the track and was mesmerized by the cars zipping around the figure-eight track.

This place could be a feeding ground for pedophiles and their unsuspecting prey, she thought.

SOUTHFIELD
THURSDAY, FEBRUARY 19, 1976

It was only eleven in the morning when Dave Nagel, a local businessman, felt a cold coming on. He made his way out the office building's front door and down the shoveled sidewalk as his galoshes crunched against the icy patches and salt sprinkled along the cement. He made his way to the parking lot, surrounded by three-foot snow banks created by the industrial plows that came during the night to clear the parking areas for the next day's customers.

Vibrant colors atop the snow bank grabbed Dave's attention. He stopped and, at first glance, thought he was viewing a discarded mannequin. His eyes focused on the object. It had a red parka with blue jeans, and wisps of blond hair blew in the wind. Half walking, half jogging, he moved closer in hopes that his fears were wrong, but each step closer confirmed his suspicions. The object was not a mannequin at all, but that of a little boy. There, neatly placed on top of the snow bank for all to see, lay a fair-haired boy who belonged to someone.

He ran back to his office and called the police. The Southfield police responded immediately to the call at Ten Mile and Greenfield due in part to their efficiency and in part because the body was literally across the street from their station.

SOUTHFIELD
THURSDAY, FEBRUARY 19, 1976

The police officers gathered around the body. They knew that Ferndale police had been looking for a boy who matched the description of the body that lay in front of them. They were all veterans, accustomed to death. They all had seen a dead body in the past, either from previous military or law enforcement service. These bodies came in the form of fatal traffic accidents or the occasional drug overdose; however, taking the life of a little boy was beyond the comprehension of even the most grizzled veteran. They knew in their hearts that they were looking at Cody Edwards, who had mysteriously disappeared four days prior.

It was as if the boy had just been plucked from the face of the earth. They now looked at the little boy put on display for the world to see. Finally, one of the officers scooped up the little boy like he was going to carry him upstairs and put him to bed.

SOUTHFIELD
THURSDAY, FEBRUARY 19, 1976

It was a dark, cold night once again. The parking lot was empty as they pulled the mannequin from the trunk and placed it on the snow bank where the body had been found before. They'd dressed it in clothing similar to what Cody had been wearing. They made their way back to the car tucked in the shadows.

"Thanks for joining me...I couldn't get anyone else," Charlie said.

"I think there's a compliment in there somewhere. Where did you learn this?" Pete asked as they climbed into his Javelin.

"I'm hoping to lure the killer back. Do you remember when all the co-eds were being abducted and murdered in and around Ypsilanti and Ann Arbor?"

"Who doesn't?"

"They used a similar technique and thought they had a hit," Charlie said. "But they never caught the guy who checked out the mannequin."

"That's right."

"The idea is that assailants will come back to their crime scene to watch. Like the arsonist who enjoys watching his handy work, they get a thrill watching the police," Charlie said.

"Makes sense. Anything from the coroner?" Pete asked.

"His initial findings confirmed that he died of asphyxiation. There was a small abrasion on his head, slight ligature marks to his wrist and hands where he might have been tied up, and his anus was swollen and had minor lacerations from an unknown foreign object or mechanical device. No semen found.

"The doctor commented that his body was in very good condition overall, despite being held captive for over four days. There were no signs of dehydration or malnutrition. But what was most odd was that the boy's clothes had been recently washed and pressed. Cody had even been bathed and his nails trimmed."

"Meticulous," Pete said.

"More than us. At our meeting this afternoon, our lead investigator said the police threw out his clothes. How could they have thrown his clothes out? What were they thinking?" Charlie asked.

"Hell if I know. They probably thought they were doing the right thing," Pete said.

"It's not smart business. They moved the body to the city morgue to conduct the autopsy there and then have the next of kin identify the body. However, sensing this case was different from others, the police, for all the best intentions but the wrong reasons, moved the body to the department's security garage to check for possible injuries and cause of death."

"Shit! What else have your guys found out?" Pete asked.

"Based upon witnesses, we believe the body was dropped off in the parking lot sometime between nine thirty and eleven in the morning. This guy has a lot of guts. He is not afraid of us. That's what scares me the most."

Pete adjusted his position in the driver's seat and took a sip of lukewarm coffee. "Why do you think he left the body in such a public place, just across the street from the police station?"

"I've got some ideas. More like impressions. Given the estimated time of day and location, it's as if he's mocking us, trying to flaunt his power and intelligence over us, telling us, 'You see, you guys aren't so smart.' He's trying to draw in the whole community—nobody is exempt."

"Do you think there is any correlation between Katie, Shelly, and Cody?"

"I'd be shocked if there was," Charlie said. "Given the brutality, there are more similarities between Katie and Shelly, but I just don't see it."

Time passed quietly as Charlie and Pete became lost in their thoughts. Pete finally broke the silence.

"You know that someday we're going to have to race our cars. I can't have you going around mistakenly thinking that your Mustang can take my Javelin." Pete tapped the steering wheel.

Charlie looked over at Pete and smiled. "Are you sure that your ego can handle it, Detective West?"

"I own these streets...Doctor," Pete said.

"Detective West, you're on. Anytime and anywhere."

"You got first watch." Pete leaned over and rolled his jacket into an impromptu pillow, resting his head against the driver's side door and closing his eyes.

Charlie sat and reflected on the case, occasionally sipping tea from her cup. She could hear Pete's breathing becoming steadier, slower, and deeper. She wondered, *How many hours has he lost or spent on stakeouts like this one? I'm sure he prefers to be home with his family.* The silence was broken when Pete, without lifting his head, quietly awoke.

"How long have I been out? Crap...what time is it?" Pete asked while turning his head around to relieve the stiffness.

"A little after two in the morning," Charlie said. "Don't worry, you haven't missed a thing."

Time dragged on. Pete and Charlie stared out the front window at the mannequin lying on the snow. "Why do you do it?"

"Do what?" Pete asked.

"This...all of this. Crimes against children are the worst assignment. How can you not be affected by it all? I've done my own investigative work concerning you. Your peers are afraid of you. You're professional, unwilling to compromise your integrity, able and willing to do the dirty work. It scares the shit out of them."

Pete nodded and paused for a while before he spoke again. "In some ways, it's fairly straightforward. I made a promise to someone in another place and time. And you?"

"Similar to you; a promise, to someone else, another place and time. The only trouble with drinking all of this tea is now I got to pee," Charlie said.

"You can always go behind the car. I'm pretty sure no one will notice at this hour," Pete teased.

FERNDALE
SATURDAY, FEBRUARY 28, 1976

Charlie and Pete slid across the polished wood pew at the back of the church, watching the congregation gathered for Cody's funeral. They watched, studying faces, looking for some clue that would lead them to the killer. The pastor started the service with a reading from Matthew 5:4, "Blessed are those who mourn, for they will be comforted," followed by Carolyn's and Kyle's recollections of their favorite stories of Cody.

Afterward, Charlie and Pete watched the casket being moved from the altar to the waiting hearse by the members of the American Legion in their uniforms, each service represented. The casket was followed by a lone marine playing the bagpipes. Carolyn, Kyle, and the pastor waited at the door, thanking all for their attendance as they departed.

Charlie noticed that the funeral had been attended by hundreds. There were relatives, friends of the family, classmates, veterans, the public who wanted to share and express their grief with the family, and, finally, those who came out of morbid curiosity. Meanwhile, an unmarked white van sat across the street from the church and filmed all the attendees as they departed the service. As the police filmed, they also checked photos of known pedophiles to see if they could spot anyone familiar.

SOUTHFIELD
SATURDAY, FEBRUARY 28, 1976

Charlie parked her car in the New Orleans Mall parking lot and made her way to where Cody's body had been placed so carefully on the snow bank, like he was being tucked in. The lullaby stuck in Charlie's head as she walked across the parking lot. "Sleep, baby, sleep…And never suffer want or need…" She looked down at the spot and found a memorial card from Cody's service lying there. A shiver ran down her spine.

Across the street, the driver watched Charlie as she picked up the funeral card. The driver put the car in gear and slowly pulled out of the parking lot.

CHRISTIAN MCMILLAN'S STORY

BIRMINGHAM
SATURDAY, MAY 8, 1976

I push down on the yellow plunger, and the 1969 Barracuda car responds to the jolt of power, racing down the yellow-colored straightaway, blowing past the other car. I can hear the cheers around me. The pimply teenager across from me starts to sweat as my car pulls away. I let up just a little on the plunger as the car enters a curve. The little car slingshots around the curve, remaining in the slot and flying down the straightaway.

I push my heavy dark-framed glasses over the bridge of my nose and allow myself to briefly look around the room. I spot him smiling, caught up with the race. I think he's perfect, almost as good as the other one. I can spot their vulnerability: anxious for attention, parents probably divorced. He looks so young and innocent. What I wouldn't give to have him for my own.

I push the plunger down farther, going for the kill. My car crosses the finish line. The cheers go up. I enjoy my victory briefly as I watch the pimply teenager walk away from the track, miserable. His friends trying to console him. They look back at me, and I look back at them with utter hatred.

I quickly mask my feelings and look for him. I spot him, noting his light-brown hair, the freckles across his face, and his red-and-white-striped shirt. I find him in the Estes Rockets aisle. I smile as I walk over to him.

"What did you think?"

"That was awesome," he says. "You destroyed that guy. He's such a jerk."

"He is, isn't he?" I say, glancing at the group of teenagers leaving the hobby shop.

I turn my attention back to him. "Hey, I was thinking about going to get some ice cream to celebrate. Do you want to come?"

He shrugs his shoulders and looks at the floor. "Ah, I don't know. My mom may get angry. I'm not supposed to wander off from the store."

I can tell he wants to go. I just need to apply the right pressure. "Don't worry, I'll have you right back. Besides, you know me. We're friends, and we're just going to get ice cream."

"You sure? If my mom finds out, she'll kill me."

"Hey, I understand. I got parents of my own, and they're always telling me what to do. My car is just out front. Let's get out of here." I steer him out the front door of the hobby shop. I casually look over my shoulder to see if anyone might have noticed us going.

"I like the white stripe on your car," the boy says.

"Thanks," I say as I unlock the doors. We hop into my car, but I have no intention of going for ice cream.

GROSSE POINTE

SATURDAY, JULY 3, 1976

"Baby..." The deep gravelly voice of Arthur Penhallow, the local rock 'n' roll disc jockey, is followed by the sound of a foghorn bellowing from the radio to inform his women listeners sun tanning at the local beaches that it's time to turn over. I shut off the car radio and step out of the car. I'm feeling great, surrounded by clear blue skies and the sun shining brightly, reflecting off the waves of Lake St. Clair.

I stretch, raising my arms to the sky. As I bring my arms back down, I run my hands through my long, dark-brown wavy hair, smiling confidently in the knowledge that the occupants would be pleased with their order. Why should I give this a second thought? They're always pleased, very pleased, with what I deliver.

I chuckle at the irony that I'm delivering stag party–like material to a bunch of old men. But I'm not delivering just any pornographic movies of men and women engaged in sexual activities and photos of large-breasted young women—that would too easy and predictable. These men are connoisseurs with a different appetite; they take great pleasure looking at films of men engaged in sexual activities with children. I walk to the entrance, standing in front of the large, white double doors with brass door knockers. I take one in my grasp and pound loudly.

The butler opens the door. His skin is pitch black and wrinkled, his eyes and teeth yellow with age.

"Yes, may I help you?"

"Hey, James, I believe the 'master' is expecting me."

"Yes, sir. Please follow me. He's in the library."

The butler reaches the library door, opens it, and stands aside to let me through.

I enter a large room with glass windows that provide a stunning view of the lake. I find myself surrounded by leather-bound books upon shelves that reach the high ceiling and dark-red leather chairs and sofas. The thick red-and-gold drapes are pulled aside by large gold cords.

Sitting in one of the leather chairs is Raymond, fastidious Raymond, with his pitch-black hair, a perfect coiffure with not a strand out of place; I've heard he visits his barber every morning for a daily clip, manicure, shave, and facial. Raymond, skin faintly glowing pink, is wearing an impeccably tailored shirt and dress pants from London and custom-made dark leather loafers from Italy. Shit, he even looks good in this heat and humidity.

"You've arrived. So glad that you are punctual," he says. "I hate it when you're late. Were you able to bring something special from our private collection?"

"I'm sure that you won't be disappointed," I say.

"No, I'm sure that you are correct, but I'll share with you something that is disappointing me..."

As Raymond is speaking, I just make out the door opening and closing behind me. I don't hear any footsteps behind me, but I can feel his hot breath on the back of my neck. I can smell his cologne. I'm afraid to look behind me.

"Christian, have you had the pleasure of meeting Abraham Lincoln?"

I slowly turn and find myself staring into the man's chest. I raise my eyes up to the man towering over me.

"Abraham, if you could be so kind as to provide an update on the dreadful murders of those children in Birmingham for Christian, that would be appreciated," Raymond says.

"Sure. Right now, all of it resides with local law enforcement, and there are no ties to us," Abraham says. "However, I want to caution you that my subordinate suspects our existence."

"Can he be persuaded?" Raymond asks.

"That'll be a cold day in hell."

"Every man has a weakness," Raymond says.

"Not this guy. He briefs me regularly, so I'll know when he's getting close. I'll try to keep him at bay by feeding him misinformation or misdirecting him."

"Abraham, thank you." Raymond addresses me directly. "Christian, you're hearing this for a reason. You must understand how embarrassing it would be for all of us to get caught up in an investigation. You've been sloppy lately. Tell me you weren't involved with this little boy's abduction and death?"

"No, no, I swear I didn't touch the kid." I can feel the sweat start trickling down the side of my face and taste the acrid bile in my mouth.

"I can't have any more of it. It's only a matter of time before the press and law enforcement take notice of your digressions. So please, be careful. Do we understand each other?"

I look at Raymond and nod my head in agreement. Then I look at Abraham. His black eyes bore a hole into me. My stomach is gurgling, and I'm struck by a sudden urge to defecate. The guy literally scares the shit out of me. I find myself hoping I can leave the room as quickly as possible.

GROSSE POINTE
SATURDAY, JULY 3, 1976

The men gathered in Raymond's darkened basement. The only thing that could be heard is the men shifting in their seats and the occasional deep breath. They stared at the screen with incredible intensity. One of the men pulled a handkerchief from his pocket to wipe the sweat from his upper lip. They were oblivious to the door opening behind them.

"Beautiful, aren't they?" asked the deep, smooth voice.

Raymond looked over his shoulder, smiled, and held out his hand to her. "They're perfect."

"Yes, they are. But you need to exercise more caution. The idiot that you have delivering the films is a poster child, no pun intended, for disaster. He's nothing like his father—he's sloppy, and one of these days he's going to get caught and ruin it for all of us." The woman moved silently across the linoleum floor.

"We are indebted to you, my dear, but we think we've got the necessary safeguards in place," Raymond said.

"Lincoln, honey, what's that charming name your man calls us?" she said.

Abraham smiled. "The Brotherhood."

"That's right...the Brotherhood." The woman stepped in front of the screen, standing before the men wearing white high-heeled shoes, her long, bare, tanned legs complimented by her white hot pants, and her perky breasts could be seen through her white blouse. Scenes from the movie could be seen playing against her body.

"My point precisely," she said. "There are suspicions about our organization. Why risk this beautiful thing we've got going for ourselves?"

"My dear, you are a better businessman than his father," Raymond said. "I, for one, am internally grateful for your organization skills, but I think you are overreacting just a tad." The other men nodded in agreement.

"Don't say that I didn't warn you," she said. "I have a bad feeling, and my instincts are usually pretty damn good."

"Duly noted, my dear. Now why don't you join us?" Raymond asked.

She smiled, walking past the men, and disappeared into the recesses of the darkened room. She returned shortly and announced. "Why watch when you can have the real thing?" she asked.

All the men's heads turned in her direction. She side-stepped to the right, exposing her gift.

The men sat forward in their seats like a pack of hungry snarling hyenas ready for the kill. Raymond smiled. "Marilyn, you continue to amaze me."

ANN ARBOR
SUNDAY, JULY 4, 1976

Small beads of sweat formed at the sides of Charlie's face and on the small of her back. She could feel the heat rising off the street as her flip-flops occasionally stuck to the black tar that had started to melt and ooze up between the gray gravel. The trees, birds, and squirrels didn't stir in the hot, humid weather. The only noise came from the little house further down the street.

She walked apprehensively along the street toward the laughter of the partygoers and music in the distance. She walked past the beat-up Volkswagen Beetles in their various shades of green, blue, and orange. She walked past the occasional Dodge Darts and rusted-out Ford Pintos that were lined up along the quiet neighborhood street. Finally, Charlie stood at the end of the driveway.

She stopped to watch two couples playing lawn badminton in the front yard. The girls were in bright flowered bikinis, with their breasts bouncing up and down as they reacted to the shuttlecock. The guys were in cut-off jean shorts, barefoot, and shirtless. Their sweat glistened in the sun. They only stopped for beer breaks to quench their thirst.

Smoke rose up over the house from the backyard. Charlie smelled the mixture of grilled meat and charcoal burning. The house seemed to be bouncing up and down on its foundation from the partiers dancing. Today was the country's bicentennial. What better reason to celebrate?

Despite the heat, Charlie felt chilled and began to doubt her decision to attend the party. Her sister had been so insistent that she had finally relented. Charlie recalled that it was her parents' and sister's insistence that had led her to this point before. *Déjà vu?*

She hesitated before she opened the front door to her younger sister's home. All of her senses were blasted with the faint sweet smell of marijuana, the bodies swaying, twisting, and grinding to the rock music. Charlie tried to control her emotions. She told herself, *Just let it go.* The rage and fear were starting to swell inside her. She tried to rationalize that it was normal behavior for some of the university's finest medical residents and interns just letting off steam.

Charlie made her way through the house looking for a familiar face. She spotted Susan talking and laughing with an athletically built handsome young man with tousled blond hair. "There she is!" Susan yelled out and reached for Charlie with her arms opened wide. Charlie awkwardly returned the hug.

"Where are Greg and the kids?" Charlie asked, looking around the tiny house.

"Greg's around here somewhere, and the kids have been with Mom and Dad for the past couple of weeks. They're going to bring them up here later so we can all watch the fireworks together. Of course, they'll come back spoiled rotten. They love it there."

Charlie nodded.

Susan looked at Charlie with concern. "Can we...? Never mind. We just finished our exams and just want to let off a little steam. So can we just lighten up for one day? Please?"

Before Charlie could answer, Susan called for the young man she had been talking with previously. "Dr. Keith Horvat, I would like you to meet my incredible older sister, Dr. Charlie Taylor. Didn't I tell you she was knockout? She's a jogger just like you."

Charlie looked impassively at her sister.

"Hey, you don't have a drink. What can I get you? Wine?" Susan pointed to the kitchen counter, which was stacked with various wines and liquor. "We've got a keg out back if you prefer beer. Keith, do you mind entertaining my sister while I get her some wine."

"Sure," Keith said.

"Susan, really, I'm fine. I don't need anything to drink," Charlie said to no avail as Susan disappeared among the other partygoers.

"So, you like to jog?" Keith asked.

"Actually, I'm a runner. I train," Charlie said.

"Well, I like to run, too."

"Charlie, huh...is that like 'Choo-Choo Charlie, the Good & Plenty train engineer, or Choo-Choo Charlie Justice, the running back?" Keith asked.

Charlie could feel the heat in her body start to rise. She knew that Keith meant no harm and was just trying to make conversation. "Neither. I was named after my father's door gunner who was killed in the war." Before Keith could respond, she added, "It was very nice meeting you." Charlie then walked away.

Keith looked at Charlie as she walked away, wondering what he had just done wrong, when Susan returned with Charlie's drink.

"What did you say to her?" Susan asked.

"Nothing. I was just trying to make conversation. All I did was asked her about her running and her first name. Is she always like this?" Keith asked.

"You mean 'bitchy'?" Susan asked. Keith nodded. "No, she used to be a lot of fun, but something happened. Keith, will you excuse me?" Susan handed him the drinks and ran after her sister.

Charlie pushed open the screen door and stormed out of the house. Her teeth were clenched, her heart was pounding, and her emotions were quickly unraveling.

"Charlie, wait!" Susan yelled. She ran across the front yard and caught her sister by the arm. "Where are you going?"

Charlie turned and faced her sister. "Susan, this was a mistake...my being here."

"Charlie, come on. It would do you some good to lighten up. There are some really terrific guys here whom I'd think you'd find interesting."

"Susan, what is so hard for you to understand? I'm tired of the folks, you, and Greg always trying to fix me up. I can take care of myself," Charlie said.

"OK, I'm sorry. We're all concerned about you. We just want you to be happy."

"I can take care of my own happiness. I don't need you or anyone else. Why can't you all just leave me alone…please? Is that so hard to understand?"

"Well, from our vantage point, it doesn't look like it," Susan said. "Maybe you should turn your own methods on yourself or, better yet, go see a shrink."

Charlie felt betrayed by her younger sister and looked at her with pain in her eyes.

"Charlie, I'm sorry. That was a terrible thing to say. God, I just want my older sister back. We use to be so close and have so much fun together. We never use to act this way. What's happened to you?" Susan asked.

Charlie looked at Susan and then turned to go.

"At least stay for the kids. They'll be bummed that they missed you," Susan said.

Charlie turned back around and collected her emotions. "Give the kids a hug and kiss. Tell them that I love them."

"What about Mom and Dad?" Susan asked. Charlie turned and walked determinedly away.

Charlie walk-jogged to her car, jumped in, and floored it out of there like a woman possessed. Returning to her home, she threw the car keys on the sofa and fell to the floor. Her telephone rang, but she didn't have the strength to answer. She curled up in a fetal position on the floor, holding onto herself. The serpent struck her, sinking its fangs deep into her body. She could feel the hot poison working its way through her body as the serpent slowly slithered its way toward her for the kill.

The poison made her feel lethargic—she had begun to lose all will. Her stomach was twisted in knots and gurgled. She knew she'd be hit with a severe case of diarrhea. The serpent moved closer, beginning to wrap itself around her. Tears flowed down her face—she was powerless for what came next. Her mind raced. Kill herself: drugs, wrists, a gun, carbon monoxide? What she hated the worst was the uncontrollable emotion of wanting to hurt others.

In her mind, she cried out for help, but there was no one to answer. She begged and pleaded for it to stop. The serpent continued to slither up her body. She heard it hiss as its pink forked tongue flicked in and out of its mouth. Charlie welcomed death to be relieved of the tortured feeling the serpent brought over her.

Charlie heard her name being called from the front door but didn't have the strength to respond. Someone was kneeling over her and applying a cold compress. She could hear her name being whispered, her matted hair being brushed away from her forehead. The cold washcloth proceeded to wipe away the sweat and tears.

Charlie's eyes were swollen, and her vision was bleary from the tears. She could barely make out the person. She could just comprehend the soothing voice and gentle touch, which began to drive the serpent away.

Charlie looked again. She could just barely make out the red curly hair, freckles, and hazel eyes. Charlie's vision began to clear. She could see the gentle smile and a concerned look. Charlie looked up at the beautiful face again. "Honey, what's wrong?" The soothing words began to work their magic.

DETROIT AND HIGHLAND PARK
FRIDAY, JULY 23, 1976

The summer had been without relief from the heat and humidity. The late afternoon sun bore down on Pete, who felt sweat trickle down his back into the crack of his ass. He tried to adjust his position, and his shirt peeled away from the black leather. Despite the discomfort, he wouldn't allow himself to give into temptation by rolling up the window and blasting the air conditioning. Life's lessons learned in the jungles of Vietnam and later patrolling the streets of Detroit had taught him not to give into self-pity or distractions.

Pete continued his way northward along Woodward Avenue from Detroit, looking at the decay and lifelessness around him. The city was on life support, having never recovered from its previous sins of racism and political corruption. He passed the beauty supply store, the nondescript tool and die shop, and the boarded-up tavern. He drove past the billboard of the larger-than-life image of the former NFL star, now local Cadillac dealer, smiling down on the motorists passing by.

He looked out from behind his shades at the dandelions growing between the cracks in the sidewalks. Litter was scattered along the avenue's island of browned grass. Pete stopped at the traffic light and saw the road covered with skid marks, the telltale sign of street drag racing. Pete smiled. He was probably responsible for a few of them. "Where are they now?" Pete asked himself with a wry smile, looking for other cars to race.

He was now thankful for picking the less popular, Penske-designed Javelin over the Barracudas, Camaros, and Mustangs. His "other car company" car had buried them all—the so-called best of the best, Plymouth, Chevrolet, and Ford—in pickup drag races along Woodward Avenue.

Besides his family, street drag racing on Friday and Saturday evenings along Woodward Avenue kept him sane. He'd find like-minded drivers all out there, trolling for action, looking to prove something: the kids with their home-made souped-up garage specials; engineers from Ford, GM, and Chrysler with Hemi engines willing to take on all comers to prove their engineering dominance and racing prowess where it mattered most—on the streets. At the stoplights, Pete could hear the high-pitched whine of the engines and the squeal of the tires as the lights turned from red to green. In a matter of seconds, it would be over.

Most law enforcement saw the underbelly of humanity—Pete's perspective was the lowest of the low. Even the strongest-willed man couldn't handle what the job required. Most ended up transferring or drinking and smoking themselves into oblivion to erase the brutal images. Pete's escape was racing. He knew it could lead to his death. There was a part of him that didn't care.

As Pete continued northward, he could see the subtle distinction between where he had been and where he was going. This was no-man's land, where the poor ended and wealth began. He looked across the median at the Ford LTD parked in an empty parking lot. He saw a man with short sleeves talking to a young boy. Preteen boys who hustled along Woodward were known as chickens, and their johns looked to score a quick blow job before they went home to their wives and kids in the 'burbs.

Many of these kids came from shattered families whose fathers had left them a long time ago to fend for themselves and whose mothers who were either strung out on drugs or turning tricks themselves. They didn't choose this lifestyle, but a trick often meant the difference between having a meal and going hungry.

Pete flicked on his blinker and pulled into the parking lot, shut off the engine, and waited. It wasn't long before Pete saw the boy trotting up to his car from his rearview mirror. The boy cautiously made his way from the alley across the parking lot, looking nervously about. The sun's rays gave light-copper highlights to his Afro. He was wearing a dirty grayish T-shirt, tattered blue jeans rolled up, and torn-up Converse All-Stars.

Life had dealt him a terrible hand. The boy, Pete knew, was the product of a white mother who was a prostitute and heroin addict and a black father who had been her pimp. Pete had heard that the boy's old man had been shanked and died in prison a couple years ago, the result of competing gangs trying to gain control of the drug trafficking in prison. There was no clue where the mother was. The boy had been in an out of foster homes, always choosing the streets. Though his name was Zachariah, everyone called him Zeb, short for Zebra. His skin had very distinctive white and brown splotches.

Pete compared Zach to his own children. They were beautiful, with flawless light-brown skin, light-brown curly hair, and emerald eyes. Strangers would stop his family and comment on their beauty. They had modeled for local department stores. Pete's protest over the money spent on their clothes fell on deaf ears as Gabrielle made sure they were always dressed perfectly, from their starched button-down shirts to their Adidas Gazelles. Pete felt a pang in his heart.

The boy came up to the passenger side, opened the door, and jumped into the car.

"Hey, Zach." Pete winced and his nose flared as the boy's body odor reached him.

"Hey, Pete, is that a gun in your pocket or are you glad to see me?"

"Please."

"Would you prefer if I said how's it hanging?"

"Neither. But I'm glad to see you."

Zach nodded his head, perhaps unsure how to handle genuine concern from an adult. "I'm making it."

"What was wrong with the last home? They seemed like nice folks."

Zach shrugged his shoulders.

"Summer doesn't last forever," Pete said. "What are you going to do when the weather turns worse?"

Zach shrugged again. "I'll make it."

Pete noted the dark shadows under his eyes, his gaunt body and sunken cheeks. Zach looked like he hadn't a decent meal in days. "What do you know?"

The boy looked around nervously. "There's a place in Berkley, a house. It's a regular Tupperware party for dudes like you."

"What do you mean?"

"Word is these rich guys hold a party at the house and bring in kids from around the area."

Pete pulled himself up higher in his seat. "Go on."

"Well, they bid on the kids, and then afterward…the usual stuff…you know."

"Yeah, unfortunately, I know all too well. Why aren't you at this party?"

Zach looked over at Pete in disbelief and then back out the front window. "They don't want a scaggy kid like me. They want good-looking kids. You know, clean. The blond hair and blue eyes go for top price."

"Got an address?"

"It's over by the middle school."

"Convenient. Anything more specific?"

Zach pulled out a dirty, rolled up scrap of paper from his pocket and handed it over.

"Where did you get this?"

"Some of us try to take care of each other."

"Thanks." Pete handed him a twenty-dollar bill.

"What's this for?"

"Looks like you could use a decent meal."

"Screw you...Pete." Zach smiled as he opened the car door and jumped out.

Pete yelled out "take care," but it fell into an empty space as Zach jogged back into the shadows. Pete pulled his car back onto Woodward Avenue, turning and making his way to the address.

HIGHLAND PARK
FRIDAY, JULY 23, 1976

As Zach rounded the corner, he was met by the big and imposing man with a deep, smooth voice that seemed to come from the depths of hell. "Did he believe you?"

"Yeah, I think so."

"Good." The man handed him a fifty. "Now get lost." He smiled to himself and walked back down the darkened alley.

HIGHLAND PARK
FRIDAY, JULY 23, 1976

The sky's brilliant hues of orange and purple faded as the sun finally started to set, bringing some welcome relief to the humidity and heat. Pete turned onto the side street of a quiet neighborhood with little brick framed houses. Lawns were not manicured but for the most part were kept well maintained. To Pete, the residents clearly took pride in their little neighborhood. He slowed down as he neared the address. Everything seemed relatively quiet—just a house among all the other houses. Drapes were drawn, outside lights off, no sign of life. Pete drove past and parked his car down the street.

He thought this might be the lead he had long waited for. Despite his heart racing, he made his way up the street casually, like a resident out for an early evening stroll. He stopped briefly in front of the house and made his way down the drive over the sidewalk to the front door and rang the bell.

It was a long time before an old man, who appeared flushed, answered the door. His shirt was slightly unbuttoned with long gray chest hairs protruding. If that weren't unsightly enough, the old man was wearing a golden-colored toupee with his wiry gray hair sticking out from the sides.

"Yes?"

"Hi, I'm here for the social activities." Pete winked and gave a big smile to the man.

The old man's Adam's apple began to bob up and down as he became more agitated. He nervously looked over his shoulder and then back to Pete. "Son, I've got no idea what you are talking about."

"Please, don't play so coy. Are you going to let me in?"

"Listen, I don't know what the hell you're talking about." The old man started to shut the door.

"Hey, is that someone yelling for help?" Pete placed his hand on the door and whipped out his police badge.

"Huh?" The old man was startled.

"Pete West, Michigan State Police. I'm coming in. I believe someone needs help."

"What the hell? I didn't hear anything. Get the hell out of my house." The old man tried to prevent Pete from gaining entrance.

Pete pushed past the old man into the darkened and eerily quiet house. The old man trailed closely on Pete's heels, trying to explain that he wouldn't find anything here. Pete stood in the middle of the family room, which was relatively clean and well maintained with old and faded furniture. He could hear music coming from the back of the house.

Pete moved even more quickly toward the back of the house. The first bedroom was converted into a sewing room—nothing. The second bedroom had various model airplanes, some hanging from the ceiling, some displayed on shelves, others in various states of assembly.

When Pete reached for the master bedroom doorknob, the old man grabbed his arm.

"Don't go in there."

Pete shrugged the little man off and flung the open the door.

"Herb, what's going on?"

Pete stared at the old woman lying spread-eagled on the bed wearing a sheer white babydoll nightie, bright-red lipstick, and rouge. He was at a loss for words.

"Ma'am, I'm, uh, really, really sorry for barging in. I thought that I heard someone cry for help."

"Honey, he's with the Michigan State Police. I tried to explain, but he wouldn't listen."

"Officer, I'm sorry. Oh God, I hope the neighbors didn't call. You can see I'm good, right? Herb and I still like to have our fun on Saturday nights. Don't we, hon?"

The old man looked away in embarrassment, mumbling under his breath.

"Ma'am, I'm really sorry." Pete looked at the old man. "Please accept my apologies. I'll let myself out."

Pete made his way to the front door before the couple could respond. Walking to his car, he cringed, knowing the ribbing he was going to take from Gabrielle.

GRACE JOHNSTON'S STORY

ROYAL OAK
SATURDAY, JULY 31, 1976

"**D**amn it, not again." I stamp my foot as another gutter ball rolls down. Two lanes down, a group of four guys are having a good time, drinking beers, getting louder each frame, and goofing around.

I sit down after my turn and Ruth, my best friend, whispers in my ear, "I think he's looking at you."

"Really? I'm too scared to look."

Ruth looks for me. "No, he's really looking this way. I think he likes you."

I squeeze her arms.

"Yow, you're pinching me."

"Sorry, he's so cute." I giggle.

"Wait…"

"What?"

"He might be looking at me."

I push Ruth in the shoulder. "He'd better not."

As we sip our Cokes and munch on fries between frames, I keep sneaking peaks in his direction. When it's my turn again, I pick up my bowling ball, wondering if he's watching.

"All right, Grace, throw a strike," Ruth says.

I try to look cool as I walk up to the line, but the ball drops from my hand with a loud thud. My friends break out in laughter, and I turn beet red. I look around to see if he noticed, but he and his friends are gone.

I search around but can't find him at all. I'm so bummed.

We continue to bowl for a little longer to finish the game, but I'm not very excited anymore. Ruth sees right through me like she always does.

"You are not moping because that guy disappeared, are you?"

"No. But he was really cute! You saw the way he was looking at me. Do you think he's too old for me?"

"Yeah. This is totally gross. What would an older guy want with some thirteen-year-old?"

"I don't know," I admit. "Maybe he thought I was older. Promise me, if we do run into him again and he asks my age, tell him I'm sixteen and I go to Dondero High School. Please, Ruth, please?"

"OK, but it's still weird and creepy."

Our friends get picked up by their parents, but Ruth and I wait for my mom outside the bowling alley. That's when I hear a voice behind me.

"Hi, girls. My name is Keith."

It's him.

"Hi. This is Ruth, and I'm Grace."

"Are you girls from around here?" Keith asks.

"Royal Oak. Do you live around here?" I ask.

"Actually, I live near Pontiac, in Auburn Heights. A friend from school lives near here, and I came down for some bowling and brews. I guess it's my lucky night."

ROYAL OAK

SUNDAY, AUGUST 8, 1976

I throw the *Seventeen* magazine on the floor with the rest scattered around. "God, I'm bored. Why doesn't he call?" I say out loud. Keith warned me not to call him at home. His parents would freak if they ever found out my age. I can't help myself. I just want to fool around with him. I dial him using our secret ring code and hang up.

Five minutes later the phone rings. "Grace, I told you not to call here."

"I know, but I'm bored," I say. "I want to be with you."

"Hey, we got to be more careful."

"I'm tired of being careful. I'm going crazy. I want to kiss you and...you know."

"Shhh. My mother sometimes listens in on my conversations," Keith says.

"Tell her it's none of her business. Don't be such a momma's boy."

"Hey, I told you that I'm living at home. I got to play by their rules."

"You're nineteen. Tell them you're an adult."

"This isn't going anywhere...What's up?"

"I'm bored. I'm lonely. I want you to come over. My mom's at work. I'm sitting down here trying to stay cool. I've got an idea. Why don't you come over and bring me some McDonald's?"

"Hey, I can't come over all the time. Besides, I've got to go out with my friends later tonight."

"I'm tired of you always going out with your friends. Why don't we go out tonight? We can go to the movies. How about a drive-in?"

"I told you that I've already made plans."

"What if I come to your place?"

"How would you get here?"

"I'd hitchhike," I say.

"No, I don't like you hitchhiking. There're too many freaks out there."

"Scaredy cat, I can tell. I don't get into the car with anyone I don't trust."

"It's too dangerous," Keith says. "I'll be really pissed if you come over here."

"Don't be a fag. I'm coming over..." I hang up the phone before he can say anything else. The phone rings as I run upstairs to get ready, but I don't answer it.

I check my face in the mirror, grab my handbag, shut the front door to the house, and run down the front stairs, never looking back. Mom would never understand about Keith and me. Besides, he's a lot hotter than any of Mom's creepy jerks.

Finding a ride isn't as easy as I thought it would be. I shout out, "What's taking so long?" And just then a dirty black pickup slows down and stops. The driver leans over and rolls down the passenger's side window. The guy has greasy curly hair and has these gray-and-black whiskers starting to show. "Need a ride?"

"No, thanks. My mom is coming any minute."

"It's awful hot out there. I've got A/C, and you can wait in here until she does show," he says.

"No, thanks."

"It's really hot out there."

"Why don't you buzz off?"

"Hey, no need to get ugly."

"Why don't you find someone your own age, pig?"

"Screw you."

I flip him the bird as his pickup races away. Another five minutes pass before the next car slows down and eventually stops in front of me. The window rolls down.

"Where are you going?" The driver, a woman, has beautiful eyes.

"Auburn Heights," I say.

"You're in luck! I'm heading in that direction. Hop in."

"Thanks."

I jump in, and the car smoothly pulls back onto the road.

"Hi. What's your name?" she asks.

"Grace. Hey, thanks for the ride. I was getting hot out there." I look around the car and then back to the driver. The heat doesn't seem to affect her. I'm hot and sweaty with my hair parted in the middle and plastered to the side of my face. Meanwhile, she looks like a TV star with her long brown hair feathered cut with large flicks and blond highlights to accent her tan. She's so different from anyone I know.

"What's wrong?"

"Oh, nothing. You must be very rich."

The driver laughs. "Why do you say that?"

"This car is really nice. You're so different...You're really beautiful, and you smell really good. I like your perfume."

"Thank you," she says. "But I'm not very rich."

"Better than us."

"Well, I'm sure that your mom and dad work very hard."

I slouch further down in the seat. "I didn't know my dad. He took off before I was born. Some of the guys my mom hangs around with are real losers. Her job is pretty lame. She's always bitching about work."

"I'm sure she tries her best. What takes you out to Auburn Heights?"

"My boyfriend."

"How old are you?"

"Thirteen."

"Wow, I'd have taken you to be much older."

"That's what most people think. I think it's because my body...you know."

She nods her head yes, and her smile makes it seem like she understands. "Aren't you a little young for a boyfriend?"

I shrug. "You sound like my mom. I guess so...maybe... He's really cute, and my friends are so jealous."

The driver smiles at me. "Don't you know that you ought to be more careful? There are a lot of creeps out there."

"Yeah, I guess so." I shrug. "You should've seen the pig who tried to pick me up before you came. He was so gross. I can tell...naturally. A creep doesn't look like you. They don't have a hot car like this. Trust me, I know."

She laughs. "Well, it sounds like you've got them figured out pretty well."

I like her laugh. "What's so funny?"

"Hey, I've got to make a quick detour. I hope you don't mind. It'll just take a minute."

"Yeah, sure. No problem." I think, *Great, it's going to take forever to get to Keith's house.*

"So I don't look like a creep," she says. "That's comforting to know. Well, here we are. Come on in, and I'll get you something to drink. I'll just be a minute."

SOUTHFIELD AND ROYAL OAK
SUNDAY, AUGUST 8, 1976

The humidity had finally begun to abate as the cool evening air moved in. This was little consolation to Kathleen Johnston as she left the mall. She made her way to the back of the parking lot where her car was parked, letting out a long breath to release the stress and frustration from what had been building over a long and exasperating day at work. Unlocking the car and settling into the driver's seat, she started the car, checked the rearview mirror, put the car in gear, pulled out of the parking space, and began a mental checklist of her life.

Job sucks? Yep.

Bank account sucks? Yep.

Bills suck? Yep.

Car sucks? Yep.

House sucks? Yep.

Love life sucks? Yep.

Sex life sucks?

"Hell yes!" she screamed out loud.

God, my life sucks. Thirty-one years old and I can barely take care of myself, and on top of that, I have a thirteen-year-old daughter I can't make happy.

Her mother had been a single mother, too. They'd always fought and argued with each other. Her mother had drunk too much and could be so loving, kind, and generous one moment and then brutal the next, passing out her own brand of physical or verbal punishment. She hadn't been able to wait to get out of the house, away from her mother and her loser boyfriends. Now life seemed to be repeating itself. Grace was a lot like her—she was too into boys and talking on the phone and was trying to grow up too fast.

Kathleen pulled into the driveway, parked the car, got out, and moped to her unremarkable duplex. Just for a moment everything was uncharacteristically quiet, almost peaceful. Kathleen opened the door; the stench of cat urine and litter box would have knocked most people to their knees, but she seemed oblivious. All she wanted to do was get out of her pathetic uniform, toke a joint, shower, and maybe eat some pizza and drink some wine.

"Grace? Grace?" she called out into the darkness as she brushed the cat aside with her foot. "Dammit, Puss, get out of the way. Grace?" Kathleen made her way through the house and opened the basement door and yelled down, "Grace, you down there?" Kathleen didn't pay much attention to Grace not being there. She was known to disappear for hours at a time.

Kathleen went to her bedroom, unzipped her dress, and stripped. She went over to her chest of drawers and opened the top one. Her hand searched around for the plastic bag containing her stash. She pulled out the dirty bag containing a few joints and mostly stems and seeds. "Shit, I need to get some more." Kathleen pushed the mound of dirty clothes from the old faded fabric chair and plopped down in their place. Sitting in her shabby bra and panties, she lit up the joint and took a long drag.

She held it for a long time before she finally exhaled. After she'd finished her joint, she peeled off her bra and panties and went into the shower.

Later, Kathleen had a towel wrapped around her head and wore nothing but a stained white cotton robe as she sat in front of her old TV watching *Cher* and drinking cheap red wine. She planned to wait until Grace arrived before making dinner, but her cravings made her stomach crumble.

Kathleen caved in and went to the kitchen and pulled down the last box of Appian Way pizza mix. She threw the ingredients together and popped the sad little pizza into the oven. By midnight, she had eaten the pizza, finished the bottle of wine, and finished her last joint. She stumbled to her bedroom and passed out on top of the dirty sheets and bedspread.

Kathleen woke the next morning with serious cotton-mouth and a vicious headache. She pushed herself off the mattress, working hard to steady herself. She tried in vain to tie her robe closed. "God, I need some coffee," she said out loud. The house was quiet, which was nothing out of the ordinary in the morning. Then she realized that Grace had never come home.

"Grace? Grace?" There was no response, just the purring of the cat rubbing up against her shins. Kathleen was concerned, but not overly worried, at this point. She remembered that just last fall Grace had disappeared with an older boy for a few days.

Although Kathleen's parental capabilities were extremely limited, her maternal instincts began to send the tiniest signals that something was wrong. When it came to Kathleen, it could be hours before the message ever got through. As morning came and went, she called Ruth and a few of Grace's school friends, but no one had seen or heard from her all day. Kathleen hung up the phone, sat back in the chair, and pulled out a crumpled pack of cigarettes. *When I get my hands on that kid, I'll ruin her fun. She'll be grounded for days—no, months.*

The remainder of the afternoon was filled with anger, but as the seconds turned into minutes, and the minutes into hours, her anger was eventually replaced by fear. Kathleen paced through the house like a big game cat trapped inside a small cage. She had already torn the house apart looking for possible signs to her daughter's whereabouts, but she wasn't able to find a clue.

ROYAL OAK
WEDNESDAY, AUGUST 11, 1976

Eventually, three days later, in sheer desperation, she called the police.

"Can you describe your daughter to me, please?"

"Well, she's thirteen years old, with light-brown curly hair and light-brown eyes. She's tall for her age and looks older."

"Has she done anything like this before?"

"Yes, last fall, but this just feels different…"

"I'm sure that she'll show up soon. They usually do. I'll send a car over as soon as possible."

Kathleen had no real family or friends. The only company Kathleen kept was with the overflowing ashtray of various-sized cigarette butts and the half-drunk cup of cold coffee. She sat in the living room staring out the window into space. The dark rings around her eyes and her almost catatonic state were the only evidence that exhaustion and stress had taken their toll. One thought ran through her mind over and over: *What have I done to deserve this?* She was not a religious person, but she couldn't help thinking that if there was a God, he wouldn't do such a terrible thing to someone who had suffered so much already.

Kathleen stared at the TV. Eventually, the combination of the doorbell ringing and the loud knocking on the door brought her back to reality. She answered the door to a two patrolmen. She asked them in.

They were polite in their questioning, but Kathleen saw the disbelief on their faces as their eyes swept the dirty house. She felt inadequate from the insincerity in their voices as the officers tried to assure her that no one had been kidnapped in years and that Grace was most likely hanging out somewhere with her friends. As they departed, she overheard them talking to each other.

"What a dump!"

"You're not kidding. Did you get a whiff of that shit hole?"

"I thought that I'd been hit in the face with a baseball bat. My favorite fragrance: Eau de Litter Box with a pinch of cigarette smoke."

"Don't blame the kid. I'd have run away, too."

ROYAL OAK
FRIDAY, AUGUST 13, 1976

Charlie rang the doorbell. The door slowly opened. Charlie looked at the catatonic mother wearing a dirty bathrobe.

"Ya?" Kathleen Johnson asked.

"Hi. Kathleen Johnston?"

"Ya?"

"My name is Dr. Charlie Taylor. I work with the Oakland County Prosecutor's Office."

"It's about time someone took an interest in Grace. The police don't ever answer my questions."

"May I come in?"

Feeling slightly self-conscious, Kathleen looked back at the dirty house and ran her hand through her greasy, unkempt hair. "Sure. I'm sorry the house is a mess. I haven't had the energy to take care of it since Grace disappeared."

"I completely understand."

Kathleen opened the door and let Charlie into the house. Charlie had been warned by the Royal Oak police, but it still hadn't prepared her for the smells and sights that hit her. Charlie quickly composed herself and smiled reassuringly at Kathleen.

"Like I said, it's a mess. Sorry," Kathleen said.

"Kathleen, I'm sorry. I can't begin to imagine what you've been going through. Can we sit over here?" Charlie said, trying to direct Kathleen to a relatively clean spot on the sofa. "Kathleen, I'm sorry to have to tell you this, but the police in Ohio have discovered the body of a young girl that matches the description of Grace."

"You're wrong. My Gracie would never go to Ohio by herself. What would she be doing in Ohio, for God's sake? No, no, no, this can't be happening."

"The police have been very thorough to this point in the investigation. They've talked with Grace's friends and neighbors and were able to piece together the following information. Grace had an older boyfriend who lived about ten miles away in Auburn Heights, and she was supposed to be hitchhiking to his place but never made it."

"Was she...you know?"

"No, she hadn't been sexually molested, and she was fully clothed."

Kathleen covered her face with her hands and began to sob uncontrollably. Charlie got up and sat next to her, put her arm around her, and provided some comfort to a woman who had seen little in her life. Charlie had tremendous empathy for the families of victims. She knew what it was like to have your life shattered in a moment and to be left all alone to face the consequences.

"I need your assistance, Kathleen. I need to know Grace better. What can you tell me about her?"

"She was my baby…my best friend. I guess we were more like sisters than mother and daughter. I had her when I was just a baby myself. I was only seventeen. Her father took off before she was born."

"What type of girl was Grace?"

"I guess she was like most girls. Growing up fast…too fast. She was more interested in boys than books."

"Did she have a lot of friends? How did she get along with her classmates?"

"She had a couple of girlfriends. But it was the boys…not just her classmates, but high school boys. Then the men got a whiff. They're a bunch of sickos, if you ask me."

"Anyone in particular?"

"There was this college boy last year. She disappeared with him for a couple of days last fall. I don't have a clue about this guy in Auburn Heights. She didn't share. I'm sure she didn't want me to know because I'd have put an end to it immediately."

"Do you mind if I look in Grace's room?"

"No, it's just down the hallway, but she spent most of her time in the basement." Kathleen showed Charlie down the hallway to the back of the house. Grace's room was not much different from the rest of the house—unkempt and dirty. Charlie walked around the room, taking in the surroundings. Charlie saw a picture of several girls in bathing suits with a lake in the background.

"Is this Grace?"

"Yeah…last summer at Mackinac Island."

"She's pretty. Do you have a better picture?"

"I've got one on the kitchen fridge. I'll get it for you."

Charlie began to search the room like she had been trained, starting at twelve o'clock and then moving in a clockwise direction. She hadn't gotten far when Kathleen returned with Grace's school picture.

"What is it?" Kathleen asked.

Charlie stared at the photo. "She reminds me of someone…someone who…" Charlie looked at the photo and was taken by Grace's resemblance to another victim.

PONTIAC

FRIDAY, AUGUST 20, 1976

"Dr. Taylor, what do you have to report?" Sydney White asked. Her staff turned their attention to Charlie, who was twirling her pen deep in thought. "Dr. Taylor? I asked you a question."

"I'm sorry...It was something that had been said previously that got me thinking," Charlie answered while continuing to twirl her pen between her forefinger and thumb.

"Stop twirling your pen and just provide your answer," Sydney White said. Charlie could see the smirks of the other staff members seeing she was receiving the same scrutiny they did on a regular basis.

Charlie glanced at the pen in her hand and smiled. "Americans doodle, and Asians twirl their pens," she said before setting hers on the table. "Grace Johnson was growing up fast. Physically, she'd already gone through puberty. She could easily be mistaken for sixteen instead of her actual age, thirteen. She was already promiscuous, not just with boys her age but with young men much older. She liked to hitchhike, too. She was a high-risk victim."

"Are you saying she deserved it?" Sydney asked.

"Absolutely not. What I'm saying is that her risky behavior increased her chances of running into trouble."

"Right, so she's like a lot of teenagers—letting her hormones get in the way of common sense."

Charlie nodded in agreement. "Yes. I apologize for being distracted, but I can't get over how much Grace looks like another victim I studied early in my career—Lauren Ring."

"Lauren Ring...I don't remember the case."

"It was September 1972. She was from St. Clair Shores, and she had been held captive for over a month before the killer left her body out in the open for anyone and everyone to discover. She was wearing the same clothes that she had disappeared in."

"Nothing strange about that," Sydney said.

"No, of course. But the clothes were very expensive and were still very well maintained. The killer had held her captive for almost a month, yet there were no visible markings except some slight bruising around her wrists."

"I don't see the connection between the two girls other than looking alike."

"Despite their age differences, there is a striking physical resemblance," Charlie said. "Both girls were restrained in a way that reduced the amount of bruising. Grace's hands were tied behind her back with a white cloth. Grace and Lauren were killed by asphyxiation."

Sydney White sat forward in her chair. "You're not implying that both girls were killed by the same person, are you?"

"No," Charlie said. "At least not yet."

"Anything else to add? What about the profile of the killer?"

"Male, twenty-five to thirty-five, something compelling about him for Grace to get in the car with him."

"Compelling?" Bill Choate, the deputy, asked.

"His looks, the car itself, his personality. Maybe he has a bad-boy persona," Charlie said.

"Anyone else have anything to add?" Bill asked. Seeing no responses, he went down the remainder of the agenda with Sydney and her staff. Charlie had gone back to the recesses of her mind, lost deep in her thoughts and twirling her pen.

FRANKLIN VILLAGE
MONDAY, SEPTEMBER 6, 1976

All the heads in the crowd turned to the top of the hill. The little ones couldn't contain their excitement and jumped up and down in anticipation. From the other side of the large hill the blast of sirens from the police cars and fire trucks could be heard—noon sharp, the signal of the annual Franklin Round-Up parade. Josh and Melissa, with their faces painted like clowns, looked up at Charlie and Annie with big smiles on their faces. Charlie pointed toward the top of Franklin Road. "Here they come."

The police cars and fire trucks with their sirens blaring were the first to crest the hill. Volunteer police and firemen threw bubblegum to the children gathered alongside the road. "Quick, grab them," Charlie said to Josh and Melissa. The kids didn't hesitate to scramble among the other kids, grabbing pieces of Bazooka and stuffing their pockets.

The local car enthusiasts were next, showing off everything from Model Ts to the latest Corvettes. A white 1965 Cadillac Eldorado convertible with red leather interior was followed by the roar of the 440 Super Commando six-barrel V8 of a purple 1970 Plymouth Road Runner with its distinctive high-mounted rear wing and decal of the cartoon Road Runner bird holding a helmet.

"You should have your car out there," Annie said.

Charlie, with her aviator sunglasses, hair pulled back into a ponytail, and even dark-brown tan, looked at Annie and smiled.

"What I wouldn't do to own some of these cars. Mine is nice, but it can't compete with these cars. Besides, here comes my favorite part of the parade."

Magnificent horses and their skilled riders entertained the crowd. They watched the powerful animals with their hides glistening in the warm noonday sun and listened to their hooves clomping against the paved street.

"We used to ride our horses," Charlie said. "Susan and I would be in our traditional British riding regalia of hunting caps, brick-red fitted jackets, and tall boots." Charlie leaned over and whispered in Melissa's ear, "See that little girl over there riding? That will be you next year, and you can ride with me."

Melissa hugged Charlie's waist tightly.

"Thanks. She'll be insufferable," Annie said.

"It's the least I can do."

A beautiful palomino with its distinguishing gold coat and brilliant white tail and mane came up to Charlie, Annie, and the kids and stopped.

The rider tipped her cowboy hat back on her head. "Charlie? Charlie Taylor, is that you behind those shades?" She wore blue jeans tucked into highly polished black cowboy boots, a large silver belt buckle with turquoise accents, and a blue-and-white gingham shirt with the sleeves cut off.

"Hi, Sally. It's great to see you. What a beautiful animal." Charlie stroked the horse's face.

"It's been about, what, five years? Why aren't you out here riding?" Sally asked.

"Too much work and too little time."

"Nonsense. Riding cures what ails you."

Charlie made introductions. "Sally, this is a friend of mine—Annie—and her kids, Melissa and Josh. Do you think you can let them ride with you the rest of the way?"

"Sure. Josh can ride with me, and Melissa can ride with my sister." Sally waved to another rider to come to her.

"We'll meet you across from the Cider Mill in the open grassy area. Sound good?" Charlie saw the hesitation in Josh's face. "Hey, Josh, don't worry. Riding is safer than going down that big icy hill." She boosted Josh up on the horse. Sally's sister rode up alongside to let Melissa get on.

"I'm not afraid," Melissa said.

"Honey, you're fearless," Charlie said.

"Hang on tight," Annie said as the riders rejoined the parade.

"Are they going to be alright?" Annie asked nervously.

"They're going to be great," Charlie said to alleviate the concerned look on Annie's face. She was studying Annie's face when the ringing of bicycle bells and the honking of horns caught their attention.

"How precious," Annie said. "I'd rather have them riding their bicycles than a large beast. I'd be a little less worried."

They watched all the kids with their painted faces covered in rainbows and flowers, Indians, pirates, or clowns and their bicycles decorated with plastic flowers, colored paper, and playing cards attached to the spokes. This signaled the end of the parade.

"That was terrific," Annie said. "It lived up to its billing. What's next? I can't wait."

"Why, the Cider Mill. It isn't a Michigan fall without going to the Franklin Cider Mill," Charlie said. "On Saturday afternoons, I still come back here to buy a jug of cider and a greasy brown lunch bag of doughnuts, salami, and cheeses. Then I return to the commons. I enjoy sitting, taking in the beautiful fall colors, watching the horseback riders, and maybe catching a Pop Warner football game."

"Sounds wonderful," Annie said.

Charlie and Annie strolled along Franklin Road with Charlie pointing out the popular landmarks. "Over there, the little white clapboard building...that's the library, and on the backside of it is the police station."

"It's so quaint. Doesn't look like much of a police station. They mustn't get much crime around here."

"Really all they have room for is the police chief's office, his secretary's desk, and a small dispatch radio. Complete volunteer force here. No, they don't have much crime here at all." Charlie pointed to a brick building. "This is the Golfdale Market. Susan and I would ride our bicycles up here and then load up on bubblegum before we continued the ride to the top of the hill to go to our elementary school."

They walked past the hardware store with its large front porch, the Standard Oil gas station with its large pumps, and Commonwealth bank. All seemed to be from a different time and era.

"I love this place. Everything seems so quaint," Annie said.

"The village's motto is 'The Town That Time Forgot.'"

"You must have some fabulous memories."

Charlie reflected for a moment. "Yes, I was pretty fortunate to grow up around here."

They eventually made their way to the open grassy area where the riders had collected. They were looking for Josh and Melissa when they heard Josh yell, "Mom, it was so awesome!"

Charlie and Annie walked up to the collected group of riders and kids.

"Sally, thanks," Charlie said. "I can tell they really enjoyed the ride."

Annie hugged her two grinning children. "It's really appreciated."

"They're naturals. When are we going to get you back out riding?" Sally asked Charlie.

"Don't have much time for it or desire. Besides, I don't know if I have any of my riding gear. My parents donated most of it to Goodwill when Susan and I went off to school."

"Nonsense. You don't have to get all dressed up to enjoy it. You can come by anytime to enjoy a ride."

Melissa looked up admiringly at Charlie. "Aunt Charlie, can you ride?"

"Missy, that was long time ago."

"Honey, don't let her fool you. She's a great rider," Sally said, winking at Charlie.

"Missy, I think the heat's getting to Sally." Charlie gave her old friend her rendition of the evil eye.

"I want to hear more," Annie said.

"Well, if Charlie had a penis she'd have competed in the Olympics and probably won," Sally said.

"Sally…" Charlie warned, looked at the children.

"The coach and parents used to freak because she'd kick all the boys' butts. You should've seen her. She was so impressive. We all looked up to her."

"Missy, Sally has a tendency to exaggerate…grossly," Charlie told the girl. "Don't you, Sally?"

"Huh, tell her or I will," Sally said, and all eyes turned on Charlie.

She sighed, giving in. At least she could explain it without the colorful exaggeration. "There's an event called the pentathlon."

"What's that?" Melissa asked. As she looked up, she put her hand over her eyes to shade them from the sun.

"Explain to her what you used to do," Sally said.

"The pentathlon is a five-sport event that consists of a two-hundred-meter freestyle swim, fencing, show jumping, running, and shooting," Charlie said.

"She's being too modest. She'd outswim, outrun, outshoot till those jerks couldn't take it," Sally said.

"Sally, thanks again for taking the kids on a ride," Charlie said, trying to usher Annie and the kids away.

"So when are you going to get back on a horse again? Let's go riding like we used to, without a care in the world."

Charlie smiled. "Stranger things have happened. Maybe I'll take you up on that offer someday. But right now I'm taking them to the Cider Mill for a slice of heaven on earth."

Charlie, Annie, and the kids waved good-bye and made their way toward the Cider Mill. "What did she mean?" Annie said.

"Don't pay any attention to Sally...she has a tendency to exaggerate."

"I don't think so. I find it very intriguing to get some additional insight into you. Let's say you're not the most forthcoming person I've ever met. You're not like most women who are always pouring out their life story."

Charlie looked at Annie thoughtfully. "Well, as Sally said, I used to train and compete with the boys in the pentathlon. It was everything that I loved to do, swimming, riding, and running. I love to compete in everything, just can't turn off my competitive juices. So if a boy beat me in an event, I'd train that much harder. I don't know...I just couldn't walk away. Well, some of the boys' parents started to complain to the coach. It got pretty ugly—teasing that went over the top, cheating, even trying to physically hurt me. I wasn't going to back down, but my parents caved in. They tried to reason with me that girls aren't supposed to do these things. I felt betrayed."

Charlie thought, *It wouldn't be the last time, either.*

Annie took Charlie's hand and squeezed it. "Thanks. And I'm sorry."

"It's not your fault. Besides, that was a long time ago. I've moved on. Come on, let's go. The best is yet to come."

Charlie directed Annie and the kids into the dark, musty building that held the waterwheel.

The kids held onto the chain link fence, fascinated as they watched the large waterwheel slowly turn. "What's this place?" Melissa asked.

"The Cider Mill," Charlie said. "I used to come here when I was little…and still do. It has this incredibly large functioning waterwheel that crushes all the bright-red-yellowish apples into this delicious golden-brown cider. You can smell the sweet apple juices from the fruit being crushed below. We'll buy small paper cups from a wall-hanging penny dispenser to drink the cider."

"Let's go," the kids yelled, and they ran inside the main building.

"Look at how many people are jammed in here just to buy some cider and doughnuts," Annie said.

Charlie paid the man behind the counter for the half gallon of cider and a dozen doughnuts. She reached into the brown lunch bag and pulled out a warm doughnut and placed it in front of Annie's mouth. "Try this."

Annie bit down on the doughnut. "Oh my God. These doughnuts and cider are to die for. I can see why this place is packed."

"I've got one more surprise. The pièce de résistance. The hardest decision is choosing between the candy or caramel." Charlie presented four apples, two of each kind.

Josh and Melissa reached for the beautiful candy apples, with their alluring, shiny, red, hard candy coating.

"Those look sinful," Annie said. "The coating looks like glass. They're almost too beautiful to eat."

Charlie smiled as the kids tried to break through the hard candy coating. "Can I give you a hand?" Charlie asked.

"Yes, please…" Melissa handed her the apple.

Charlie took the white waxed paper and wrapped it around the side of the apple. She then tapped it against the pavement, skillfully creating a crack in the candy coating. "There you go." She gave the apple back to Melissa.

"I think Josh is determined enough to conquer it on his own," Annie said, tousling Josh's hair as she watched the boy doggedly trying to bite through the hard candy coating.

"You're not exempt either." Charlie gave Annie a caramel apple.

Annie bit into the thick, gooey caramel coating. The apple juices erupted and flowed down her hand and arm. "Ah, I'm a mess." Annie laughed out loud. "You're spoiling us."

Annie smiled at Charlie and then took the apple in Charlie's hand and pulled it toward her. She took a large bite and tried to keep the juices from leaking out of the corner of her mouth. "I don't know what I'm most worried about…the next dentist appointments, the inevitable stomachaches, or if they are going to have any room for dinner."

"Don't worry, Mom, I survived the Round-Up for numerous years," Charlie said. "Kids are so much more resilient than we are. Besides, this is the last day of summer. You and the kids are back in school tomorrow."

Charlie watched with fascination and delight as Josh and Melissa continued making a mess—their mouths red and sticky as juices ran down their arms. She thought how lucky they were…to be carefree, with no worries, to be loved and safe.

Then, turning her head, she looked in the direction of where she had been spent the better part of a night looking at the grisly crime scene just a few hundred meters away. Katie Hill had been spending time with her girlfriend, maybe her first love, and then in a matter of hours someone had snatched her, sexually assaulted her, and brutally murdered her. Life could be cruel and quickly turn on you.

"Hey, are you in there?" Annie waved her hand in front of Charlie's face.

"Sorry, I was just thinking…"

"I know. Why don't we save it for another time?"

They spent the rest of the afternoon playing carnival games and watching the firefighters take on the police in their classic water hose duel. As the warm fall sun started to fade away, they sat down on a large blanket and ate delicious barbeque and fresh sweet corn for dinner.

As night fell, Charlie and Annie packed the kids into the car for the drive back home. Charlie flipped on the headlights and headed for the highway.

"Thanks again for a great day," Annie said.

Charlie looked at the kids in the rearview mirror. "They couldn't be more precious."

ALLISON WALKER'S STORY

"**N**o. No. No." I try to run, but my legs won't move. They're like lead. I've gotta run, I have to get away. I can feel him coming. "Stop smiling. Stop it! Please, stop it!"

Run, run, I tell myself. "No, stop! No, please don't…"

He holds a gun, points it at my face. I'm tired, exhausted, and scared. I raise my hand up in defense. I scream…

"Allison…Allison, wake up, honey. It's only a bad dream."

"Mom…Mom, he's after me."

"Who, honey? Who's after you?"

"I can't see his face…It's always the same dark room."

"Now, honey, don't worry. It's just a dream. You've been under a lot of stress. You need to try and relax. Take deep breaths and think happy thoughts."

I hug my mom tight until I fall asleep.

BIRMINGHAM

FRIDAY, NOVEMBER 26, 1976

"Mom, I don't want to go to the doctor's," I say as we drive in my mom's car.

"Honey, she's going to help you with your nightmares."

"What if she wants to give me a shot?"

"Allison, you're twelve. I hope that you aren't afraid of shots anymore. Besides, she's not that type of doctor. She specializes in helping people with their mental issues."

"I'm not crazy!"

"Honey, no…no…She's going to help you with your bad dreams. Here we are," Mom says.

"This is close to dad's house. Can we go there after, just to say hi?"

"No promises."

We walk into the doctor's building. It smells funny. I hear the sound of a dentist drill, and I start to get nervous again. What if she thinks a shot will make me feel better? Every time I go to the doctor they tell you that the shot will make you feel better and that shots don't hurt. I hate shots…they hurt.

The office is really different from any doctor's office I've seen before. It's like our living room. There are no nurses, just a nice lady behind a desk who smiles at us.

While my mom checks us in, I go over to the fish tank to look at all the pretty fish. After a few minutes, I hear my mom talking to someone, so I turn around.

"Hi, Mrs. Walker. Dr. Alex Simpson."

"Hi, Dr. Simpson. I'm Judy Walker, and this is my daughter Allison," my mom says, turning toward me and nodding at me.

She's so pretty and smiles at me.

"Hi, Allison."

"Allison, say hi to Dr. Simpson," my mom says.

"Hi."

"Allison, that isn't polite," my mom says. "You need to speak louder. I'm sorry…"

"Oh, she's fine, Mrs. Walker. Allison, when I was your age, I hated going to the doctor because they always had you taking off your clothes, and then they poked at you and wanted to give you a shot."

I nod my head and shrug my shoulders.

"I promise you that I won't give you any shots. Instead of a shot, how would you like a cup of hot chocolate?"

I smile.

"Great. Why don't we get ourselves a cup of hot chocolate, come back to my office, and talk? Does that sound good to you?"

I nod my head yes. I hear my mom laughing.

"Come on…" The doctor holds her hand out to me. "Do you like anything in your hot chocolate?"

I wasn't sure what to say.

"I like a little cinnamon in mine, but when I was your age I liked marshmallows."

"I like marshmallows, too," I say.

"Great. The little ones or the big puffy ones?"

Back by her office is a small kitchen that has all these snacks and candy in jars. We make our hot chocolate together.

"Welcome to our special place. Where would you like to sit?"

Her office is so neat. There is a couch, a big comfortable chair, and beanbag chairs, plus stuffed animals, toys, and blocks. I sit on the floor, and she sits down across from me and smiles. We talk about favorite TV shows and books.

"What is your favorite book?" She asks.

"I love Nancy Drew. I read her stories over and over again."

Laughing and nodding her head, she says, "I love her, too. You remind me of Nancy. You're independent and strong willed," Dr. Simpson says, taking a sip of her hot chocolate.

"When I was your age one of my favorite books was *The Arabian Nights.* One of the stories is about a boy named Aladdin, his magic lamp, and the genie inside. Aladdin rubs the lamp and a genie appears and grants his wishes. If you were Aladdin, what would your wishes be for the genie?" she asks.

I shrug my shoulders. I'm scared, but she makes me feel so good inside. I haven't felt like this in a long while. I feel special. "You promise not to tell?" I ask.

"That's an excellent question, Allison. I promise not to tell. Your secrets are safe with me."

I take a deep breath. She has the prettiest eyes.

"I wish that my mom and dad weren't divorced, that we were happy again."

"Have you ever talked to your mom and dad about your feelings?"

"They're always too busy."

"Allison, it may seem like your mom and dad are always too busy, but I bet if you asked them to talk with you they'd be more than willing to."

I look down at my cup.

"If you wanted the genie to grant you another wish, what would that be?"

"I want them to stop hitting each other."

"Your mom and dad hit each other?"

"They're always yelling at each other and saying mean things. One night, my dad got so mad that he slammed the door."

"What do you do when they are arguing with each other?"

"I try to make them stop. Sometimes I go to my room and hide under the bed."

"Do you tell your mom or dad how you feel?"

"I…I try, but they just don't listen. I try to be good. I think maybe if I'm really good then maybe they'll get back together."

"Allison, I know how painful divorce can be, but you need to understand this has nothing to do with you."

"Did your parents divorce?" I ask rubbing my hand.

"No…no, my mother died when I was a little girl."

"Did it hurt?"

"Yes, it was a very painful time."

"How…how did you…"

"How did I manage?"

"Yeah…"

"I was a lot like you," Dr. Simpson replied. "I found places to hide. My favorite was a secret place in the basement where nobody could find me. But you need to understand, Allison. We can't hide from our pain and anger. We need to learn how to cope with our problems. Does that make sense?"

I nod my head.

"Good. With your permission…I'd like to form a team… you can call me anytime you think the pain is too bad. This will be our safe place. Fair?"

"Yeah…I guess so."

"Good. I'm glad that we've got that settled. Can I share something else with you?" Dr. Simpson asks.

I shake my head yes.

"You are a very pretty young lady."

I look at my cup and blush.

"When I was your age, my body started to change, and I became very overweight and the kids could be really mean, calling me 'fatso' and 'piggy.' Their words were very hurtful, but that wasn't the hardest part. Along with all my physical changes, I started to menstruate, but I was too scared to tell anyone. I'd never like that to happen to you. Sometimes it's easier to tell a friend than maybe your mother."

Feeling a little nervous, I start to fidget in my chair. She smiles at me.

"Have you started menstruating?"

I'm feeling really nervous and embarrassed.

"Allison, you've got nothing to be embarrassed about. It's all part of growing up."

"No…but…"

"But, what?"

"Well, my best friend started her...you know."

"You mean her period?"

"Yeah...so, I went to the drug store and bought my own..." She smiles knowingly at me. "I didn't want to have any accidents...so I keep them in my purse."

"Does your mom know?"

"No..." I shake my head.

"Well, I'm sure she'd appreciate it if you shared your feelings with her. Moms can be a big help, especially when you begin to menstruate."

"What did you finally do?" I ask.

"You mean when I started to menstruate?"

"Yeah...I mean what did you do? Since you didn't have a mom or anything."

"Well, my father eventually remarried. I had a stepmother and an older stepsister. I asked my older stepsister what to do. Like I said, if you feel uncomfortable about going to your mom, you can always ask me. Now let's finish up our hot chocolate. I notice you're eyeing my jar of licorice rings. What's your favorite color?"

"I like the orange ones."

"I like the black ones."

I shake my head. "They're gross."

"On the way out, why don't you grab a couple for your trip home? I'm really excited having met you and look forward to our partnership. Let's go out and talk to your mom. I know that she's very concerned about you."

"You're not going to tell her about...you know?"

"No, your secret is good with me. I'll only tell her what you want me to."

ROYAL OAK
WEDNESDAY, DECEMBER 22, 1976

Everything seems wrong...not like it used to. Mom's not home. I'm tired of watching my little sisters. I don't want to go to church tonight. I hate them so much.

Why can't things be like they used to be? We had been spending Wednesdays at my dad's house since the divorce, but that's changed. My mom wants us to go to stupid church.

I look over at the small pile of Christmas gifts already under the tree. They've ruined everything. I gotta go to church. Tomorrow, we go to dad's house to celebrate Christmas with him. I hope his stupid girlfriend isn't there. Christmas Eve is Mom's birthday, and we're going to my grandmother's house for dinner and to celebrate her birthday like we always do.

But it just doesn't feel the same. It's not right. All I want for Christmas is for my parents to be together: for us to be a family like we were.

I don't want any presents. I just want to run downstairs on Christmas morning to see my parents standing there, together: Dad with his arm around Mom, a big cup of coffee in her hands while he takes pictures. All of the Christmas tree lights on, all the presents in three piles—one for me, one for each of my sisters—just like it used to be.

They've ruined my life. How can they do this? What did I ever do wrong to them? They're so selfish.

I hear the front door open and Mom comes in, stomping the snow off her shoes.

"Hi...I need your help."

"What's for dinner?" I ask.

"What would you like?"

"I don't know."

"How about some beanie weenies?"

"Fine..." I shrug my shoulders.

"I need your help. We've got to get going so we can make church."

"Do we have to? It's so boring."

"Yes, we do. Now give me a hand, please."

I take the bags out of her hand and put them in the middle of the living room. Then I lie down on the couch and start looking at my magazine.

"Allison, honey, I need your help setting the dinner table."

"Mom, why can't Greta do it? Besides, it's her turn."

"Because I asked you to do it. I really do not want to have this discussion right now. I'm busy getting dinner ready, and I need your help."

"Why can't Greta do it? Why do I have to do it all?"

"Please, Allison, can we just have a little cooperation? It's Christmas time. Please, as a gift to me."

The phone rings. Before my mom picks it up she looks at me. "The table—now, young lady."

She answers the phone. "Hello? Really…you know how much this means to the kids." She looks over at me, and I can see by the disappointment on her face and by the tone in her voice that she's talking to my dad.

"Great…OK, but this is so typical of you. Leave me to clean up your messes." She slams the phone down.

"Was that Dad?" I ask.

"Yes."

"What did he want? Why didn't you let me talk to him?"

"Allison, we'll talk later. Right now, I need you to help me get dinner ready."

"I just want to know. What did he want?"

She sighs. "He called to say that he wasn't going to be able to see you tomorrow like you normally do. You'll celebrate Christmas with him on Sunday."

I'm so mad. I'll show them.

"I hate you, I hate all of you. I hate Christmas. I hate this place."

I look at her. I can feel the tears start to run down my cheeks. I see a tear in the corner of her eye. The hate is starting to go away. There is a part of me that wants to hug her and say I'm sorry. But I can't. I don't know why, but I can't.

"Allison, if that's the way you really feel, then leave this house and do not come back until you are ready to apologize and be a member of this family. Do you understand me, young lady? If that's how you really feel, then get out of the damn house right now."

I scream and stomp up the stairs and slam the door to my room.

I'll show her. She doesn't know what I can do.

I put on my bright-green parka and pack my backpack with my favorite striped blanket and book. Without stopping, I stomp as hard as I can back down the stairs. I pause at the front door and look back at my sisters' sad faces.

I slam the front door and then jump on my bike. I just start to ride, pedaling as hard as I can go and pumping as hard as I can. My legs hurt trying to pedal through the slush and snow. I don't care—I just keep pedaling.

Dark outside. The cars along the main road are heading home. Home. I can't go home…I'll go to Dad's. Dad will understand everything. He'll call Mom and explain everything to her. It will be all right.

I'm riding, weaving, and sliding on the sidewalks. I've been riding for a long time, but I don't seem to be any closer to Dad's house. Scared, I keep pedaling harder. I'm looking for something familiar. I pedal faster. Everything looks different at nighttime. I start to cry.

My legs hurt. I'm tired and hot. I want to be back home with my mom and sisters. But I can't go back.

BIRMINGHAM
WEDNESDAY, DECEMBER 22, 1976

Headlights from the car captured the girl riding frantically. Like a curious shark circling with its dark-gray, menacing dorsal fin cutting through the darkened ocean waters, the driver purposefully pulled ahead of her and waited. Stepping out of the car, the driver waved and called out to the girl. The driver then, like a great white, picked up speed, with its eyes rolling over the moment before the strike.

ROYAL OAK
WEDNESDAY, DECEMBER 22, 1976

"Greta, tell Allison to come in, wash her hands, and get the table set."

"Sure, Mom." Greta opened the front door and yelled to no one and everyone at the same time. "Allison! Allison, time for dinner!"

"Greta, if I wanted you to yell and disturb the neighbors, I could have done it myself. Now where is your sister?"

"She's not here, Mom."

"What do you mean she's not here? It's dinnertime and pitch black outside. Where could that child have disappeared to?"

"Mom, her bike's gone, too."

"What? Come back inside before you catch cold."

Allison's mother, Judy, set the table and served her two other children their dinner, but the minute they were finished, she threw on her coat and began a frantic search of the neighborhood for her daughter. Her search did not provide any clues to where Allison had gone. Judy grabbed her car keys and drove to her ex-husband's house in Birmingham.

En route, she looked for her daughter, hoping to see her pedaling her bicycle.

This is the only place she would go. She has to be making her way to Rick's.

But there was no sign of Allison along the way. She found the doorbell hidden by a large Christmas wreath and rang it.

Rick opened the door.

"Sorry to bother you, Rick. I know you are busy, but this is really important. Is Allison here?"

"Hi, Jude. No, she's not. What's up? Are you and the girls all right?"

"Allison and I had an argument over helping me with the chores, and it escalated pretty quickly. I think she was pretty pissed that you weren't going to see her on Thursday. I told her to leave the house and go outside. I thought she'd be sitting on the porch, but when we went to call her in for dinner, she had disappeared and taken her bicycle with her."

"Sounds like the apple hasn't fallen very far from the tree. Sounds a lot like somebody else I know who drove her parents crazy," Rick said.

"Great, I'm looking for a little support here, not to have my childhood thrown in my face. It's tough enough when there were the two of us, and it's near impossible with just me. Besides, you don't see her every day."

"Never mind. I was just trying to add a little levity to the situation. I'm sure she's fine," Rick said. "We both know too well how Allison can be when she gets in one of her moods. I'm sure she'll turn up here or she'll be back at your place by the time you arrive, but I'll be sure to call you if she shows up here."

"You're probably right. She scares me a little. She's twelve, for God's sake. What will she be like when she's sixteen?"

"Please call me if she shows back up at home, and I'll do the same. If it'll help I'll change my plans and have the girls tomorrow for Christmas. I know how much Allison looks forward to our Christmas together. She won't miss that."

"Thanks, Rick. I'm sure you're right. That girl, I'm going to clobber her."

God, I've got to find my baby, Judy thought as she got into her car and started making her way back home. She drove along Woodward Avenue, stopping along the way at possible businesses that Allison might have visited—the grocery store, the drug store, and the hobby shop that was the local teen-agers' favorite haunt. There was no sign of Allison. She was nowhere to be seen.

Judy called the Royal Oak police a little before midnight. The police did not seem very concerned. They figured that Allison was a runaway who most likely would return in the morning. Judy hung up the phone and realized that her frustration and hurt had long evaporated and been replaced with concern and fear.

She opened the front door and stepped onto the front porch. She wasn't sure why; maybe it was in hope of finding some sort of sign or asking for God's divine intervention. It was a cold, foggy night, and the dampness in the air caused Judy to shiver. She wrapped her sweater around her body, but nothing seemed to ease the cold that had settled in for the evening.

ROYAL OAK

THURSDAY, DECEMBER 23, 1976

Judy didn't sleep well that night, and as the morning came, she found herself sitting by the phone. She spent the morning calling all of Allison's friends, but no one had seen or heard from her. Time moved on, and the rest of the day brought no signs of Allison. Judy got her two other daughters dressed in their Christmas best and drove them to their father's home. Judy was still optimistic that Allison was fine and that when they arrived at Rick's house she would find her sitting by the fireplace reading her favorite book and Rick would proclaim that the prodigal daughter had arrived.

Rick Walker hugged his daughters Greta and Dawn as they entered his home. "There are warm Christmas cookies on the kitchen counter," Rick said as he gathered up his daughters' coats and scarves.

"Rick, is Allison with you?" Judy asked.

"No. I was hoping that she'd be with you and maybe you just forgot to call. Why don't you join us, too? You know that Allison would never miss this time together," Rick said.

The meal had been finished, the table cleared, and the dishes washed, but still there was no sight or sound of Allison. Judy began to sob, voicing her concerns. "Rick, what has happened to our baby?"

"Hey, I'm concerned, too. I'm sure she is fine," Rick consoled.

Judy could no longer control her worst fears, thinking, *Something terrible has happened to Allison. Am I to blame?* She thought back to Allison's terrible nightmares—she shook her head to try and erase the thought that they might have been a premonition.

ANN ARBOR

SATURDAY, DECEMBER 25, 1976

"You've spoiled us all," Annie said as she stood alongside Charlie and handed her a cup of hot tea. The two women watched as the kids tore through the wrapping paper, stopping only a short time to admire one gift before they moved onto the next present.

"This is just what the doctor ordered. I love to see such innocence, such happiness on their faces, not a care in the world. It's the best gift you could have given me."

Annie ran her hand along the soft flannel robe's collar. "You're way too generous…"

From the TV blared, "This is an NBC news update. The teenage girl who's missing Christmas still hasn't been found. Allison Walker, the Royal Oak teenager who disappeared three days ago, remains missing. The Royal Oak police department thought initially that the teenager who had left home on Wednesday evening after she had a fight with her mother was a runaway. They're asking that everyone be on the lookout for the twelve-year-old. When last seen, she was wearing a bright-green parka, blue jeans, and snow boots. If you have any information on where Allison may be, please contact the Royal Oak police department."

"God, what's this world coming to? This is so sad. Her poor family." Annie sipped from her turquoise coffee mug.

"I know her. I just didn't realize it was Allison that they were referring to," Charlie said.

"You know her?"

"Yes, my father is an acquaintance of her father. I met Allison when she was just a young girl. They're a really nice family."

Annie looked up from the TV to Charlie. Charlie was staring back at Josh and Melissa.

"Thank God they're safe and sound. I don't know what I'd do if something happened to them," Annie said.

"I'll never let anything happened to them. I'm sorry, but I'll probably go into the office later and see what I can find out," Charlie said.

"Then let's make the best of our time together," Annie said, placing her arm around her.

TROY
SUNDAY, DECEMBER 26, 1976

"Breaker, breaker, 1-9. I have a 10-200, at I-75 and Big Beaver, over."

"This is the Troy police, 10-2, over."

"10 20, I 75 and Big Beaver, over."

"Roger, 10-20 at I-75 and Big Beaver, over."

"Roger, 10-38, appears to be a body, over."

"Roger, 10-38 being dispatched along with a patrol car. Can you provide more information? Over."

"Roger, I've pulled off the road it looks to be a body alongside the highway...breaker, breaker...wearing a bright-green parka, over."

TROY
SUNDAY, DECEMBER 26, 1976

Charlie got in her cold, damp car and started the powerful engine. The streets were lonely and empty at this time of day. She was able to get across town and onto I-75 quickly. She powered her car southeast to where Allison had been dropped off.

As she approached the scene from the opposite direction, Charlie noted how inconceivable the drop-off point was. Maneuvering her car off I-75 bound onto Big Beaver and back onto the northbound I-75 service drive, she pulled her car off the road behind the numerous police cars and news agency vans.

As she made her way to the crime scene, she was approached by a handsome, well-groomed Troy policeman. "Dr. Taylor? Ma'am, if you follow me this way, please."

"Excuse me, Officer. How'd you know that I was Dr. Taylor?" Charlie asked as they walked toward the crime scene.

"We received a call from Detective West of the Michigan State Police who informed us that you were on your way."

"OK, but how did you know that I was Dr. Taylor?"

"You matched his description."

"I'm afraid to ask what that might be," Charlie said.

"He said to look for a woman, Asian like, five feet three inches to five feet four inches tall, attractive, well dressed, with a very determined look on her face and driving a hot car. You're the only who matches that description."

"Thanks…I think."

Charlie stood over the blood-covered snow bank, taking notice of the fragments from Allison's green-and-orange ski cap. The detective walked up to Charlie and introduced himself. He handed the plastic shell case to Charlie.

"A twelve-gauge," Charlie asked.

"Yes, ma'am."

"Do you have any leads?"

"No, no witnesses. The trucker found her around eight forty-five this morning. Based upon the snowfall and accumulation on her, we think he placed the body here around six thirty this morning," the detective said.

"Thank you, Detective. I'm on my way to the coroner's. If you find anything else, please let me know," Charlie said and walked away.

PONTIAC
SUNDAY, DECEMBER 26, 1976

Charlie slid into the red leather booth and reached over to Pete's soda glass and took a sip of his Cherry Coke. She took note of the other patrons of the Big Boy restaurant and then looked back at Pete.

"I knew her...not well. My dad and hers are acquaintances," Charlie said.

"This sounds heartless, but this gets me out of having to go to church two days in a row. I can only ask for so much forgiveness," Pete said.

"Have you been to the scene?" Charlie asked.

"I just came from there. Looks like the killer dropped Allison's body off sometime early this morning based upon the amount of snow on her. She was wearing her backpack with her favorite blanket still packed inside. It appears Allison died from a shotgun blast to the head. Have you been to the scene?" Pete asked.

Charlie took a nibble of her tuna fish sandwich, put it down on a plate, and wiped her mouth with a white paper napkin. "Just before, I went to the coroner's. After we break away from here, I'm going to see the family." Charlie watched Pete wrap his large fingers around the white-and-red-diamond wax paper as he took an enormous bite from his double meat cheese Big Boy sandwich, washing it down with a large swig of Coke.

"What? Would you like some?" Pete said, holding onto the sandwich with both hands and making a gesture of offering it to her.

Charlie smiled, shaking her head no.

"The autopsy revealed that the killer had tried to smother her but was not successful," Charlie said. "Allison must have come to when the killer laid her body along the highway. The killer must have been shocked, placing Allison's body along the road, only to see her miraculously come back to life."

"He probably shits his pants," Pete said.

"I agree. I think he lost it and shot her in a panic," Charlie said. She paused as she collected her thoughts. "But I'm beginning to get concerned—really concerned. Dr. Schmidt determined that her body had been cleaned and washed prior to her death. Her clothes washed and pressed."

Pete was about to take another bite of his burger but instead placed it down slowly. "Go on. You've got my attention."

"For one moment let's take the shotgun out of the equation and let's say the killer had successfully asphyxiated Allison. Allison is abducted for several days. She is relatively well taken care of, wearing the same clothes that she disappeared in, which are cleaned and pressed. She was left out in the open for the public to discover and for everyone to see. Sound familiar?"

Pete took a sip of his Coke. "Are you trying to tell me that Cody Edwards and Allison Walker were abducted and murdered by the same perpetrator?"

Charlie pushed her half-eaten sandwich away from her, sat forward, and clasped her hands. "There are more similarities than we'd probably like to think about."

"I get the eerie similarities with the bathing, the clothes being pressed, and dressing. But we've got a boy and girl. He was molested...Allison?"

"No...no, she wasn't. I know I don't have a one hundred percent correlation, but I can make a very reasoned argument that we may be dealing with the same perp."

"I'm not saying you're jumping to conclusions, but I'd like to see more…"

"I'm going to open the aperture on the geography and time frame. Lauren Ring, sixteen, looked more like a thirteen-year-old. She was held for almost thirty days, but her expensive clothes were still in good condition. She had been asphyxiated and left in an open field." Charlie sat back in the booth.

"But what about Katie? She was sexually assaulted, possibly by a mechanical object, left nude, and skull crushed. Physically she was a big girl," Pete said.

"Right next to the Cider Mill. In the open," Charlie said.

"Cody, a boy, mechanically assaulted…"

"Asphyxiated and body left in the parking lot of a supermarket," Charlie said.

"Now Allison, not sexually assaulted, shot to death," Pete said.

"Kept for four days, attempted asphyxiation, bathed, fingernails clipped, clothes pressed and left alongside a major highway."

"Shit…" Pete exhaled.

"You forgot one other—Grace Johnson. Who wasn't sexually assaulted, asphyxiated…"

"Why so many years between Lauren's and Katie's murders?" Pete asked.

"Who knows how many other kids we may have missed because no one has put two and two together. Maybe there was some event that triggered all these recent abductions and murders," Charlie said.

"I don't know which one is more disheartening, that we've had a rash of unrelated abductions and murders or that a single person might be responsible for all of this," Pete said.

"I may be wrong. I hope to God that I am. We know that serial killers' MOs improve with time because there's a learning process for them, just as there is for us. However, their signature remains the same. For this guy, his signature means leaving these kids out in the open for all of us, and I mean all of us, to find."

"None of this is any good. I hope you're wrong because we both know what it means…Merry Christmas."

"Pete, if I'm right—Happy New Year."

Her next stop was to visit with Judy and Rick Walker.

ROYAL OAK
SUNDAY, DECEMBER 26, 1976

Charlie pulled into Judy Walker's driveway and surveyed the area.

What a terrible way to start the New Year. This poor family. I can't fathom the pain and anguish they must be going through. She made her way up the wooden stairs and knocked on the door.

A voice yelled through the closed door, "Can't you leave us alone? Please, just give us some peace and quiet." Charlie recognized Rick's voice, though it was muffled. "We need to time to grieve. Can't you just leave us alone?"

"Rick? I'm not with the press. I apologize. I should've called before I came over. My name is Dr. Charlie Taylor. I don't know if you remember me, but you and my dad worked together on—"

The door opened and Rick's haggard face appeared. "Charlie…sure, sure. I'm sorry, I thought you were one of those bloodthirsty journalists. This is really a bad time. Can I ask what brings you here?"

"I'm here because of Allison. I work for the Oakland County Prosecutor's Office. I'm a psychiatrist who specializes in assisting the police in developing a profile of the perpetrator based upon the victim, the crime scene, and other factors. I know this is a difficult time, but the sooner I can speak with you and Judy, the better."

"Please, come in." Charlie handed her coat to Rick and then made her way to Judy, curled up on the couch. She knelt before Judy and took her hand. She looked at Judy, noting her bleary, bloodshot eyes and red nose. She seemed to have aged ten years since the last time Charlie had seen her.

Charlie sat down next to the grieving mother and gave her a hug.

"Judy, I'm so sorry for your loss. You, Rick, and the girls are in my thoughts and prayers."

Judy nodded her head. "Please find out who did this to my little girl."

Rick came back into the room with coffee. "Thanks, Rick." Charlie held the cup in both hands. "Judy, I can't make any promises, but I'll do whatever I can to be of assistance. What have the police told you?"

"Frankly, to say the police have been incredibly disappointing would be an understatement," Rick said, "First, they didn't take Judy's call seriously. To them, Allison was just another kid pissed off at her parents, trying to teach us a lesson. Then they tried to blame Judy because she told Allison to leave the house until her attitude improved. Give me a break! What parent hasn't said that to their kids a thousand times? They also try to make it seem like it's my fault, that I'm an absentee father."

Charlie nodded. She had experienced how law enforcement could sometimes make victims feel like they were responsible for the crimes against them. "I understand your hurt and frustration. It would be very helpful to me if I had your insight on what happened."

"I'd just come home from work and Christmas shopping," Judy said. "I was a little frantic. I was trying to get dinner ready, feed the kids, and then get us out the door so we could make church services in time.

"I'd asked Allison to help with some chores. About that time, Rick had called saying he'd have to postpone his Christmas with the girls. When I told Allison, it seemed to have really unhinged her."

"What was Allison like?"

"She was a great kid," Rick chimed in, standing against the fireplace mantle. "She was a very protective big sister, but she could be very stubborn and determined."

"Like Rick said, Allison could be very stubborn. It wasn't long before she was yelling some very hurtful things at me."

"I'm sure she didn't mean them," Charlie said, taking Judy's hand. "Unfortunately, that's pretty age appropriate."

"Well, I told her to leave the house until she could be a part of the family. So she stomped upstairs, packed a few clothes, her blanket, and her favorite book." Judy choked back tears.

"Her favorite book?" Charlie asked.

"Nancy Drew. She must have read it a dozen times," Rick added.

Charlie smiled and nodded. "Can you continue, Judy?"

Judy blew her nose into a tissue. "I'm OK. Well, I sent Greta to call Allison for dinner, but she didn't answer. So, after dinner, I went looking for her. I figured she would either head to one of her friends' house or Rick's place."

"Judy called all of Allison's friends, but nobody had seen her," Rick said. "Although one little girl thought she had seen Allison near the hobby shop—you know the one off Woodward?"

"Yes, I'm familiar with it. Did Allison go there?" Charlie asked.

"She'd go there occasionally, but it wasn't a regular hang-out for her. She'd go there mostly out of curiosity to see if any of her friends were hanging out there," Judy said.

"Was anyone else able to verify Allison had stopped at the hobby shop?" Charlie asked.

"No, none of the employees remembers seeing Allison that evening," Rick said.

"We also told the police about Rick's dojo being near there and the possibility that she ran into someone she might have known," Judy said. "They said they would check on it, but I got the impression that they didn't take the suggestion very seriously. I also told them about Allison's counselor, who she saw in one of the office buildings nearby. Again, they said they would look into it, but I'm not very hopeful."

"You mentioned that Allison rode her bicycle. Has anyone seen it?" Charlie asked.

"No, no one has seen it." Rick said.

"What did it look like?"

"It was a girl's bike," Judy said, "purple, with handlebars—"

"High handlebars," Rick cut in.

"...with a purple curved seat decorated with silver sparkles."

"Banana seat," Rick said.

"Why would anyone in their right mind do this to my precious daughter?" Judy sobbed. "What kind of animal attacks little kids? She was just a baby! My baby—and I want her back! I want her back now and that monster caught and put away." Charlie gently rubbed Judy's back.

"Is there anyone I should speak with you think might be helpful?"

Judy shook her head no.

"Thanks, Judy." Charlie hugged the grieving mother.

Rick retrieved Charlie's coat and handed it to her. "There is something else you need to know," he said quietly so Judy wouldn't hear. "She's taking this very personally. The fact that the two had words before Allison's abduction and murder is eating away at her. I try to console her, but it's of little use. Here is the number to her counselor."

"I'll do whatever I can," Charlie said. The card read. Dr. Alex Simpson. "Will you give me permission to discuss the specifics about Allison with him? It may not be important, but you never know where the facts may lead us."

"Sure. But Alex is a woman, not a man," he said. Charlie chided herself. She knew a thing or two about people assuming she was a man because of her name.

As she stepped outside, the cold air slapped her in the face, bringing her out of her thoughts and back to reality. It was about six in the evening—the same time that Allison had jumped on her bike and began that fateful ride four days before. Charlie decided to spend the rest of the evening trying to replicate her ride.

Charlie got into her car, turned on the dome light, and pulled out the AAA Auto Club map of the area out of her glove box. *Kiddo, which way did you go, and who took you? Give me a clue, a sign, something. Well, I guess I'm going to have to work on assumptions.*

Charlie studied the map, her finger tracing along the possible routes. *She most likely followed the same route her mom and dad traveled to go between Rick's apartment in Birmingham and Judy's house in Royal Oak. It was dark; she'd stay to the well-lit main roads and avoid the snow and ice. Most people tend toward their dominant side when they are navigating, so I'll assume that she is right-handed.*

Allison's first decision from her house would be to either a right or left on Mayfield. Right would take her along Mayfield to Vinsetta Boulevard to Woodward Avenue—a little more scenic route. A left would take her to an immediate right on Fernwood Road and then a right on Catalpa Drive to Woodward Avenue. Either way, both intersect Woodward Avenue at almost the same location.

Charlie started up the car and threw the map on the passenger seat. Charlie was about to make the right turn when she stopped herself and sat back in her seat. Charlie said out loud, "But Allison wasn't thinking clearly—she wasn't upset, but furious. She's fiercely independent, so she most likely didn't take the routes her parents would have traveled. She'd have gone her own way."

Soon Charlie found herself traveling north on N. Main Street. "How can nobody see this little girl riding her bike in December after six in the evening? Dammit, somebody saw her. She was a target of opportunity…or was she?"

Charlie hadn't gone very far when something came to her attention. Two boys were looking at a bike leaning against a building. Maybe it was the boys' actions or that she just had a conversation about Allison's bike, but whatever it was, something registered in Charlie's brain. She pulled a hard right into the law firm's parking lot.

Charlie got out of her car and made her way to the boys. "Hey, guys, what have you've got there?"

The two boys looked at her furtively. The one with the Detroit Lions Honolulu-blue stocking cap began to stammer. "Ma'am, we weren't doing anything wrong."

"Nobody said that you were."

"We just saw this bike sitting out here and wondered what it was doing here," the older of the two boys added.

"A reasonable question. Are you guys from around here?"

"Yes, ma'am. We just live up the street," the older boy replied.

"Great. Did you see this bike here before?"

"No, ma'am," the older boy answered, and the younger boy shook his head.

"Can I see it? I'm looking for a girl's purple bike, raised handlebars, white banana seat with flower decorations on it."

The boys jumped back from the bike as if they had just been shocked. "We…we didn't mean any harm. We weren't going to take it," the older boy said.

"Relax, guys. I'm happy that you found it. It belongs to a very special girl, and I just want to make sure it gets back to her. I've got a favor." Charlie reached into her coat pocket and pulled out a small gold case, opened it, and took one of her business cards from it. "I want you to go home and have one of your parents call the Royal Oak police…"

The younger boy hit the older boy. "I told you we're going to get in trouble. Now we're going to jail."

"Shhh…" The older boy glared at the younger boy.

"Hey, guys, no one is in trouble. Here's my card with my name and position. Now, have your mom or dad call the police and tell 'em what you found and that it has to do with Allison. They'll understand. And for your troubles, here's a little something." Charlie gave them a ten-dollar bill.

The boys looked at the bill and then at Charlie, and then they started to run. The older boy kept hitting the younger one, saying, "I told we wouldn't get in trouble."

Charlie sat in her car, listening to the radio, foregoing the rock 'n' roll stations to listen to WJR's Jimmy Launce Jr. while marking her map with the location of Allison's home, the location of the bike, and where her body was dropped off. Then she started to do the same with the other victims—Grace, Cody, Shelly, Katie, and Lauren.

A knock on her driver's side window caused Charlie to jump. She had so focused on the task at hand that she hadn't noticed the patrol car pull in behind her and the officer approach her. Charlie stepped outside of her car.

"Sorry for startling you," he said.

"No, no problem. I just got caught up in my work," Charlie said.

"Can I get your name, ma'am?"

"Dr. Charlie Taylor. I work for the Oakland County Prosecutor's Office. I had just come from speaking with Allison Walker's parents when I happened to notice two boys looking at a bicycle. I know the police hadn't recovered Allison's bicycle, so I was intrigued. When it matched the description that her parents had given me, I thought it was important enough to have you called."

"Thanks, ma'am. I'll take it back to the station and have one of the detectives show it to her parents to confirm if it's Allison's."

"Thanks, Officer."

The patrolman started to walk away, rolling the bike toward the car. As he opened the trunk, he asked. "Ma'am, if you don't mind, can I ask what you're doing out here? I mean, you're from the prosecutor's office."

"Same as you—looking for the killer," Charlie said as she hopped into the car. She sat back in the driver's seat and thought for a moment. "This place has been crawling with cops lately," she said out loud. "The killer definitely has mine and everyone else's attention—Cody's funeral card, Allison's bike. What's next?"

Charlie decided to continue her drive along Woodward Avenue. She took in all the sights and the memories they brought with them: the imposing Shrine of the Little Flower and the occasional masses she and her family would attend there. Charlie looked to her left across Woodward—nothing could be more foreboding than the Roseland Park Cemetery, stretching for more than half a mile.

Charlie finally made it to Thirteen Mile Road. *Did Allison actually go from her street, cross over both Woodward Avenue and Thirteen Mile Road, to get to the hobby shop? Seems unlikely. She'd been riding for over a mile, maybe second-guessing her decision, scared, looking for a friendly or familiar face. Maybe the hobby shop brought her a sense of comfort. Had Allison made it this far riding her bike in the cold and dark? Had she stood in this same place four days ago?*

Charlie pulled into the parking lot and surveyed her surroundings. Thirteen and Woodward, the crossroads that brings Berkley, Royal Oak, and Birmingham together. Beaumont Hospital loomed largely in the distance.

Charlie looked at her watch. She could get back to Ann Arbor in about ninety minutes. She didn't feel like eating another dinner alone but didn't feel like driving the few miles to her parents' house. She walked over to the payphone and made a call to Annie.

"Hey, it's me. It's getting late, and I'm starved," Charlie said. "Are you interested in getting a bite to eat?"

"Sounds terrific. What did you have in mind?" Annie asked on the other end of the line.

"I know a little off-campus bar not far from your place that's known for its great jazz combo and excellent food."

"It's a Sunday night, the day after Christmas. Do you think they're going to be open?" Annie asked.

"Yeah, you're probably right. Damn," Charlie said. "Where are you now? I'm in Birmingham. I can probably make it back to Ann Arbor in about ninety minutes."

"I've got a better idea," Annie said. "I'll meet you at your place, and I'll throw something together by the time you get back."

ANN ARBOR
SUNDAY, DECEMBER 26, 1976

Charlie hit the brakes, and the car started to slide on the icy road. She turned into the skid and righted herself before she careened into the ditch. Charlie chided herself for not tapping the breaks. She couldn't believe she had almost missed her driveway.

She hadn't recognized her own home with the outside Christmas lights glimmering off the pristine snow. She got out of the car and looked at the Christmas tree in the front living room window with its sparkling lights and complementary red and gold decorations.

Charlie watched the blue smoke from the fireplace slowly drifting upward into the clear, dark sky. It looked like an unattainable picture from a Hallmark card, not the usual darkened and cold home that awaited her most nights. She was comforted.

Charlie stomped her feet to shake off the snow before she entered her house. She was excited at the prospect of what waited for her on the other side. She opened the front door and was struck with the mixed aromas of pine from the Christmas tree and garland, the wood burning from the fireplace, and garlic. She was moved by an overwhelming feeling of joy. She hadn't felt this way in a long time—a very long time.

"Wow, you made it. Great timing. I was worried about the weather and road conditions that you might have an accident in that beast of yours," Annie said as she walked from the kitchen, removing the apron. "I've seen you drive."

Charlie looked at her friend. Annie was wearing white woolen stretch pants and a deep blueberry silk blouse that complemented her arresting red hair and complexion. "I almost did," she said. "Luckily it would've happened right in front of my own house."

Annie shook her head in mock disbelief. "I never quite understand why you drive that car in the first place. Come on. I've got some wine waiting for us."

Charlie followed Annie into the living room. "Bullitt."

"Bullet?"

"Bullitt, not Bullet. Actually, there is a very rational reason. I'd seen *Bullitt* with Steve McQueen, and I fell in love with the man and the car. The car is the first real paying job gift to me—a dark-green 1968 Mustang Fastback GT."

"It all makes perfect sense now," Annie said. "Who doesn't love Steve McQueen in *Bullitt?* Who doesn't want to be Jacqueline Bisset?"

The two women sat down next to each other on the 1950s moss green sofa listening to the soft jazz music playing in the background. Charlie reached down and took one of the wine glasses from the low, sleek teak table. She sipped the merlot wine.

"Hungry?" Annie asked.

"I'm famished. But I'd like to relax just a bit." Charlie leaned her head back against the couch and closed her eyes.

"Whenever you're ready, just let me know. I just need a few minutes to cook the noodles."

"Whatever it is, it smells incredible."

"It pales in comparison to the fabulous Korean meals that you've treated us to. It's really nothing, just some salad, garlic bread, and spaghetti."

"Where are the kids?"

"They're with Garrett and his parents celebrating another Christmas," Annie said. "He was a lousy husband, but he's a great father. Despite our shortcomings as a couple, we both want to make sure the kids are well taken care of."

"That's smart," Charlie said, nodding her head in agreement.

"I'm sorry, I can't wait any longer. I'll go get our salads." Annie got up from the sofa and moved to the kitchen.

Shortly after finishing the salads, Annie served the spaghetti and garlic bread. For the rest of the meal, the women exchanged an array of small talk—music, fashion, books, and movies.

"That was a fabulous meal. Coffee and a cordial of Amaretto?" Charlie asked.

"I'll take the Amaretto. I'd be up all night long if I had caffeine now. This is so nice to be able to have an actual adult conversation and not having to constantly referee."

Charlie smiled at Annie and then turned and took down small-stemmed glasses from the wall cabinet and filled them with the almond amber liquid. She looked into Annie's hazel eyes as she handed her a glass. Their hands touched. Charlie started to get an uneasy feeling in her stomach.

BIRMINGHAM
WEDNESDAY, DECEMBER 29, 1976

Charlie parked her car next to the white brick building with large white columns in the front. The office space was like a lot of others in the area, its occupants consisting mostly of doctors, dentists, and the occasional lawyer. Charlie found Alex Simpson's name listed on the outside of the door. She pressed the buzzer and was startled by a garbled mechanical sound.

"The office is closed for the holidays."

"I'm sorry to bother you. My name is Dr. Charlie Taylor. I have an appointment with Alex Simpson."

"Who did you say you are?"

"Charlie Taylor, and I'm trying to speak with Alex Simpson. I was given her name by Rick Walker in reference to his daughter, Allison.

"Just a minute. Come up."

The buzzer sounded, and a loud click unlocked the door. Charlie opened the door and was greeted by off-white walls, linoleum floors, and a strong antiseptic smell. She heard heels clicking on the floor above her, and Charlie looked up to see a very attractive woman looking down at her over the railing.

"Hi, thanks for letting me in. I'm sorry for any inconvenience. I'm Charlie Taylor. I'm looking for Alex Simpson."

"You're in luck. You found me. Come on up. My office is at the right of the stairs."

Far from the frumpy, middle-aged woman Charlie expected to see, Alex Simpson looked like a *Cosmopolitan* cover, smiling confidently. Her thick brown hair was curled away from her face. She wore a well-tailored navy-blue blazer, faded flared blue jeans, and a white blouse opened to the second button. Charlie couldn't help but be impressed by her. Charlie watched as Alex sized her up.

"As I said on the phone, I'm with the Oakland County Prosecutor's Office, and I'm looking into the death of Allison Walker. Did Rick or Judy Walker call you?"

Alex started down the hallway with Charlie walking along side of her. "They did. It's my understanding that I'm to share with you what Allison and I talked about. Sorry about the whole door routine. The speaker system is inadequate, but we've got to take the necessary precautions. The area has been hit with a rash of break-ins recently. Drug addicts are targeting professional buildings such as this one, trying to get their hands on any drugs. Just last week, not far from here, a doctor and his nurse were held at gunpoint. It was pretty unnerving for all concerned, to say the least. How are Judy and Rick holding up? I've been meaning to call them. They must be devastated."

Charlie nodded as they walked down the hallway. Alex opened the door and stepped into her office. The reception area was warm and inviting with a touch of sandalwood fragrance.

"Can I get you something to drink? I've got coffee, tea, soda, juice, water…pretty much a little of everything."

"Tea sounds great."

As she waited for Alex to bring back their tea, Charlie looked into the receptionist's room. The walls displayed diplomas from prominent universities, along with several certificates and letters of appreciation from local communities. *That's smart of Alex,* she mused. *The waiting room and reception room are geared toward the parents, making them feel comfortable and reassured that their troubled children are in safe, capable hands.*

Alex returned and handed Charlie a large mug filled with a creamy white drink. Alex took a sip of her tea. "Let's move back to my office."

Alex and Charlie entered what looked more like a comfortable living room than a typical psychiatrist's office. "I was expecting to see the usual chair and couch motif," Charlie said.

"They're fine for adults but weren't effective for me working with children and teenagers. It's imperative in my work to be able to establish a rapport. I see a wide variety of kids: sexual abuse, drug or alcohol addiction, promiscuity, homosexuality, divorce—like Allison."

"I imagine it would be challenging. You're to be commended for your work," Charlie said.

"It's pretty rewarding to see that I'm making a difference."

"What can you tell me about Allison in general?

Alex took a moment to contemplate her answer. "Allison and her mom came to see me because Allison was having terrifying nightmares. In the nightmares she was being chased, caught, and shot by some unknown man. At first, my approach was similar to that of Carl Jung. My assessment was that her dream was her subconscious trying to deal with the divorce of her parents. She really loved the concept of the ideal family that her parents had created for her.

"Her 'death dream' was not really a prediction or foreshadowing of what would come, but the death of her family as she knew it and wanted it to be. Needless to say, there is something strikingly eerie about it all."

"What kind of kid was she?" Charlie asked.

"She was a very smart, determined, and strong-willed young lady, especially for her age. The fact that she was willing to leave her home just before dinner when it's cold and dark to ride her bicycle somewhere gives you a good indication of her personality."

"Let's assume for a moment that she wasn't abducted. Would Allison have gone off with a complete stranger?"

"Unfortunately, the community does not comprehend the danger of these predators. Yes, I mean predators. We all tell kids to be wary of strangers, but these predators can be a favorite relative, a trusted family friend, or a recognized professional such as a doctor, teacher, priest, policeman, or fireman. They are not evil looking—just the opposite. They are charming and engaging, and they know how kids tick better than we do. They are extremely adaptable to their environment.

"To answer your specific question, it's very possible. In her agitated state, she may have been very susceptible to a warm and understanding smile. Most likely, the predator saw her riding her bike. He picked the right moment to intercept her, when she felt vulnerable and needed comfort and help. A kind word, an offer of a ride, and just like that she's gone."

"Her parents believe that she was en route to Rick's place," Charlie said. "Would you agree?"

"Yes, I believe so. I don't think she would go to another location to kill time."

"Rick and Judy thought it was a possibility that she might have run into someone she knew."

"That's certainly feasible. It would have made the abduction that much easier."

"If you have any recommendations on who I should speak with, I'd appreciate the information. That's all the questions I've got for the moment. Would you mind if I stopped by or called if something else pops up?"

"Not at all," Alex said.

"Alex, do you mind if I ask you a personal question?"

Alex leaned back as though anticipating a question that might take more time answering. "Go ahead."

"How did you get started?" Charlie asked. "I mean, how did you decide to become a psychiatrist?"

"The trite answer is because I like working with people, especially kids. But the old cliché is probably closer to the truth: I had some serious issues that I needed to address in my life, so I came to this profession in an attempt to cure myself. It's funny how much our families impact our lives. I can't begin to tell you how much bad parenting begets bad parenting, an endless cycle of abuse. I see screwed-up kids who eventually become screwed-up adults who eventually become parents themselves."

PONTIAC
FRIDAY, DECEMBER 31, 1976

Charlie anxiously waited for Sydney White's arrival, along with the rest of the staff. She was reviewing her notes when Sydney burst into the room and slammed her fist on the table.

"What the hell is going on around here? Can anyone give me some answers? We've got five kids who were either abducted or murdered off our own streets for us to deal with. Five kids. The press and public are all over us. I can honestly say that I don't blame them. The police's incompetence is unacceptable."

The staff members shifted uneasily in their seats as Sydney continued her tirade. "At least Dr. Taylor is out on the streets trying to find something out," Sydney said. Her index finger pointed like a sharp stick at each of her staff members. Sydney's nostrils flared, and her chest heaved.

Charlie saw that a bad situation was getting uglier by the second, so she spoke up. "I have something," she said, and all eyes turned to her. "I believe it's the same person abducting these children—with the exception of Shelly Coleman. Shelly was an opportunity rape and murder. There are the massive blows and shots to her head, and he leaves her at the crime scene. This type of killer is a young male, impulsive, into girly magazines, preens over his vehicle, typically drives a pickup truck, but in this case it was a Cadillac."

"Dr. Taylor, we've been through this before," Sydney said.

"I know we have, but maybe it's time that you started listening," Charlie said, challenging her boss.

Sydney didn't even blink. "Doctor, what you just said about Shelly Coleman's perpetrator could be said about Katie Hill's."

"Fair point," Charlie said, "and I'll get to that in a minute. The perpetrator is very bright, with a high IQ. We're not dealing with some idiot. He is very charming, in that he is able to lure the children. Then the monster emerges. There are no commotions at the abduction points, which are done out in the wide open. The same can be said about when and where he deposits the body. This isn't about sex; he's sending us a message. Katie's murder was to send another type of message. There was unmatched excitement and pleasure in Katie's murder. I think it was revengeful in some way."

"So what do you suggest, doctor?"

"I think we need to educate the public, especially the kids."

"I'll concede that you may be right, but no way in hell I'm going to tell the public there is a serial killer on the loose. We'll have a panic in the streets. Dr. Taylor, start working up the profile. Gentlemen, start looking for this person. I don't care if it's New Year's Eve, get the hell out of here and go find me a killer. Doctor, I'd like you to stay behind."

After the men had left the office, Sydney turned on Charlie. "Don't ever undermine me in my office. Is that clear? I'll make sure that you never work in law enforcement again."

NICOLE HERNANDEZ'S STORY

"**M**om, can I get a magazine? Please?"

"Nicky, honey, I'm not crazy about you going across the street by yourself."

"Mom, please? I've helped you around the house," I say.

"Baby, I know. You've been a big help, and I really appreciate it."

"Mom, pretty please? I'm bored. The 7-Eleven has the new *Tiger Beat*. Please, can I go? I'll be careful. I'll come right home."

"I like *Tiger Beat*, too," she says.

"Really?"

"What, you think I'm too old?

"No, no, I'm sorry. I didn't mean to say that! Sorry, Mom."

"I remember how excited I used to get when a new magazine came out," she says. "I used to save up my nickels and dimes, and when I had enough money I'd beg my Nana or Papa to go to the store, too."

"But I saved up my allowance," I say.

"And I'm proud of you for doing that, sweetie. You're growing up so fast."

"Then why can't I? I'll be safe. I'll wait till the crosswalk light changes."

"You win," she says, relenting at last. "But why all the excitement?"

"Donny and Marie are on this month's cover!"

"Donny and Marie? I'm surprised. You mean you're not into Leif Garrett or Shaun Cassidy?"

"Oh, they're OK, but I really like Marie. She's so pretty. She can do everything," I say.

"I like Donny and Marie, too. Donnie's a little goofy. Marie really has his number." Mom chuckled.

"I like the way Marie is always making Donnie look silly," I say.

"All right, honey, you can go. But look out for traffic. Pick out your magazine and come right home. Be safe. Cross your heart?"

"Cross my heart and hope to die."

BERKLEY
SUNDAY, JANUARY 2, 1977

The driver watched the beautiful little brunette girl cross Twelve Mile Road. "She's perfect," the driver said out loud. The driver gripped the steering wheel, fighting the urges that stirred deeply so soon after the last one. The driver's restraint caved in to the knowing pleasure that would come from having another. The driver pulled the car into the parking lot and followed the little girl into the convenience store.

BERKLEY
SUNDAY, JANUARY 2, 1977

Maria glanced at the clock and thought, *It's not like Nicky to be late. Where can that stinker be?* She looked out the window across the apartment complex grounds. It was a quiet Sunday afternoon. *Nothing could possibly happen to her. Could it?*

Maria glanced anxiously at the clock again. She tried to reassure herself that it hadn't been too long since Nicky had left. Her stomach began to toss and turn. She threw on her coat and went looking for her daughter.

Maria made her way out of the apartment and headed for the crosswalk. The traffic was light; only a few cars on the road zipped past. She looked apprehensively across the four-lane road in hopes of spotting her daughter. As the cold wind whipped through her hair, she brushed the premature gray strands out of her eyes and squinted, hopeful to see her daughter's bright parka in the store.

As the light turned to green, she made her way across the road. *This is so unlike Nicky. She's probably still mooning over Donny and Marie inside the 7-Eleven.*

She couldn't see Nicky anywhere in the store. She asked the clerk stocking cookies on the shelf, "Did you see a little girl in here just about ten, fifteen minutes ago?"

The store clerk paused for a minute. "Yeah, I think so."

"What do you mean 'yeah, think so'? She has brown hair, big beautiful brown eyes, and a bright-purple parka. She was here to buy a magazine."

The store clerk rose up from his knees as he started to grasp the seriousness of the situation. "I'm sorry. Yeah, I think she was in here…I get kids…"

"Nicky, honey," Maria Hernandez called out. She turned and saw the teen magazine on the newsstand with Donny and Maria's toothy grins on the front covers. She gripped the aisle shelving as her knees buckled.

BERKLEY
SUNDAY, JANUARY 2, 1977

"Your theory is looking more accurate every day," Pete said as they exited the 7-Eleven.

"I'm surprised that he took one so quickly," Charlie said. "There's usually a cooling-down period, but this doesn't seem to be the case here."

They stopped in front of Pete's car. "Any reason…any logical reason?"

"I think it may have something to do with the personality and maturity of the children," Charlie said. "Allison was pretty hard headed, and she'd started her period. Maybe the killer thought she wasn't pure enough, that something was missing. No connection with the child."

"What's next for you?" Pete asked.

"I'm going to speak with Nicole's mom. Take care. I'll let you know if I find out anything interesting."

BERKLEY
SUNDAY, JANUARY 2, 1977

Charlie made her way across Twelve Mile to the apartment complex where Nicole and her mom lived. The ground was frozen hard, and bitter cold wind had picked up. She looked up at the building that faced Twelve Mile with all its lights on and then back at the 7-Eleven. Again the killer had been able to abduct a child out in the open without anyone noticing. A patrolman opened the apartment front door for her.

"Thank you, Officer."

"My pleasure, Doctor. The mother's apartment is on the third floor, 303B."

Charlie walked up the stairs to get some exercise in. She was feeling stressed and lethargic. She contemplated going for a run when she got home regardless of the time. Charlie arrived on the third floor barely breathing hard.

She opened the dark-gray door into the lit hallway. She walked down the well-worn light-gray carpeted hallway; the wallpaper design of greens and grays was beginning to fade, and she could hear sounds of muted TV broadcasts coming from behind the doors. Charlie arrived at 303B and knocked. The door cracked opened, and an older man peered from behind the slight opening.

"Sorry to disturb you. My name is Dr. Charlie Taylor. I'm with the Oakland County Prosecutor's Office. I'm assisting the police with the disappearance of Nicole. I would like to speak with Mrs. Hernandez."

The old man looked back into the apartment, hesitating before opening the door wider. "Please come in," he said. "I'm Nicole's grandfather. Maria is trying to get some rest. The constant haranguing from the police and news folks has only exasperated the situation."

"I understand. Then perhaps you would be willing to answer some questions for me?"

"I don't know, but I'll try." The old man showed Charlie into the living room area. They had just sat down when they heard a voice from behind a bedroom door.

"Dad, who is it now?"

"It's a doctor," he said. "She's with the prosecutor's office."

The door opened, and Maria came out. She was in her early thirties, though her prematurely gray hair was matted down on one side, her eyes cloudy, nose red and sore looking. Maria sat down on the floral-print sofa beside her father. Charlie explained to Maria who she was and what she did.

"Nicky is my oldest from my first husband," Maria said. "I've got two other children from my second marriage."

"Five of you live here?" Charlie asked.

"No, just me and the kids. I'm in the process of getting another divorce. I'm terrible in selecting men, but I have great kids," Maria said.

"Tell me about Nicole."

"Nicky's a great kid. She never complains or fusses. Even as a baby she hardly cried. The way she looks at me...she has the biggest, most beautiful soft brown eyes. She just seems to understand what I'm going through and doesn't want to be a burden."

"She sounds like she's a beautiful soul," Charlie said.

"Oh, that's perfect way to describe her...a beautiful soul. I work very close to here, and sometimes I've got to work late, but she never complains. She does whatever I ask her to do. She's such a help around the house."

"You mentioned Nicole's father. Does she have any interaction with him?"

"No, we haven't seen him in years. He took off when Nicky was very young. We were all very young—three babies living together."

"So you don't think it's possible that he might want to have wanted to see Nicole?" Charlie asked.

"I'd heard he moved down to Tennessee or someplace like that a long time ago. He wouldn't even know where to find us."

"How about the father to your other children? Maybe not wanting to cause harm to his own children, but wanting to get back at you, he takes Nicole."

"Frank's a loser, but he'd never do anything to harm Nicky," Maria said. "They were great friends. He always said if he ever had kids of his own that he wanted them to be just like Nicky."

"This has been very helpful, Maria. I appreciate your willingness to talk with me. Your father is right. I know it's very hard, but you need to get some rest. I can write you a prescription for a sedative to help you sleep."

Maria shook her head. "I don't want to be too groggy in case Nicky calls. I need to be strong for her just like she's always been for me."

"I understand...Here's my card. If anything else comes to mind, please let me know." Charlie got up and hugged Maria good-bye.

"You're different from the rest," Maria said.

BIRMINGHAM
MONDAY, JANUARY 3, 1977

Pete sat in his library and drained the remains of his second cup of coffee. The house was still and peaceful. Gabrielle and the kids had not gotten up yet, still reaping the benefits of the long holiday break. Usually, he would have relished this opportunity to appreciate his newspaper and coffee undisturbed—a chance to collect his thoughts before leaving for his office. But this day hadn't even started, and he was already exhausted.

He had spent the rest of Sunday afternoon and all evening trying to make progress on the case while it was still hot, fielding the endless calls from senior law enforcement officials and politicians. Everyone wanted answers; everyone wanted results; everyone was nervous. He said a prayer for Nicole's safe return and for her family. He believed in God but was not a particularly religious man. This time, though, he needed all the help he could get.

Pete threw the *Detroit Free Press* down on his desk in frustration. Charlie might be right. What a way to start the New Year. Another child abducted on a Sunday along a busy road just a stone's throw from her home.

His conversation with Charlie had triggered something in him. He had worked into the early morning hours in preparation for his Monday morning meeting with Abraham. He organized his notes, photos, and tips from the relevant cases into several binders. He placed the binders into two large carrying cases. He was assembling a picture of unbelievable evil.

Pete got up from his desk, looked into the large mirror that hung on the wall, and began to tie his tie when he heard the door to his office open. He looked into the mirror and saw Gabrielle entering the office. She was wearing his tartan flannel pajamas. He admired her beauty.

"Good morning, Sleeping Beauty. Hope I didn't wake you."

"Here, let me do that for you." She grabbed him by his navy-blue and maroon striped club tie and pulled him toward her as she straddled the corner of the desk. She deftly tied a full Windsor.

"When are you going to upgrade your wardrobe?" Gabrielle brushed an imaginary piece of lint from his starched light-blue button-down. She looked admiringly at Pete in his gray flannel slacks, cordovan tassel loafers, and matching belt.

"If it's good enough for Kennedy, it's good enough for me," he said. "Someday this fashion will be all the rage. Then I'll look prophetic. But until that time, I refuse to wear those obscene leisure suits, anything made with polyester, rayon, or any other synthetic material. I'd rather be caught dead than wear those clothes."

Gabrielle gently ran her finger through his clipped, sandy-brown hair to his temples and sideburns with their touch of gray. "You used to be so cool. You know growing your hair out just a bit, a little more fashionable, wouldn't hurt you."

Pete kissed his wife passionately. He looked at the knot. "Perfect as usual."

"Me or the knot?"

"Both."

"Another long day?"

"Afraid so."

"Do you think you'll find her? That poor child. Her poor mother," Gabrielle said.

Pete clipped his holster with a pistol to his belt. "I'm used to seeing the scum of the earth, but this could be worse, a lot worse. We may be dealing with a monster. Do me a favor—drive and pick up the kids from school from now on. I don't want them to go anywhere without our supervision."

"They're not going to like it. They're going to want to know why they can't ride their bikes all over like they always do. What do I tell them?"

"The truth," Pete said. "I'm sorry, I don't mean to be an alarmist, but it's just not safe anymore."

"Be safe. We'll be here when you get home."

"I know. That's what keeps me going." Pete kissed her and headed out the front door.

LANSING

MONDAY, JANUARY 3, 1977

"We've got no clue," Abraham Lincoln answered as he inspected the gloss on his nails from his latest manicure.

"What are you going to do about it?" the deep husky voice asked over the phone.

"I got word this morning that the governor will convene a task force if it looks like the Hernandez girl was taken by the same guy," Abraham said.

"Do you think it might be Christian? He can be so reckless at times. I wouldn't put it put it past him."

"Of course he's reckless. He's twenty-eight years old. What twenty-eight-year-old male's libido isn't out of control? Besides, I don't think it's him. Its not his style," Abraham said.

"You don't think or you don't know? There's a big difference."

"Listen, Marilyn. I know the difference. You don't have to lecture me. But no, I don't think it's him. He usually trolls in the Tri-City area—Flint, Saginaw, Bay City. He sometimes heads up near Alma and Mt. Pleasant. I can't get anything out of my vast network of sources, so this is somebody definitely different and unusual," Abraham said.

"You're the expert. I just don't want any of this to blow back on us. I've been thinking that maybe we should curtail our operations for a bit."

"Raymond and the rest of our clients won't like it."

"Screw them. I'm in charge, and I say what goes. What about this task force? What would they be responsible for doing?"

"Most likely we'll be put in charge. As you can imagine, the Ice Princess and the Cowboy will put on a good face publicly, but there will be holy hell to pay privately. They'll be screaming that we're infringing on their territory. So we'll be put in charge to run the thing, and we'll get support from all the local cities and county."

"Aren't you concerned that they might find out something about us? What about your man?"

"Naw, they'll pull in all the low-hanging fruit, the known pedophiles, and question them. They'll get so overwhelmed with tips that they won't be able to see the forest for the trees. As far as my man, I've got something special planned for him. I'm going to put him in charge of the investigation; the sheer work load will bury even him."

"If that fails?"

Abraham chuckled. "If all else fails? I've got a plan that will take care of everything. And that will be that."

"Abraham, that's why I love you," Marilyn said. "If I ever was going to be attracted to a man, you'd be at the top of the list."

"If I ever was attracted to skinny old white women, then you'd be my first, too," Abraham said as he hung up the phone.

The big man leaned forward and reached across the desk for the football. He picked it up with one hand and spun it in the air. He still hadn't made up his mind about the Vikings and Raiders. The "Purple People Eaters" looked great against LA, but it was hard to argue with the Raiders and how easily they had handled the Steelers the Sunday before. He smiled and thought to himself, *The Raiders...I like their killer attitude.*

Abraham looked over at the wall clock and knew Pete would be arriving shortly for their weekly Monday morning meeting. Pete was always on time, so determined. Marilyn might be right. He'd have to watch Pete's actions more closely.

CHRISTIAN MCMILLAN'S STORY

I lie back down on my bed and stick the doughnut in my mouth. I look at the teenage girl on the front page of the *Birmingham Eccentric.* I read the article with interest: Another girl had been taken just days after the last one. The article reports the circumstances surrounding Allison Walker's murder and now Nicole Hernandez's abduction.

The article goes on to report that the police have no clue as to the identity of the perpetrator or perpetrators. Parents and city officials have begun to express their fears. Police have advised parents to speak with their children about and what to say concerning the dangers of talking with strangers. I think to myself that it may make my desires a little more difficult to achieve, but not impossible. I stuff the last remains of the doughnut into my mouth and brush the crumbs off my faded flannel shirt.

My bedroom door creaks open, and I hear the feet tread softly across the thick padded carpet. The little white terrier paws at the bed. I pick him up and place him on my lap. "How's my Buddy doing?"

Buddy wags his tail, which makes his whole butt shake.

"You're such a good dog." I scratch his head. "You were so helpful the other day."

Buddy laps up the doughnut crumbs from my bed.

"Covering my tracks again. Thanks, Buddy. Sorry, dude, but I got to put you back into the basement. I've got to travel up to Flint for some work."

I take him downstairs, open the basement door, and push the dog's butt with my foot.

Then I grab my car keys and heavy coat and go out the side door. Hoping to get in and out of my car without any of my parents' neighbors noticing, I instead hear someone behind me. "Christian! Christian! Happy New Year! When do your folks get back from South America this time?"

PONTIAC
FRIDAY, JANUARY 7, 1977

Charlie's face was haggard as she rubbed her tired eyes and sipped her warm Vernors. Drinking the amber ginger ale was like drinking gold. It soothed her. She couldn't remember the last time she had a good night's sleep or a meal she didn't feel compelled to wolf down, afraid that her pager would buzz at any moment. What she wouldn't give for a run, even in this weather, and a hot shower.

Charlie looked around the conference room. The normal anxiousness had evaporated. There was no energy for it. Everyone was flat-out tired and irritable. Sydney walked in and sat at the head of the table.

"What is the latest on Nicole's disappearance?" Sydney asked.

Charlie noticed the fine lines around Sydney's eyes seemed to have deepened. Her normally clear blue eyes were cloudy and bloodshot. A few strands of her platinum silver hair had escaped. Charlie raised her hand.

"Yes, Doctor?"

"I think she's still alive," Charlie said confidently, causing everyone to look up in astonishment.

"Well, Doctor, that's the first bit of good news that I've heard. You've got my undivided attention. Let's have it."

"I've made a theory based upon the premise that the killer is the same person who abducted Cody Edwards and Allison Walker. Most child molesters and abductors live, work, and operate in the same area as their victims. Additionally, most children are murdered within hours of the abduction. But this hasn't happened in either of the previous cases. In the cases of Cody and Allison, the killer left both children in very open areas, knowing that the bodies would be discovered quickly instead of burying them in a hole someplace.

"From the autopsy reports, both victims seem to be well cared for. Neither was dehydrated. Their clothes were washed and pressed, and the bodies were bathed. Even their nails had been clipped and washed. The kids were not in high-risk areas, nor were they high-risk victims. They all were very average, well-behaved kids."

"All right, Doctor, both Cody and Allison were held for only four days each. It's already been six days for Nicole. Why the difference?"

"The difference is based upon each victim's behavior. Cody wanted to be a marine, so he probably fought hard, hence the ligature marks on his wrist and ankles. He'd heard from veterans how they survived in POW camps. He probably thought it was his duty to try and escape.

"Allison, a precocious girl, was entering a rebellious stage. We can understand that she'd fight back at every opportunity.

"Nicole, on the other hand, is a lovely sweet girl and, by her mother's own account, is very mindful and respectful of others. So I believe that Nicole hasn't fought back, allowing the killer to spend more quality time with her. She may even be bonding with the killer and providing him some comfort."

The grizzled detective sitting across from Charlie looked at her skeptically. "Doc, I never gave your hocus-pocus much credibility. Now you want us to believe this eleven-year-old is bonding with this asshole? Let's be honest, doc, this asshole gets his rocks off abducting and having his way with these kids."

Charlie studied the detective, with his hard-to-ignore bulbous nose, visible pores, and blotchy complexion from too much alcohol. The folds of his neck hung over his shirt collar. She wondered when the man was going to keel over from a heart attack. Charlie spoke clearly and purposefully. "I disagree completely. These abductions aren't about sex."

The man rolled his eyes and scoffed. "Doctor, with all due respect, I've been doing this since before you were a twinkle in your daddy's eye. This guy is a garden-variety straight-up perv," the detective said, his jowls shaking with each word that he spoke.

"Go ahead, Doctor," Sydney said, holding up her hand before the conversation became any more contentious.

Charlie paused for a moment and looked the detective in the eye. "Do you know the chosen occupation for serial killers?"

The old police officer shook his head and squirmed slightly in his chair. "Why don't you just tell me?"

"Ministers, police officers, and counselors," she said. "It's a power trip with them. It gives them a sense of control over their victims. Our killer derives pleasure from taking care of the children while at the same time is not afraid to send authorities and the public at large a message for us 'to go screw ourselves' by leaving the bodies out in the open. We have time, but what I can't tell you is how much."

"What type of person are we dealing with?" asked one of the other detectives.

"Here's where I'm going to buck some of the conventional wisdom of my peers," Charlie said. "I believe we can safely assume we're dealing with a serial killer. From my research, we know that most serial killers are white males, have no formal education, have normal or above-average IQs, live alone or with their parents, and are unmarried or unattached. They are age twenty-five to thirty-five, passive and quiet; they work in menial jobs and often do poorly in school."

Charlie pushed her papers together so they created a neat stack with all the edges aligned. She looked at everyone in the room. "I'd ask that you seriously consider the following. First, this person is very intelligent. Look at his MO. He's abducted the child from one location, kept the child in another location, and dropped the body in yet a third location, thereby leaving us with virtually no clues—very little to go on. Furthermore, serial killing requires a particular kind of studious discipline. The killer is only going to get better."

"So what you're telling us is that our chance of him getting overconfident and sloppy, thus leading to his apprehension, is less likely," another detective added.

"Correct," Charlie said. "Second, the killer has something attractive about him: his personality or a certain amount of charisma that the children trust or are attracted to. Maybe the killer is one of us with a badge or poses as one of us. Maybe the killer is wearing a uniform like a policeman, fireman, doctor, or priest that wins over the children. By all accounts none of the abductions seem to be forced. Therefore, I've concluded that all the victims were unlikely to realize they were in any danger."

"Why the hell now? What's made this serial killer decide to start? What set him off?" the deputy county prosecutor asked.

"Great question. Unfortunately, I don't know. It may have been some life event that triggered them to begin. On some rare occasions they may go dormant for a while, but what I do know is that the killer is going to continue to go after kids. He won't stop unless he is captured, dies, or is incarcerated. Men will eventually wane with their sexual potency. However, on the odd chance it's a woman, they only get better with age."

"You mean it might be a woman?" Sydney White asked.

"Why not? The theory is not so farfetched," Charlie said. "Each child was well fed, bathed, and the clothes washed and pressed. Allison had started her menstruation cycle. She was able to change out her tampons. Doesn't that sound more like a woman's nurturing side than a man's?"

"I find this hard to believe," the old detective said. "You're telling me we might have a crazed woman out there?"

"Yes, I understand how it may be hard to imagine, but in her mind she cares about these kids," Charlie added.

The room was quiet for a moment.

"I've been in conversation with the governor," Sydney said at length. "He'll create a task force, led by the state police, if in fact Nicole was taken by the same man...or woman." She looked over at Charlie.

Bill Choate, Sydney White's deputy, added, "This will be a monster—trying to coordinate everyone's efforts. We all know how local law enforcement can be very protective of their territory. Everyone is going to want to lay claim to catching this guy, so they might not be forthcoming with all the information associated with these crimes. Getting everyone to collaborate is going to be a real challenge."

"We'll cooperate fully while still continuing our efforts here," Sydney said. "I want to make one thing clear. We'll not cooperate with the sheriff's department. I don't want that asshole—the Cowboy—getting a crumb of credit. For God's sake, this past week he claimed at a recent out-of-state convention that he and his office are the only ones capable of solving these crimes. He had the nerve to spout off about our decisions to call in additional experts while his office had the same capabilities and resources. Adding insult to injury, he said we are wasting of taxpayers' money. I'll see that bastard pays," Sydney White said.

Bill asked, "Anything else? Let's find this little girl and put an end to this madness."

As the staff departed, Bill called to Charlie. "Sydney and I would like to have a word with you privately."

Charlie sat back down. Once the staff had cleared the conference room and the door was shut tight, Sydney and Bill joined her at the table.

"How accurate is your assessment? That we are dealing with the same person—a serial killer," Bill said.

Charlie looked at Bill and Sydney. "Yes, I think we are dealing with a serial killer and that he or she will continue to strike at us through the kids. There are a couple of things going on. He or she is trying to make us pay for failing him or her in the past. The killer feels that somewhere or sometime in her past we've abandoned her when she needed our help. I'm still struggling with the idea of a relationship of nurturing and taking care of the preteens while seeming to have a physical attraction to the older girls."

Sydney let out a sigh and looked out the window of the conference room. "I probably should have followed your advice sooner and taken the necessary precautionary steps to at least inform the public. We've might have been able to prevent Nicole's disappearance."

Charlie saw a more vulnerable Sydney for a moment and added, "It's not too late."

"I want you on the task force to work closely with Bill," Sydney said. "Keep him informed at all times. I also want the two of you to develop an educational program to inform both parents and children. When can you have a preliminary plan to me?"

"Forty-eight hours," Bill answered.

"Charlie, one more thing."

"Yes?"

"Catch me a killer," Sydney said.

Bill smiled. Acknowledgment from Sydney did not often come to those she hadn't let into her inner circle.

Charlie left the conference room and made her way to her own clinically sterile office—white walls; bright, garish fluorescent lighting; metal bookcase and filing cabinet. She looked at the file folders on her desk labeled Lauren Ring, Katie Hill, Shelly Coleman, Cody Edwards, Grace Johnston, Allison Walker—and her newest addition, Nicole Hernandez. She knew the contents by heart.

Slumped in her desk chair, Charlie looked out the window at the beginning of a dreary winter day. She pulled out the large set of files and let them drop to the desk with a thud. These were the files of potential suspects. She had been reviewing the case files against known suspects for anything that might match. It was long and tedious process of trying to cross-reference similarities.

Charlie hadn't looked up from the files and her notes in quite some time when her secretary knocked on the door. "Sorry for disturbing you, Dr. Taylor, but unless you have something else for me, I'm going to go home."

Charlie looked at her secretary. "What time is it?"

"It's five o'clock."

Charlie covered her face with her hands and tried to wipe the weariness away. "Thanks, Theresa. No, go home, and have a great weekend."

"Thanks, Dr. Taylor. You need to get home yourself and get some rest. Or go out and do something. You look like you're in need of a break, or at least some type of distraction."

"You're probably right, but so much work and so little time," Charlie said.

"I've been a secretary in this building for a long time, and I've seen it happen to the very best. They just burn themselves out by working an insane number of hours."

"Or die trying," Charlie said.

"Or quit. We're all rooting for you—the women in the building," Theresa said. "We want to see you succeed."

"Women's solidarity?" Charlie asked.

"Exactly."

"What about Sydney? Isn't she one of us?"

"She's more like a man in woman's clothing. At first, we all thought it was cool how she won, and we were behind her one hundred percent when she came into office, but she turned us off. She treated us worse than the men."

"Thanks for the support," Charlie said. "I hope that I don't let you down."

"You won't, Dr. Taylor. Now go out and have some fun. See you Monday." Theresa closed the door to Charlie's office and departed. Charlie thought about calling someone and then decided against it. Charlie picked up the next folder in the pile. There was plenty of work to be done.

She took some colored magic markers out of her desk and started drawing on the walls. She had the names of the victims listed chronologically along the left side and associated facts across the top. She then placed check marks in the appropriate places. Soon the two groups of victims emerged.

The murders of Katie Hill and Shelly Coleman were violent, messy, and brutal in the way they were raped and murdered. In her second group were cases where children were abducted without notice and asphyxiated but were well cared for over a long period of time. In this group was Lauren Ring, Cody Edwards, Grace Johnston, Allison, and now, possibly, Nicole Hernandez.

Charlie looked at the check marks for any connection between the two groups of victims. Her eyes began to close. She tried to will herself to stay awake. *It's only ten in the evening; I used to put these hours in during residency without a problem.* Again her eyes slowly closed, her chin hit her chest, and she was gone.

Charlie awoke from her stupor with a sharp pain in her neck. She stared at the obnoxious telephone ringing on her desk. Her eyes were burning as she tried to make out the clock. It was just past midnight. She concentrated harder on the phone and reached out for it.

"Dr. Taylor speaking." Her voice was scratched and tired as she rubbed the rheum from her eyes.

"Are you all right? You sound like crap. I've been trying to reach you all night. I was getting worried."

"Annie?" Charlie asked.

"What are you still doing at work?"

"I've been...been studying the facts...looking for patterns...that would provide some sort of insight all night...I must have dozed off," Charlie said, noticing her mouth felt like it was filled with feathers and stale breath. She looked for some water to wash the feeling away.

"I was hoping that we could get together for a drink or something, but that plan's shot to hell."

"Sorry. A drink…right now a drink sounds fabulous, but what I could really use is someone to rub my aching shoulders and back. My neck is killing me."

She started to focus on her writing and marks on the wall. Charlie discovered that her creative energies were at their best the first forty-five minutes after she awoke.

"Hello? Are you there? Are you even listening?" Annie asked.

"I'm still here," Charlie said, staring at the wall.

"What do you think?"

"About a drink? A drink would be nice," Charlie said as the marks began to take shape.

"I thought we could get dressed up and have a girls' night on the town. Who knows—maybe you'll get lucky and find someone to rub your shoulders and back. Tomorrow? I'll pick you up," Annie said.

"Tomorrow sounds great. I'm sorry, Annie, I've got to go." Before Annie could respond, Charlie hung up the phone.

Charlie studied the marks on the wall. *I'll call it my "Rule of One Off,"* she thought. *There isn't a perfect correlation among them. All of the victims were girls, with the exception of Cody. All were abducted in winter except Grace. All were taken on Sunday except Allison…a Wednesday. All were not sexually molested except Cody. All were preteens except Lauren.* Charlie thought about Katie and ruled her out—there was something exceptional about her abduction and murder. *All were held less than a week except Nicole.*

Charlie thought she might be onto something. Her thoughts bounced around her head. *Sundays and*

Wednesdays—sounded like doctors' days off. Doctors wear uniforms that kids would recognize. What if the doctor or health professional happened to be an attractive woman? Even law enforcement wouldn't suspect a good-looking professional woman. Women are nurturing by their nature. She goes where the kids are—she's watching, waiting, stalking like some tigress waiting to pounce on her prey.

ANN ARBOR
SATURDAY, JANUARY 8, 1977

Charlie heard the doorbell and looked out her front window. The gentle snow flurries had given way to heavy wet flakes—the storm had arrived. She inspected herself in the mirror and adjusted her black cashmere sweater and black-and-white diamond pencil skirt along with her expectations. She pulled on her red high-heeled boots and opened the front door.

"You're getting wet. Come in."

"I think that's supposed to be my line," Annie said, stepping into the foyer and brushing off the snow that clung to her coat.

"Just give me a second. I need to grab my coat and we can take off—unless you'd like to grab a drink here first?" Charlie asked. "What?" Charlie was taken aback by Annie's intense glare.

"You look fabulous," Annie said.

Charlie blushed while she admiringly looked at Annie with her forest-green coat and fire engine–red lipstick and nail polish.

"You can start by taking my coat." Annie unbuttoned her coat and revealed her outfit: a cream-colored, off-the-shoulder, cowl-necked sweater dress; black silk stockings; and large, gold hoop earrings.

Charlie placed Annie's coat in the closet and slid the door closed. The two women made their way to the family room.

"What can I fix?" Charlie asked.

"Plenty," Annie said, curling her legs underneath her buttocks.

NICOLE HERNANDEZ'S STORY

"**D**o you think my mom misses me? I think she needs me." I dabble my fingers into the warm, sudsy water.

"I'm sure she does, Nicky. I know that I'm going to miss you." The woman washes her back.

"I'm going to miss you, too."

"Thanks. You've been the best, too." She pours the white soap from the green plastic bottle and rubs it all over my body.

"Look at my fingers. They're all wrinkly," I say. "I look like an old lady. Let me see yours."

"Just a little bit more…We just want to make sure that you're super clean. We don't want your mom complaining, do we? I've got your clothes cleaned and pressed."

"I think she'll be happy to see me."

"Get out of there so I can dry you off. We don't want us looking like a prune, now, do we?"

"When can I see her?" I ask.

"We'll have our last dinner together and then I'll take you home."

"Cross your heart?"

"Cross my heart."

"Hope to die?"

"Hope to die."

FRANKLIN VILLAGE
FRIDAY, JANUARY 21, 1977

In the dark, cold, early morning hours, the road was empty except for a lone car driving cautiously. The driver avoided any sudden turns and pumped her brakes to make sure she maintained control of her car. She finally reached the intersection, made a left turn onto Telegraph Road, and headed south. She exhaled and began to relax.

She enjoyed this time by herself. She'd driven almost a mile when she saw Temple Beth El, the synagogue with its Minoru Yamasaki cutting-edge design rise up from the ground. She continued along Telegraph, passing the subdivisions on her right. She could barely make out the fenced fields and the big red barn. She continued past the woods and Franklin River winding through it.

She was fast approaching Thirteen Mile Road. The light changed from red to green; she slowed anyway. She took the turn wide and slow onto Thirteen Mile Road heading west.

She thought to herself, *Perfect, unlit—everyone is sleeping comfortably in their little suburban homes.*

She approached the final destination quickly. She slowed the car down, made the turn into the deserted road, and turned off the headlights and interior lights. She exercised caution not to hit the brakes and give away the location. The car continued to creep along the road.

"Dammit!" She hadn't realized the end of the cul-de-sac was approaching so fast. She could see the outlines of the darkened houses and a few of the front door lights. The back bumper scraped the bank of snow as she made a three-point turn.

Don't overreact. Get a hold of yourself.

Finally, the car stopped, facing north again with large pine trees blocking any possible light reflecting off the car. She opened the trunk and carefully lifted the body out as if Nicole were still sleeping.

She placed Nicole's small body on top of the bank of snow, adjusted her coat, and made sure her pants were still tucked into her boots. She then carefully packed snow up against the body as if to tuck Nicole into bed on a cold winter's night. The killer gently closed Nicole's eyes, folded her arms, and kissed her goodnight. The killer whispered the words "…little lamb is on the green…with snowy fleece so soft and clean…" Erasing her footprints from the snow, she made her way back to the car.

The car turned back onto Thirteen Mile Road, and she felt elated as she spotted the street sign. *Won't that throw them for a loop?*

FRANKLIN VILLAGE
FRIDAY, JANUARY 21, 1977

"Hey, be quiet and sit down," the bus driver yelled.

"Mr. George, what do you think is wrong?" a little girl asked.

George looked out the window as the bus drove past the ambulance and all the police cars and news vans. "Honey, I don't know, but I'm sure everything is all right."

The schoolchildren pressed their faces to the windows as they watched the commotion.

FRANKLIN VILLAGE
FRIDAY, JANUARY 21, 1977

The latest snowfall covered her like a soft white comforter, and the snow was carefully pushed up around her like she had been tucked in at night. Charlie looked down at Nicole and then turned and walked back toward the two detectives.

"Pete," Charlie said, holding her hand out to Pete.

"Abraham, this is Dr. Charlie Taylor. Charlie, this is Lieutenant Colonel Abraham Lincoln," Pete said.

"Dr. Taylor, it's a pleasure. Pete's spoken very highly of you. From my understanding in conversations with both Pete and Sydney, you pegged this as the work of a serial killer long before anyone else," Abraham said.

"Thank you, Lieutenant Colonel," Charlie answered.

"Pete will have an official kickoff meeting in our headquarters, but you might as well get ahead of the game. Everyone already knows that you'll be leading the investigation," Abraham said.

Pete nodded. "Do I have the authority to put who I want on the team?"

"We'll discuss the specifics tomorrow at the headquarters. Obviously the county, sheriff, and local LE are going to want a piece of the action. We're going to be relying on their manpower, so we'll have to be accommodating to a certain degree," Abraham said.

"I want Dr. Taylor as part of the team."

"Done." Abraham nodded his large head in the direction of Charlie. "Her boss and I already discussed her participation with the task force. She definitely will be an integral member of the team. Do you need anything else from me?" Pete shook his head. "Then I'm heading back up to Lansing," Abraham said and bid them farewell.

Charlie and Pete listened to the snow crunching underfoot as the imposing man made his way to the car. Pete pointed out the street sign. "Charles Lane…Coincidence, or is the killer trying to tell us something?"

"I hope that it's more than coincidence. That means maybe I've touched something inside of her." Charlie looked around. "Who's that over there?" she asked, pointing to an obviously distraught man leaning up against one of the squad cars.

"It's the mailman. He discovered the body. Pretty shook up. We're checking his story out now," Pete said.

"The killer hasn't changed her signature. I bet the coroner will find that her body was bathed, nails trimmed, asphyxiated, and she wasn't sexually assaulted. This isn't about sex; this is about power, control. She's caring for them," Charlie said.

"Caring for them? Seems eerily appropriate," Pete said, rubbing his chin.

"When we are growing up, who has the greatest control over us?"

"Dear old mom."

"Well, she isn't these kids' mothers, so she's more like a caregiver, nanny, or babysitter," Charlie said.

"I know that we should have listened to you when you said we have a serial killer living and operating in our area," Pete said. "But you really think it's a woman?"

Charlie kicked at the snow with the tip of her boot. "The more I look at the facts surrounding the case, the more I lean in that direction. I'm trying not to let my theory get ahead of the facts."

"I'm more and more convinced that it's a pedophile or a ring of pedophiles," he said.

"I know how much you want it to be the Brotherhood, but I think you're going to be disappointed," Charlie said.

"Why do you say that?"

"First, our killer has a certain amount of 'savoir faire.' Second, most child molesters have to resort to a physical abduction or force. Not in our case. The killer is able to lure the kids in. The kids are not picking up on any negative vibes. There seems to be a certain amount of trust."

"So how do we stop this guy or gal?" Pete asked.

"Do you know Bill Choate, assistant district attorney?"

"I've heard of him."

"Bill and I have already started an education program with local law enforcement going into the schools and teaching 'stranger danger.' We also have a program of safe houses with a cardboard plaque with a red hand on it that's posted in the front windows. So kids out in public who feel they're in danger can run to these houses. We are going to have to increase our efforts. It won't stop her, but hopefully it'll slow her down. You?"

"The only evidence we have seems to be where the car backed into the snowdrift to turn around. We'll see if we can identify what type of car it is."

"Not much to go on," Charlie said.

"You're right. Whoever it is has covered all of his or her tracks," Pete said. He blew into his gloves to warm his hands.

Charlie nodded in agreement. She thought how careful and meticulous the killer had been.

"I've got several meetings in Lansing to get the task force off the ground. Birmingham has given us an unused elementary school off Fourteen Mile, between Lasher and Lincoln, for our use," Pete said.

"Valley Woods?"

"That's the one. We'll have our first meeting there on Monday."

LANSING
SATURDAY, JANUARY 22, 1977

The Michigan State Police headquarters was buzzing with activity for a Saturday morning. There was no denying it anymore—there was a serial killer on the loose. Pete entered the headquarters and was buzzed through the double doors. He nodded at the sergeant as he passed his desk and made his way to the elevators. The elevators took him to the top brass of law enforcement.

All the heavy hitters were assembled at the office. Colonel Miller Sheard, the director of the Michigan State Police; Lieutenant Colonel Abraham Lincoln; Martin Hershberger, the attorney general; Sydney White; and a man Pete didn't recognize dressed in a conservative navy-blue pinstripe suit and maroon tie. He correctly assumed he was a representative from the governor's office.

Colonel Sheard directed everyone to his large conference table.

"You all know each other and why we're here, so I'll forgo introductions and get down to business. The governor, attorney general, and I have been in consultation since Nicole Hernandez was abducted. Now that her body's been discovered, the possibility exists that her death may be linked to Allison Walker and Cody Edward. We need to get out in front of this. People are worried. Our switchboard is getting hundreds of calls a day.

"This task force's specific mission is to prevent any more abductions, to find the killer or killers, and to put them behind bars. The governor's office is in the process of requesting federal dollars, and the FBI is ready to help us. We'll lead the task force, but local law enforcement will play a big part of it."

Sydney White interrupted. "It's my jurisdiction. I think that my office is more than capable of leading the task force. We've got strong relations with the local police and can run this task force as well as anyone else."

Before the governor's representative could chime in, Colonel Sheard responded, "Sydney, we've already been over this before. We know your folks are very capable, but the governor has the authority to direct who runs the task force, and in the best interest of all concerned, it'll be run by us."

"In the best interest of all concerned...give me a break," Sydney said. "We all know the governor wants to make sure that he and his boys get all of the credit."

"Stop it, both of you." The governor's representative addressed the group in a levelheaded manner. "We're all under tremendous pressure to solve these murders. There are over seventy police forces varying in size from five to over five thousand. In each murder, the child was abducted in one jurisdiction and left in another. He or they are playing us against one another. Everyone will share in the credit. I'll make sure of it. Now can we continue?" He indicated that Colonel Sheard should take over.

"I've selected Lieutenant Colonel Abraham Lincoln to be in charge of the task force from here in Lansing. Kenton Fisk will take care of the planning, operations, and administrative responsibilities in the elementary school. This will free up Pete West, who will run the actual investigation. We're all familiar with these men's capabilities. There aren't better cops around."

Everyone nodded in agreement.

As the participants were walking out of the office, Sydney White pulled Pete to the side, her voice hissing into his ear.

"Listen, West, I expect you to keep me informed at all times. Is that clear? Don't mess with me."

Pete smiled as he watched Sydney White walk away. He thought to himself, *What a piece. Less than five minutes, and the politics have already started.* Pete headed for the elevator. He stopped short when he heard his name being called. It was Abraham and Colonel Sheard, waving him back into the office.

"Sorry to put you in this position, Pete, but this investigation is incredibly important, and there isn't a better investigator in this state," Colonel Sheard said as he put his arm around Pete's shoulder. "Finding the killer may be easier than dodging the political land mines. We'll try to provide you with as much cover as possible so you can focus on the investigation. The governor and everyone at headquarters are expecting you to solve this."

"You keep me informed and let me know what you need," Abraham added. "We'll keep the Ice Princess out of your hair."

Pete and Abraham left together and walked toward Abraham's office.

"What did you think of my latest report?" Pete asked. "Were you able to find anything else about the island up north and its possible owner?"

"Umm, nothing yet, Pete."

"I can feel it. Finally, we're starting to close the gap. It's the same feeling I had when I played ball and fought in 'Nam. It's hard to explain why; it's just there."

"Well, I'll keep asking around. This is my stop." Abraham held his hand out as they stopped in front of his office. "Keep me posted."

GROSSE POINTE
SATURDAY, JANUARY 22, 1977

"Yes?" Raymond asked.

"Have you been tracking the news?" Abraham asked.

"Yes, I have. Sorry to hear about the little girl. I have no use for them; they are as troublesome as their adult versions. So what's the concern? This should have nothing to do with us."

"Raymond, Marilyn is concerned that all of this attention may get back to us. I've addressed her immediate issues, but her concerns have some validity."

"So what does she expect us to do?" Raymond asked.

"She wants us to start covering our tracks. We need to make sure that none of our actions can be attributed to us."

"I find this conversation boring and unwarranted."

"We want you to close down your little operation on the island and close ranks."

"Doesn't this all seem a little premature?" Raymond asked.

"No, it's smart business. You can never tell with these investigations where they will go. Sometimes they grow a life of their own."

"Yes, yes, but you know how much I receive from our enterprises—the financial gain we all benefit from."

"Raymond, listen. I'll do my best to make sure we stay ahead of the investigation, but I can't promise it'll be enough."

"What else?"

"You need to consider making sure that you can access your money without the FBI knowing where it's located."

"The task force is made up of capable men?"

"Yes. West is the officer in charge, and he's hungry and driven to find this killer. However, the local police abilities vary. They have some good guys, but they lack the experience in dealing with these types of crimes. I'm sure they will be spread thin rather rapidly, causing their bosses to utilize less experienced and capable officers."

"All right, all that you have told me sounds reasonable. However, I don't know if I'm ready to shut down everything, especially when it seems to be going so very well."

"One other thing," Abraham said.

"Yes?"

"Christian. The idiot just may have something to do with these killings. At first, I thought that he was so damn sloppy that he couldn't have done it. Now I'm not so sure."

"Christian assured me that he wasn't involved," Raymond said, "but your concern about his sloppiness is not without merit."

"We can't expect his parents to keep paying off victims and bailing his ass out of jail. At some point, people will no longer be able turn a blind eye to him. He's weak and lacks sophistication. I could see him spilling his guts to the state troopers to save his own butt."

"When the time comes, I'll defer to you on what actions that we should take in regards to Christian," Raymond said. "I'm sure that you'll use your best judgment—I trust you. Now, I'm going to have to put an end to our call. I have a previous engagement that I must attend to."

There was a light knock on the door just as Raymond hung up the phone.

The door opened slowly, and a slight young boy timidly walked into the room. Raymond used all of his strength to conceal his pleasure.

"There you are, young man. Come to Uncle Raymond. Come here and sit on my lap. We'll read a story together and have such fun."

BEVERLY HILLS
THURSDAY, JANUARY 27, 1977

Charlie walked into the elementary school that now served as task force headquarters. She made her way to the school's administrative offices and knocked on the door of the vice principal. "Yes?" a voice called from within.

Charlie opened the door. She looked around the office as she sat down. "The office and furniture seemed more intimidating when I used to get sent to the vice principal's office. I'd get really nervous."

"I can't ever imagine you doing anything wrong." Pete smiled.

"Well, Mr. Boy Scout, we're not all perfect. Some of us got to adulthood from very different paths—a little different from homecoming king, football star, and war hero," Charlie said.

"I hope that you've got some good news to tell me. I could use it," Pete said.

"I'm afraid not; it's a mess. The county coroner conducted the autopsy and came up with the following findings. Nicole was asphyxiated. There was no penetration of the vagina or anus, but he claims to have found the presence of semen," Charlie said.

"Why am I getting the feeling that I'm not going to like what comes next?" Pete asked.

"If it wasn't so serious, it would be almost comical. He says that the killer was so excited that he ejaculated prematurely with such force that the semen found its way into her. It's so absurd. I called Sydney and told her how damaging this could be to her and the county. Although she's trying to manage the damage, she is doing the right thing and sending the samples to the FBI. We should know in a couple of days. I suspect they won't find anything," Charlie said.

"What else?" Pete asked.

"Nicole's mother doesn't think that she dressed herself. Something to do with the way her pants were tucked into the boots and her shirt tied in the back versus in the front," Charlie said.

"So the killer must have dressed her after she was dead—a real piece of work, this guy," Pete said, shaking his head.

"What's next?" Charlie asked.

"Feel like traveling?" Pete asked.

"Some place warm and exotic?"

"Right on both accounts; it's a little farther south, so it has to be warmer than here, and it's definitely exotic. In fact, it's right up your alley."

"Sounds enticing. What did you have in mind?"

"I was given the name of an inmate by the Illinois State Police. He specializes in trafficking child pornography. I thought he might be able to shed some light."

"You're full of surprises. He sounds like a keeper, just my type of guy. What else?"

"Nothing, besides good old-fashioned police work—running down every tip. We're getting hundreds of calls a day."

"Encouraging," Charlie said.

"A big fat maybe: most of the tips are people with grudges. Wife can't stand the husband, so she calls in her husband. Doctors calling in their patients, patients calling in their doctors, and neighbors against neighbors—everyone is turning on one another. You get the picture. Everyone is scared, and fear is feeding on itself."

"The killer is feeding off the fear that they're creating. She's taking satisfaction from all of this. No one is immune," Charlie said.

Pete massaged his temples. "I could use a break. Let's go for a walk. I'll show you around."

Charlie and Pete walked to the end of the school hallway.

"This room will serve as the squad room," Pete said. "This office will be the commander's office when Lincoln is in town, the cafeteria will serve as the operations center, and these rooms will serve as the interview rooms and tip processing and phones offices. And in the back, we'll place the terminals and computer room." They watched the buzz of activity through the windows.

"At this rate, I'm going to have to pull in our computer specialist. We're going to have to automate in order to cross-reference the tips. We're noticing some duplicate tips, and we just don't have the manpower. We'll get overwhelmed very quickly," Pete said.

"You know, the killer may be out there among them," Charlie said ominously, looking at the volunteers scouring about.

"You've been a bundle of good news. Now there's a killer on the task force?"

"Serial killers are drawn to law enforcement. What better way to see that your work is being appreciated than first-hand? It just adds to the thrill, the excitement."

Pete and Charlie continued their walk down the hallway to the heavy double doors in the front. As they walked through them, they were hit with a blast of cold air. The schoolyard and parking lot were covered in shadows from the fading afternoon winter sun. They surveyed the quiet suburban area.

Charlie turned to Pete. "We're on a fishing expedition—no pun intended. We've established Operation Lure, working with schoolchildren, parents, and teachers to get any recollection of possible unwarranted contacts or approaches by unsuspected pedophiles or homosexuals. We'll see if we catch anything. We're also going to every school talking with the children and parents, telling them to watch out for strangers. Police presence at the elementary and junior high schools and established safe houses for children to flee to. But I'm thinking about bringing in some additional help."

"I hope it helps." Pete rubbed his hands together for warmth.

"Now, get back inside before you catch pneumonia," Charlie said.

BIRMINGHAM
WEDNESDAY, FEBRUARY 9, 1977

"So, who is a stranger?" Alex asked a roomful of children.

"A stranger is someone we do not know," the children yelled at the top of their voices.

"You guys are really awesome," she said. "What do we never let a stranger do?"

"We never let a stranger get too close, whether he or she is in a car or walking."

"Wow, you are going to be tough to trick." Alex pulled out a piece of candy and approached a little girl. "Hi, I've lost my dog, and I really need your help. I'll give you this piece of candy for your help."

The little girl was overwhelmed by the attention and started to reach for the piece of candy. Her classmates shouted, "No! Don't do it. She's trying to trick you."

Alex laughed. "Excellent, last one. If a stranger tries to grab you, what do you do and say?"

The school auditorium yelled in unison. "Run away. Yell, 'That's not my daddy, that's not my mommy, fire, fire.'"

"Bravo! You've learned your lessons really well. I'm really proud of you," Alex said, smiling at the children.

As the kids filed out of the auditorium, Charlie caught up to Alex. "You were terrific."

"Thanks. Glad to be of assistance."

"I could really see the kids responding to you," Charlie said.

"They're fabulous. It's nice to be with healthy, well-adjusted kids at times. Let's say it rejuvenates me."

The parking lot was filled with a line of cars with anxious mothers waiting outside to pick up their children. "Crazy, isn't it?" Alex observed.

"Can't blame them. I'd be doing the same thing," Charlie said. "Time for coffee?"

"I'd love to."

"There's a Sanders in town. Do you know where it is?" Charlie asked.

"Sure, I'll meet you there."

Charlie jumped into her Mustang and headed for town just a few blocks away. She parallel parked a block down and tossed a couple of coins in the meter.

Alex was waiting for her under the pink-and-white awning of Sanders. Charlie felt a pang of guilt as she admired Alex.

"Wow, you're quick," Charlie said as she arrived.

"Fast car," Alex said with a wink.

"It must be. You smoked me."

"Your car isn't too shabby either. I think it goes well with your image," Alex said as she opened the door for Charlie. "Please, after you."

The lunch counter was empty this time of day, and four of the five booths were unoccupied.

Charlie said, pointing to one of the booths, "Does this work?"

"Perfect." Alex slid into the booth with pale pink upholstery.

"So many delicious choices," Alex said.

"I know what you mean. I love everything here."

The women hadn't sat long when the waitress came up to take their order.

"I'm going to splurge and treat myself," Alex said. "I'll take a hot fudge cream puff with butter pecan ice cream and a glass of ice water."

"I'll take an ice cream sundae with pink peppermint stick ice cream and dark chocolate hot fudge, and hot tea," Charlie ordered.

"Thanks, now I don't feel so guilty," Alex said as the waitress took their menus. "I really shouldn't indulge myself like this, but once in a while, I feel I owe it to myself. You, on the other hand, look like you don't have to worry about what you eat."

Charlie smiled. "Only if you knew what I went through. Actually, I run…I run a lot."

"Well, whatever you're doing, it's working. I'm way too lazy for any type of physical activity."

"Now I'm the jealous one. You don't exercise and you look the way you do," Charlie said.

"You should have seen me as a kid and teenager. I was huge. Miss Piggy huge, but I didn't have the self-confidence to pull it off like she does."

"I never would've guessed," Charlie said.

The waitress returned with their dessert. Alex forked a large bite of cream puff, held it up, and looked intently at it. "My childhood was less than idyllic. I'd eat to ease my pain and loneliness."

"We do what we can to ease our pain and survive," Charlie said. "Is that why you got involved in child psychology?"

"I was pretty screwed up, looking for answers. I sort of fell into it. My mother died of cancer when I was five. I remember lying in bed at night praying for my mom to get better, squeezing my hands so tight that my blood would run from my hands until I fell asleep. But God never answered my prayers. She just got grayer, with dark rings around her eyes, and weak. She had always smelled so sweet, but then she just smelled…smelled of something horrible like the garbage left in the summer sun, rotting.

"I did the usual kid things. I promised God that I would be good, that I'd never cause any trouble. I even asked God to make me sick instead of my mother, I told him that I was strong and could take whatever He could dish out. That somehow my parents could live without me, but we needed my mom. How did He expect us to survive without her?

"I remember the night my aunt came in to tell me that my mother died. I kept yelling at her, 'No, no, you're lying. I hate you.' She sighed and left the room. I rolled over and cried. I thought, 'Why did she have to leave us?' But nobody was listening—not even God."

Charlie empathized with Alex's raw feelings. She'd felt the emptiness brought on by depression. She was pain-fully aware of the feelings of loneliness and abandonment. Charlie's sleeve slid up a few inches to reveal the faint white scars among the fresh red cuts. "I'm sorry. I didn't mean to dredge up old memories—especially bad ones."

"No, it's good for me. I need to exorcise the devil," Alex said.

Charlie nodded her head in acknowledgment. "Any time you need someone to talk to, let me know."

"I appreciate it. I really do. It's hard to find someone who really understands. Hey, I just got an idea. What are you doing for dinner?"

"I hadn't even given it much thought. I was going to swing by the office and then make my way home."

"Are you from around here?" Alex asked.

"I grew up here, but I call Ann Arbor home."

"That's a lot of driving, especially in this weather. Why don't you come to my place for dinner? I rarely entertain and would really enjoy your company."

"After all this ice cream, I don't think I could eat another bite," Charlie said. "It's enticing, but not very practical." She felt a pang of guilt. She could feel herself being physically and emotionally drawn to Alex.

"I'm not talking about eating right away. We can have some wine, pleasant conversation, pick at our neuroses...just joking. I promise to keep it light and fun." Alex snapped her fingers. "Better yet, you can spend the night. We'll make it into a slumber party."

Charlie's head started to spin with images of her and Alex lying around in pajamas.

"This is a really tempting offer, but I don't like the idea of showing up to work in the same clothes two days in a row. Too many people would notice and begin to speculate and gossip."

"We're about the same size. You can borrow some of my clothes."

Charlie's feeble defenses were beaten. "You win; you convinced me."

"Great. I've got to make a quick stop by my office, and then we'll go to my place."

Charlie tailed Alex to her office. She started to have second thoughts about her decision and felt her conflicting emotions swell. The two cars pulled into the office parking lot.

"It'll only take five minutes," Alex said.

"I can wait for you out here."

"No, don't be silly. Come on up."

The two women made to their way into the office building. The last patients of the day were leaving the various offices. Charlie held the door for a mother and her little boy who had tears in his eyes and was gently rubbing the side of his face. Charlie overheard the mother scolding her son. "I told you what would happen if you don't brush your teeth regularly and keep eating all that junk food. You've got no one to blame but yourself."

"Enlightened parenting," Alex said. "My office is filled with the results."

"Poor kid. I think my mother wrote the book on it," Charlie said.

Alex unlocked the door to her office, and both women walked into the comfortable waiting room.

"How do you like private practice?" Charlie asked.

"It's great. I was really nervous at first whether I was going to be able to make a go of it…pay the bills. I didn't know the first thing about the business end. I learned from others and through trial and error and somehow made it work."

"You seem to have become very successful. My office is a dreary dungeon compared to this place," Charlie said, admiring the décor.

"I love the freedom it affords me. I can come and go as I please—no one to answer to. Best thing is no office gossip. You should think about it yourself."

"I'm a bit of a masochist. I wouldn't know what to do with myself if my life didn't contain some type of pain and drama."

"I'll just be a minute."

Charlie walked over to Alex's diplomas and certificates posted on the wall. "I didn't realize you went to Wayne State."

"Yeah, I went there for both undergraduate and medical school," Alex responded from her office. "And you?"

"I was there for a couple of years. Then I transferred to Michigan." Charlie started to feel the serpent slowly unwinding itself and slithering toward her.

"We're about the same age. Do you remember the incident involving that girl?"

"It doesn't ring a bell." Charlie was becoming flushed. Her stomach flip-flopped.

"It was all over campus. She was gang raped at the fraternity house," Alex said. "The things they said about her were terrible—a reference to driving a train."

Charlie's knees began to quiver. She was trying to quell the nauseous feeling. "It must have happened after I left," she said.

"It must have. I don't know how you could have missed it, I felt so sorry for her. People can be so vicious. I wonder whatever happened to her."

Charlie's hand shook as she reached into her purse and pushed the button on her pager. The device began to beep.

"Is that yours or mine?" Alex asked.

"It's mine. The office." Charlie pulled out the little black device and looked at the display. "Do you mind if I use your phone?"

"No, help yourself. You can dial direct."

"Thanks." Charlie picked up the handset to the push-button phone on the receptionist's desk and pressed the numbers. "Our office still uses those old ugly black rotary dial phones. Private practice is becoming more alluring," Charlie said while listening to the dial tone. "Yes...right now...I'm in Birmingham...I'll get there as quickly as possible."

Alex came out of her office while Charlie finished her call. "Sounds important."

"My boss has called for an emergency meeting that I've got to attend. I'm sorry, but I'm going to have to take a rain check on our slumber party."

"Why don't you come to my place after the meeting?"

"I'd hate to do that to you. She's pretty unpredictable, and the meetings can go on forever. There's no telling when I'd get out of there."

Alex frowned, gave Charlie a hug, and whispered into her ear, "Another time, then."

"I look forward to it," Charlie said, smiling. She closed the door to Alex's office and fled the building as quickly as she could.

JOLIET, IL
TUESDAY, FEBRUARY 15, 1977

"You're a long way from home, aren't you?" the man asked as he casually crossed his leg, drew on his cigarette, and inhaled the smoke. He tilted his head back, opened his mouth to form an *O*, and let out a throaty whisper. Perfect smoke rings floated across the interrogation room.

"My name is Detective Pete West, and I'm with the Michigan State Police." Pete sat forward in his seat and interlocked his large fingers.

"How I may be of service to you, Detective West?"

"Dr. Taylor and I are investigating the abductions and murders of three children in the suburbs of Detroit," Pete said.

"Ah, the Motor City. Great music. Criminal what's happening to the city." The man smiled at Pete and Charlie. "No pun intended."

"Mr. Wentworth, we were given your name by the Illinois State Police. We are exploring the theory that a child pornography ring might be using the children to make films and photos," Pete said.

"I understand the logic of why you might think that, but I'm highly skeptical," he said, pausing to stub out his cigarette.

Charlie read the file in her lap. William Wentworth, advertising executive, Chicago, Illinois. Convicted on multiple accounts of purchase and distribution of child pornography. Charlie looked up from the file and keenly studied the man sitting across from her.

He had a clean, handsome face, and his jet-black hair with just a trace of gray was combed neatly. He was dressed in his prison-issued dungarees and light-blue denim shirt with his collar buttoned. She knew that time in prison—suffering from bad food, bad air, and harsh treatment from his fellow prisoners—would eventually erase any remnants of his good looks and charm. He'd be an old, broken man when he was released.

Charlie slid a piece of Juicy Fruit gum across the table. She watched as William Wentworth peeled off the familiar yellow wrapper and foil paper, rolled the gum into a ball, and popped it into his mouth. He nodded at Charlie and winked his thanks.

"Mr. Wentworth—" Charlie started to speak.

"Let's not be so formal," he said, looking at Charlie.

"William…"

"Please, my friends call me Rusty. Yours?"

"Charlie."

"Nice. Charlie, what would you like to ask?"

"Why are you skeptical of the theory?" Pete asked, interrupting Charlie's next question.

"People in my business are in it for several reasons—part business, part pleasure. For them, it's the best of all worlds. They make incredible money and take care of their sexual desires. It's really a no-brainer. The pictures and films usually have three destination points: New York, LA, or New Orleans. However, they're probably curtailing their actions because of the pressure from ongoing investigations.

Pete sat back, showing his disappointment with the answers they were getting. Charlie sensed an opening and asked, "Do you have any ideas of who might be doing this?"

Rusty put on his best salesman smile. "We rarely get women as beautiful as you, Charlie." Charlie watched as Rusty contemplated his next response and said gravely, "It's a psychopath."

"What led you to that conclusion?" Charlie asked.

"Look at where he's leaving the kids' bodies," Rusty said. "Right out in the open. He's begging you or taunting you to catch him. One other thing: He enjoys what he's doing—he's not going to stop."

Pete pushed himself away from the table and made his way to the interrogation door. Rusty appeared amused as he watched Pete depart the room. "Intense, isn't he?"

"It's his crusade," Charlie said. "He's been trying to catch a phantom ring of 'executive' pedophiles. Similar to your enterprise." Charlie got up and started for the door.

"It's not a phantom," Rusty said, staring off into space.

Charlie stopped and turned. "What are you saying?"

"What's in it for me?" Rusty asked as he shook a cigarette free from the packet and put it into his mouth.

"Neither of us is in a position to negotiate. I have no authority with the Illinois Department of Corrections."

"Don't sell yourself short, Charlie. A beautiful woman like you can move mountains."

"Please spare me your patronizing—it won't work."

"My apologies. If you would ask the warden that I get my own cell separate from the general populous, it would be a wonderful thing to my ego and health. My peers do not take too kindly to my kind in here."

Pushing herself away from the table, Charlie got up and started to walk away. "I won't make you any promises," Charlie said.

"Hang on, doc...don't get your panties in a bundle. I like you," Rusty said, beckoning Charlie back to the table. He took the file folder and pen from her hands and scribbled several names on the outside jacket.

Charlie read the names. "Why?"

"Maybe there is no honor among thieves. Maybe this place is getting to me. Or maybe I found a soul."

Charlie took the file and walked out of the room and met Pete waiting in the hallway. "What was that all about?" Pete asked.

"Your first real lead on the Brotherhood." Charlie punched Pete in the chest with the file. He took the file and looked at the names scrawled across the folder.

CHRISTIAN MCMILLAN'S STORY

The sky has a light-gray pallor, clouds crowd out any midday sun, and the snow lies black and dirty along the sides of the road from the exhaust and mud. I'm trolling the streets in my dark-green Chevette with custom decaling. We continue the usual loop around Woodward Avenue to the Detroit Zoo, east on Nine Mile Road, and then north on Greenfield. I think to myself, *Driving, looking, like a pack of dogs looking for a kill.*

"Dammit!" I punch the dashboard in anger.

"What's eating you?" John asks.

"Nothing. Just keep looking." A sense of desperation runs through me.

"I've got to get home pretty soon. We've already been to the hobby shop, parks, and movie theater. This is boring. I think Buddy has to pee," John says.

I glare at John. "It's all of them. Damn cops, warning everyone. Parents, kids—everyone's looking over their shoulders. I'll show 'em. I'll show 'em all."

I pull the car over to the side of the street. "Get out." I don't even bother looking at John. "Get out of the car!"

John is barely out of the car when I slam my foot on the gas pedal, propelling my car back into the street, back into the gray chasm. My body is aching, longing, for something to destroy.

BIRMINGHAM
THURSDAY, FEBRUARY 24, 1977

Pete answered the desk phone, its color the pea green of baby food. "Yes, Detective Pete West speaking."

"Ralph Grier, detective, Flint Police. We've just apprehended two adult males for sexually assaulting four boys and carrying numerous rolls of child pornography."

"You definitely piqued my interest."

"Both are real pieces of work—repeat offenders. I think you may be interested in one of them, if not both. The one's acting all tough like he's some badass, implying that he's well connected. He keeps threatening us with lawsuits."

"I've seen and heard that before."

"I'm sure you have. Your reputation is pretty well documented. It was his attitude about being well connected that got me thinking about you. He's from down around where you live…"

Pete sat up in his chair. "You piqued my interest again. Does the perp have a name?"

"McMillan. Christian McMillan. And the other loser is Gray. John Gray."

"Ralph, I'd greatly appreciate it if you would have both of them sent to the Oakland County Jail. I'll make the coordination."

"I don't know. This is pretty big for us, especially given what's going down in your area. If it pans out this is the guy, do we get the credit?"

"I'll personally make sure that you get all of it."

"Detective West, you've made yourself a deal."

PONTIAC
THURSDAY, FEBRUARY 24, 1977

Pete entered the battleship-gray interrogation room, which smelled of urine, sweat, frustration, and fear. A deputy stood ramrod straight against the wall, his starched uniform and polished shoes ready for inspection. The room contained a single table and two steel chairs with thin gray padding across from each other. Seated in one was a man around twenty-five, leaning back and trying to act nonchalant. He took a drag from his Kool menthol cigarette. He had on chocolate-brown wide-wale corduroys, a light-blue button-down shirt, and heavy work boots. He looked like an accountant, bookish, with thick, wavy black hair and small, dark eyes peering through black, thick-framed glasses. The only thing missing was the pocket protector and slide rule. However, they weren't meeting to discuss tax returns.

Pete sat down across from the man. He studied the file, flipping the pages and letting out a sort of half whistle with no tune associated with it. The man blew smoke in Pete's direction. Pete closed the file and looked at the young man.

"John, I'm Detective Pete West, Michigan State Police, and the lead investigator for the task force investigating the abductions and deaths Cody Edwards, Allison Walker, and Nicole Hernandez."

John looked puzzled. He took the cigarette out of his mouth and blew the smoke in another direction. His right leg started a furious pumping motion.

"I don't know what you're talking about. I didn't have anything to do with those kids. I'm...I'm here on child pornography charges."

"We'll get back to those in a moment. You're a pretty tough guy. Pretty extensive file you have here." Pete placed his fingers on the dark-brown file folder. "Says here that you like to get behind the child and put him in a choke hold."

"Yeah, but I—"

"Strike one, John. All the kids were killed by asphyxiation, same MO as you. You came up behind the kids and choked them. What happened? Get a little too excited and go too far?"

"No, no. You got to believe me. I had nothing to do with it."

"Where do you live?"

"Birmingham."

"Strike two, John. All the kids were abducted and killed in and around Birmingham. You know the area."

"Stop, stop. This is insane."

"Strike three: You can't seem to keep a steady job, giving you ample time to take the kids and then kill them at your leisure."

"I had nothing to do with it. You gotta believe me."

"John, would you like another at bat? We have reason to believe the children were used to take pornographic pictures and movies. Strike one, you were just arrested on carrying child pornographic material."

"I'm telling you that I had nothing to do with it."

"John, do you own a gun or ever go shooting?"

"I know where you're going with this one. I didn't—"

"Strike two. Allison Walker was asphyxiated, but the killer didn't go far enough this time, so she started to come to at the drop-off point. The killer then took a sixteen-gauge shotgun and blew the top of her head off."

John jumped out of his chair, sending the chair skidding across the interrogation room. The deputy started to move quickly toward him, but Pete held up his hand, and the deputy halted in his tracks and returned to his position.

"The evidence is overwhelming, John. When the court finds you guilty of multiple murders, you're going to be sent to Jackson. Jackson's nothing like this place. This place is Club Med compared to Jackson. Don't take my word for it. Ask the deputy over there." Pete nodded to the deputy in the corner.

Pete smiled and sat back in his chair. "Do you know what 'prison justice' is?"

The young man shrugged his shoulders, trying to regain his composure. "I'm not afraid," he mumbled.

"John, I couldn't care less if you're not afraid. You see, there is nothing we can do to protect you at Jackson. Frankly, whatever happens to you there, I think that you have it coming. But you need to know that inmates don't care for pedophiles, especially the murdering kind. Many of them are fathers themselves. They worry about assholes like you raping their children while they're in there. They can't do anything to protect their own, so they do the next best thing. When a pedophile is brought to their house, they initiate their own version of justice. Given the fact you're from Birmingham and your parents have money, they'll be screwing you more than one way."

"I can handle myself."

"Putting choke holds on kids, and then pulling their pants down and having your way with them, isn't exactly handling yourself," Pete said, and he watched the fear starting to creep back into the man's façade.

"I'm not saying shit to you. I want my lawyer."

"Fair enough. Sorry we wasted both our time. See you at trial. Do me a favor: When I leave here, I want you to keep saying out loud, 'I'm still a cherry,' while you're still alive."

Pete slowly picked up the file, pushed his chair back, and stood up. The young man's shoulders began to shake, and he mumbled a few words.

"What was that, John?"

"What can you do for me?"

"Start talking. If what you say is true, that you didn't have anything to do with the murders, I may be able to find you a better neighborhood to live in." Pete sat back down at the table.

"We all know you. Big, badass Pete West. We've got a dozen names for you."

"Thanks. I'm not interested in what your ilk calls me."

"You've got no clue."

"Humor me."

"I'll humor you. The joke is on you. CB! We use the fucking CB radios to track your location. We always know where you're at. 'Roger 10-4, Detective "Badass" is jerking off at this location.' Get it? So you can come in here and threaten me, but we're all over the place. You don't understand. We're college students, bankers, lawyers, factory workers, clergy, teachers, coaches, and, best yet—police. You're trying to stomp out a raging fire with your shoes."

"We've got you," Pete said.

"Yeah, you may get one or two of us occasionally. Sometimes, we purposely give you one just to keep you off our scent."

"John, where is the big-shot lawyer? How do you know you're not being thrown to the lions right now? How long have you been sitting here?" There was silence in the room for what seemed like an eternity.

John bit his nails. "It's all Christian. I was just along for the joyride. He's the one who picked up the kid and the film.

He's always bragging about working for these rich assholes. He says they're really powerful. They pay him big money to deliver the goods."

"These influential men that Christian works for, do they have names?"

"No. He's real hush-hush about it. He says there's one dude who scares the shit out of him."

"What about the others?"

"I just know that he goes up to Traverse City a lot. Says one of the guys is so rich he owns a whole island up north. They fly these underprivileged kids in, and then they've got them trapped up there. The usual stuff goes on." John took another drag from his cigarette.

"Would you like a cup of coffee or something?" Pete asked.

"Yeah," John said.

Pete nodded for the deputy to leave and get a coffee. Pete didn't say a word until the deputy returned with two Styrofoam cups of black coffee. John stubbed out his cigarette in an aluminum foil ashtray.

"Where were you and Christian supposed to take the film?"

"I don't know. He's been acting really queer lately."

"Why do you think that is?"

"I don't know. Christian can be a real asshole, but he's been worse lately. I don't know. Everyone's really jumpy with these kids being abducted and murdered."

Pete sat forward and crossed his arms on the desk. "What do you mean?"

"It's one thing to get your rocks off, but none us talk about murdering them. It's just not our thing. I mean…"

"What aren't you telling me?" Pete asked.

"I don't know."

"Knock the shit off."

"You gotta believe me. I didn't have anything to do with their disappearances. Girls aren't my thing, but…I want some guarantees that I'm going to be taken care of. I told you, Christian…those guys…they can get away with murder."

"I can't guarantee anything, but if you start talking here and now, you just might get yourself a better neighborhood to live in."

"We-well, Christian always talked about kidnapping a kid, having him to all ourselves. You know—whenever, whatever."

PONTIAC
THURSDAY, FEBRUARY 24, 1977

Pete stood outside of the interrogation room, through the two-way mirror observing the man sitting at a table and chairs similar to the last room. He contemplated his interrogation game plan. His direct approach had jarred John into providing some plausible information and leads. Pete was about to enter the room when he felt a presence next to him.

"What brings you here?" Pete asked.

"You know cops can't keep a secret." Abraham took a sip of coffee from a thin silver thermos.

"We've got 'em dead to rights on the child pornography and a charge of molestation."

"So what makes him so special?" Abraham asked.

"He's special on so many counts." Pete stared straight ahead, his arms crossed behind his back, tapping the back of his legs with the case file. "I think he's good for the kids."

"What makes you think so?" Abraham said calmly.

"Choking out the kids, his partner stating that he's wanted to abduct kids for a while and hold them as his sex slaves, the pornography, repeat offender, lives in close proximity to both the abduction and drop-off points, no serious employment—can come and goes as he pleases, uneducated but intelligent. He fits the typical profile. I've got them running a check to see if he owns a shotgun."

"Sounds promising."

"It gets better. I think he's the next step in getting to the Brotherhood. I've got a name at the top and now at the bottom."

"We'll want to do a lie detector test," Abraham said. "I'll arrange it."

"Lloyd Colston's the best."

"You know that you can't take the words of a convicted felon seriously," Abraham said.

Pete nodded. "Rusty had nothing to gain by giving Charlie those names, but I'm sure glad that he did." He smiled as he opened the door and walked into the interrogation room. The pencil in Abraham's hand snapped in two pieces.

PONTIAC
THURSDAY, FEBRUARY 24, 1977

"Mr. McMillan, my name is—"

"I know who you are," Christian said.

"I'm starting to get a complex," Pete said.

"You're not supposed to be here. My lawyer's not present."

Pete could see the look of utter contempt on his face as Christian spoke.

"I've got nothing to say."

"I'm sure that you have plenty to say. You just might not be willing to say it to me." Pete smiled as he shifted forward in his seat.

Pete watched as Christian turned his body slightly to the right so he wouldn't be looking at him directly. "Why am I still here? My lawyer said that my family has already posted bail. You have no right to keep me here."

"Christian, we'll have you out shortly, but you know how incompetent we are. Sometimes it takes paperwork a little time to go through all the offices, and worse, sometimes the paperwork just gets lost, so we've got to start the process all over again."

"You're an asshole."

"You do know me well."

"I don't know how that film got in my car. It's John's. If you drop the charges...I'll testify against him that they're his films."

"That's for the Flint police to decide. You'll be moved back up there after we finish here."

"Can you do that? My lawyer will have a field day with you."

"Christian, I'm not worried about you and your lawyer, because when I get finished with you, you'll have greater concerns.

"Now, Christian, I'm one of the law enforcement officials who think you are responsible for the abduction and murder of Cody Edwards. Cody was just your type."

"Bullshit." Christian's nostrils were flaring.

"In fact, I was told that you had a fantasy of kidnapping and holding a boy for a long time to do whatever and whenever you'd like."

"Bullshit, bullshit." Christian clenched both of his fists.

"There are others who think that the same individual abducted and murdered all three children."

"Bullshit, bullshit, bullshit."

"I'll take that as a no that you had nothing to do with the abductions and murders of the three kids. But I've got a pretty good feel for this stuff, been at it for a while. I really like you for Cody's murder. You were taking pictures and making films of the kids and it went bad."

"Cody—that's only one of the three kids," Christian said.

"You're good at math. I'm convinced that you and others are responsible for the deaths of the girls and Cody."

"No way."

"No way, what? You had nothing to do with the girls, but the others did?"

"What others?"

"The others you're working for or with?"

"I've got no clue what others you're talking about," Christian said.

"Sure you do."

"Are you hard of hearing? I don't know who you're talking about."

"All right, let's start with Raymond Evreux," Pete said. "Tell me about Raymond."

Christian's eyes flickered just for a moment. "Never heard of him."

"Let me paint a picture for you, Christian. You're on bail, pending trial for sexually assaulting four different boys in Flint. Given the public sentiment over these recent children's abductions and murders, there is no judge or prosecutor who is going to let you off the hook this time. All your parents' money isn't going to get you out of this predicament. You see, if you cooperate with me, give me the information that I'm looking for, it just may go a long way to reduce the time you spend behind bars. Trust me, this time you're going down."

"Am I supposed to be intimidated by you? You guys are so full of bullshit. Now get me the hell out of here."

"Tough talk, Christian. I personally may make an exception and visit you in prison after someone has made you their bitch. So, tell me about Raymond Evreux and the others."

Christian paused as his open hostility subtly started to soften. He appeared to be thinking about what he was going to say.

The door to the jail's interrogation room opened just as Christian was going to speak. Pete carefully looked at

Christian, trying to decipher the sudden change in his demeanor before he looked over his shoulder.

"Pete, do you mind if I join you?"

Pete smiled. "No, Abraham. I was just asking Christian about Raymond Evreux and the Brotherhood."

ANN ARBOR
SATURDAY, FEBRUARY 26, 1977

Charlie and Annie entered the bar, their eyes adjusting to the dimly lit interior, the blue smoke of cigarettes slowly drifting upward. The jazz combo finished their set. As the hostess led them to their table, as if on cue, several of the men sitting at the bar turned their heads and looked at them appreciatively. The hostess seated them in a comfortable booth and placed menus in front of them.

"I haven't seen you in ages. How are the kids?" Charlie asked.

"Tell me about it. They're terrific. They ask about you all the time. We liked it better when you weren't this super crime fighter: leaping over tall buildings in a single bound, faster than a speeding locomotive," Annie said.

"I'm sorry. It's been brutal, and we're none the closer to catching this person," Charlie said, running her hand through her hair.

"That's terrifying. I think about my own kids. I don't know what I'd do if they were ever taken," Annie said, putting down the menu and looking off into space.

Both women were caught up in their own thoughts for a moment before the silence was broken.

"Shit, I'm sorry; this is supposed to be a break from your work and I've got us talking about your work. I can be so socially inept at times. So, what looks good? I'm starved," Annie stated.

"I'm thinking a half rack of ribs, house salad, cottage fries, and a glass of merlot," Charlie said as she closed the large leather-covered menu and placed it back on the table.

"I hate you," Annie said, pursing her lips in a kissing suggestion.

Charlie raised her eyebrows, looking pointedly at Annie. Annie smiled and pretended to continue studying the menu. "I need to take up running, but it's so boring," she said. "I'm going with the Cobb salad."

"If you'd only…" Charlie started to say.

"The only thing that runs on me is my stockings. Besides, anything that touches my lips goes straight to my hips."

"I won't even go there," Charlie said, winking at Annie.

"The story of my life—no one seems to want to go there."

"I don't know about that. The wolves over at the bar are eyeing you pretty closely." Charlie nodded in the direction of the bar.

"Great, that's what I can look forward to: depressed, overweight, married men hitting on me. What about you?" Annie asked. "I think the one with the toupee is kind of cute. He may be just what you've been missing in your life."

Charlie shook her head. "Stop it. You're so bad. Besides, I've got too many issues. Don't need any more complications in my life. Enough about me, back to you. I'm only saying that if you ran a little, you wouldn't have to eat 'boring' salads all the time. You wouldn't feel guilty about the occasional splurge," Charlie said.

"Didn't you know? I live my life vicariously through you. I can only hope to lick the barbecue sauce off your fingers later," Annie said, winking, as the waitress had arrived with pen and pad in hand.

Charlie gave her order and amusingly watched Annie try to decide what to eat.

"I'll have the same thing, thank you," Annie said, as she closed the thick menu and handed it to the waitress. "Don't say a word. Besides, I can't always live my life vicariously through yours." Annie looked at Charlie thoughtfully. "It's good to see you smile. I've been worried about you."

"I appreciate it. I'll manage. I've been through worse, much worse." Charlie, pensive, looked away and tried to concentrate on the music.

The waitress arrived with their drinks and salads.

Charlie took a sip of her bold merlot as she watched Annie take a bite of the salad.

"This is the best house salad I've ever eaten," Annie said, looking up at Charlie while pointing at the salad with her fork. "The lettuce is cold and crisp, and the blended flavors of thin-sliced red onions, chunks of Roquefort blue cheese, crumbled bacon, and house dressing is incredible," Annie said, stabbing the salad with her fork.

When Charlie and Annie left the bar, it was pitch black, with stars shining brightly. Annie put her arm through Charlie's as they walked to Charlie's car.

"It's freezing out here," Annie said, shivering.

"Up for a drink at my place?" Charlie asked.

"Thought you'd never ask."

The drive was short and quiet in the cold, dark night. Charlie started to get a nauseous feeling in her stomach. It wasn't long before they arrived. Charlie and Annie pulled off their boots and hung their coats up.

Charlie flicked on the lights as she walked through each room. "I'm going to get the fire started."

Annie went over to Charlie's wet bar. "Do you want to stick with wine, or would you like something stronger?"

"Something stronger."

Once the fire was lit, Charlie and Annie stretched out in front of the fireplace, sipping their Cognac. The warmth of the fire removed any remnants of the cold outside. Charlie pulled a throw blanket down off the leather sofa and placed it over Annie. They looked thoughtfully at one another.

"Doctor, I get a strong sense there is something on your mind that you're not telling me." Annie said.

Charlie smiled. "It's nothing...really."

"Tell me," Annie said, reaching her hand out to Charlie and gently rubbing her arm.

"Some things are better left unsaid; moreover, it's not safe." Charlie rolled over onto her back, staring at the ceiling.

PONTIAC
WEDNESDAY, MARCH 2, 1977

"What's this?" Pete asked Abraham.

"His release papers."

"What jackass judge signed these papers? This guy's a repeat offender."

"What can I say, Pete? Money seems to cure all."

Pete watched through a two-way mirror as the technician hooked the wires up to Christian. "Abraham, why isn't our guy doing this?"

"He wasn't available. Additionally, the county insisted on it. We've got to play nice. You know the deal."

"Is he any good?"

"I'm told he's as good as ours."

"And if he isn't? Listen, Flint still has the molestation charges, but they still have to prove it, and we will have nothing on him and will have to let him go." Abraham looked over at Pete.

Pete flicked the button so he could listen to what was being said between the operator and Christian.

"Christian, I'm Detective Lloyd Colston. Have a seat. For this to work, I need to get to know you."

Christian shrugged his shoulders and nervously looked at the polygraph machine.

"How are you doing?"

"I guess I'm OK. I'm a little freaked," Christian said, shrugging his shoulders and running his hand through his hair.

"Most people are at first, but no need to worry. The machine takes that into consideration," Detective Colston said. "Let me explain how this all works. We're going to spend some time just getting to know you, ask about your education level, occupation, and health. For example, are you taking any medications? Then I'm going to make a determination if I will get valid responses from you. The machine doesn't prove your guilt or innocence—only a court of law can do that. What it will do is tell if I'm getting an appropriate response."

Christian nodded and exhaled.

"Is your name Christian McMillan?"

"Yes."

"Where you born on December 23, 1949?"

"Yes."

"Do you live in Birmingham?"

"Yes."

"Is today Wednesday?"

"Yes."

"Are the lights on in this room?"

"Yes."

"Did you volunteer to take this test?"

"Yes."

"Have you ever lied to get out of trouble?"

Christian paused for a moment.

"Have you ever lied to get out of trouble?"

"Yes."

"Have you ever deceived anyone who trusted you?"

"Yes," Christian said as a small bead of sweat formed on his temple.

"Have you ever committed a crime?"

"Yes, I told you about it."

"Please, Mr. McMillan, either yes or no."

"Ever committed a crime without getting caught?"

"No," Christian said, breathing hard.

"Besides the four other acts, did you ever indulge in an unnatural sexual act?"

"Yes."

"Did you ever think of abducting children?"

"Yes," Christian said as his heart rate spiked.

"Have you ever choked someone?"

"No."

"Did you cause the abduction and death of Cody Edwards, Allison Walker, and Nicole Hernandez?" Detective Colston studied the graph.

"Hell, no." Christian bowed up in his chair.

"Please, Christian, just yes or no answers."

"Do you know who caused the abduction and death of Cody Edwards, Allison Walker, and Nicole Hernandez?"

"No."

"Were you involved with someone else to plan the abduction and death of Cody Edwards, Allison Walker, and Nicole Hernandez?"

"No."

"Thank you, Christian, that completes the examination," Detective Colston said as he studied the graph carefully. He tore the graph paper off the machine and laid it across the table. He continued to study the paper.

"Well, what does it say?" Christian asked anxiously.

"Christian, you're not involved in the abductions and murders of Cody Edwards, Allison Walker, and Nicole Hernandez."

"Yes," Christian shouted, jumping up out of his chair and shooting his arms straight up into the air.

"Shit," Pete said, watching Christian leave the interrogation room. "I know he's involved somehow."

"I'm sorry. I know that you wanted it to be him. What now?" Abraham asked.

Pete looked at him. "Back to square one. We continue to check out every tip. We're wholly dependent on someone turning this guy in. He's left us with absolutely nothing—no witnesses, no fingerprints, no evidence—not a shred of it." Pete stormed out of the room.

PONTIAC
WEDNESDAY, MARCH 2, 1977

Abraham stepped into the interrogation room, and Detective Colston looked up at him.

"How bad was it?"

"He wasn't flat-out lying, but some of his answers were deceptive. He shouldn't have been cleared. What are you going to do about it?"

Abraham didn't respond. He turned and walked out of the room.

PONTIAC

FRIDAY, MARCH 4, 1977

"For the first time in my life, I feel that I've lost control," Sydney White said as she looked out her office window at the street below. "I can't influence or manipulate a person or event in my favor."

Charlie and Bill Choate exchanged looks, surprised, at Sydney's rare glimpse of vulnerability. Bill was the first to respond. "That's understandable. We're operating under the theory that no one can ever keep a secret. The task force is receiving over two hundred tips a day. We're chasing every lead possible. Something will break. Someone will come forward."

Charlie chimed in. "Adding to what Bill just said, this has been unique on a psychological level, too. Serial killers always stay with the same type of victims. The fact this killer is choosing both preadolescent boys and girls is distinctive. It tells me that the type of child is more important than the gender. She's picking these kids for a reason. I don't think the abductions have been random. She's stalking these kids. She knows what she wants."

"Why us? Why not pick up one of the street kids down in Casa Corridor?" Sydney asked, turning to face Bill and Charlie. She gestured for them to take a seat.

"She's trying to send a message," Charlie said. "Location is important for several reasons. In most cases, taking kids from a wealthy suburban neighborhood symbolizes cleanliness and purity. Look at the press coverage both locally and nationally. Look at how everyone has been affected. Everyone is terrified. The other trend is she's keeping each child progressively longer. She's getting more comfortable, maybe even confident."

"Can't tell by the weather outside, but winter is almost over. Do you think he or she will strike again?" Sydney asked, referring to the recent newspaper theories that the killer only struck during the winter months.

"I do. I don't buy into the winter-only analysis," Charlie said.

"God help us," Sydney responded.

BIRMINGHAM
SATURDAY, MARCH 5, 1977

Charlie's strides were easy and comfortable as she made her way south along Oxford Street. It was an uncommonly pleasant day in a long, dreary winter. Charlie ran alongside Poppleton Park expecting to see the park full of kids playing, taking advantage of the unseasonably warm day and sunshine. Instead, the large manicured park was empty; the streets were empty.

There were no children to be seen anywhere—no laughter, no screams of joy. Charlie saw the "Red Hand" placards displayed prominently in the windows of stores and homes.

She could see what she had previously only felt: The city was gripped with fear.

Charlie continued her run. She entered the park and began a series of intervals: sprint one hundred yards, drop to the ground and complete ten push-ups, sprint, drop to the ground, and execute twenty-five sit-ups. She was muddy and wet, and, despite the exhausting routine, she was starting to feel strong—revitalized. She was doing a set of push-ups when a polished boot appeared in front of her.

Charlie dropped to her knees and pushed herself up so she was sitting on her haunches. Her sweatshirt and pants were wet and muddy, her hair was stuck to the side of her face, and steam started to rise from her body.

"Impressive," Alex said.

Charlie looked at Alex, in her three-quarters cashmere white winter coat, matching hat, and gloves. Dark-brown curls came just over her collar. "You look sensational. As far as I go, I can think of a lot of adjectives, but 'impressive' isn't one of them. Please don't get too close. I'd hate to be responsible for getting mud on your beautiful outfit," Charlie said as she stood up.

"I've been watching you for a while."

"Surely you can find something better to do with your Saturday afternoon."

"Oh, I don't know if I'd agree with that."

Charlie looked at Alex. "How are you doing?"

"I'm doing well, but I'm getting the feeling you've been avoiding me. You don't return my calls, and you have someone else schedule my school visits. Did I do something to offend you?" Alex asked.

"No, I apologize. I've just been really busy," Charlie said.

"That's a relief. I was becoming paranoid."

Charlie shivered and started to jog in place.

"Look at me…worried about my own narcissistic insecurities while you're fighting off hypothermia," Alex said. "The least I can do is offer you a hot shower and a place to change."

"That's a very generous offer, but I really couldn't. I'll be fine…really," Charlie said.

"Charlie, it's not an issue. I love entertaining," Alex said.

"I was just about to jump into the car, crank up the heater, and make my way back home."

"Nonsense, I won't be responsible for your death."

"I didn't bring a change of clothes with me," Charlie said, trying to deflect Alex's persistence.

Charlie watched as Alex looked at her. "We're about the same size. You can borrow some of my clothes." Alex said.

"Alex, actually my folks live very close by so I can shower and grab some old clothes there. I thought I was neat, but if your house is anything like your office, I'll feel terrible if I tramped dirt into it."

"Stop being childish. I have a mudroom right off the garage. You can take your clothes off there and toss 'em in the laundry. By the time dinner is over, they'll be clean and dry. You can return home fresh as a daisy."

Charlie could no longer fend off Alex. "All right, I'll follow you. Try to keep me in your rearview mirror. I've experienced your racing skills before."

Charlie ran across the park, pulled out her keys, and opened the door. She jumped in the car and sat back in the driver's seat. The feeling of wet, cold clothes against her back made her shudder. Despite her objections, Charlie was excited about spending time with a peer—woman, psychiatrist. For a brief moment, Charlie let her wants get the best of her.

She hadn't been intimate with someone in a while, and it left her body wanting. She thought she could only run and work so much before she might do something stupid and cave in to her desires. She knew nothing would come of it. She started her car and listened to the engine roar—it always made her feel good.

Charlie followed Alex's car, winding through the side streets, avoiding all the main thoroughfares. They arrived shortly at the appealing home. Charlie parked her car along the curb in front of the house. She noticed even in the last dregs of winter that the house seemed warm and inviting. Alex had parked her car in the garage and waited for Charlie to walk up the drive.

"This is nice, really nice. I like the paint scheme," Charlie said, admiring the house before she walked into the garage.

"I'm glad that you like it," Alex said as she unlocked the back door.

Charlie took off her shoes and was anxious to get out of her wet clothes. Charlie entered the little laundry room with the standard Westinghouse washer and dryer, ironing board, and empty hampers. "You can strip out of your clothes here—just toss them into the washing machine. I'll go get a robe for you to put on."

Charlie peeled off her sweatshirt, sweatpants, and socks and tossed them into the washing machine. She smiled to herself, thinking, *I bet she doesn't have any lint in the trap either.*

"What's so amusing?" Alex asked as she walked back into the mudroom carrying a plush white terrycloth robe.

"A hunch," Charlie said, reaching for the robe.

"What?" Alex crossed her arms, looking a little defensive.

"I thought that you wouldn't have any lint in your trap."

"And?"

"Not a speck of dust," Charlie said. She unhooked her bra, covering her breasts with her forearm, and threw her bra into the washing machine. She pulled on the robe and tied it in front. Charlie reached underneath the robe, pulled down her panties, and tossed them into the washer.

"Just getting out of my wet clothes and putting on the robe already works wonders," Charlie said.

"Come on, follow me," Alex said.

"It's a beautiful home. It has great bones."

"Here we go." Alex looked comely as she stood against the wall with her arms crossed behind her back and right knee slightly bent. Charlie peeked into the room and timidly entered it. She took in the rich golds, dark chocolates, and deep reds.

"Bathroom is on the right; the closet is right over here." Alex pointed to the louvered doors. "Help yourself to anything you want to wear. I keep my lingerie here," Alex said, opening a drawer.

"I won't be long."

"Take your time. I'll have some wine waiting for you when you get out."

There was a single candle burning on the bathroom sink. Charlie turned on the light, closed the door, and slid back the frosted shower door. She turned the faucet handles, and the water came rushing out. Charlie tested the water with the tips of her left hand as her right hand adjusted the hot and cold handles.

Charlie stepped into the shower, pulled up the handle, and was blasted with the hot water pouring from the showerhead. She let the water hit her head and shoulders, feeling it cascade down her body. Her muscles felt relief from the warm, therapeutic water. She turned to face the shower and leaned forward, resting her head against the tile, and let the water pound the top of her shoulders and neck. She closed her eyes. The door slid open.

Alex stood behind Charlie and gently placed her hands on Charlie's shoulders. Charlie could feel Alex's breasts pressed against her back. Alex whispered into Charlie's ear, "Do you want me to leave?"

Charlie turned her head, a thousand conflicting thoughts and feelings racing through her mind. Charlie shook her head. "No...this isn't wise."

Alex looked at Charlie attentively.

"We're targeting homosexuals," Charlie said.

"Slight difference—we're after men who prey on children and not two beautiful women who are enjoying each other's company. I know I didn't have anything to do with the abductions. Did you?"

Charlie shook her head no.

"I'm not going to tell. Are you?"

Charlie started to speak. Alex's hand came up and covered her mouth. She gently bit Charlie's ear and slowly kissed her neck. Alex picked up the shampoo bottle and poured a small amount into the cup of her hand. She rubbed her hands together and began to work the shampoo into Charlie's hair, gently massaging her head.

"That's wonderful." Charlie leaned back into Alex.

"Good. You've had too much pain in your life."

Charlie could smell the citrus essential oils as Alex took the lemon fragrance body wash and poured an enormous amount into her hand. Her hands glided all over Charlie's body as she washed her.

"That's even better...oh...oh, I can't believe it." The sensation of warm water, silky soap, and Alex's gentle touch as her hand glided over Charlie's body caused Charlie to moan, her body shuddering.

Alex held Charlie in her arms and gave her soft little kisses on her chin, nose, and forehead.

Alex's fingers grasped Charlie's buttocks. Charlie's body shuddered from the pent-up sexual pleasure driving out of her body. "I wasn't expecting that," Charlie said, trying to catch her breath.

"A dangerous, unforgiving, and wonderful cocktail," Alex whispered into Charlie's ear as she held her tight against her.

"Warm sudsy water, beautiful bodies, and pent-up desires?" Charlie asked.

"Life," Alex said before kissing Charlie on the lips.

Afterward, Charlie and Alex lay on their sides next to each other in bed, the silk sheets, blankets, and covers sprawled across the bed and floor. Alex's left arm wrapped around Charlie's body, holding her breast. Alex took Charlie's hand and gently twisted it to look at her wrist and saw the fine, slightly raised red marks crisscrossed with white, razor-fine scars.

"It helps hold the depression at bay," Charlie said.

"The other day…" Alex began to say.

"Yes, I remember the incident all too well."

"It was you," Alex said.

"Choo-Choo Charlie…the girl who wanted it…wanted to drive the train," Charlie said, her body racked with pain and anguish.

"Can I ask you what happened?" Alex said soothingly as she propped herself up one elbow and gently caressed Charlie's arm.

Silence filled the room. The shadows danced on the walls to the flickering candle lights. Charlie and Alex lay still.

"He was a friend of the family. Both our parents thought we'd be a good match. Truth be told, I don't think he had any more interest in me than I did in him. My parents had been so insistent and were joyful when I finally caved in and accepted the invitation.

"It was a beautiful summer night, a big party at the fraternity house. I thought to myself, what was the harm? There were people everywhere. They had a garage band in the basement. Kids were dancing, laughing, and drinking, the occasional joint being passed around.

"He took my hand, and we squeezed through the crowd. He got me a cup of punch and told me that he'd be right back. I think he was thankful that I didn't object. I actually saw him make a beeline for another girl sitting in the corner. He probably thought that I couldn't see him or that he was such a player that he was working two women at the same party.

"Most girls might have been upset at the idea of being dumped, but I was glad. I wouldn't have to make some type of lame excuse of not wanting to go back to his room. I wouldn't have to fend him off. Besides, I liked watching the girls in their summer dresses dancing around. He must have felt a sense of obligation or guilt—didn't want word getting back to his folks that he hadn't showed me a good time.

"He must have been gone for an hour or hour and a half. By that time, I was standing against the wall. I was tired of watching the drunken sloppiness. I don't know why I even stayed as long as I did. I guess I was concerned that he would say something to his parents and it would get back to my parents. I was just about to leave when he came up and handed me another cup of punch.

"I must have been thirsty or feeling a little dehydrated, because I gulped it down pretty quickly. I didn't think anything at first, but then I got this killer headache. I told him that I needed to sit down. My head was pounding.

"He guided me upstairs and opened the door to this small single room. He helped me sit down. I just put my hands to my face. My head was pounding, I couldn't focus, and my arms and legs started to feel like dead weights. He lifted my legs up and told me to lie down until I felt better.

"I couldn't move. I was having this out-of-body experience. I could hear whispering in the hallway outside, but nothing was registering. I must have blacked out. I could feel something happening to me, but I couldn't tell what. It's like when the dentist shoots your mouth full of Novocain. You can feel the pulling and tugging, but there's no pain. You just know the pain is coming.

"I woke sometime in the morning. My dress had been pulled up over my head, my bra pushed up to my neck, and my panties were wrapped around one ankle. I was bruised and bloodied. My vagina was on fire.

"I don't know how I did it, but somehow I managed to get up, get dressed, and go back to my dorm room. I slumped in the shower, clothes and all. I just wanted the water to wash all the dirt away. I showered five times that day, threw the clothes away, but nothing seemed to work.

"I'd figure out what had happened, but wasn't going to say anything. I was mortified. I didn't want to cause my parents any pain. I was just going to melt away.

"Later that day and every day after, my phone would ring. I'd answer it, but all I'd get was either deep breathing or train whistle noises. I'd just crumple to the floor in shame, the tears pouring out of me. I tried acting like nothing happened and just go about my business, but I could feel the stares and hear the whispers. It was then that I decided to go to the police and provost."

"What did they say?" Alex asked.

"That I didn't stand a chance. They were all so condescending—each and every one of them. I was mistaken. I was overreacting. They were boys just being boys. They meant no harm; things just got out of hand. When I wouldn't back down, it got worse.

"Who was everyone going to believe—the white, good-looking, wealthy, fraternity premed students or the hapa girl? They said that everyone still remembered Pearl Harbor and how sneaky the Japs were. I told them I was Korean and not Japanese. They said the gooks were just as bad. Japs, chinks, gooks—we're all slanty-eyed, conniving liars. They said it was just best if I went away," Charlie said.

"Those assholes, they're so predictable. What about your parents?" Alex asked as she reached over Charlie and handed her a tissue.

"I tried confiding to them, but they were in denial. My mother and I have always been at odds. The only one who understood, really understood, was my grandmother. She knew the moment I walked into her room," Charlie said as she wiped her eyes and then gently blew her nose.

"How about the bastard who set you up? What did he have to say for himself?"

"He denied having anything to do with it," Charlie said. "I sort of believed him. I think he didn't realize how ugly it was going to get. It was just going to be him and a couple of his close buddies."

"What a first-class jerk," Alex said. "Did you ever see him again?"

"Once, at a family function. He came up to me privately and professed his innocence. I threw a drink on him and walked away. I heard later from my parents that he and his fiancée were killed by a drunk driver," Charlie said.

"Serves him right. How can you work with the police after what they did to you?" Alex asked.

"It's because of them. I couldn't care less about them. It's about the victims and their families. It's why I'll never rest, it's why I'll do everything in my power to comfort, bring some type of relief and closure to the victims and their families," Charlie said.

Alex leaned over and wiped tears from Charlie's face. Alex closed her eyes, kissed her lips, and made love to her. She tried to wipe away the pain they both felt, even if it was for a short time. The two women lay intertwined in each other's arms and legs.

"When did you first know?" Charlie asked.

"That you were a lesbian?"

"That, too. When did you realize that you were into women?" Charlie asked.

"God, I must have been eleven or so…You know how it is…you find yourself looking at the models in the lingerie section of the Sears catalog, getting…excited.

"She lived at the end of the street. She must have been sixteen or seventeen…she was my babysitter. My parents and stepsister would go out for dinner. I was so lonely, feeling rejected. My stepmother had told her that I needed a bath and to make sure that I had it before I went to bed. I remember sitting in the bathtub, and she was sitting on the toilet seat cover watching me.

"She stood up and started to take her clothes off. She got in the tub with me, and we washed each other. She'd have me touch her. I was so embarrassed and thrilled I thought I was going to pee."

"How did you know about me?" Charlie asked.

"I had this sense…feeling maybe it was wishful thinking on overdrive. I'm glad that my suspicions were right," Alex said.

Charlie smiled and pushed Alex on her back. "I'm glad that you were persistent."

Charlie awoke sometime around dawn. The room and outside were still dark. She looked at Alex lying on her side, lightly snoring. Charlie slid out of her side of the bed and walked around to Alex's side. She pulled the covers up over Alex's shoulder.

She found the bathrobe lying in a heap and put it on. She quietly moved out of the bedroom and closed the door lightly. Charlie walked down the hallway, admiring Alex's interior design expertise.

Charlie walked across the cold kitchen floor. She opened the door to the mudroom and felt the cold draft. Charlie pulled closed the terrycloth robe's lapels. On top of the dryer were her running clothes, bra, and panties—washed and folded.

Charlie pulled off her robe and started to dress as quickly as possible, the cold air making her nipples erect and giving her a sudden urge to pee.

"Where are you going?"

Charlie startled jumped backward. "I need to get home."

"Defensive measures kicking in again?"

"No, I've really enjoyed our time together," Charlie said as she hooked her bra.

"Good—so did I. The way you tried to leave so quietly without saying good-bye, I was worried that you might be having buyer's remorse for what happened last night. See you again?"

"I promise."

"You sure that you have to go?" Alex asked.

"Unfortunately, I do. I've got a pile of work waiting for me."

"Can I at least fix you some breakfast or some coffee for the road? I feel bad you leaving on a cold morning without a hot meal to send you off."

"That's very thoughtful, and you've been more than gracious, but I really need to get going," Charlie said. She kissed Alex on the mouth and gently squeezed one of her breasts.

"Get out of here," Alex said and slapped Charlie lightly on the ass.

Charlie opened the back door to the garage. Alex pushed the garage door opener. The women watched the garage door slowly rise. Above the whirling and clanging sounds of the motor, Alex said, "There's a person I think you should check on…Marilyn Smith."

Charlie turned looked at Alex. "Marilyn Smith?"

"You know, the bigwig auto executive."

"Yeah, yeah. Why, what do you have?"

"I had a client who told me about her 'aunt Marilyn' and their sleepover parties."

"Can I have the client's name?"

"You know I can't share that information with you, but I can tell you I think there are a lot of similarities with what my client said and what's happening to these kids."

"Such as?"

"Like them bathing together and fixing her favorite food. I've given the killer a lot of thought. I've developed my own profile. Remember, you're not the only psychiatrist." Alex placed her arm around her body to prevent her robe from opening as she leaned over to kiss Charlie good-bye.

BEVERLY HILLS
MONDAY, MARCH 7, 1977

Charlie dunked her "dunker" elongated glazed donut into her coffee. Detectives of the task force were sitting around a large conference table in the makeshift squad room waiting for Pete to begin the meeting. There was the usual morning chatter about the Tigers' spring performances, wives and kids, and the humorous incidents in the execution of their investigations.

"Good morning, Charlie and gentlemen. I'm sorry for running late," Pete said as he entered the squad room and took the seat at the head of the table. He needed a shave, and his shirt was wrinkled. He looked tired, face drawn, with dark circles around his eyes.

"Before we go around the table and you provide us with your updates, I'd like to share a couple of observations…concerns. I would like to caution you against wishful thinking, false hopes, and complacency. I know there is talk that spring is around the corner and that the perpetrator might not strike again. In fact, I've talked with some of our best investigators who are convinced that they may have already talked to the killer and that he or she—" Pete looked in Charlie's direction "—is laughing at our ineptitude and will wait until next winter to deposit a child's body along a roadside.

"Surprisingly, we've only received two false confessions. At any time a suspect could come in here or we could receive a tip that leads us to the killer. We're receiving hundreds of tips each day, and to date we have over three thousand seven hundred.

"Although we haven't caught the killer yet, we've received information about a large in-state pedophile ring and possibly a tip to an automotive executive. We're doing good work, and I wanted you to know that I appreciate all the hard work and dedication. We're not going to let these families down. So, please keep it up. Kenton Fisk will now go over the tips procedures."

"Thanks, Pete," Kenton said. "We're bringing the computers in from Lansing this week, so we're going to have to institute a new tips policy." Groans could be heard. "Yeah, I hear you, but the additional work will pay dividends and save us a lot of time and hassle in the future.

"The tips will be given priorities—green, amber, and red—based upon your assessments. The highest priorities will be given mainly to us, the best and most seasoned investigators. We are expected to investigate these leads ASAP. The next priority is medium, and they will be executed when there are no outstanding or open high-priority tips to be investigated. The lowest priority will go to our least experienced investigators for examination.

"The tips are entered into an automated system by the subject's name, address, and tip number. The system then checks to see if the subject's name has been previously reported. Now, here's the beauty of automation. If the CRT indicates a record, you'll confirm that it's the same suspect and cross-references other pertinent information, as a result saving you additional work.

"I've also added some other files to help in our work: a surveillance file for cars that have been identified near the abduction sites; a suspect file that contains the known travel patterns of previously convicted pedophiles; and, finally, a school questionnaire that Dr. Taylor developed for teachers to assist their students in filling out the form. Dr. Taylor?"

Charlie picked up from there. "In addition to all the safety classes for children, parents, and educators, the form is to be filled out by the children with the help of their teachers." Charlie handed out copies of the forms to all the members.

"These will serve as another source of incident forms," she said. "We're asking them to tell us how many times strangers have asked to give them rides, offered candy, taken their pictures, or asked for help. From this report and others being worked up, we're developing a pattern of contact. We've also reached out to the FBI and other law enforcement organizations to get a list of known paroled pedophiles who have moved to Michigan and currently reside within the state."

The meeting went on for another hour, with each local law enforcement lead investigator providing an update on his investigation. Charlie found these interactions helpful because another agency might have a piece of the puzzle that another jurisdiction might need to solve the murders. As the meeting broke up, Charlie gathered her papers and placed them into her leather briefcase. She was about to leave the squad room when she heard her name being called.

"Dr. Taylor?" It was one of the investigators who had been highly critical of her observations.

"Yes, Steve?"

"I want to apologize."

"For what?" Charlie asked, picking her briefcase up off the table.

"I was really critical of you and said some pretty shitty things behind your back," he said.

"Don't give it a second thought."

"I was really offended at first when you stated that priests could be involved. I'm Catholic, and I just couldn't fathom how a man of the cloth could do such things. Well, I was wrong. We've got names of at least a dozen priests who have done heinous crimes. I've got kids of my own, and I send them to Catholic schools. I'm beside myself."

"Thanks for having the courage to apologize, but please do not worry about me. I've had worse things said about me, and I'll probably have more said later." Charlie extended her hand.

BEVERLY HILLS
MONDAY, MARCH 7, 1977

Charlie stood outside Pete's office while he talked on the phone. Pete looked up at Charlie and waved her inside. Despite his disheveled appearance, his voice sounded almost buoyant. Pete hung up the receiver, stretched back in his chair, and placed both hands behind his head.

"You seemed rather pleased," Charlie observed.

"I haven't felt like this in a long while."

"What's up?"

"I just got back from Traverse City. A reporter for the *Traverse City Record-Eagle* has been doing some investigative research. She got wind of some unseemly behavior on North

Fox Island. She has done some superb investigative work and saved me a tremendous amount of time and energy.

"They've been able to connect the dots on Raymond Evreux's operation. Raymond Evreux, multimillionaire, son of a wealthy family from Grosse Pointe and resident of Ann Arbor, with the help of like-minded friends, created a camp for underprivileged boys.

"This guy's amazing. There have been articles written about him and his generous charitable donations to several organizations in support of boys. However, he was a regular contributor to a magazine that was dedicated to the liberation of boys and boy-lovers. The pedophiles used this magazine to contact each other.

"Raymond read from another contributor about his concept of a camp for boys, and Raymond just happened to own a remote island, so it seemed like the perfect fit. The two established the camp for underprivileged boys under the auspices that it is a 'church' camp, so they are a nonprofit organization."

"This is insane," Charlie said, sitting forward in her seat.

"It gets better. They've even conned welfare departments into making payments for the support of the boys. Right now, they have the county paying up to one hundred and fifty dollars, the state up to four hundred dollars, and the Feds up to seven hundred dollars per child per month. They've created an organization that has tax exemption and gets paid by local, state, and federal authorities to rape boys and make child pornography films. I haven't even scratched the surface on what they make on these films and pictures."

"This is tragic," Charlie said. "Those poor boys. Not only do they come from disadvantaged economic circumstances, but these guys are crushing any or all hope these kids may ever have. It's disgusting."

"I also have reason to believe that they may be shipping these kids out of state," Pete said. "There seem to be big markets in New York, Los Angeles, and New Orleans. John told me that I had no idea how big this organization was. He was right. I completely underestimated the size and scope of the Brotherhood."

"What's your next step?"

"I've begun to compile the evidence to convince the prosecutor to take it to the grand jury."

"I'm torn. On one hand, I'm happy for you that you've been right all these years—there is a Brotherhood—and on the other hand, I'm sad that it's terribly true."

"Just like 'Nam. Guys with too much power, money, and connections, and they believe they are untouchable. Maybe they are? And the kids just keep getting used. Just like 'Nam."

Charlie wrapped her arm around Pete's waist.

MARILYN SMITH'S STORY

I kick off my shoes and put my feet up on the desk. I read the current and projected sales report. This is going to be a banner year. My thoughts are interrupted when the intercom system buzzes. I swing my feet down, reach over, and hold the intercom button down.

"Yes, Janet?"

"Mr. Campbell, Bloomfield Hills Dealership, is on line two for you."

"Thanks, Janet."

I pick up the phone and push the flashing button down. "Yes, George?"

"I could kiss you."

"I'm flattered."

"You're a genius. Those styling changes that you had them make are the answers to my prayers—smaller car, more fuel efficient, but no sacrifice to the interior. I've got Mercedes Benz owners lining up to trade in their cars for ours."

"Congratulations. It feels good, doesn't it? I'm reading our sales production report right now. We're projected to produce over three hundred thousand units, and we're well on our way to selling our six millionth car."

"You truly are your old man's daughter," Campbell says. "Why don't you come by the dealership on Saturday?"

"By Friday I'm thinking of celebrating and going to Red Fox for prime rib and plenty of dry martinis," I tell him.

"It hasn't been the same since Hoffa disappeared."

"Just adds to the intrigue."

"If I didn't know better...I wouldn't be shocked if you have something to do with it," he says. "Your old man hated him."

"My father was an SOB—he hated everyone."

"So why can't you come by on Saturday?" Campbell asks.

"Depending on how bad the hangover is, I'm either going to sleep in and relax around the house or maybe go to the club and play bridge."

"Why do you always have to make things so complicated, Marilyn?"

"Why don't you just tell me what's on your mind, George?"

"You're not making this easy on me."

"I rarely go easy on anyone," I say. "Another of my father's traits."

"God, it's a thing of beauty."

"What's a thing of beauty?"

"Well, as a token of my undying gratitude, I've got a car for you," he says.

"How thoughtful...tell me more."

"I know how you like them big with a large trunk."

"Just like my men. I'll see you Saturday," I say as I hang up the phone, thinking, *Could this day get any better? Sales through the roof, and now someone is giving me a new car.*

My intercom buzzes again. "Yes, Janet?"

"Ma'am, the caller didn't identify himself."

"Hang up on him."

"I'd normally do that, but he said it was urgent, and his voice…"

"What about his voice?"

"It frightened me. It sounded menacing," she says.

"All right. I'll take the call. Why don't you call it a day and get out of here?"

I push the flashing button. "I told you never to call me here unless it's an emergency."

"It is. He knows all about Raymond and North Fox Island."

BIRMINGHAM
TUESDAY, MARCH 8, 1977

I punch the garage door button, close the car door, and make my way into the house. Before crossing the kitchen floor, I manage to kick off my high heels and toss my purse across the kitchen table before I am attacked.

"Ah, Schultzie, get down. I missed you, too," I say as I scratch behind the ear of my miniature Schnauzer.

I head straight for the cupboard, pull out a highball glass, reach into the freezer for a few ice cubes, and watch them rattle and clang the sides of the glass. Opening the bottle of my Glenlivet Scotch whiskey, I pour myself a stiff one.

I move through the house to the family room. I stare at the cold and empty fireplace, toss the drink back, and feel the liquid burn my throat. The whiskey only seems to fuel the fire inside of me.

I think to myself, *Damn them. How could they be so selfish and risk everything we've achieved? No one ever underestimates Jack's little girl. I plot how their deaths should be arranged. I'm definitely my old man's daughter. He was a brutal and unloving man—a martinet. I remember all too well how his belt would come off, and my brothers and I would take the lashings across our buttocks. Daddy could be a sadistic bastard. What would he have done?*

I grin as my thoughts become more perverted. *Sweaty men with hairy chests and pawing hands leave me cold. Women aren't much better. At least they're willing to spend some time and energy in foreplay, but women aren't without their own issues. They can be whiny, possessive control freaks.*

Yes, I'm my old man's daughter. I cross to the wet bar and pour another whiskey. *We had so much in common—cars, whiskey, cigars, and children. Give me a little one—their innocence is so refreshing.*

Unlike my father's sadistic behavior toward them, there's a part of me that really loves my little angels. I'm not doing them any harm. My butterfly kisses are just an expression of my love and tenderness. The poems that I write to them express my devotion. I'm not some maladjusted freak—a pedophile who causes harm or pain. I'm just allowing them to understand and express their own sexuality. It's been too long.

The front doorbell rings. *Who in the hell can that be?* I walk to the front of the house. I pause in front of the mirror for a moment, smooth my dress, and pat into place a few stray strands of hair.

"Schultzie, quiet," I say to stop the racket.

I look out the big bay window of my living room to see who it is. I turn on the front porch light and open the heavy oak door. Standing in front of me is a woman with her back turned.

"Yes?" I say.

"Ms. Smith?"

BIRMINGHAM
TUESDAY, MARCH 8, 1977

"Yes, but before you get started, I want you to understand that I don't contribute to door-to-door charities, I've already given my old clothes to Goodwill, and I'm not interested in becoming a Mormon. Anything else?"

"Ms. Smith, my name is Dr. Charlie Taylor. I'm from the Oakland County prosecutor's office. I'm with the task force looking into the abductions and murders of Cody Edwards, Allison Walker, and Nicole Hernandez."

"That's all well and good, Dr. Taylor, but what does that have to do with me?"

"There's been a complaint lodged against you. I thought it would be more considerate if I came here and we discussed it privately versus calling you down to the task force headquarters for all to see. May I come in, Ms. Smith, so we can discuss—?"

"It's been a very long week. Can't this wait?"

"Ms. Smith, I understand and appreciate your feelings. We receive hundreds of complaints and tips every day. I'm sure you understand that we have to investigate all of them. Most times, they're cleared up very quickly. May I please come in?"

Marilyn's response was slow in coming as she looked at Charlie and seemed to register her options. Then she opened the door wider for Charlie to enter into the home. "Please, come in. Can I take your coat?" she asked.

"You have a beautiful home. Live here alone?" Charlie asked as she slipped out of her winter coat and observed the immaculate home.

"Thank you. Yes, I live here by myself. Well, not exactly. Schultzie keeps me company. Don't you, boy?" The Schnauzer's stubbed tail wagged back and forth in response to being recognized.

"He's adorable. Schultzie," Charlie asked, holding her fist down for the dog to come and smell her.

"We can sit here if that's OK with you," Marilyn offered as she looked at Charlie suspiciously.

"Yes, this would be great." Charlie sat down on the vintage French-style sofa in dark-gold linen upholstery. "I would imagine that your position has tremendous demands and your home provides you a certain amount of refuge."

"Can I get you a drink?" Marilyn said as she held up her own glass and gently shook it so that the ice cubes swirled around in the glass.

"No, thank you," Charlie said, crossing her leg over her knee.

"I assume that you won't tell me who made this complaint?" Marilyn said as she sipped from her glass.

"That's correct."

"Well, can you tell me what I'm supposed to have done?"

"Unfortunately, I'm not at liberty to state the circumstances or the content of the complaint. In very generic terms, allegedly you were personally involved in the abduction and murder of the three children," Charlie said. She noticed that Marilyn's knuckles turned white as she squeezed her glass tightly. Charlie took out a notepad and pen from her purse.

"I can tell you…"

"Ms. Smith, congratulations on your promotion. I'd imagine being a woman in a man's world and the high visibility your position brings must place you under tremendous pressure."

"Thank you, but it's nothing I can't handle…but I don't see…"

"Seems like a fascinating and demanding job," Charlie said. "To me cars are like a work of art—they stand on a pedestal for all to view and judge. We buy them to reflect our styles and tastes."

"That's a nice way of putting it. The work is very demanding, but I'm passionate about what I do. Our customers are very loyal, and I owe it to them to provide the very best product that I can—one miscalculation and all can be lost. The competition is fierce and is getting worse every day.

"These last few years have been brutal. We're just recovering from the oil crisis, inflation is out of control, loans hovering around six point two-five to six point five, a decline of interest in muscle cars—and let's be honest, the buyer is becoming more fickle. I can't take their loyalty for granted. What does your father drive, Dr. Taylor?"

"He's a Buick man through and through," Charlie said. "Nothing but a Riviera for him."

"A wise choice over the years, although I'm not crazy about this year's model. Do you like cars?"

"Every year I'd look forward to going to the showroom with my dad and picking out our new car. Months prior I'd study everything there was about the new models, an effort in futility because all he ever was going to pick was a Buick despite my arguments to the contrary."

"It's very rare that I find a woman who is really interested in cars. Most pick out a car like a new pair of shoes and handbags—color and style is all that matters. No real appreciation. What do you drive? Mustang…'67," Marilyn said, craning her neck to look out the window at the car.

"'68 Fastback," Charlie said.

"Bullitt?"

"Bullitt."

Marilyn nodded. "I hate that movie. It did more for the Mustang. I would've figured you for a Trans-Am or Corvette."

"I'm partial to the Stingray's '63 through '67, although the '56 and '61 are beautiful," Charlie said.

"Please excuse me a moment. I'd like to refresh my drink. You sure there's nothing that I can get for you?" Marilyn asked as she stood up.

"I'm fine, thank you." As Marilyn went to the wet bar, Charlie got up and walked around the room to admire the décor. The tables were highly polished, and everything was perfectly placed. Charlie couldn't find a speck of dust. She was reading the titles on the bookshelf when Marilyn returned.

"I always loved Nancy Drew," Charlie said, pointing to the familiar yellow book spines with the picture of the young woman detective.

Marilyn strode up next to Charlie. "For my nieces when they visit," Marilyn said as she drew on her Tiparillo cigar and blew the smoke out with a smile. I didn't get to the top by being a lady," she said. "I'm always proving that my vagina is every bit as tough as their balls."

"You could've inspired their advertising. Single?" Charlie asked.

"Never had time for hard dick and bubblegum. Most guys are too intimidated by my drive and success."

"The life of a professional woman?"

"I wouldn't have it any other way," Marilyn said. "And you?"

"The life of a professional woman," Charlie echoed, moving back toward the sofa and sitting down. "I just have a few more questions for you."

"Really? I was starting to enjoy the conversation."

"Do you ever entertain other children here besides your nieces?"

Marilyn drew on her cigar and blew out the smoke. "My nieces stay here on the weekends, but by Sunday afternoon I'm ready for them to leave."

"I know what you mean. I've two nieces myself. I wish that I still had that much energy. Does anyone else stay here?"

"I also entertain business associates' daughters sometimes. My associates like the idea of their daughters associating with a successful woman. These days some men want the best for their daughters; they want their girls to take advantage of women's liberation. Mark my words, these girls are going to have education and employment opportunities that we did not think was possible."

"When the kids come for their visits, what type of activities do you do?"

"The usual. Depending on their ages we'll play Monopoly, Scrabble, or gin rummy."

"Do you ever bathe with them?"

Marilyn looked down at her drink and stubbed out her cigar. When she raised her head, her eyes bore into Charlie. "These absurd accusations about me are utterly false, and I find the idea repulsive."

"I'm sure you do. Thank you for your time and willingness to speak with me," Charlie said. She closed up her notebook and placed it and her pen in her purse.

"I hope this puts an end to any unfounded accusations," Marilyn said.

"I'm sure it does, but occasionally we have to double-check the information," Charlie said as she put on her winter coat and offered her hand.

Charlie rewound the conversation in her head as she walked back to her car. She was uncertain of what had just taken place. However, Marilyn Smith did warrant further examination. Charlie chalked it up to intuition.

Charlie was about to place the key into the door lock when she looked back at house. Marilyn was looking intently at Charlie, with her left arm wrapped around her waist and her right hand holding the cigar at the corner of her mouth. She smiled, blew the smoke out of the side of her mouth, and turned and disappeared into the house.

BEVERLY HILLS
WEDNESDAY, MARCH 9, 1977

Barricaded in her office, Charlie surrounded herself with work, trying to guard herself from distractions. Charlie had been drawn to Alex and, for that matter, Marilyn. Charlie thought about her physical attraction to both women. Charlie could see herself having a relationship with Alex. They were so alike, yet maybe they were too alike.

Thoughts of Annie crossed Charlie's mind, too. Charlie loved her spunky friend but knew that it could never be more than friendship. Charlie had been burned in the past when she had opened up to straight friends about her sexual preference. An awkwardness or discomfort would spring forth between them, and it would only be a matter of time before their friendship would be severed.

Charlie hated giving in to her emotions.

She focused on the work at hand and continued to look for patterns. She tried not to be swayed by the numerous conflicting theories swirling in the papers and task force headquarters and focus only on the facts. Lauren and Katie were from St. Clair Shores and Roseville, Macomb County, abductions well east of the current abductions in Oakland County. However, their bodies had been left at one of the major east/west mile roads; Lauren near Twenty-Seven Mile Road and Katie at Fourteen Mile Road. There was something sexual about their abductions and murders.

Grace was a transitional victim. She looked older than her actual thirteen years of age, and her physical similarity to Lauren had been striking. Yet her death was similar to those of Allison and Kristen. She hadn't been sexually assaulted, her hands were bound behind her back with white strips of cloth, and she'd been asphyxiated. Maybe the killer had been attracted to her the same way she was to Lauren, but when she found out Grace's real age that changed the dynamics.

For the younger children, the pattern was even more pronounced. Cody was taken from Nine Mile and left at Ten

Mile, Allison from either Twelve, Thirteen, or Fifteen Mile Roads and left at Sixteen Mile, and Nicole at Twelve Mile and left at Thirteen Mile. She saw how the abduction of the kids straddled Woodward Avenue as the killer moved northward. Charlie started to think the next victim might be a boy closer to Fifteen Mile Road on the north east.

She sat back in her chair and took a sip of her tepid tea.

BIRMINGHAM
THURSDAY, MARCH 10, 1977

Tom Woodson tossed the *Detroit Free Press* on the floor in disappointment with the lack of progress made in the search for the children's killer. *Maybe I should talk to him, but he has a good head on his shoulders.*

"Shaun, can you come down here, please?"

"Yeah, Dad." When Shaun entered the kitchen, he asked, "Am I trouble?"

"I want to talk about these kids who've been abducted," Tom said.

Shaun nodded. "Our teachers and the police have been talking to us about what we should do if someone approaches us."

"That's good to hear. Son, it's incredibly important that you understand that you have to be on your guard at all times. Don't talk to anyone who offers you candy or asks for your help because his dog is missing. If anyone approaches you, run as fast as you can and yell 'fire' at the top of your lungs. Do you understand me?"

"Sure, Dad. I'd never let anyone get close to me. I'd run away."

"That's good to hear." Tom Woodson relaxed a little. "Little League tryouts are next week. Are you ready?"

"I can't wait."

ANN ARBOR
FRIDAY, MARCH 11, 1977

The weather matched Charlie's feelings—gray, cold, damp, depressed. She opened the front door to her house and breathed a sigh of relief. Her house always brought a sense of serenity and purpose to her world, which she could find little solace in now. She spent her nights at various stakeouts, and during the days she met with the parents. Her updates brought little reprieve from their pain and suffering. The mothers were bundles of nerves, looking exhausted.

She couldn't share her suspicions with them—there were still too many unresolved issues. Charlie just wanted to let them know that someone was their advocate. They needed to know there were dedicated professionals committed to finding the killer of their children. Taking time, listening to their frustrations, she reassured them that every effort was being made.

Charlie dropped her bags in the foyer with little enthusiasm or motivation to carry them to her bedroom and unpack. For some strange reason, the house seemed colder and somehow unfamiliar. She began to turn on the lights as she made her way from the front of the house to the family room.

She entered the living room and reached for the long wooden matches in their red cylinder tube, thankful that she had prepared the fireplace with wood, newspaper, and kindling. As she struck a match, the sulfur filled her nostrils with its pungent smell. With little thought she reached down and held the flame to the newspaper.

The paper began to crackle, the blue flames leaping and fluttering like sheets drying in the wind as the smoke drifted upward through the chute. Charlie made her way to the wet bar and poured herself a Scotch.

House silent except for the fire crackling and the furnace groaning, Charlie sat down on the brick ledge in front of the fire and sipped her drink. She pulled up her sleeve and looked at her latest artwork. The heat radiated from the fireplace, and Charlie could feel her back getting hot.

The fine hairs on the back of her neck began to rise. Charlie was struck with a creepy sensation that someone was watching her. She looked out the bank of windows into the darkness but could only see her exhausted reflection staring back at her. Despite the roaring fire, Charlie felt cold and vulnerable. Charlie thought, *Is it the same person…the killer?*

SHAUN WOODSON'S STORY

Mom is getting ready in front of the mirror, talking to us over her shoulder while she checks her hair. "Dad and I have dinner in town with one of his clients, but we won't be late. Joel, you have the concert tonight. What time are you taking off?"

"We're leaving around eight. We probably won't be home till late," Joel says, raiding the fridge, barely paying attention.

"All right, young man, but I'm not thrilled about you going to a concert on a school night. I don't want to repeat previously covered territory. I just want you to appreciate that your dad and I've got the utmost trust and confidence in you to do the right thing. Next?" She glances at Daniel, my brother, who is carefully stepping over my legs spread out over the kitchen floor as though I weren't even there. "Daniel, you've got babysitting duties at the Wrights', and you're expected there shortly. OK, take off and behave yourself."

"Thanks, Mom, I will," Daniel says, taking a chocolate cookie from the bowl, taking a large bite out of it, and stepping back over me as he makes his way from the kitchen to the front door.

"And last but certainly not least..."

"He's certainly least; he's just a pipsqueak," Joel says before he takes a drink from the milk carton. He gently kicks me and then walks away.

"That's enough, young man," Mom berates, trying to restore order. She looks down at me, and I roll the basketball down to my knees and back up. "Shaun, you're holding down the fort," she says. "We'll be home not long after Joel leaves for the concert, so don't get any ideas in your head, like having a wild party."

"Aw, Mom." I hug her and then run for the front door to shoot baskets outside.

I wave to everyone as they leave. I continue to shoot baskets until it's too dark even with the garage and front porch lights on. I go inside trying to decide what I'm going to do next. I run upstairs to Joel's room. I can smell the mixture of Right Guard and British Sterling coming from his room.

"Can I borrow some money to go to the store to buy some candy?"

"Sure, pipsqueak. I've got some change on top of my dresser," he says as he looks at me, smiles, and buttons up his shirt.

I grab the thirty cents and run from his room before he changes his mind. Joel can be worse than Mom and Dad sometimes. I realize that he may lock me out of the house, so I run back upstairs, open the door, and poke my head inside of his room.

"Hey, leave the door open so I can get back into the house. OK?"

"Sure, buddy. Now get out of here so I can finish," he says, tucking his shirt into his jeans.

"Thanks, Joel. Have a great time at the concert."

I leave the house, grabbing my skateboard lying by the side of the driveway, and push off the street to get me rolling. I work on my latest tricks. It's a great night out, and it feels neat to be able to go to the store on my own. I ride through the parking area watching for cars and shopping carts.

I grab my orange skateboard and head into the store through the back door. I go straight to the candy section. They've got a great selection—Black Jack Taffy, Squirrel Nut Zippers, and Mary Janes. I look at the packets of baseball cards. Maybe a pack of Beemans or some Bazooka? I can't make up my mind. I reach for a family favorite, Bonomo's Turkish Taffy, when I hear a voice behind me.

"Tough choices?"

I look up at the smiling face. "Yeah."

"You must have strong teeth to eat taffy."

"I don't know," I say. "We always put it the freezer and when it gets frozen real hard we throw it against the bricks by the fireplace and it breaks up into little pieces. Then it's easier to eat the small pieces."

"Very clever. I'll have to remember that the next time I buy some. Personally, I'm partial to a Chunky. I love chocolate, raisins, and nuts all in one candy bar. Well...?"

"Shaun."

"Well, Shaun, it was certainly nice talking with you."

"Thanks." I wave good-bye and go to pay for my candy.

The candy only costs twenty-five cents, so I put the nickel in my pocket and go outside. I hop on my skateboard and start to roll when a voice yells at me.

"Hey, kid, that's a great looking skateboard. Can I see it?"

I look over to see a teenager about Joel's age waving me over. He's leaning up against a dark-green car with an older guy driving. A cute little white dog bounced around the back seat barking at the people walking by the car. I was going to say yes and make my way over to him when I remember what my dad and teachers warned me about. Then I look around. I'm in a parking lot with lots of people. What can the harm be?

BIRMINGHAM
WEDNESDAY, MARCH 16, 1977

Julie and Tom Woodson arrived home from having dinner just a short distance from their home and found a few lights on and the door ajar. As they walked up the sidewalk to the front porch with the moon shining over them, Tom put his arm around his wife, thankful for her company and the good life they lived. They weren't overly concerned that the door was open; the kids were always leaving the door open despite their occasional threats.

"Shaun, we're home," Tom called out. But there was no response to his repeated calls. Julie began to search the house to see where Shaun might be, but she couldn't find him.

"He's not here, Tom."

"He's probably at a friend's house and will return shortly. You know Shaun. He isn't likely to stray far from home."

"But that's my point. It's strange. Shaun is always leaving notes telling me where he's going and when he'll be back, but I can't find any notes," Julie said. "You're probably right. I'm turning into a worrywart. It's just that these kids' disappearances have me freaked out."

Tom grabbed the *Detroit Free Press* off the sofa and settled himself into his favorite chair in the family room, with its knotted-pine walls and the chairs and sofa in navy blue with tartan throws of navy, kelly green, black, and white. He made his way through the sports section, hopeful that the Tigers were going to have a good season. He thought of baseball and opening day just around the corner, which led him back to thoughts of Shaun and his baseball tryouts. "Julie, is Shaun back yet? What time is it?"

Julie came into the room. "It's nine thirty. I'm concerned, Tom."

"Yeah, you're right. I'll jump into the car and look around the neighborhood. Why don't you call his friends to see if he isn't hanging out there?" Tom suggested.

Tom grabbed the car keys and strode out the door—the flimsy screen door bounced off the doorjamb behind him as he walked down the sidewalk. Tom drove around the neighborhood searching for Shaun, but he couldn't find a trace of him. Tom pulled the car into the driveway of Shaun's best friend.

He looked at the darkened house and knew Shaun wasn't there. His worst fears were beginning to materialize. Tom looked at the house with his hands on his hips, heart racing, and prayed they were all overreacting. Tom returned home to Julie and his son Daniel. He hugged his wife and son.

"It'll be all right." Tom said.

"Tom, I'm worried. This isn't like him. What are we going to do?" Julie said.

"Honey, I don't have a good answer right now. I'll let the police know. In the meantime we keep calling and looking for him till we find him. We don't stop until he's safely back home." Tom said.

"Hello, Birmingham Police Department," a woman's voice answered.

"Hi, my name is Tom Woodson. I'm concerned that my eleven-year-old son isn't home," Tom said, trying to keep his emotions in check.

"When did you last see him?"

"A little after this evening when my wife and I left for dinner."

"Did anyone else see him?"

"My oldest son, before he left for a concert, which would have been around eight."

"When did your son last see him?"

"He's not home yet, so we don't know."

"Sir, I'll let a police officer know, and they'll be in contact."

"That's it? That's all you're going to do?" Tom asked.

"Yes, sir."

"You've got to be kidding me. We've got a killer running around out there. My son who is the same age as the other children is missing. All you're going to do is let a policeman know?"

"Yes, sir."

"This is insane."

BIRMINGHAM

THURSDAY, MARCH 17, 1977

"When did you get the call?" Charlie asked Pete as he got out of his car.

"Early this morning. The parents had called the Birmingham police last night, but the operator didn't forward the information until very early this morning," Pete said, shaking his head in disbelief. "I've already received several calls from Lincoln. We're bringing some additional support to include several helicopters and special radio equipment. We're occupying Poppleton Park," Pete answered as they strode up the Woodson driveway.

"What do we know?" Charlie asked.

"We're soon to find out," Pete said as he reached for the front doorbell.

A woman answered the door. Charlie could see that she hadn't slept much if at all the night before.

"Mrs. Woodson? Detective Pete West with the Michigan State Police. This is Dr. Charlie Taylor, my associate. We are with the MSP task force."

"Thank you to the both of you for coming," Julie Woodson said. "Won't you please come in?"

Julie Woodson took Pete's overcoat from him. Even without makeup, she was an attractive woman in her midforties wearing a navy-blue turtleneck and blue jeans. She kept her dishwater-blond hair short and stylish.

Charlie took the time to look around the modest and comfortable home. She walked over to the living room wall where all the family photos hung. There were photos of all the kids at various school ages, family trips taken, and holidays being celebrated. The photos were a collage of a happy, well-adjusted family.

"My husband is in the family room," Julie said. Charlie and Pete followed her into the family room.

Tom Woodson stood as Charlie and Pete entered the room. He was a handsome, middle-aged man. He was dressed in a brown plaid Pendleton wool shirt and dark-chocolate-brown wide-wale corduroys. "Tom Woodson."

"Detective Pete West," Pete said as he shook Tom's hand firmly.

Tom Woodson extended his hand to Charlie. "Dr. Charlie Taylor," Charlie said as she returned the handshake.

"Please have a seat."

Charlie and Pete sat in chairs facing the Woodsons, who sat together on the sofa. Julie slipped her hand into her husband's as they sat on the edge.

"I'm with the Michigan State Police, and Dr. Taylor is a criminal psychiatrist for the Oakland County Prosecutor's Office."

Noticing the Woodsons' bodies tense, Charlie tried to reassure them by quickly adding, "Please know that our presence here doesn't mean that anything has happened to Shaun, but we do not want to take any chances. I hope that you understand."

"Please, we welcome your assistance in finding our son," Julie said.

"We need to get some background information. Can you tell me about yourselves and the children?"

"Certainly. I work for Franklin Allen, the advertising agency in town, and Julie works at Niemen Marcus in the Somerset Mall," Tom said. "We have three kids. Joel is eighteen, a senior, and Daniel, sixteen, is a sophomore, and Shaun is a sixth grader."

Pete wrote in his notebook. "Can you run me through what happened last night?"

Tom nodded. "I had a business meeting with a client, and we decided to make it into both a business and social engagement, so our wives joined us. We left the house around six to meet the couple at a local restaurant."

"Then what happened?" Pete asked.

"Daniel had a babysitting job just a couple of streets over, and he left for that," Julie said, trying to maintain her composure.

Tom continued. "Joel got home late last night around midnight and what he told us is Shaun came up to his room around seven forty-five and asked for change to go to the store to buy some candy. Shaun asked him to keep the front door open so he could get back in. Joel left shortly after that to go to his concert. We got back home around nine and discovered the house empty. Julie called all of Shaun's friends, and I went around the neighborhood looking for him." His voice started to quiver.

"When you left, what was Shaun doing?" Charlie asked.

"He was playing basketball," Julie said, looking at her husband.

"That's right, honey. He was shooting hoops out in front of the house," Tom added.

"Was that normal for Shaun to be playing outside?" Charlie asked.

Julie let herself smile. "Shaun is small for his age, and having two older brothers you'd think he might be intimidated, but that isn't Shaun. He loves sports. He's always playing something. He's always competing."

"Can you describe the clothes that he was wearing?" Charlie asked.

Julie closed her eyes, visualizing her son's outfit. "He was wearing his red hockey jacket, green pants, a navy-blue shirt, and white tennis shoes."

"Do you know how he might have traveled to the store?" Charlie asked.

"I didn't see his skateboard out on the front lawn, so I assume he took it with him," Tom said.

"What type of boy is Shaun?" Charlie asked.

"I know all mothers think their children are special, but Shaun is a real joy. He's so thoughtful. He always leaves me notes telling me where he's going and when he'll be back. He always gives me a hug, and he has this incredible smile." Julie wiped a tear from her eye with a handkerchief wrapped around her finger.

"Where are the other boys now?" Charlie asked.

"They're trying to get some rest," Julie said.

"Do you have any ideas of who might have taken Shaun? Would anyone have any motive to hurt Shaun? Maybe someone upset with a business deal?"

Both parents vigorously shook their heads and adamantly said they knew of no one.

"With your permission, we'd like to keep a detective here just in case a kidnapper tries to contact you," Pete said.

"So, you don't think this could be the monster who's taken the other kids? The term sickens me. You know…what the press is calling…" Tom asked.

"It's too early in the investigation to tell. We don't want to make any assumptions or miss any opportunities. We'll be going now, but we'll check back in periodically," Pete said.

Tom and Julie walked Charlie and Pete to the front door. Tom handed Charlie and Pete their winter overcoats. Julie stood in front of Charlie as she buttoned up her camel-hair coat and tied the belt around her waist. Julie took Charlie's hands in hers. "Please find my baby before it's too late."

Charlie hugged her. "We'll do our best."

Charlie and Pete silently walked to the end of the driveway. Charlie looked back at the quiet home. Less than twenty-four hours before, it had been a contented and blessed household. She now wondered if it had been cursed.

"We're bringing in the store clerk this morning. The Birmingham police already have numerous public safety announcements asking for potential witnesses to come forward. It's going to be a zoo around the office. What about you?" Pete asked

"I'm going to walk to the drug store," Charlie said, looking down the quiet road. "I like retracing the victims' routes and crime scenes. It gives me a sense…a feeling of the victim and the killer."

BIRMINGHAM
THURSDAY, MARCH 17, 1977

Charlie pulled the map from her pocket and unfolded it. She studied the marks of the children's homes and the abduction and drop-off locations. She wrote Shaun's name next to the crosses that marked his home and abduction location. She put the map and pen back into her purse and lifted up the collar on her coat.

The weather was particularly ugly this time of year, neither winter nor spring—cold, damp, and uninspiring.

Charlie turned left out of the driveway and headed west along Shaun's street. She walked along the paved sidewalks, looking at the quaint homes with their inhabitants just starting to stir, getting ready for school and work. Charlie could only imagine the horror they would feel when they realized the child of one of their neighbors had been snatched from this beautiful street.

She'd covered the few blocks quickly and came to the N. Adam intersection. She looked around trying to visualize Shaun the night before—waiting at the corner for traffic to clear, standing on his skateboard and propelling himself across the street. Charlie crossed the street and continued moving westward along Knox Street.

She arrived at the back parking lot of the grocery store and pharmacy. She watched the commotion of police cars and news reporters. She didn't want to enter the fray, so she made her way around to the front of the store. Charlie stood at the intersection of Maple Road and Woodward and looked across the street at the restaurant with its name written in the familiar white script. Shaun's parents had been eating their dinner less than the length of a football field away from the location their son had been abducted. Charlie asked herself, *Did the killer know?*

BEVERLY HILLS
THURSDAY, MARCH 17, 1977

"How are the parents holding up?" Abraham asked.

"Well, they're showing incredible resilience. They're planning a televised plea this evening," Pete said.

"Interesting."

"Dr. Taylor thought it may help—appealing to either the killer or someone who can lead us to the killer. She's been coaching them on what to say."

"It certainly can't hurt. Do we have any witnesses?" Abraham asked.

"There was a woman who thinks she saw a boy who matched Shaun's description talking to a man in the parking lot. She was unloading her groceries into her trunk, and they weren't more than twenty feet away."

"That's encouraging. Can she provide a description of the man?"

"Yes, she described him as twenty-five to thirty-five years old, approximately five feet ten inches to six feet. He had longish dark-brown curly hair with long sideburns."

"Did she offer any other information?" Abraham asked.

"She thought the man was standing next to a navy-blue AMC Gremlin with white hockey stick decals along the side."

"Have some of the guys contact all the AMC dealerships. We need to find the owner of this Gremlin."

"Already started. You know how witnesses can be. I just hope this lead doesn't turn into a red herring," Pete said.

"This is the most promising lead we've had to this point. We can't afford not to follow it," Abraham said.

"The FBI and several of the local car dealers believe they identified the type of car that may have made the impression in the snow bank where Nicole Hernandez's body was dropped," Pete said.

"And?"

"It wasn't an AMC Gremlin. More like a Cadillac or a Buick Riviera," Pete said.

"Typical for this case—nothing ever pans out," Abraham said, shaking his head in disappointment. "What else?"

"The task force is starting to feel the pressure. Since we made the announcement yesterday, we've already had over twenty-five hundred tips. The process is starting to overwhelm us. We're trying our very best to keep up with all the leads. We also are having some dissension among the ranks. Some of the detectives from the municipalities haven't bought into the idea of a serial killer. Adding insult to injury, they're airing their views to the press."

"I'll talk to the police chiefs to see if I can have them nip this in the bud," Abraham said, writing a note on a pad of paper.

"Thanks, but I won't hold my breath," Pete said. "While you're at it, ask them to stop sending their inexperienced detectives."

"What are you talking about?"

"Some of the municipalities are sending brand-new detectives here so they can get experience on someone else's dime. At the same time, they've got their best detectives trying to solve the crime in their jurisdiction. Nice?" Pete sat back in his chair and closed his notebook.

"Crap. I'll see what I can do," Abraham said, scribbling in his notebook again. "I'm afraid to ask, but anything else?"

Pete sat forward. "Has the attorney general made any decisions on my friend from Grosse Pointe?"

"No, he hasn't made any decisions. I'll let you know as soon as he does. But in the meantime, just keep the ball moving down the field."

Pete closed his eyes momentarily, thinking his opportunity to catch the Brotherhood could be slipping through the cracks.

"Up for a beer?" Abraham asked.

"No, thanks. I've got a ton of paperwork to go through. I'm going to try and get home before the kids are asleep. I haven't seen them in ages. They're usually sleeping when I leave in the morning and asleep when I return."

"You can't expect to keep going eighteen hours a day, Pete. Nobody works as hard as you or does a better job than you. This is the largest task force that's ever been established in the United States. We're learning a lot of valuable lessons."

"It's only good if we catch the killer. All the rest is just window dressing," Pete said. He got up from his chair and shook hands with Abraham.

Pete made his way back to his office and stared down at his usually clean and neat desk, now cluttered with phone messages. To Pete, his messy desk was symbolic of the case: so much information, but of little value.

Occasionally taking a sip of cold coffee from a Styrofoam cup, Pete continued to work late into the night, reviewing the high-priority tips, taking notes, and establishing the priorities for the task force for the next day when he would return early in the morning. He finally turned off the light and headed out the building to his car across the street in the public parking lot. It didn't take him long to reach his darkened house.

BIRMINGHAM

THURSDAY, MARCH 17, 1977

Pete opened the front door slowly, trying not to disturb anyone. The lights were off but for a single lamp in the living room welcoming the tired warrior. Out of habit, he made his way through the darkened hallways to his home office, where he removed his revolver from his belt. Pete rubbed his hands across his face and through his hair while letting out a long exhale. He thought, *I won't be beaten. I won't let my guard down.* There was no one who ever worked harder than him, and this was going to be no exception—not an opponent, not the enemy. Pete relished the role of underdog against all odds.

He quietly made his way up the stairs, avoiding the steps that let out their telltale creaks and groans. A sliver of light shone from the crack in the door of the master bedroom. Beyond the door, he could hear the familiar voice of Bill Bonds, the local ABC anchorman, giving the latest details of Shaun's abduction.

He moved right past the bedroom door and went to his daughter's room. He opened the door quietly and then stood there for a while looking at her sleeping peacefully in bed. She was only six but already had an attitude. She was an exquisite girl with light, coffee-colored skin and hazel eyes. He knew that Gabrielle and he would pay the price when she turned sixteen. He closed the door and went to his son's room, which was littered with sports memorabilia, equipment, and clothes. His son lay spread-eagled across the bed with the covers kicked to the floor. The transistor radio's single white earpiece still in his ear, the boy had obviously fallen asleep listening to the Red Wings game. Jackson was the same age as Shaun. The killer could just as easily have taken Jackson as he had Shaun. Pete's drive began to falter as he was bombarded by waves of exhaustion. He took off his tie and threw it among his son's piles of clothes. He lay down next to Jackson and slept.

BIRMINGHAM
THURSDAY, MARCH 17, 1977

Gabrielle thought she had heard Pete come in, but when he didn't come into the room she thought that she might have imagined him returning home at a decent time. She knew how driven Pete was with his work, and the latest abductions and murders were driving him to work insane hours. She had seen Pete at his best and worst, and she knew that he was driven as if they were his own children abducted. She got out of bed and poked her head into the hallway.

"Pete?" she called quietly into the darkness.

There was no response. She could hear the faint sound of snoring from her son's bedroom. As she approached the bedroom door the snoring got louder. *Who could sleep through that racket?* She opened the door and found Pete and Jackson, a bundle of arms and legs and a symphony of noises. She picked up the blanket and covered her husband and son, and then she departed the room as quietly and as unobserved as she had entered.

PONTIAC

FRIDAY, MARCH 18, 1977

"We have decided to take some extraordinary measures to try and catch the killer," Sydney White declared to her staff. "Bill, pass out a copy of the confidential memorandum."

Bill Choate handed out the documents to the staff members. Charlie took her copy and began to read. The memorandum was addressed to law enforcement officers assisting in the investigation of the missing boy, Shaun Woodson. It authorized all local law enforcement agencies assisting in the investigation to conduct stop and search in order to save the life of Shaun Woodson and apprehend his abductor. The memorandum also went on to direct the conduct of the officers during the stop and search. In conclusion, it stated that officers who conducted a stop and search must be able to defend their actions that led to reasonable suspicion. The memorandum was signed by Sydney White, Prosecuting Attorney, and William Choate, Chief Assistant Prosecutor.

"We didn't do this without some reservation," Bill said. "However, I think most people will be sensitive to and understanding of the stop-and-search policy."

"Everyone is scouring Oakland County for the Gremlin and the dark-complexioned man with long, dark-brown wavy hair and long sideburns. We finally got the lead that we've been looking for. It's just a matter of time before we catch this son of a bitch," the detective with the red bulbous nose sitting across from Charlie said.

"If you knew everyone was looking for you and there's a fairly accurate description of you, don't you think you might change your appearance and ditch the car?" Charlie asked.

"Don't fret, Doc. These guys aren't that smart," the detective replied.

"Well, up to this point, the killer's been very smart. He hasn't left us with a single clue, and now he's been seen by several witnesses."

"What ya driving at, Doc?"

"The killer was there all right or Shaun wouldn't have disappeared, but I think the witness saw Shaun talking to this man, providing the perfect opportunity for the killer to slip in when no one was looking and then abduct him. We still don't know for sure where Shaun was taken from. The cashier thinks she remembers seeing a boy who fit Shaun's description. The witness believes she saw a boy matching Shaun's description talking to this man. He easily could have been on his way home when he was taken. People were flowing in and out of a busy parking lot, but no one saw Shaun being taken. I've walked the route between Shaun's house and the store. There are a lot easier places to snatch him from than a busy parking lot. That's what I'm driving at."

The detective's nose turned a dark blood red, and he was about to speak when Sydney cut him off. "Thanks, both of you."

BEVERLY HILLS
FRIDAY, MARCH 18, 1977

Charlie parked her car in the school parking lot, feeling exhausted, frustrated, and desperate. She stepped out of the car, her hand instinctively clutching her purse to ensure the package had not disappeared. She went into the school, which was abuzz with activity, and made her way to Pete's office. She watched him in action—simultaneously talking on the phone, shuffling papers, and handing out instructions to detectives standing in his office, cool under fire. The detectives acknowledged Charlie as they left the office. Pete glanced up and waved her in.

Pete stood behind his desk, his hands on his hips, and smiled. "Nice job prepping the Woodsons; their broadcast was very effective. Now the *Detroit News* and other organizations are offering a hundred thousand dollar reward, and there's the artist's composite of the potential suspect. It's even zanier around here. By the way, last night on TV, Tom Woodson's plea for his son's safe return and still being able to try out for Little League was a nice touch."

"Trying to make a connection with the killer," Charlie said, falling into the chair in front of Pete's desk. "I know from my research that with most child abductions and murders, the victims are usually white females from middle-class neighborhoods, around eleven to fourteen years of age, which partially tracks with our killer with the exception that she's abducted two boys. She seems to be stuck in adolescence—hence, she's gender neutral."

Pete sat down and leaned back in his chair.

"She shows a form of protection and remorse in the way she cleans the bodies and clothes and then leaves the bodies out in the open. Her actions—in some bizarre and incomprehensible method—are a declaration of love for the children.

"I've even questioned my own analysis and profile, so I've reached out to several experts from around the country," Charlie said. "I was trying to get a fresh perspective. There are some differing thoughts among us. One camp believes that the profile of our killer is a male, part-time worker or unemployed—doesn't have to punch a clock, lives in some type of fantasy, and has little or no adult interaction or relationship. The other camp, of which I'm a member, believes this person is a male, possibly bisexual, incredibly intelligent, white collar, physically attractive, outgoing, and narcissistic. He's very familiar with the area, too."

"One exception," Pete said.

"Yes, I believe the killer is a female," Charlie said.

Pete sat forward in his seat, resting his arms on the table, and wrapped both his large hands around his coffee mug. "We can't seem to agree or come to any type of consensus," Pete said.

ANN ARBOR
SATURDAY, MARCH 19, 1977

"Where do you find the energy?" Annie asked, breezing into Charlie's living room.

"I'd go insane if I didn't," Charlie said as she took a sip of her orange juice.

Annie slipped her arm around Charlie's waist.

"Sorry, I'm gross," Charlie said.

"I don't mind. How far did you go?" Annie took the glass from Charlie's hand and sipped the orange juice.

"About seven."

"You're disgusting."

"Didn't I just say that?"

"No, you said gross."

"What's the difference?"

"As far as I'm concerned, everything," Annie said.

"I like the solitude. It frees my mind."

"I like the look." Annie admired Charlie's lean muscular legs and arms in her formfitting gray polyester running shorts and black tank top.

"I need a shower," Charlie declared as she disengaged from Annie's embrace and started walking toward the back of the house.

"I'll fix us breakfast while you get cleaned up," Annie yelled as she watched Charlie strip out of her sweaty running clothes, toss them into the laundry, and then disappear into the bedroom.

Annie thought, while looking in the large mirror hanging from the wall, *You could bounce quarters off that, while I'm like a red lobster with all the meat in my tail.*

Later Annie and Charlie sat around the kitchen table eating their breakfast of lightly buttered toasted English muffins, yogurt topped with blueberries, and coffee while reading the morning and afternoon papers.

"More coffee?" Charlie offered as she raised the coffee pot.

Annie placed her hand over the top of her mug. "I'm good."

Charlie looked up from the editorial page at the sound of muffled sobs. She looked over at Annie, who was wiping a tear away from the corner of her eye.

"Honey, what is it?"

Trembling, Annie wiped away the tears and handed Charlie the paper.

Charlie took the paper and began to read…An open letter from Julie Woodson. Charlie read the mother's heartfelt words pouring out onto the paper. She wrote about how she was going to hold him tight and kiss his freckled face and then fix his favorite dinner of fried chicken, mashed potatoes, corn, and chocolate milk followed by his favorite desert of fudge brownies with chopped walnuts and served with plain milk to wash them down. The letter continued on about the activities they would do together upon his return. She eloquently wrote of her thanks to the local law enforcement and her earnest plea to the community to assist law enforcement in their efforts. She closed with, "…Pipsqueak, we love you and can't wait for your safe arrival."

Charlie looked away, hiding her anguish and professional embarrassment. She thought about how the Woodsons had shown such great composure and resolve through this ordeal.

"What do you have in mind?" Annie asked.

Charlie grabbed Annie's arms. "Can you take care of the house?"

"Sure, but..."

"I've gotta pack and get out there. Give the kids all my love," Charlie said. She kissed Annie on the cheek and headed off to her bedroom. She quickly stuffed her overnight bag full, tossing some books in on top of her clothes and personal items.

"I've got to end this...I've got to end this right now," Charlie said as she closed the front door behind her.

OBIRMINGHAM
SATURDAY, MARCH 19, 1977

She was in her car, like she had been all the other nights, binoculars pressed against her eyes, watching, waiting, looking. Charlie lowered her binoculars and tried to adjust her position to ease her back pain. She opened the book that had motivated her, *Casebook of a Crime Psychiatrist* by James A. Brussel, MD. The book detailed how the New York City Police Department was at its wit's end after sixteen years of being unable to catch New York's Mad Bomber. So they decided to try something new and solicited the assistance of Dr. Brussel, a Manhattan psychiatrist. Dr. Brussel was skeptical at first of his own abilities; however, after studying the case file, he developed the profile of the bomber that eventually assisted the police in arresting George Metesky.

Like Dr. Brussel, Charlie started to think about the killer's modus operandi. *She took the kids from very public locations with no sign of forced abduction. She returned with the kids to her home. Would she change the location from her home to some sort of other location to lessen the likelihood of her being identified?*

Charlie started to reflect on the killer's signature.

She leaves the kids out in the open, bathed, cleaned, and well taken care of. What message is she trying to send? What is the significance of the fact that neither girl was sexually assaulted, but Cody was? Had something happened in her past to cause her to treat the boys differently than the girls? If we don't find Shaun, and fast, he is going to be placed alongside a road for everyone to see. Would her MO evolve? Charlie had so many unanswered questions.

Despite her discomfort, Charlie was overcome by exhaustion and dozed off. She awoke cold to the bone and aching all over. Every stiff muscle voiced its complaint as she tried to move. She rubbed her neck and rotated her head to alleviate the pain.

She had seen no movement inside the house and was unsure if this was the most efficient use of her time. Perhaps she had taken Shaun to some other location. Maybe Charlie's intuition and research had failed her. Maybe a different course of action would be necessary.

She started the car and put the heater on full, knowing what would come next. A blast of cold air hit her like a ton of bricks, jolting her awake. She decided to head to her parents' house, to crawl into some clean sheets. Even a few hours would provide relief. The very thought of a toilet and a hot shower immediately boosted Charlie's morale.

Charlie arrived at her parents' home at six that morning and rang the bell. It took a while for her parents to respond. Her father opened the door, looking at her with complete surprise when he finally realized it was his willful daughter standing in front of him.

"Charlie, are you all right? Your mother and I weren't expecting you this morning."

"Thanks, Dad. I apologize for getting you up out of bed."

"No problem, Charlie. Come on in. Is everything alright?"

"Everything's fine. I've been on a stakeout. I just ran out of gas and need a place to warm up, catch some sleep, and rejuvenate the batteries."

Charlie peeled off her coat and kicked her shoes off. Her mother stood at the top of the stairs, looking down at Charlie and her husband in disbelief.

"*Uhma, mi-ahn-ham-nee-dah*," Charlie said in Korean. "Please, go back to sleep. I'll explain everything later."

Her mother responded with her usual, "*Aigoo.*"

Charlie walked with her father up the stairs. He awkwardly gave his daughter a kiss on the forehead. "Goodnight, kiddo," he said, trudging down to his bedroom.

In the bathroom, Charlie stripped out of her clothes, relieved her bladder, and brushed her teeth, and then she went to her old room and dove under the clean sheets and warm blankets.

Despite her fatigue, she lay still staring up at the ceiling for a while, feeling a sense of loneliness. She thought about how lonely and scared Shaun must be right then. It was still dark outside—no sun, no moon, no stars. She tried to imagine what it must be like for these kids. Life must seem helpless to be without hope. Her thoughts were of Shaun. *When would he arrive home?*

Moments later, she threw off the covers and trudged down to her grandmother's room to retrieve the pink synthetic mink blanket. Charlie returned to her bed and curled up with the familiar smell and feel of the blanket.

BIRMINGHAM
SUNDAY, MARCH 20, 1977

From somewhere in the dark came the little voice.

"What are you reading?"

I eventually looked up from the newspaper. "Nothing important, just getting caught up on the news. Please be quiet so I can finish my reading."

"My wrist hurts, and I'm thirsty."

"Well, if you'd listened and been more cooperative, then I wouldn't have had to tie you to the bed. Shaun, the last boy who stayed with me didn't listen either, so I had to give him a boo-boo. Now, you don't want me to give you a boo-boo? Do you, young man?"

"No, ma'am," Shaun said.

"Now please be quiet."

"Yes…"

"That's a good boy." I looked at Shaun as the tears rolled out of the corner of his eyes. I finished reading the letter written by Julie Woodson.

"Do you like chicken?"

"Yes, it's my favorite…especially Kentucky Fried Chicken and chocolate milk."

"Well, I think it's time for you to go home. Wouldn't you like that, Shaun?" The killer could hear the whimpering coming from the dark. "Shaun, wouldn't you like to go home, sleep in your own bed?"

"Do you mean it?"

"Of course I mean it. But first, we're going to celebrate our last night together. We'll have a big party. We'll eat chicken and corn and drink as much chocolate milk as you'd like."

"Thank you."

"I can't have your mother thinking I'm a bad host. Of course, you'll need to take a bath; your nails need to be scrubbed and trimmed. They were disgusting when you came here. I'll need to wash and iron your clothes again. I've got so much to do. You be good while I'm gone."

BEVERLY HILLS
MONDAY, MARCH 21, 1977

"You look beat. It looks like you haven't slept in days," Pete said, noting the dark rings around Charlie's eyes.

"I'm fine. I'm really worried that we're running out of time. I just don't think she'll hold him as long as she did Nicole," Charlie said, scrunching her face as she took a sip of the bitter, burnt coffee.

"We're no further along either. It's like we're chasing a ghost," Pete said, looking at his coffee then at Charlie. "Taste likes the usual cop coffee to me."

"Maybe we should be checking closer to home."

"Meaning the killer lives here?"

"Exactly," Charlie said.

"You might be right, although we've gotten zip from the roadblocks. We've been checking on every Gremlin owner in the county with absolutely nothing to show for all the work. A big fat red herring, if you ask me," Pete said.

"I sound like a broken record repeating myself, but these are low-risk, well-behaved, good kids. All of them are attractive, preadolescent, innocent and trusting, sexually safe, clean, and pure. To the killer, these are the nice kids. Their abduction and murder sends a message.

"I think the killer knows these kids. I used to think they were just opportunity abductions, random, but the killer is too methodical. She's tracking them. They're premeditated. That's why they haven't been forced. She's not afraid; she's bold, and this is her territory.

"The killer isn't dragging the kids into the bushes and discarding the bodies. No, she's probably taking the kids to her well-kept home in a clean car—she's meticulous.

"The kids probably had no sense of danger; that's why she was able to get Nicole, and now Shaun, in spite of all of our efforts to warn kids about going with strangers. The kids are wary of the boogeyman, a man, but not a woman, an attractive woman."

"I thought your gender was supposed to be nurturing," Pete said.

"She is...in her mind. She wouldn't compare herself to a man because this person believes she is doing no harm to the children. She loves the children. She's nurturing, caring, and looking after their well-being."

"Is this why she's bathing them and cleaning their clothes?" Pete asked.

"It's clearly part of it, but I also think she's aroused by the way the warm water caresses her own hair. It excites her."

"Why here?"

"There may have been something that happened to her in the past, so she has a predilection to kill," Charlie said.

"But why now?"

Charlie shrugged. "Most likely there's been a recent event that triggered her to spiral out of control."

"Is there something that will make her stop?"

"Why should she? Up to this point, she's been incredibly successful. She's studying everything about this case, and she is serious about her business. She's tracking every move we make, just like her victims. The only way we stop her is if we arrest or kill her."

"I used to like talking with you," Pete said, shaking his head. "Lately, you only leave me feeling more uneasiness. Did you see the papers this weekend?"

Charlie shook her head no and leaned back against her chair.

"They think it might be the work of a fanatical cult with both men and women involved for some religious or sexual gratification," he said. "At first, I didn't pay much attention, but then I started to objectively look at it. Their theory has a lot of validity to it.

"I came in yesterday and looked up the dates the kids were abducted, and many of the dates are associated with Pagan holidays. We are dealing with multiple personalities, not just one, which is the reason for some of the inconsistencies in each of the abductions. Finally, your theory of a woman being involved has not been lost on me. I agree," Pete said. "How many guys do you know who could take care of four kids for numerous days, especially the girls? The killer held Nicole for nineteen days. Nineteen days. We also know that Allison was having a period and that she had a clean tampon inserted. Really, how many guys are going to walk into a grocery store or pharmacy and purchase tampons?"

ANN ARBOR
MONDAY, MARCH 21, 1977

"It's time. New York, LA, and New Orleans are not interested in any of our wares. We're toxic as far as they're concerned," Abraham said.

Marilyn didn't acknowledge the comment.

He continued. "I never thought I'd see the day, but I just received word that the attorney general is going forward with the indictment on Raymond."

"Shit. He should have left when he had the chance."

"His ego got the best of him. He thought that all his political connections and money made him untouchable. He'd have been right, but these abductions and murders of these kids have everyone freaked."

"Can they get to us?" Marilyn asked.

"No, I've covered our tracks. But you need to watch yourself. She's gunning for you."

"Who, Taylor? I can handle her."

"She's been parked outside of your house day and night—watching."

"I can't have these murders coming back to me."

"I know…I've got a couple of loose ends to tie up…then the task force will be shut down," Abraham said and hung up the phone. He picked up his National Championship football and twirled it in the air. His large hands squeezed it tight as he caught it.

LIVONIA
WEDNESDAY, MARCH 23, 1977

The floodlights shone down on the activity below them. "Who discovered the body?" Charlie asked as she watched the lab crew snap photos, place markers near the body and skateboard, and look for evidence.

"A couple of teenage boys around eleven on their way to a party," Pete said, standing next to her with his fist jammed into his pockets. "They had made a wrong turn on Gill Road and were about to turn around when one of them spotted the body."

"I heard his body was still warm," Charlie said.

"When the paramedics arrived, they did everything they could to revive him," Pete said. "Didn't want to leave anything to chance," Pete added as he shifted his weight to his left leg.

Charlie walked over and squatted next to the body and then carefully lifted one of Shaun's arms. "Based upon lividity, I'd put the death about six hours ago, sometime between six and eight this evening. The ME will be able to provide a more precise measurement once he examines him."

Charlie looked closely at Shaun's fingertips. "His nails have been trimmed and cleaned. Julie showed me a photo of Shaun taken on the day of his disappearance. He was holding up his science project, and you can see that his fingernails were long and dirty."

She pushed back his jacket sleeve and then lifted his pant leg. "He has indentations around his ankles and wrists where he probably was bound by some type of ligature." She gently pushed back Shaun's hair. "He has an abrasion to his left temple similar to Cody. No other apparent physical damage to the body. So I'd make an educated guess he was asphyxiated like the other children."

Charlie continued her examination of Shaun's body. He was in the same clothes that he had been wearing the night he was abducted. She could see they had been recently washed and pressed. She looked closely at Shaun's jacket and lifted something from it.

Pete took his hands out of his pockets and walked closer. "What do you have there?"

Charlie brought her hand up closer to her eyes for a closer examination. "It's hair...definitely not human hair. Looks like cat, possibly dog, hair. The lab will have to make a determination," she said, dropping the hair into a plastic bag. Charlie stood up and looked at the scene and surrounding area. Shaun's body had been discarded in a ditch alongside Gill Road just shy of Eight Mile Road. "We were getting close."

"Maybe he or she is just screwing with us," Pete answered.

"She placed the body at night versus early morning," Charlie said. "The body is in Wayne County, possibly to avoid the roadblocks or to create more tension between the two jurisdictions. Or maybe she's starting to feel the investigation closing in on her."

"You think?"

"I'll come back later when it's brighter out, but Shaun's body hasn't been carefully laid down or displayed like the others. His body has been discarded in a ditch along with his skateboard." Charlie thought, *What am I missing?*

Pete, echoing his own sense of inadequacy, said, "Don't beat yourself up. You're not alone. We all feel like crap right now. We all feel terrible that we weren't able to get to him sooner."

"Going to the coroner's?" Charlie asked as Pete turned to leave.

"No, I've got some things to take care of this morning."

GROSSE POINTE
WEDNESDAY, MARCH 23, 1977

Raymond slumped in his favorite chair, the newspaper crumpled at his feet. Tears ran down his face. He hadn't bothered to shave for the past few days as his façade came crumbling apart. He was alone in the house. The servants had been sent away or released from their employment. The furniture was covered with sheets. Raymond sat powerlessly in his library as his little scheme fell to pieces. He could no longer find solace in the sanctuary of his palatial home.

The *Traverse City Record-Eagle* had conducted a four-month investigation in conjunction with the Michigan State Police and uncovered his enterprise at North Fox Island. The exposé revealed how a wealthy benefactor, the owner of the island, would fly in unsuspecting, disadvantaged children in his private plane. The paper went on to explain how the children were forced into sexual acts and photographed for pornographic magazines. What seemed like a dream come true for these underprivileged kids quickly evolved into a nightmare.

Raymond's connections and political influence could not stop the tidal wave. No one was going to risk their necks no matter how much money was sent their way.

Raymond had been warned. Like dominoes lined up one behind the other, the clientele started to fall in rapid succession. The first domino to be pushed was Christian. Law enforcement had used their leverage against him, and he had caved.

The phone rang, startling Raymond.

"Yes?" he answered.

"Have you moved your financial assets to those Caribbean bank accounts?" the deep voice asked.

"Yes, it's all been taken care of. My lawyer has assured me that I can access those accounts anywhere in the world, and the feds won't be able to find my location."

"Good. When do you depart?"

"Shortly. I'm waiting for the limousine now. What about the others?"

"Screw the others. This is about self-preservation. I couldn't care less about those guys, but I've got something for our little informant. Now, I expect to see my money in my account shortly or I'll hunt you down and make your life a miserable hell. Remember, others may not be able to find you, but I can and I will, anytime, anywhere. Am I clear?"

Raymond heard the horn of the limousine honking in his driveway. "I've got to go, the car's arrived. I'll be in touch. We had too much of a good thing going on to give it up now. I'll just relocate to Europe where they are more progressive about these things."

Raymond hung up the phone, turned off the light to the library, and made his way down the long hallway with the dark wood paneling and closed the door.

Yes, this opportunity to go to Europe is something to be relished. This will be good. He stood a little straighter, shoulders back as his gait became faster. He opened the front door and spotted his black limousine, which would transport him to the airport and then a flight to New York and finally Paris. *Ah, Paris, magnifique!*

Standing beside the limousine was a well-dressed man who smiled when he saw Raymond. He was composed and physically fit, with short blond hair.

My day keeps getting better and better, Raymond thought to himself. *Even the trip to the airport is going to be pleasant.*

"My bags are just inside the door. Do you mind getting them for me?"

"Mr. Raymond Evreux, my name is Detective Peter West, Michigan State Police. You're under arrest. You have the right to remain silent…"

BIRMINGHAM
WEDNESDAY, MARCH 23, 1977

After Charlie had left the Wayne County morgue, she drove through the quiet neighborhood where the Woodsons lived and pulled into their driveway. She turned off the engine and stayed seated for a moment to compose herself. Charlie knew most cops and law enforcement officials dreaded having to tell families the bad news and sometimes avoided it. There was no protocol or training for them to call upon. In some odd way, it was part of her own healing process. Charlie could empathize with them; she knew the pain and anguish.

She walked up the driveway, knowing that just days before Shaun had been in the same spot shooting hoops without a care in the world. She made her way up the sidewalk and imagined him running out the door with the change in his hand, stuffing it his pocket, picking up his skateboard, and skating to the pharmacy.

She pressed the front doorbell and waited for it to be answered. She only hoped the press had not beaten her here. Julie Woodson, looking pale and exhausted, answered the door.

"Dr. Taylor."

"Hi, Mrs. Woodson. May I come in and speak with you and your husband?"

"Certainly."

The Woodsons and Charlie made their way to the kitchen.

"Coffee?" Julie Woodson asked, holding up the pot of coffee.

"No, thank you," Charlie said, standing in the middle of the kitchen.

Julie pulled out the wooden chair and sat down. She stared at her cup of coffee and ran the tip of her finger along the edge of the cup. Tom remained standing, leaning against the kitchen counter with both palms flat on the counter.

Charlie started to speak. "I'm afraid I've got some terrible news."

Julie grasped her coffee cup, her knuckles turning white. Tom took a deep breath, his hands turning into fists.

"The little boy found last night on Gill Road—was that Shaun?" Julie asked.

"Yes, it was," Charlie said.

Julie's lower lip began to quiver, the tears welling in her eyes. She softly mumbled, "Oh God."

Tom walked over to the kitchen sink and looked out the little kitchen window at the barren yard. "What's next?"

"We'll need for someone to come down and identify Shaun," Charlie said.

"I'll do it," Julie said, gaining her composure while starting to stand.

"It can be a relative, a close friend, or maybe even a trusted neighbor," Charlie said.

"Thank you, Dr. Taylor, but that is my son and my responsibility," Julie said, coming over to Charlie and hugging her.

"At least let me drive you there," Charlie suggested.

"Thank you, I'd appreciate that."

"I need to go upstairs and tell the boys," Tom said, walking way with his shoulders slumped.

Julie and Charlie watched Tom for a moment.

"He has been crushed by all of this...he feels like he's failed us because he wasn't able to protect his child. Now, please excuse me, I need to go upstairs and be with my family," Julie said, leaving the kitchen.

Charlie watched Julie for a moment before making her way through the house and out the front door. Charlie opened the car door, slid into the front seat, and rested her head against the steering wheel. The tears poured out of her eyes as the serpent began to make its way out of the dark recesses of her mind.

Good for Pete, Charlie thought. The buzz was all around the office of the breakup of a large pedophile ring. There was water-cooler speculation that identifying and catching the killer couldn't be far behind. Despite the trials and tribulations of the past year, he'd finally succeeded in identifying and arresting the members of the Brotherhood.

Bill Choate opened the meeting. "To date, we've stopped and searched over one hundred and seventy-five vehicles, looking for males twenty-five to thirty-five years old who remotely resemble the sketch of the potential killer. We've found and interviewed every AMC Gremlin owner in Oakland County, and not a damn thing.

"I've just received news that the governor and attorney general are thinking of reducing or maybe even closing down the task force. We've almost used up the whole two million."

Sydney White then addressed the group. To Charlie, Sydney's veneer was a reflection of the effect the cases had had on all of them. Her control and perfect appearance had gone from being slowly chipped away to nearly shattered. The thin lines around her eyes and mouth were a little deeper and more prominent. Her perpetually furrowed brow was a mirror to the toll of these cases.

"For the first time in my life, I feel powerless," she said. "The killer—this beast, whoever he is—holds the key. He's dictating the rules. Despite all of our efforts, we're not any further in the investigation than the day Katie Hill's body was discarded in Franklin twelve months ago. I thought we'd taken every measure humanly possible."

Sydney turned to her lead investigator. "Let's hear it."

The large man trying to maintain equanimity opened his notebook and read from his notes. "The boy's body had been discovered last night around eleven by two young men on Gill Road, just south of Eight Mile, which places him in Livonia in Wayne County."

Bill Choate added, "The killer did us no favors. Now we'll have to coordinate our efforts with Wayne County."

"A change in the killer's MO?" Sydney asked.

"The killer may have changed her MO for a couple of reasons," Charlie said. "We're getting close and she needs to throw us off the scent. Our road checks are cutting down on her freedom of movement. She was rushed or forced to change her tactics.

"However, what hasn't changed is her signature. Like all the kids, Shaun was found in the same clothes that he had been abducted in. They had been washed and pressed. His body had been thoroughly washed, his fingernails and toenails clipped. His body was pristine.

"Unlike the others, his body had not been carefully presented: His arms weren't folded, and there was no snow to tuck him into. The killer did leave his skateboard right next to him, as if Shaun was going to jump up from a nap, grab his skateboard, and start skating like he had the night he disappeared.

"Just like the other kids, the cause of death was asphyxiation," Charlie continued. "There are some slight ligature marks on his wrist and ankles, and a slight abrasion to his head, similar to Cody. Like Cody, he had been sexually assaulted, his anus being dilated. It doesn't appear to be from a penis, but something mechanical. There was one other thing the autopsy discovered," Charlie said.

"Yes, what is it?" Sydney asked impatiently.

"The autopsy revealed that Shaun's last meal was eaten about an hour or so before he died. It was a chicken dinner and chocolate milk."

The room remained silent for what seemed an eternity. Finally, Sydney broke the silence with a barely audible whisper. "That'll be all for today."

ANN ARBOR
THURSDAY, MARCH 24, 1977

Charlie, still wearing her coat, her purse tossed at her feet, sat in her cold, dark family room staring out the sliding door windows into the darkness. Her phone rang, and she looked over at it, annoyed, and wondered if she should answer it. On the fourth ring, she pushed herself up off the couch and picked up the receiver.

"Yes," Charlie answered. Her voice cracked painfully from her being up almost twenty-four hours.

"God, you sound terrible," Alex said over the phone.

"I haven't slept in hours," Charlie said.

"I thought so. I'm really sorry to hear about Shaun. I know how driven you are and how much this case has taken control of you. I thought you might like some company... maybe a shoulder to cry on."

"That's very thoughtful, but I wouldn't be much company. I'm going to fix myself something and try to get some rest."

"You sure? I can be good medicine for what ails you."

Charlie smiled for a brief moment. "Alex, I really appreciate the offer, but I'm just going to let myself crash and burn."

"Well, if you're in town anytime soon...give me a call. I enjoyed our last time together."

Charlie said, "You're much too kind and thoughtful. I'll call you sometime...I promise." Charlie barely had the strength to hang up the phone and soon passed out from exhaustion.

Charlie could feel something warm and soft being wrapped around her cold and exhausted body. She could feel the heat on her cheek from the fireplace and smell the burning pine. She tried opening her tired, dried-out eyes, but her eyelids wouldn't cooperate. She was finally able to lift her right eyelid and focused on the person standing over her.

Charlie smiled and pulled the blanket up under her chin. "I don't deserve you. I'm no good...I only hurt and disappoint those closest to me," Charlie said, kicking off her shoes and stretching out on the couch.

"Let me be the judge," Annie said. She helped Charlie out of her coat and readjusted the blanket.

"Trust me…you'll only get hurt…It's safer this way…No one…" Charlie drifted off.

BIRMINGHAM
FRIDAY, MARCH 25, 1977

Like a seedling in spring breaking through the remnants of last winter's snow, the sun broke through the dirty gray clouds as the Woodsons departed the Holy Name Catholic Church. The family, a paragon of stoicism, was supported by a procession of relatives, friends, and well-wishers behind them.

"Recognize anyone?" Pete asked.

Charlie shook her head. "I've been studying hundreds of files and pictures. No one looks familiar."

"I heard there was a commotion this morning."

"The funeral director went in to check on Shaun, and he saw someone ducking out of the home."

"Did he see the person?" Pete asked, turning to look at Charlie.

"As far as he could tell, the person hadn't touched the body."

"Could be some nutcase. Still, it's unsettling. That poor family—as if they haven't been through enough pain and anguish. You don't think it could've been…?"

Charlie shrugged her shoulders. "I'm not so sure what I'm supposed to think anymore."

BIRMINGHAM
FRIDAY, MARCH 25, 1977

The indistinguishable dark sedan made its way through the picturesque subdivision. As it drove past the house without hesitation, the driver noted all that was going on around the neighborhood—nothing. Kids were in school, husbands at work, wives shopping or working out. The second time around, the car did not hesitate as it pulled up the drive far from any observation points from the street.

Abraham got out of the car, taking the case with him. He looked around briefly and then made his way to the back door. He removed several picks from the locksmith kit—tools of the trade—had his way with the lock, and opened the door silently. *So much money, yet such lousy security precautions—fools.*

He stepped into the home and then stopped, waited, and listened. He could hear a man singing terribly off-key. He smiled, knowing the singer was occupied. He glided over the thick white shag rugs, silently moving past the Oriental lamps in black, red, and golds and the tastefully upholstered furniture. He stealthily made his way up the spiral staircase.

The singing continued. Abraham paused at the door, adjusted his gloves, and then pulled the gun from the case and dropped the case in one smooth motion, pushing the door open.

The singer, Christian, was like a little field mouse sensing danger; the hairs on his neck stood on end. As the presence became more certain, he turned and jumped in his chair.

He stammered out, "You! What are you doing here? How did you get in?"

"Long time no see, Christian. You know why I'm here. And, in the end, it really doesn't matter."

Christian's eyes widened when he saw the gun.

"My-my-my parents are wealthy. You can have anything in the house. The charges will be dropped like they always have. Those kids will never testify; my parents will see to it, like they have in the past."

"You really are a fool, Christian. You and that idiot put our whole operation in jeopardy with your little stunts. We can't have you doing this. There's just too much at stake."

"I never heard a complaint when I supplied you with all those pictures and movies," Christian said. "You guys made thousands off me. You and the others got your rocks off."

"Christian, Christian, Christian. Must I really explain it all to you? What is so hard to understand? We can't afford you identifying us to the police. Why did you persist in molesting those kids? Weren't the private parties and camp enough?"

Christian was seething with anger and frustration. His hands balled up, his knuckles turned white, and his fingernails dug into his palms.

"Why? I'll tell you why," Christian said. "Every Christmas my parents left me at that godforsaken school during the holidays while they partied their asses off across Europe. Then, when all the kids had left with their parents and the staff departed, *he* would call for me.

"He would have me join him in his private library, where he would educate me on the finer things in life, and he would call for me. It started out as looking at classic paintings as he caressed my head. His hand would glide along the back of my head, going farther down. I hated that bastard. He raped me!

"I can still feel his cold, clammy hands all over me. When I told my parents, they'd laugh. Can you believe it? They'd laugh and say what a vivid imagination I must have. They'd say how ungrateful I was for the first-class education that I was receiving and how much they spent. Those morons had no clue what type of education I was receiving.

"So you ask why I did it? I did it for them, to them. I want others to feel the pain that I felt every Christmas, the pain of abandonment, the shame. And I wanted them to know what it feels like to be deserted in the middle of nowhere, to be left alone with that monster. Nobody raised a finger to help me, so to hell with them all. I wanted them to feel pain."

Laughing hysterically, Christian fell to his knees. He covered his face with his hands, sobbing.

The shot was no more than a pop. Abraham completed the coup de grâce efficiently and effectively. He then placed the gun in Christian's hands, knowing that the police so desperate to catch the killer would assume he had committed suicide. He then removed the hand-drawn picture of Cody screaming in terror from his coat and tacked it to the wall. He removed the ligatures from his coat pocket and threw them in Christian's closet.

He walked out of the house, leaving the impressive neighborhood as he had arrived—unobserved. He pulled into the shopping center, parked alongside the public pay phone, and got out to make his call. Closing the door to the phone booth, he dialed the number from memory.

"Yes?" Marilyn asked.

"It's completed. They'll never suspect anything."

"Thanks." The line disconnected. Then Abraham Lincoln closed the door to the telephone booth and got into his dark sedan.

BIRMINGHAM
MONDAY, MARCH 28, 1977

"Pete West, Detective, Michigan State Police." Pete cradled the phone between his shoulder and head and continued to fiddle with the paperwork on his desk. He paused to ensure he had heard the speaker at the other end correctly.

"You say the maid and a family member found him this morning?...Shot?...Suicide? You sure?...It's only circumstantial evidence, but you're right, it sure looks incriminating. Thanks for the call...Yes, I'll be right over. I want to have a look for myself."

As Pete pulled into the driveway of the palatial home of Christian McMillan's parents, he wondered how someone with this financial advantage could ever stoop so low as to be involved in child pornography and the molestation of little boys. Pete, having grown up in relative affluence, was taken by the beauty of the home. The artwork and furniture were the best money could buy.

Pete and the local detectives made their way upstairs and down the hallway to Christian's bedroom. Pete stood in the doorway and visually swept the room to get a feeling for its occupant. The room was rather unkempt considering that a maid visited the house three times a week to clean. His mind wandered back to Charlie's profile of the killer. The disheveled state did not seem to match characteristics they thought the killer would have. This was not the meticulously clean room they'd except to find—far from it.

The young detective made his way over to Pete. "Sir."

Pete shook the young man's hand. "Hal, what do we have?"

"Christian McMillan, thirty-year-old male, single shot to the head. Looks like a .22 caliber fired from a rifle. He's been dead for about two days."

"A .22 is hardly a round to kill yourself with—too great of a chance to make mistakes. More like the round of a professional hit man. Have we found any other .22 caliber bullets in the room besides what's in the gun?" Pete asked.

"Yes, there's a box on the dresser alongside a box of shotgun shells," the detective said, pointing to the boxes.

"What about a shotgun?"

"Nothing yet. We're still searching the house."

"What else?"

The young detective pointed to the drawing tacked to the wall just above Christian's head.

"I saw that when I walked in." Pete walked over and studied the picture of a little boy screaming in pain. The drawing's resemblance to Cody was disturbing.

"One other thing." The detective pointed in the direction of the closet opposite of them.

As Pete approached the closet, he immediately spotted the white cords on the floor.

"Let's make sure they're tested for blood," he said. "Anything else?"

"We found a little white terrier in the basement. Someone must have been looking out for the dog because they left enough food and water for it to survive."

Pete left the home and made his way back to the car. He knew from his conversations with the Berkley detectives that Christian had been a promising suspect. They thought he had been responsible for Cody Edwards's abduction and murder, but he had passed a polygraph test. He had just been released from jail prior to Shaun Woodson's abduction and murder. Pete was even more convinced that his promising suspect was now the actual killer.

As Pete drove away, he wrestled with what he'd just seen. He could understand why Christian would appear responsible for the boys' abductions and murders, but what about the girls? The autopsy said the boys had been penetrated by something mechanical. Christian was all about molesting and raping boys, so why change completely? Pete let out a sigh; nothing seemed to match in the cases.

BEVERLY HILLS
FRIDAY, APRIL 1, 1977

Charlie walked into Pete's office. He was filing papers and placing the brown folders into a box. Pete looked up. "I guess you got the word?"

Charlie nodded.

"We've run out of money, so it's time to close up shop," Pete said as he continued to place the files into the boxes.

"What happens with all of this?" Charlie asked.

"Next week, all the files will be moved to my MSP office. I'll continue with the investigation as time permits. The thought from on high is that our killer won't strike again until next winter, and if he or she does, we'll immediately reestablish the task force."

"Pretty risky, if you ask me."

"I agree. What about you?"

"Same here. I'll continue to work for the prosecutor's office. Sydney has taken a liking to me."

"Lucky you. Doesn't happen too often," Pete said, winking at Charlie. "Didn't you have another lead? What's her…?"

"Marilyn Smith? There's something there, something not quite right. I just can't place my finger on it."

Pete nodded in agreement. "I know the feeling. Christian McMillan looks so good for all of it, but now we will never be able to touch him. No prosecutor will go after a dead man, especially a well-connected dead man, because he can't defend himself."

"Families are getting screwed in this whole deal," Charlie said.

Pete placed another file into the box. "Yep, we did some good, but we may never know the answer. That about does it for me here; I'll finish tomorrow," Pete said, placing another file into the box.

Charlie and Pete walked out of the school building together. They both stood for a while looking at the idyllic neighborhood that surrounded the elementary school.

"Where you off to now?" Pete asked.

"Heading home. And you?"

"Something I haven't done in a while." Pete smiled and headed to his car.

Charlie watched as Pete's tires squealed and the engine whined as he sped out of the parking lot.

ANN ARBOR
FRIDAY, APRIL 1, 1977

Instead of heading home, Charlie decided to give herself a break and walk around the beautiful university campus. The effects of spring break were undeniable. Classes had finished, and the students had fled. What a difference a couple of hours made in her university town.

Spring was in the air; the warm sun began to dissipate the cold gray clouds that left everyone feeling dismal and lonely. Even Charlie's spirits were lifted by the feeling of a new beginning. Charlie thought the best thing she could do for herself now was to go for a run. She hopped into her car, jumped on the gas pedal, and sped home.

Before she lost the race to pessimism, Charlie tossed off her clothes, threw on her running gear, and headed out the front door. She hoped this run would jog loose something in her mind. She started out sluggishly, but soon anger replaced her lethargy, and she started running at a faster clip. Charlie, even more determined, thought she should run pissed off more often.

It wasn't long before she was flying through her neighborhood streets. Even the usual dogs that often gave chase remained in place, sensing her vibes that she shouldn't be messed with today. Her legs hurt and her stomach cramped, but she refused to throttle it back down. She was going to exorcise the demons within her.

Arms pumping, legs outstretched, Charlie sprinted the last stretch of road. She raised her arms into the air as she crossed the imaginary finish line. She was soaking wet. Gulping for air, side stitches couldn't shake her feeling of elation. Charlie thought, *Running is a lot like sex: when it's good, it's really good, leaving you sweaty, breathless, and in ecstasy.* She went through the garage, took off her shoes and clothes, and threw the clothes into the washing machine.

Parading in her panties and bra through her house, Charlie grabbed a glass of water and headed for the shower. She pulled the shower curtain closed and let the warm water pour over her body. She lathered up, grabbed the long wooden-handled scrub brush, and let her body have it. She cleansed her body inside and out.

As the water started to go from hot to warm to tepid, Charlie turned off the showerhead, realizing she had used up all of the hot water.

She went into her bedroom, which was decorated in various shades of chocolate browns, purples, and grays. Forgoing a bra and panties, she threw on a men's navy-and-white-striped Oxford button-down shirt. She loved its soft feel against her skin. She pulled on favorite jeans, the ones with the tears in the knee, and some soft plush cotton socks.

As she made her way through the house, everything seemed to feel almost normal. It was a sensation that she hadn't felt in a long time. Pouring herself a glass of merlot, she plopped down on the floor. She was tempted to start a fire but decided against it and just lit some candles and looked at her notes.

The run, the wine, or the bathing had energized Charlie's thought process.

Charlie thought about her own skills of sympathy, intellectual curiosity, dogged determination, and a strong intuition. Her intuition was strongest when she ran or prayed. Her gut would send her signals.

Charlie went back through all the conversations and articles she had compiled during her inquiry. She perused her notes, turning the pages slowly, thoughtfully.

A particular article caught her attention. It was an artist's rendition of the local area map, identifying the location of the abduction and drop-off points of each victim.

The main streets created a triangle with Nine Mile Road at the base or opposite, Greenfield Road the adjacent, and Woodward Avenue the hypotenuse. In the middle of the triangle sat Beaumont Medical Center. Charlie stared at the map. *Could it be that simple? Dammit, April Fools.* Charlie blew out the candles, grabbed her keys, and made her way to the school library—her other home.

Charlie pulled into the empty parking lot, hoping to God that someone was still there. As Charlie rushed to the door, she put her hand on the handle and found the door locked. "Shit," Charlie said under her breath. Then Charlie noticed someone standing on the other side of the door, frowning and shaking her head no.

"Charlie, no way; it's spring break, and we all need a vacation, especially me," Amy, one of the librarians, said through the glass door.

"Please, Amy. It's very important. What if I told you that it was a matter of life and death?" Charlie pleaded with the tiny Asian woman with the large wire-framed glasses.

"Aren't we being a little melodramatic?"

"It's about the kids in Birmingham," Charlie said, pleading evident in her voice. "I just need to get to the microfiche reader."

"I've seen your name mentioned in the papers several times." Amy hesitated for a moment and then unlocked the door. "I'd like to get home at a decent time."

Charlie hugged her and gave her a quick peck on the cheek. "You're the best."

"That's what you're always telling me, but it doesn't seem to get me anywhere," Amy shouted at Charlie as she raced up the stairs.

BEVERLY HILLS
SATURDAY, APRIL 2, 1977

Charlie walked into the almost-deserted task force head-quarters. She walked down the darkened hallway, her footsteps echoing off the cinderblock walls. Looking into Pete's unlit office, she debated the pros and cons and left a note for him on his desk. Charlie retraced her steps and left the building with her head hanging down—lost in her thoughts.

BEVERLY HILLS
SATURDAY, APRIL 2, 1977

Pete waved good-bye to Gabrielle as he jumped into his car. He turned the key, and the powerful motor leaped to life. He adjusted the rearview mirror out of habit and thought to himself that he almost felt normal for the first time in over a year. He and Gabrielle had enjoyed an intimate night for the first time in a long time. He had slept in and enjoyed being able to sit down for breakfast with his wife and the kids. It was late in the afternoon, and he was in no rush to return to work, but he knew that it was a necessary evil.

When he arrived to the school parking lot, he was not surprised by its emptiness. Pete walked into the converted cafeteria looking for a sign of life. He saw one of the detectives on loan from Berkley and waved to him and made his way to one of the remaining volunteers manning the phones.

"Any messages?" Pete asked.

"Sorry, I don't have anything for you," the volunteer responded.

As Pete started to walk away, she yelled out to him. "I'm still getting people calling in with tips. What do you want me to do with them?"

"Just follow procedures and we will farm them out appropriately," Pete said as he turned toward her.

"I wasn't sure what you wanted me to do, so I left some on your desk. I guess folks haven't gotten the word that we're shutting down," she added.

"I'll take care of it...thanks..."

"Suzie," she said.

"Thanks, Suzie," Pete said as he turned and made his way to the office.

Pete flipped on the light switch and saw his desk littered with notes. Pete thought, *I guess she wasn't kidding.* Pete sat down at his desk and started to thumb through the notes when he noted one that looked different from the rest.

"Pete, I found the missing piece. It all fits. I just need to figure out why she did it." He looked at her note and saw the name. Pete started to open and slam the drawers to the large gray metal desk. "Goddamn it. Hey, someone get me a phone book. I need an address this minute!"

Suzie ran into the office. "Are you all right, Detective?"

"I need a phone book…now," Pete demanded.

BIRMINGHAM
SATURDAY, APRIL 2, 1977

Charlie walked up the familiar drive and sidewalk, trying to keep her emotions in check. She stepped onto the front porch, looked around at the neighborhood, and rang the doorbell. Shortly, Charlie could hear the footsteps approaching the front door, the bolt turning back, and the door opening. Charlie smiled and looked into the woman's genuinely surprised eyes.

"Wow, what a pleasant surprise. Come on in," Alex said warmly as she opened her front door to let Charlie in. "There's a part of me that thought I would never see you again, especially at my front door."

"I admit I haven't been very considerate, and here I go barging in on you like this. I should've called first at least, but I've gotten a little carried away with all of this," Charlie said.

"I can see that…you're almost vibrating," Alex said.

"All my electrical neurons are firing at once," Charlie said as she took off her coat and handed it to Alex.

"Is your visit professional? Or do I have a cause to celebrate and you actually came to see me?" Alex asked, taking Charlie's coat and hanging it up.

"Actually, it's both," Charlie said.

"Then, I'm going to have a glass of wine to celebrate. Care to join me?" Alex said as she turned and faced Charlie.

Charlie looked at Alex in her well-worn jeans and untucked white dress shirt. Her long brown hair cascaded to her shoulders in soft curves. Even without makeup, she was captivating with her delicious good looks. Charlie could feel her body responding to her attraction to Alex.

"I'll take some hot tea if you've got any," Charlie replied.

"Will Earl Gray do?" Alex asked.

"One of my favorites," Charlie said.

"Come on, follow me," Alex said as she moved from the foyer to the kitchen. "It was tragic about Shaun. How's the family holding up?" Alex asked as she filled the teapot with water from the tap.

"Paragon of strength and faith," Charlie said, her back leaning against the kitchen counter and her arms crossed.

Alex took a mug down from the kitchen cabinet and a spoon from the drawer and placed sugar and cream bowls on a tray. Alex looked at the tray and around the kitchen to make sure she hadn't missed anything. "I think I've got everything. Let's go sit in the living room; it's much more comfortable there," Alex said as she picked up the tray.

"Have a seat," Alex offered as she nodded at the sofa and placed the tray on the coffee table in front of them.

Charlie sat down and felt comfortable in the orderly surroundings. Charlie could empathize with Alex's desire for control and a sense of order when her normal life dealt with so much pain and confusion. Charlie thought everyone needed their refuge.

Alex picked up her glass of dark burgundy wine and pulled a leg up under her. "I hate to belabor the point, but I'm really surprised to see you here," Alex said.

"I know that I have not been very considerate or thoughtful of your feelings, especially when you've been so generous in giving your time to work with the kids and the way you made me feel. I haven't felt that way in a long time," Charlie said.

"We're so much alike and have so much in common. I've always felt we're kindred spirits," Alex said, taking a sip of wine and resting her head against her right hand.

"I'm glad that you took the initiative. I was feeling the same way, but I was just scared to reach out. I'm tired of my life being filled with pain and anguish. Have you ever thought it would be nice if we could be like…" Charlie said.

"Heterosexuals?" Alex asked.

"I think that I'd give up my life in a heartbeat to be June Cleaver…hell, I'd settle for Harriet Nelson and willingly put up with screwball Ozzie. I look at my parents' and sister's relationships and try not to be envious, but it seems so damn unfair that I'll never get to have something as special as they do."

"You never know—things are constantly changing… maybe there will be a time for us," Alex said.

Alex took a sip of wine and eyed Charlie closely. "Out with it. What's the real reason you're here?" Alex asked.

Charlie fidgeted in her seat, looked down at her mug, and then took a sip of the fragrant tea. "Am I that blatantly obvious?" Charlie asked.

Alex looked at Charlie thoughtfully. "No, you're never blatantly obvious, but you do have a certain amount predictably," she said.

"It's a good thing I don't gamble," Charlie said.

"Too conservative...you need to bluff once in a while. Keeps people guessing, on their toes," Alex said.

"I've been hurt by enough people, and disappointed the others...I'd prefer the distance...I'd rather be aloof than seen as unpredictable," Charlie said.

"I didn't say lie; just make sure they don't understand or comprehend what's really true," Alex said. "Enough with all the drama."

"I think I've put it all together...the pieces of the puzzle," Charlie said.

"You think you've solved it?" Alex asked, sliding her leg out from under her and sitting forward.

"Ever since you gave me Marilyn Smith's name, I've watched her and looked up every possible piece of information that I could on her. I've staked her out. I even went to her house and confronted her to see her reaction," Charlie said.

"Go on...this is getting interesting. Maybe I've misjudged you," Alex said.

"Well, I value your opinion as a psychiatrist, especially someone who is familiar with the impact of sexual abuse on children. I'd like to bounce what I've got off you."

"I'm glad to be of assistance," Alex said, sitting back in her chair.

"First, I don't buy into the theory that this is some maladjusted homosexual male who's confused about his sexuality. This person is very confident and knows exactly what she's doing. She is very confident and successful."

"Well, Marilyn is certainly a very successful businessperson," Alex said.

"Clearly she shows signs of early abandonment, which is why she's attracted to the preadolescents and seems to want to take care of them. Most likely, it stems from her mother dying or neglecting her as a young child," Charlie continued.

"I'd agree with that assessment," Alex said, nodding in agreement.

"What I can't figure out is why she sexually assaults the boys. She doesn't have a penis, so is that why they were abused with something 'mechanical'?"

"Could be for several reasons, but the act of penetration means she probably wanted to cause them greater psychological harm."

Charlie nodded her head. "You confirmed my suspicions. So maybe the killer was harmed or violated by a boy or the boys remind her of a painful experience with another male in the past."

"That's a reasonable assumption. If I didn't know better, we easily could be talking about you." Alex said.

"I spoke with her younger brother, who shared a very troubled and disturbing upbringing," Charlie said.

"I'm not surprised. Like we discussed before, families can be either incredibly positive or destructive in children's development."

"The last piece I'm trying to put together is her access to children…" Charlie was about to finish her thought when out of the corner of her eye she saw movement—a beautiful calico cat making its way into the living room. It began to purr as it rubbed up against Alex's legs.

"She's beautiful…I don't remember seeing a cat the last time I was here," Charlie said.

"She doesn't take to strangers…she must like you or she'd have stayed hidden until you left," Alex said as she picked up the cat and began to stroke her back.

Charlie's heart began to beat faster. She sat back in her chair to collect her thoughts.

"What is it?" Alex asked.

"It's probably nothing," Charlie said.

"Don't stop now," Alex demanded.

"We found cat hairs on Shaun's jacket," Charlie said, her heart racing faster.

"I don't think I read that anywhere in the paper," Alex said as she stopped petting the cat and looked at Charlie.

"You wouldn't have. We kept it out on purpose," Charlie said as she crossed her legs confidently. "There's other information that we purposely withhold so we can differentiate between those who are really involved and those who aren't."

"Clever," Alex said.

"Not really, in comparison…she really had us fooled until now," Charlie said, feeling her temples beginning to throb.

Charlie placed the mug on the table in front of her and leaned forward. "You see, we were all blind, especially me. She bet on her ability to manipulate all of us. She used it all: male bias, vulnerability, love, sex."

"I'm getting the impression we're no longer talking about Marilyn," Alex said.

"I never was. All of those things happened to you…didn't they?" Charlie said in an accusatory tone.

Alex laughed. "Charlie, you've got a lot of issues, but I'm not one of them."

"Why? Those kids didn't deserve what happened to them," Charlie said.

The cat sensed something was wrong, hissed, and instinctively dug its claws in.

"Shit!" Alex picked up the cat and tossed it off her lap. She got up off the seat, walked back into the kitchen, and poured herself some more wine. "You've got it all wrong," Alex said as she walked back into the living room toward the couch.

"They all knew you, didn't they?"

"I have no clue what you're talking about," Alex said as she stood over Charlie.

"Sure you do. I was wondering how you got to Nicole and Shaun, but when I thought it about logically it made perfect sense."

"You've got no idea what you're talking about," Alex said.

"They—"

The blow was swift and vicious. Alex lashed out at Charlie's face. Charlie raised her arm and turned her head and then fell back into the sofa. The side of her head exploded with pain.

Charlie could taste the blood in her mouth and felt vulnerable. Alex struck again and again. Charlie kicked at her, striking her in the chest and sending her backward. Charlie pushed herself out of the sofa as Alex struck again. The blow crashed into Charlie's shoulder.

Charlie cringed with pain and ducked before the next blow struck her. She looked into Alex's eyes; they were coal black, absent of any life, pure evil. Alex grabbed at Charlie's throat and squeezed. Charlie grabbed her wrists, but she couldn't release her grip. Charlie felt herself starting to go numb. In a sheer act of desperation, she poked Alex in the eye.

Alex's grip released. Charlie then sent a blow to Alex's solar plexus. In a desperate attempt, Alex grabbed Charlie by the hair, pulled hard, and shook her head from side to side. Charlie could feel the strands of hair being pulled from her scalp—the pain was incredible. Charlie struck back, hitting her hard in the stomach.

Both women stood apart, sizing up the situation.

"It's over. I've told others of my suspicions. Even if you kill me, you won't be able to get away with it. It's over."

"It's never over, Charlie." Alex swung wildly at Charlie's head. Charlie ducked, and the blows glanced off her head and shoulders. Charlie struck again, sending Alex back on her heels. Alex swung again, missing contact as Charlie ducked. Alex fled the room.

Charlie, in pain and shock, paused to catch her breath before going after her.

All of a sudden, all the lights went out in the house.

Feeling vulnerable, Charlie allowed a moment for her eyes to adjust to the darkness. She moved forward cautiously from the living room into the kitchen. She saw a door open in the corner.

Charlie stared into the rectangular wall of blackness. Absolute silence, quiet, stillness, calm. Charlie's body, in contrast, was a symphony; the kettle drums of her heart pounding against her chest, the clanging of cymbals in her ears. Sweat trickled down Charlie's temples into the corners of her eyes, creating a stinging pain and temporary blindness. Her mouth felt like she'd been eating a glob of paste, bitter and foul. Trying to avoid detection, Charlie closed the gap with the killer. Each step was painstakingly selected. Time stood still. Charlie knew Alex was waiting for her, playing this cat-and-mouse game. *Who is the prey?* Charlie asked herself.

Charlie reached the bottom of the steps, surrounded by complete darkness. The cool, clammy air surrounded her body like a wet blanket. Charlie shivered, her eyes adjusting slowly, making out shapes in the darkness. A chair there, a sofa over there, but no movement, no sound. She tried to control her breathing with little effect. Creeping steadily along, Charlie peered into the shadows—nothing.

A light suddenly illuminated Charlie; she had nowhere to hide as Alex stepped forward and fired the shotgun. The roar of the blast was deafening as white-hot pellets ripped into her, flesh searing like a fresh piece of meat thrown onto a hot fire. Charlie was thrown backward from the force. The pain was intense. Charlie grasped at reality, feeling it slip away.

Alex stood over her, smiling. Charlie, trying to catch her breath and speak at the same time, gasped, "Those kids didn't deserve to die. Their parents don't deserve to go through the rest of their lives in pain."

"You of all people should know the pain I felt. Why can't you understand?"

"We may have shared something, but we're nothing alike."

"We're exactly alike. All we want is to be loved and comforted," Alex said.

"I try to put my pain to good use," Charlie said as her breathing became more rapid.

"Well, I've got news for you—it's not working too well. You're either running or cutting yourself."

"They're just kids…they're dependent upon us," Charlie said as she tried to fight the nauseous feeling.

"Nobody protected me. Where was my protection? I cared for those kids. I did them a favor. Their lives would have only been filled with disappointment, pain, and hurt. I loved them, I loved them all. I'm not some pervert. Nicole and I would spend hours in the bathtub together, butterfly kisses, having sleepovers. She really liked it here. You would've, too," Alex said, raising the gun and pointing it at Charlie's head.

Charlie closed her eyes.

A brilliant flash of white light, the gunshot reverberated throughout the basement. The basement returned to darkness, silence; the air was filled with the metallic smell of blood and sulfur.

Charlie felt a cool hand gently push her hair out of her face. With her remaining strength, she tried to focus on the person kneeling over her. She was offered soothing words of encouragement. Charlie gave a slight smile of acknowledgment. "Thanks," Charlie exhaled.

"Don't talk. The ambulance is on its way."

"Is she dead?" Charlie asked.

Pete looked over in the direction of the killer and then back to Charlie. "Yes, Alex is dead."

ANN ARBOR
SATURDAY, APRIL 9, 1977

Charlie sat in her living room, curled up in her favorite armchair, and watched winter slowly evaporate through her window. She was at peace for the first time in thirteen months, maybe longer. She was convalescing from her wounds.

She took a sip of her coffee and reflected on the past year as the steam rolled around her face like wispy clouds. Charlie registered the noise of a cupboard being opened and closed, the sound of a cup being placed on a counter, and the hissing sound coming from the coffee pot as a drip of coffee hit the warming plate.

Annie entered, wearing only one of Charlie's flannel pajama tops, looking luscious. "You look so peaceful. Do you mind if I join you?"

"Please."

Annie padded across the living room and did a pirouette in front of Charlie.

"As good as Jacqueline Bisset?"

"Better."

"Steve McQueen, right," Annie said, teasingly sitting down at Charlie's feet with her head resting against Charlie's knees.

"I'm not into guys by any stretch of the imagination, but he's still pretty hot," Charlie said.

"How did you sleep?" Annie asked.

"You mean when I finally did sleep, how did I sleep?"

"Yes," Annie said.

"Well, it's the first time in a long time that my mind and body were able to completely relax and unwind. Luxurious? Yes, it was luxurious. I needed that," Charlie said.

"Me, too," Annie replied.

"I just never realized. I'd always assumed that…"

"Some great detective you are. How could you not notice? A horny fanatical Chihuahua, snarling and foaming at the mouth while humping your leg, couldn't have been more noticeable than me."

"I had resigned myself to the idea that my life was going to be pretty lonely. I'm so thankful and appreciative of your friendship, support, and understanding. I'm scared that I don't deserve you," Charlie said.

"Shhh, Charlie. I love you."

The two women sat quietly enjoying the harmony. After a while, Annie asked, "Why do you think she did it? And how did you figure out it was her when everyone else seemed to be stumped?"

Charlie stared out the window and ran her fingers through Annie's hair. "What made her do it?" Charlie softly repeated. "I think it was a set of bizarre circumstances that created this evil elixir: her mother's death at a young and vulnerable age, abandonment by her father, and mistreatment by her stepmother and friends. Alex might have turned out completely different if just one of those things were changed."

"How sad and tragic. What made her start?"

"It was her father's death and his leaving the estate to his wife—her stepmother. It was the final act of betrayal by someone she loved dearly. As bizarre as it seems, she really did love the younger children. The older ones were just revenge for previous wrongdoings."

"So how did you know it was Alex?" Annie asked.

"This is going to seem so over the top, but call it intuition. A series of facts that had been roaming around in my head finally all came together—click. I had the picture. However, I had to be more careful. I almost made the same mistake with Alex that I did with Marilyn Smith. I let my personal feelings get in the way. I made the critical error of establishing a theory first and then trying to make the facts fit my theory when all along I should have just followed the facts. I may have been able to prevent Nicole's and Shaun's deaths."

"Don't be too hard on yourself," Annie said.

"She'd been involved with these kids…they all had had contact with her. I'm still putting the pieces together, but for me it started with Lauren Ring almost five years ago. Lauren was a beautiful teenager who was conflicted over her sexuality, so I'd guess that she had spoken with Alex at some point. Fast forward ahead five years: The police had written off Katie Hill's and Shelly Coleman's deaths.

"Because of the eyewitness accounts, I came to the same conclusion they had about Shelly. However, with Katie I wasn't so sure.

"I was struck by how much Jane Almonte, her best friend, looked like Lauren. I went back and talked with Jane, and she confirmed that Alex had been her counselor and how she had gotten strange vibes from her. I think Alex was jealous of Katie because Katie had become Jane's lover, hence the brutality of the attack."

"Jane might have ended up dead instead of Katie," Annie said.

"Yes, all the girls were very similar in nature—teenage girls who were underdeveloped for their age. That is why I was thrown off by Katie because she was a very well-developed young woman."

"Poor girl…wrong place and time. What about the rest of the kids?"

"Alex had been doing some volunteer counseling in schools. That's where she met Cody. He had been distraught over his parents' divorce. Allison was the easiest connection. Alex was her counselor.

"Nicole and Shaun had thrown me off until I started to look at it from a kid's perspective. They both had been told by their parents, law enforcement, and special educators about stranger danger. So why would they go with a stranger after everything they'd been told?"

"You don't mean—?"

"Exactly," Charlie answered. "They had seen her. She had spoken at their schools. She wasn't a stranger. Then, later on, I had been going through my notes and was looking down at the map and realized the hospital sat in the middle of the triangle, which triggered me to think about someone in the medical profession, which led me to Alex's doorstep."

"She was evil."

"She was, but I could see so much of me in her. The pent-up anger, frustration, wanting to lash out," Charlie said. "We'd both trusted people in our lives who had done terrible things to us. I don't condone what she did, but I understand where she was coming from."

"You're nothing like her," Annie said, looking at Charlie.

The two women sat in silence for a while, sipping their coffee.

"So what's next?" Annie asked.

Charlie ran her fingers through Annie's hair and gently pulled Annie's head back. Charlie bent over and kissed her passionately on the lips.

"Mmm, I like that," Annie responded.

Charlie sat up a little straighter in her chair, wincing when she hit a sore spot.

"I really haven't given it much thought," Charlie said.

"What would you like to do for the rest of the weekend?"

"Really?"

"Yes, really."

"Just a leisurely day with you and the kids," Charlie said. "You know, puzzles, board games, pop popcorn, drink hot chocolate."

"They'd love it. But only on one condition. You've got make some bulgogi for dinner. The kids and I love it."

"That's the easy stuff. I've got some great meals planned for us. Tomorrow, we'll get the kids up early so they can hunt for their Easter baskets. Afterward, I'd love for us to get dressed up, maybe even put on a skirt and some makeup, drive over to Birmingham, show up at Easter mass, and surprise my folks."

"Sounds heavenly." Annie smiled. "No pun intended. Church?"

"The Woodsons' strength and convictions as a family and in their faith made me think that maybe it's time to forgive and reach out. After, we'll go out to breakfast at the Maple House, gorge ourselves on smoked bacon and thick slices of French toast covered with powdered sugar and maple syrup, and wash it down with coffee. Maybe even order one of their incredible apple pancakes," Charlie said with enthusiasm.

"Sounds sinful."

"Then we'll all come back here, play card games, read, just hang out. At night, we'll read them stories, tuck them into bed. Then start a fire in the bedroom, crawl under the covers, and not come up for air until the next morning," Charlie said.

"Sounds divine."

BLAIR CARRILLO'S STORY

Ahh…" Jill yelled.

"See? How do you like it?" I ask as I continue to hit Jill with my pillow.

"Stop, stop…I quit. You win," Jill says.

"Girls, time for breakfast," Jill's mom yells to us.

We run downstairs and sit at the kitchen table. Jill's mom serves us pancakes and bacon. I love eating at Jill's because they always have different syrup flavors. I like mixing strawberry and blueberry together.

"Blair, we promised we'd call your mother after breakfast."

I nod my head yes as I take a big bite of pancake and take a drink of milk.

"Honey, our phone is broken. You can use the pay phone across the street. I'll give you the change. Do you know your home phone?"

"Yes, ma'am," I say.

After breakfast, Sally's mom hands me some change, and I run out the front door for the pay phone across the street.

BIRMINGHAM
SUNDAY, SEPTEMBER 16, 1979

The rustling of the leaves fell silent as the gentle breeze stopped blowing through the branches, and the birds stopped their cheerful chirping. Time seemed to come to a standstill. The girls were having a fun weekend of sleepovers and laughter. Maybe, just maybe, if they hadn't been having so much fun, they would have noticed how the neighborhood had become silent. They said their good-byes and waved to each other as Blair left Jill's house to use the telephone. As she ran across the street to the phone booth and was about to open the door, she heard a voice call out, "Hey, where are you going?"

She hasn't been seen since.

Postscript

Although the Internet is full of speculation and theories, no person or persons have been identified or convicted of these heinous crimes.

A composite drawing of a possible suspect was developed based upon eyewitness accounts from those who saw a boy matching Timothy King's description with a man in the parking lot of the pharmacy where Timothy was last seen before his murder on March 16, 1977. The possible suspect was described as a white male, twenty-five to thirty-five years old, with a dark complexion, shaggy hair, and long sideburns and seen near a blue AMC Gremlin with a white hockey stick decal on the side. Additionally, several varying psychological profiles were developed of the killer.

No one understands why the crimes started so suddenly or why they suddenly stopped, but one thing stands clear: the deaths of Mark Stebbins, twelve, of Ferndale; Jill Robinson, twelve, of Royal Oak; Kristine Mihelich, ten, of Berkley; and Timothy King, eleven, of Birmingham paralyzed the county. I would be remiss if I didn't mention the tragic deaths of Donna Serra, sixteen; Cynthia Cadieux, sixteen; Jane Allen, thirteen; Sheila Srock, fourteen; and Kimberly King, twelve. Although their deaths happened prior to, concurrently with, or after the deaths of the other four, they were never attributed to the Oakland County Child Killer; however, they are just as tragic and worthy of our consideration and prayers.

The task force disbanded on December 15, 1978.

Selected References

<u>Books</u>:

Bugliosi, Vincent, and Curt Gentry. *Helter Skelter: The True Story on the Manson Murders.* New York: W.W. Norton and Company, 1974.

Cribari, M. F. *Portraits in the Snow: The Oakland County Child Killings...Scandals and Small Conspiracies.* Denver: Outskirts Press, 2011.

Douglas, John, and Mark Olshaker. *Cases That Haunt Us.* New York: Scribner, 2000.

Douglas, John, and Mark Olshaker. *Mind Hunter.* New York: Scribner, 1995.

Keppel, Robert D., and William J. Birnes. *The Riverman: Ted Bundy and I Search for the Green River Killer.* New York: Simon and Schuster, 1995.

McIntyre, Tommy. *Wolf in Sheep's Clothing: The Search for a Child Killer.* Detroit: Wayne State University Press, 1988.

Vronsky, Peter. *Female Serial Killers: How and Why Women Become Monsters.* New York: Berkley Publishing Group, 2007.

<u>DVD</u>:

"Decades of Deceit: A True Story of the King Family Search for the Oakland County Child Killer." Unedited comments, dated April, May, and July 2013. Copyright by Tim King Fund 2013. DVD.

<u>Selected Internet Sources Specifically Dedicated to These Crimes:</u>

Ashenfelter, David. "Decades after Oakland County Child Killings and No Peace for Victims' Families." *Detroit Free Press,* June 17, 2012. http://www.freep.com/article/20120617/NEWS03/206170515.

Ashenfelter, David. "Did the Top Suspects in the Oakland County Child Killer Case Get Away with It? Evidence Shows They May Have." *Detroit Free Press,* June 18, 2012. http://www.freep.com/article/20120618/NEWS03/206180330/Did-suspects-Oakland-County-Child-Killer-case-get-away-with-it-?odyssey=obinsite.

Ashenfelter, David (text), and Martha Thierry (graphics). "Revisiting the Crimes." *Detroit Free Press,* June 16, 2012. http://www.freep.com/article/20120617/NEWS03/120613060/Oakland-County-child-killings-Revisiting-crimes.

Broad, Catherine. https://catherinebroad.wordpress.com/.

Brody, Lisa. "Unsolved Mystery: Oakland County Child Killer." *Downtown Birmingham/Bloomfield,* October 2010. http://issuu.com/downtownpublications/docs/downtown1010.

Catallo, Heather. "Photos Released of Oakland County Child Killer Suspect's Suicide Scene." WXYZ, January 10, 2012. http://www.wxyz.com/dpp/news/local_news/investigations/occk-suicide-scene#ixzz2p3YksKcJ.

Dagner, Helen. *OCCK Headquarters.* http://cloakdagner.proboards.com/index.cgi.

Dagner, Helen. "OCCK_HD_Archieves_Pt 1.avi" (WXYZ David Newman's Peabody Award–winning radio broadcast "Winter's Fear: The Children, the Killer, the Search"). Online video clips. YouTube, April 24, 2011. http://www.youtube.com/watch?v=iP3nrWKEaWE&index=1&list=PLatCZMr5qtTe5sZFDTSPGS_nw_5b3wl6K.

Kauffman, Brian. "Oakland County Child Killer." *Detroit Free Press*, n.d. http://www.freep.com//videonetwork/1691865510001/Oakland-County-Child-Killer.

Keenan, Marney Rich. "King Family Believes They Know Who Killed 11-Year Old in 1977, but the Police Are Slow to Act." *Detroit News*, October 26, 2009. http://dreamcatchersforabusedchildren.com/2009/10/finding-timmys-killer-family-seeks-answers-32-years-after-sons-death/

Keenan, Marney Rich. "Finding Timmy's Killer: Family Seeks Answers 32 Years After Their Son's Death." *Detroit News*, October 27, 2009. http://dreamcatchersforabusedchildren.com/2009/10/finding-timmys-killer-family-seeks-answers-32-years-after-sons-death/.

McCall, Cheryl. "A Shadowy Child Killer Claims Four Victims and Holds Detroit's Suburbs in a Grip of Fear." *People* 8, no. 23 (December 5, 1977). http://www.people.com/people/archive/article/0,,20069681,00.html.

Oakland County County Child Killer, American Legion Serial Killers, email correspondence. *Detroit Free Press*, October 15, 2012, http://www.freep.com/assets/freep/pdf/C41960561018.PDF.

"Possible Early Murders." n.d. http://greatadthulhu.angel-fire.com/page2.html.

Schock, David B. "February 17, 2009—A Reporter Remembers." Delayed Justice, February 17, 2009. http://www.delayedjustice.com/?p=1154.

TrueCrimeDiary. "SecretsandLies." June 14, 2011. http://www.truecrimediary.com/index.cfm?page=cases&id=132.

Wikipedia. "Oakland County Child Killer." n.d. http://en.wikipedia.org/wiki/Oakland_County_Child_Killer.

Other Internet Sources:

Bellamy, Patrick. "Robert D. Keppel, Ph.D. An Interview." Crime Library Criminal Minds & Methods, n.d. http://www.crimelibrary.com/criminal_mind/profiling/keppel1/1.html.

Brown, Pat. "Serial Killer Myths Exposed." Crime Library Criminal Minds & Methods, n.d. http://www.crimelibrary.com/criminal_mind/profiling/s_k_myths/index.html.

Madden, Melisa Ann. "George Metesky: New York's Mad Bomber." Crime Library Minds & Methods, n.d. http://www.crimelibrary.com/terrorists_spies/terrorists/metesky/1.html.

McCrary, Gregg. "Profiling JonBenet Ramsey's Murder." Crime Library Minds & Methods, n.d. http://www.crimelibrary.com/notorious_murders/famous/jonbenet_profiled/1_index.html.

Ramsland, Katherine. "Angels of Death: The Female Nurses." Crime Library Minds & Methods, n.d. http://

www.crimelibrary.com/notorious_murders/angels/fe-male_nurses/6.html.

Ramsland, Katherine. "Criminal Profiling: Part 1 History and Method and Part 2, Interactive." Crime Library Minds & Methods, n.d. http://www.crimelibrary.com/criminal_mind/profiling/history_method/index.html.

Ramsland, Katherine. "Dr. Steven Egger: Expert on Serial Murder." Criminal Library Minds & Methods, n.d. http://www.crimelibrary.com/criminal_mind/profiling/steven_egger/1_index.html.

Ramsland, Katherine. "Female Mass Murderers." Crime Library Minds & Methods, n.d. http://www.crimelibrary.com/notorious_murders/mass/female_mass_murderer/1.html.

Ramsland, Katherine. "Female Offenders." Crime Library Minds & Methods, n.d. http://www.crimelibrary.com/criminal_mind/psychology/female_offenders/1.html.

Ramsland, Katherine. "Geographic Profiling." Crime Library Minds & Methods, n.d. http://www.crimelibrary.com/criminal_mind/profiling/geographic/1.html.

Ramsland, Katherine. "Interview of Gregg McCrary, The Murder of Marilyn Sheppard Fifty Years Later." Crime Library Minds & Methods, n.d. http://www.crimelibrary.com/notorious_murders/famous/sheppard3/index.html.

Ramsland, Katherine. "Roy Hazelwood: Profiler of Sexual Crimes." Crime Library Minds & Methods, n.d. http://www.crimelibrary.com/criminal_mind/profiling/hazelwood/2.html.

Ryder, Steven P., and Johnno. "Jill the Ripper." Case Book: Jack the Ripper, n.d. http://www.casebook.org/suspects/jill.html.

"Serial Killer Characteristics." True Crime Stories: Resources for Writers, Crime Stories, Investigations and Forensics, September 2, 2008. http://truecrimes.wordpress.com/2008/09/02/serial-killer-characteristics.

Shurter, David. "Sent to Me By a Friend in Michigan about the Oakland Child Killings…" AP, November 4, 2010. http://davidshurter.com/?p=1166.

Stuffy-Nose Man. "What Questions Do They Ask You on the Police Polygraph Test Before Employment?" Yahoo Answers, n.d. https://answers.yahoo.com/question/index?qid=20090110081936AAP5LzB.

Toy Soldiers. "Are There Women Pedophiles?" May 9, 2009. http://toysoldier.wordpress.com/2009/05/09/are-there-women-pedophiles.

TrueCrimeDiary."SecretsandLies."June14,2011.http://www.truecrimediary.com/index.cfm?page=cases&id=132.

Wikipedia. "Oakland County, MI." n.d. http://en.wikipedia.org/wiki/Oakland_County,_Michigan.

Reports:

Michigan State Police. "A Major Case Team Manual." Law Enforcement Assistance Administration Police Technical Assistance Report, August 1977. https://www.ncjrs.gov/pdffiles1/Digitization/53805NCJRS.pdf.

End Notes

i. Fortune 500, a database of 50 years of FORTUNE's list of America's largest corporations, http://money.cnn.com/magazines/fortune/fortune500_archive/full/1977.

ii. http://www.cranbrook.edu.

iii. Oakland County Child Killer Task Force, Michigan State Police Report, https://www.ncjrs.gov/pdffiles1/Digitization/53805NCJRS.pdf

iv. Ashenfelter, David (text), and Martha Thierry (graphics), "Revisiting the Crimes," *Detroit Free Press*, http://www.freep.com/article/20120617/NEWS03/120613060/Oakland-County-child-killings-Revisiting-crimes (licensing agreement with PARS International on behalf of the *Detroit Free Press*).

v. "Sleep Baby Sleep," Lullaby Link, http://www.lullaby-link.com/sleep-baby-sleep.html.

67907658R00261

Made in the USA
San Bernardino, CA
30 January 2018